The W*indhaven*

Windhaven Plantation... a family heritage and a manifest destiny... as it passes from one generation to the next, as it survives the Civil War and the Reconstruction period, as it plays host to great passions and torn loyalties—always, the plantation, the land, and its legacy endure. . . .

> "A soaring, magnificent series of books . . . I was caught up in every volume."
> —Leigh Franklin James
> *Saga of the Southwest* Series

> "History comes to life in this engaging series about a family with noble aspirations . . . the Bouchards are an inspiration!"
> —William Stuart Long
> *The Australians* Series

> "Early America means a lot to me, and I was captivated by this imaginative account of one family's close association over several generations with the rich and beautiful country along the Alabama River and in South Texas. The Bouchards are a memorable clan, larger than life."
> —Donald Clayton Porter
> *The Colonization of America* Series

The Windhaven Saga:

Windhaven Plantation
Storm Over Windhaven
Legacy of Windhaven
Return to Windhaven
Windhaven's Peril
Trials of Windhaven
Defenders of Windhaven
Windhaven's Crisis

WINDHAVEN'S CRISIS

Marie de Jourle

PINNACLE BOOKS

WINDHAVEN'S CRISIS

An original Pinnacle Books edition, published for the first time anywhere.

Produced by Book Creations, Inc., Lyle Kenyon Engel, Executive Producer.

First printing, July 1981

ISBN: 0-523-40724-6

Cover illustration by Bruce Minney

Printed in the United States of America

PINNACLE BOOKS, INC.
1430 Broadway
New York, New York 10018

Dedicated to Ilona von Dohnányi

ACKNOWLEDGMENTS

I am indebted to Professor Joseph Milton Nance of the Department of History, Texas A & M University, College Station, Texas, for his invaluable assistance in furnishing authenticated data; also to Mary H. Barton of Carrizo Springs, Texas, for her documentation on the topography and the history of the area.

I would also like to express my appreciation to Lyle Kenyon Engel and the conscientious staff members of Book Creations, Inc., who have unerringly guided my efforts throughout the *Windhaven* novels. Indisputably, much of the reader's enjoyment of this series can be attributed to their devoted, behind-the-scenes collaboration.

Finally my most appreciative thanks are due to Fay J. Bergstrom, undeniably the nation's best transcriber, without whose attentive critical aid I could never dictate my manuscripts.

—Marie de Jourlet

WINDHAVEN'S CRISIS

THE BOUCHARD FAMILY AT WINDHAVEN PLANTATION

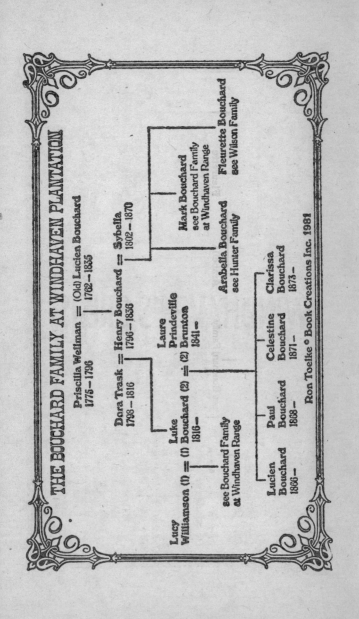

Priscilla Wellman == (Old) Lucien Bouchard
1775 — 1796   1762 — 1835

Dora Trask == Henry Bouchard == Sybella
1798 — 1816   1796 — 1856   1802 — 1870

Laure
Prindeville
(2) Brunton
1841 —

Luke
Lucy == (1) Bouchard (2) ÷
Williamson (1)   1816 —

see Bouchard Family
at Windhaven Range

Mark Bouchard
see Bouchard Family
at Windhaven Range

Fleurette Bouchard
see Wilson Family

Arabella Bouchard
see Hunter Family

Lucien   Paul   Celestine   Clarissa
Bouchard   Bouchard   Bouchard   Bouchard
1865 —   1868 —   1871 —   1873 —

Ron Toelke ° Book Creations Inc. 1981

THE BOUCHARD FAMILY AT WINDHAVEN RANGE

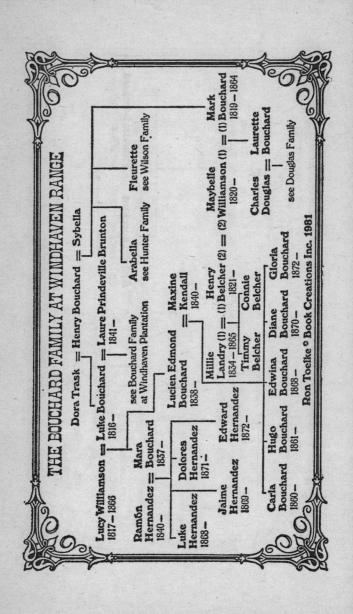

Dora Trask = Henry Bouchard = Sybella

Lucy Williamson = Luke Bouchard = Laure Prindeville Brunton
1817 – 1866   1816 –   1841 –

see Bouchard Family at Windhaven Plantation

Arabella see Hunter Family

Fleurette see Wilson Family

Mark (1) Bouchard 1819 – 1864

Mara Bouchard 1837 –

Ramón Hernandez 1840 –

Lucien Edmond Bouchard 1838 – = Maxine Kendall 1840 –

Henry (1) Belcher (2) = (2) Williamson (1) = (1) Bouchard
1821 –   1820 –

Maybelle

Charles Douglas = Laurette Bouchard

see Douglas Family

Dolores Hernandez 1871 –

Edward Hernandez 1872 –

Luke Hernandez 1868 –

Jaime Hernandez 1869 –

Millie Landry (1) 1834 – 1865

Tinmy Belcher

Connie Belcher

Carla Bouchard 1860 –

Hugo Bouchard 1861 –

Edwina Bouchard 1868 –

Diane Bouchard 1870 –

Gloria Bouchard 1872 –

Ron Toelke ° Book Creations Inc. 1981

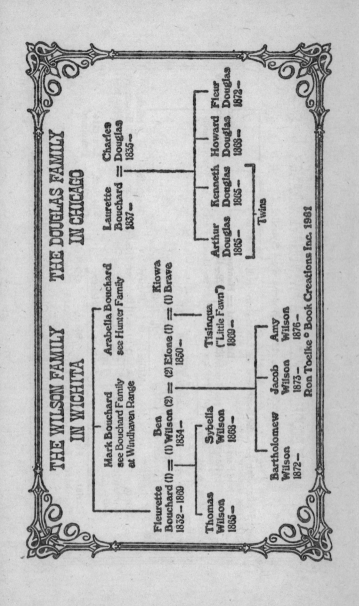

THE WILSON FAMILY IN WICHITA   THE DOUGLAS FAMILY IN CHICAGO

Mark Bouchard
see Bouchard Family at Windhaven Range

Arabella Bouchard
see Hunter Family

Laurette Bouchard 1837– == Charles Douglas 1835–

Fleurette Bouchard (1) 1832–1869 == (1) Wilson (2) == (2) Elone (1) == (1) Brave
Ben 1834–
Elone 1850–
Kiowa

Tisinqua ("Little Fawn") 1869–

Thomas Wilson 1865–

Sybella Wilson 1868–

Bartholomew Wilson 1872–

Jacob Wilson 1873–

Amy Wilson 1876–

Arthur Douglas 1865–

Kenneth Douglas 1865–

Howard Douglas 1868–

Fleur Douglas 1872–

Twins

Ron Toelke © Book Creations Inc. 1981

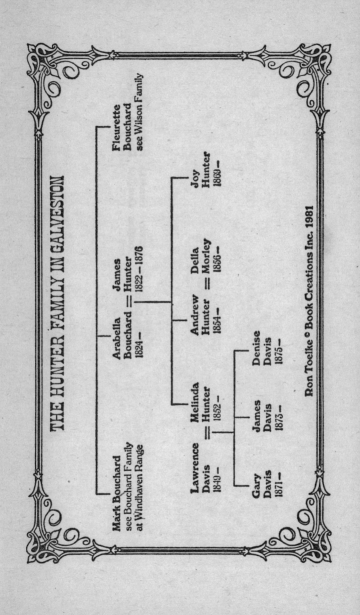

THE HUNTER FAMILY IN GALVESTON

Mark Bouchard
see Bouchard Family
at Windhaven Range

Arabella Bouchard 1824– = James Hunter 1822–1876

Fleurette Bouchard
see Wilson Family

Melinda Hunter 1852–

Andrew Hunter 1854– = Della Morley 1856–

Joy Hunter 1869–

Lawrence Davis 1849– = Melinda Hunter

Gary Davis 1871–

James Davis 1873–

Denise Davis 1875–

Ron Toelke © Book Creations Inc. 1981

PROLOGUE

"It's a mighty cool evenin', Miss Judy, ma'am, 'n dat sky look like we might have a storm." Old Josiah respectfully touched his forehead to the tall blond girl as she entered the rickety stable over which he presided and where he slept at night. The stable also quartered Judith Branshaw's spirited pony and two milk cows. Beyond it was a small pigpen where a young sow watched over her litter. A hundred yards away stood the dilapidated old farmhouse that Judith's father had built.

After the death of Judith's parents two years earlier, Josiah and the three other freed blacks had loyally stayed on to help the girl eke out a meager living from her few acres of cotton and produce. They had originally come to the farm with her parents, twenty-five years before, when Martin Branshaw and his young wife had come up from New Orleans to live near Martin's cousin on the outskirts of the little Alabama town of Tensaw.

"I know, Josiah." Judith gave him a quick smile, her large dark-blue eyes warm with affection. "I declare, you and Nate and Jerry and Tom watch over me as if I were a baby. I'm all of twenty-one and I've managed—thanks to all of you—"

"Yassam, dat you sho'nuff have, Miss Judy. 'T'ain't right, though, 't'ain't right at all that a nice, sweet gal like you should go on runnin' this farm all by herself, no ma'am." He dolefully shook his head. "'Scuse me for speakin' out of turn, Miss Judy, ma'am, but you know yourself what folks in Tensaw keep sayin'."

Judith Branshaw was five feet, nine inches tall, her face oval, with a pert nose and determined chin. Her mouth was full and sweet, but it tightened now and her eyes narrowed coldly as she angrily retorted, "I've heard it till I'm sick of

1

it, Josiah. Yes, I know. These pious God-fearing townsfolk think I'm a fallen woman, because I keep running Daddy's farm and staying here without any white kin to look after me. But I'll tell you this, Josiah, I feel safer here with just you four hardworking, loyal helpers than I'd ever feel with anybody in town, and that's a fact."

"Jist the same, Miss Judy, ma'am—" Josiah started to protest.

"Please saddle my pony for me, Josiah," she broke in, softening the brusque tone with a warm smile. As he reluctantly nodded and headed for the stall, she added in a confidential tone, "Besides, maybe Mr. Fales'll propose to me sometime soon, and then my disapproving neighbors won't have any more chance to gossip about me."

"I hears you, Miss Judy." Josiah led the black pony out of its stall and expertly put on the sidesaddle. "Dat be the fella from Stockton who been sparkin' you?"

"The very same, Josiah. Last Friday, he told me to meet him tonight near old Fort Mims by the river, after sundown. Said he had something important to ask me." Her eyes sparkled with a sudden happiness. "So you see, Josiah, if it's what I think it's going to be, I'll be marrying him and selling this farm to you and Nate, Jerry, and Tom. And I promise I won't ask much for it. You almost deserve it for nothing, considering the hard work you've put into it ever since you started working for my poor daddy."

Josiah helped her up into the saddle, holding the pony's reins tightly in one hand, frowning as he digested the news. "I dunno, Miss Judy. Sho, we'd mighty like to have dis here li'l piece of land for ourselves, only not if you jist up'n married any man jist to get away from Tensaw. 'Pears like to me—n' Nate thinks like I do—dis here Mistah Fales, he don't never come roun' here so we kin size him up 'n see what he looks like. It's allus you ridin' over to Stockton, or down by the river, to meet him when he wants." He shook his head dubiously, his frown deepening. "Mebbe I got no right to say dis, Miss Judy, but effen I was young 'n white like dat Mistah Fales and cared for a purty, sweet gal like you, I'd come callin' on you, not make you traipse off every time to see me, 'n dat's a fact!"

As she adjusted her shawl around her shoulders, she smiled down at him. "You're mighty nice to pay me such a compliment, Josiah. But in a way it's just as well Mr. Fales doesn't come calling on me here, the way folks are so quick

2

to jump to conclusions. Why, they'd be saying, like as not, I was just carrying on with him—and I'm not."

Josiah indignantly clucked his tongue and shook his head. "No need for you to tell me dat, Miss Judy. Why, we know'd your mammy and pappy before you wuz born, 'n we kin 'member back to when you wuz a li'l baby. You allus been the nicest, sweetest gal in the county. Dat's why we jist don't wanna see you come to git mixed up with any flighty fella dat mightn't do the right thing by you."

Judith Branshaw's eyes misted. Deeply touched, she leaned down to pat his shoulder reassuringly. "I said before, Josiah, you mustn't worry so about me. I'm sure he's not flighty. And now, you look after things until I get back, and then maybe I'll have wonderful news for all of you. I surely hope so!" With this, wheeling her pony toward the west, she rode off toward her rendezvous.

It was evening of January 13, 1873. Lincoln's most successful Union general, Ulysses Simpson Grant, was about to start his second term as president. At the helm of a reunited nation, he would preside over the punitive carpetbag government which was doing great harm in the South, yet which—despite the anguished protests of reputable citizens from the former Confederate states—he fully supported. Yet the new year augured well for the prosperity of this vigorous young country. The Great Bonanza silver mine had been discovered in Nevada. The Remington Fire Arms Company had begun to manufacture the typewriter, after having bought the rights from its inventor, Sholes, for a paltry twelve thousand dollars. The Bethlehem Steel Works had established its huge plant in Pennsylvania. Transportation by rail was increasing, connecting cities and towns and bringing staples and luxuries to thousands. By leasing the Lake Shore and Michigan Southern Railroad, Cornelius Vanderbilt now controlled the railroad from New York to Chicago. But despite all this, 1873 would be a year of crisis. . . . .

Nate, a stocky, bearded man in his late fifties, came out of the little cottage he shared with the two other blacks and headed for the stable. "Dat Miss Judy jist ridin' off, Josiah?" he inquired.

"Sho was, Nate." Josiah scratched his chin reflectively and shook his head. "She say she goin' to meet dis here

3

Mistah Fales. She say she think he gonna pop de question fr sho tonight."

"I don't like dat none at all, I don't, Josiah," Nate gloomily confided. "It ain't none of our business, but jist the same, I done heard things 'bout dat man in Stockton."

"What things, Nate?"

The bearded black scowled and spat. "You 'member I went to help ma fren' Eben kill a passel of coons jist aftah Christmas?"

"Sho do," Josiah emitted a delighted cackle. " 'N you brought us back two of dem tasty critters for our supper. Even Miss Judy liked coonmeat the way I fixed it for her—the sweet chile!"

"Dat ain't all I meant, Josiah. Eben hired hisself out to some of dese here rich white folks in Stockton, 'n when I tol' him Miss Judy was sorta sweet on dat Mistah Fales, Eben said he didn't think nuttin' was gonna come of it."

"Why he say dat, Nate, why, man?" Josiah anxiously inquired.

" 'Cause dis here Mistah Fales, his ol' pappy left him a big plantation, but not much cash. He been scrapin' a long time to pay de folks he got workin' fer him, Josiah. Eben says he don't think Mistah Fales gonna marry no gal dat ain't got herself rich folks to put up the cash Mistah Fales needs to run his place," Nate patiently explained.

Josiah emitted a low whistle and shook his head, then turned to look in the direction in which his young mistress had ridden off. "I don't like the soun' of what you jist tole me, Nate. If dis here Mistah Fales got Miss Judy's hopes high to marry her, 'n den he let her down, it gonna break her heart fr sho!"

"I knows dat, Josiah. I sho does wish Miss Judy'd take herself off to N'Awleans. She'd sho'nuff fine herself a proper man dere. Ain't nobody in Tensaw I know of is good nuff for Miss Judy."

"Dat's so," Josiah dispiritedly agreed. Then, with a sigh, he added, "Mebbe yoah fren' Eben, he might be wrong 'bout dat Mistah Fales. Mebbe things gonna turn out all right. I sho does hope so, fer her sake, Nate."

"I does too. Ain't gonna be easy dis year to make any money on cotton. Price keep goin' down, 'n cost of what we need keep goin' up. Even if Miss Judy gits herself married 'n sells us dis place lak she tole us she'd do, dere's gonna be

4

hard times ahead for all of us, Josiah. You jus' hear what I'm tellin' you."

It was a ride of about seven miles from the little farm to the abandoned site of old Fort Mims on the banks of the sluggishly flowing Alabama River. Sixty years earlier, on a stiflingly hot August day, a thousand Creek warriors had massacred more than five hundred whites, Indians, and blacks congregated in the inadequate fort. And eighty-four years earlier, young Lucien Bouchard had camped near the site of the fort on his journey to the fertile lands of Econchate, where he would live among the Creeks.

Judith Branshaw slackened her pony's gait as she came within sight of the ruined fort. The pitiless erosion of time had left only a jagged rectangle of rotted timbers nearly hidden from view by the luxuriant moss, weeds, and grass. It was outlined by clumps of pignut hickories and bitternut. Just north of it stood an old, gaunt, lightning-scarred pine.

The soft, thick darkness of early nightfall made this rendezvous an eerie one, but the tall blond girl was exhilarated by it. She had met David Fales in the general store at Stockton not quite a year ago, and she had been attracted to him at once because of his good looks and courtly manners. In the ensuing months, having learned that she rode her pony, Beauty, nearly every day, he had ridden out on his own sturdy dappled gelding, Aaron, to meet and chat with her.

Having lived a sheltered, isolated life with her parents, she had known nothing of men, save to be wary of their glib promises—her mother had taught her that. But David Fales had conducted himself like a perfect gentleman; never once had he tried to kiss or embrace her. Then, early last month, he had hinted that he was in love with her, and that he would count himself proud to be her sweetheart. Judith had naively replied that her sweetheart would be her husband, to whom alone she could give all her love. As they had walked hand in hand through the forest, having tethered their mounts to a live oak tree, he had suddenly turned to her, taken her into his arms for the first time, and kissed her on the mouth, saying, "I'll make you happy, Judy honey, I promise that. Trust me. Soon, I'll share my plans with you."

She had felt herself respond eagerly to his embrace and kiss, and told herself that this, indeed, was love. And in the intervening weeks, she had impatiently waited for him to divulge these plans, which she believed would make her his wife and free her from the lonely life of the impoverished little farm and the gossiping neighbors who condemned her for her courageous quest for independence. *Tonight*, she happily thought to herself, *it will all come true; it will have been well worth the waiting!*

She dismounted from her pony, patting its sleek head with one hand, while she held the reins loosely in the other. "Good girl, Beauty," she murmured. "He'll be here soon, I know he will."

Behind her there was the sound of brush being trampled. She turned, with an expectant little cry of "David!" only to drop the pony's reins and clap her hand to her open mouth. Before her stood four men in white hooded robes. The dark, cruel eyes of the burly leader glowered at her through the slits of the hood.

"Wh—who are you?" she quavered.

"Are you Judith Branshaw, girl?" The leader's voice was hoarse and vibrant with cruel anger.

"Yes, I am. What business is it of yours? Why are you dressed like that?"

"To dispense justice and to punish wickedness, as you'll find out, Judith Branshaw. Turn loose that pony and come along with us!"

"No, I won't! You've no right to—stop it—Beauty—no—oh, you brutes—how dare you treat me this way—" For one of the quartet had pulled the reins out of her hand and cut the pony across its withers with a hickory switch. With a loud whinny of pain, the terrified animal bounded off along the riverbank and disappeared.

Judith turned to run, but her assailants had anticipated that. Two of the others, stocky and short, seized her by the wrists and dragged her, struggling, kicking, and indignantly crying out, back into the forest till they reached a clearing.

The leader followed, folding his arms across his chest, while the third accomplice hurried to a gray stallion tethered nearby and came back with a coil of rope. The other two men drew out her wrists to be tightly secured with one end of the rope. The third man slung the other end over a thick, high-perched branch of the towering pine tree and squatted down, holding it tautly with both hands. Judith was forced to stand on tiptoe to ease the chafing tension of the coarse rope. She turned her fear-filled face over her shoulder to entreat the leader: "Why are you doing this to me? What have I done? For God's sake, tell me why!"

"You low bitch, you can't guess?" the leader sneered. He cuffed her with the back of his hand across the mouth, drawing blood and a strangled cry of pain from the helpless young captive. "The whole town knows all about you, *Miss* Judith, girl. Living way out of town with those four niggers, keeping away from decent, God-fearing white folks so's you can have yourself a high ol' time with them in your bed." His voice grew viciously ingratiating. "Tell me, Miss Judith, which one of those four niggers gave you the best poke, hmm?"

"That's a filthy lie! I've never been with any man, and I won't, until I marry!" Judith hysterically cried, arching and swaying to ease the torturing bite of the rope against her slim wrists.

"We know better, girl. Right now we're going to show you how we punish dirty nigger-loving sluts like you. Peel her down, boys," the leader ordered.

The two men approached the distraught girl. Despite her frenzied twistings and kickings and shrill, tearful protests, they ripped off her dress and camisole, leaving her in pantalettes, gartered stockings, and shoes. They sniggered coarsely.

"Wal, I'll be hornswoggled—she's wearin' trousers, jist like a man! Sho nuff, she is at that—so why don't you see if she *is* a man?"

Naked to the waist, her face scarlet with shame and wet with tears, Judith tried desperately to kick the hooded man who thrust his hand down under the waistband of the batiste pantalettes. But his companion, stepping behind her, hugged her above the waist with both arms, effectually hampering her attempts to evade this supreme indignity.

"She's a gal, all right," the first man lewdly announced, as he rubbed his hand up and down. "Got my hand right on her cute li'l hairy snatch, I have!"

"Oh, my God! Cowards, brutes, you filthy cowards to treat an innocent girl this way—take your hand away—oh, David, my God in heaven, David, where are you?" Judith shrieked, as she writhed and shuddered, twisting her contorted face this way and that in the poignant hope of seeing her beloved there to save her.

"Innocent, hell! All right, I said peel her down!" the leader commanded impatiently.

7

A shriek burst from Judith's mouth as the man in front of her ruthlessly ripped the pantalettes down to her calves and then stepped back. A faint ray of moonlight, filtering through the forest, touched her delicate skin with a soft glow, and the eyes of her four assailants glistened with lust.

"First, Judith Branshaw, we shall punish you in the name of the God-fearing people of Tensaw," the leader intoned, as he gestured to the second hooded man, who handed him a slim hickory switch. He made it whistle in the air, then muttered, "Best put that shawl round her eyes 'n mouth, it'll quiet her a mite, as she's purty likely to start screeching like a hoot owl 'fore much longer."

This done, he stepped back and, savoring the anticipation of what was to follow, slowly lifted the switch in the air, poised it a long, torturing moment, then cut it viciously across her lovely hips.

A wild cry of pain was torn from Judith. She lunged forward, while a bright crimson welt leaped across her shuddering flesh. Slowly, with obvious relish, the hooded leader flogged her, gloating over her convulsive, uncontrollable gyrations, her screams and babbled entreaties for mercy. When he finally flung aside the switch, her hips, buttocks, and upper thighs were cruelly welted and bleeding. Judith sagged, her head bowed, her bosom heaving, feeble moans escaping her lips which, in her suffering, she had bitten to the blood.

"And now, girl, so's you'll learn that a white man can service you better'n any low nigger, we're goin' to give you a little fun. But remember, when we're done, you'd best move out of Tensaw for good. Or the next time we might not be so easy with you. All right, you boys, lay her on the ground and spread her legs for me," the leader ordered in a thick, unsteady voice.

Judith was scarcely conscious, in the midst of her pain, that the two hooded men were laying her down on the ground and gripping her ankles to spread them wide apart. But as the leader and each of his henchmen had their way with her, she uttered clamorous shriek upon shriek, until the forest resounded with her cries of agony.

When all four had finished with her, they left her, mounted their horses, and rode away into the quiet night.

She lay sprawled on her back, arms flung beyond her head, the trailing rope still remorselessly biting into her cruelly bruised wrists. She moaned wanly; then, turning herself over painfully onto her belly, she lifted her head and looked around. Presently there was the sound of a man's voice: "Judith! Oh my poor Judith, what have they done to you?"

He came toward her, a tall, wiry, blond man in his early thirties, with well-groomed spade beard and an elegant little moustache, in riding breeches, shining new black boots, and red riding jacket. For a moment, he stood staring down at her naked body, pursing his fleshy lips and caressingly stroking his beard, then repeated, "Judith—Judith, my dearest—can you hear me? I was late for our appointment—I never dreamed they'd be so cruel to you!"

Slowly, dazed with her suffering, Judith raised her swollen face, still covered by the knotted shawl. "David—David—I prayed you'd come—to save me from them—oh, those dreadful men—they—they wh-whipped me, D-David—and then—oh, my God, oh, I want to die!"

He knelt down and carefully unknotted the shawl, casting it to one side. His mild brown eyes fixed avidly on the smooth estuary of her back and the contrast between its unmarked sheen and the savage pattern of livid welts that marred her thighs and buttocks. Very lightly, he put out his right palm to glide it over her rounded hip, and shuddered, licking his lips. Affecting a deeply solicitous tone, he inquired, "But surely, they—they left you after—after they had whipped you?"

Judith had dragged her bound wrists toward her; now she laid her face against her arms and slowly shook her head, while choked sobs wrenched her. "Oh God—if only they had—no—they—they—f-forced me—oh, David— why were you so late?"

Gently he slowly turned her over and laid the shawl over her loins, yet his eyes feasted on her heaving bosom. His left arm under her shoulders, he again passed his right palm over her bare flesh, as he murmured, "I'm sorry, Judy dearest. I never thought—all I thought they'd do is whip you and have done—"

Slowly, she turned her head to stare at him, her face stricken with mingled pain and lack of comprehension. "You—you were there—you saw?" she at last quavered.

"Yes—forgive me—"

She made an effort to sit up and groaned at the seething, hot pain the movement cost her. Her dark-blue eyes scanned his effetely handsome face as if for the first time.

9

Then, fighting for breath and control of her voice, she demanded, "You said—you said—all you thought they'd do was wh-whip me and have done—then you—you must have known that they were here waiting for me—David—David—don't let me think what I'm thinking—"

"It'll be fine, you'll see," he glibly sought to reassure her. "I told you you'd be my sweetheart. Well, you will be. We can't get married, but I'll take good care of you—"

"W-what are you saying?" she gasped, as she tugged at her bound wrists. "Please—get this rope off—it's hurting my wrists, please, David."

"Yes, of course, dear." He drew a penknife out of his breeches pocket and cut the rope. She watched him intently, her face suddenly aloof, harsh with the twisting of her pain and degradation. "There. I'll get you some water from the river—"

"No! Don't leave me now—I—I want you to tell me what you mean, David. You just said we can't get married. Why?"

He shrugged noncommittally, tightening his grip around her slim, bare shoulders. Again, his right palm strayed down her shivering naked body, smoothing the dimpled belly. She uttered a hoarse, indignant cry and, with all the strength she could muster, struck his hand away. "Stop it! Do you understand me? Now I'm beginning to understand for the first time, David Fales! You—you never wanted to marry me from the start, did you?"

"But I couldn't, Judy dear. I mean—well, you've no money, only that little farm, and everybody knows it won't ever be profitable. And then your reputation—I mean, what are people to think, your living out there all alone with four niggers—"

"I see! That's what you think, too, isn't it? But you'd like me to be your sweetheart—naked like this in your bed, I suppose?"

"Yes, of course, and I'll take very good care of you—"

With a cry of agonized desperation, she struck him across the mouth with all her might. "It was you who sent those men to whip me and force me, wasn't it? I can see it now—oh, what a stupid little trusting fool I've been all this past year! All you really wanted was for me to be your trollop, wasn't it?"

"But I couldn't marry you now, my dear," he smugly answered, as he drew out a cambric handkerchief and patted his mouth, eyed it to see if her blow had drawn blood, then replaced it. "For one thing, my own plantation is in debt, and I'm marrying Henrietta Aylmers, who'll bring me a very handsome dowry. And for another—since we may as well face up to it now, Judy dear—you're damaged goods."

"You—you—you horrible, conniving bastard—and you're a Southern gentleman, are you?" she spat at him.

He rose to his feet, his face cold and contemptuous. "How could you expect a decent man to marry you, after you've been living alone with those niggers since your parents died? Do you think I could face the smirks, the gossip, the innuendos of the townspeople if I married you—I myself always wondering if perhaps you hadn't been to bed with your hired black help? No, my dear, no respectable Southern gentleman will ever want to marry one of your kind."

"Get away from me! I don't ever want to see your lying, treacherous face again. You must surely have hired those men to do all this to me, David Fales! I'll sell my farm to my loyal blacks and I'll leave Tensaw forever!"

He shrugged again. "As you please, my dear. Though I was prepared to make you a suitable offer—it would give you financial security so you wouldn't have to sell yourself to any man who came along with the price—"

"Damn you to hell forever, you stinking bastard—you're worse than those men ever could be!"

"I'm sorry you choose to look at things that way. But I've a last piece of advice for you. You might think of moving to Montgomery. There are plenty of rich Northern carpetbaggers there who'll take a fancy to your charms."

She dragged herself to her feet, panting and groaning, dragging the ripped pantalettes up over her loins, tying the shawl with shaking fingers over her heaving bosom. "I just might do that, David Fales," she gasped. "Maybe they'll help me find a way to pay *decent* Southern gentlemen back! And now, be kind enough to get out of my sight before I try to kill you!"

He uttered a mocking laugh, untethered his gelding, and rode off into the night, leaving her standing weeping in the dark forest.

CHAPTER ONE

It was a Wednesday morning of the first week of February, 1873. The Alabama sky had been covered with thick clouds all night long, and the rumble of thunder far to the south had been heard occasionally. About an hour before sunrise, however, a brief, sharp storm had dispelled the intolerable sultriness of the air, and the day had dawned bright and clear.

As she arose this morning and went to look out her window at the sunlit fields surrounding Windhaven Plantation, Laure Bouchard thought of going for a ride with her sons—Lucien, almost seven, and Paul, four. She would leave behind with their capable and devoted nurse her little daughters, Celestine, not quite two, and baby Clarissa, who had first seen the light of day on the seventh of the past January. When, however, she proposed this outing at breakfast, bearded Luke Bouchard, now rapidly graying but still as wiry and hale as ever in his fifty-seventh year, mildly remonstrated, "My darling, it's been only a month since Clarissa was born. I don't think the doctor would approve of your exercising so soon afterward, and I'd be inclined to agree with him."

To this, Laura, with a merry toss of her golden hair, teasingly riposted, "There you go again, dear Luke, being the old sobersides I took you for when I first met you."

"Nothing of the sort!" Luke was nettled by that old joke, which had been a kind of marital goad to him ever since their first meeting in New Orleans eight years earlier. Without being aware of it, Luke had always sought to prove to his young second wife that the complacency and gentleness of his first marriage to soft-spoken Lucy Williamson had not made him at all sedate and unimagina-

13

tively predictable, as she sometimes liked to say in jest. And thus far, even Laure had been forced to admit, he had assuredly proved his point.

Aware of his irritation, Laure gave him a bewitchingly apologetic smile as she softly rejoined, "No, forgive me, my darling, I was only teasing. The truth is, it bothers me to have you so concerned about my well-being, since I'm in wonderful health. Ever since he bought out old Dr. Medbury's practice last year, that young Dr. Kennery has looked after me well, and he assures me now that I'm in the best of health. He believes that a woman should begin to exercise as soon as she feels she's regained her strength. It will speed her restoration."

"Well, I suppose that I must give way to modern medical opinion," Luke wryly agreed, as he walked around to the other end of the table and bent to kiss her forehead and then her mouth.

Laure's arms wound round him as she drew him down to her. "Besides," she whispered, "just to show you I didn't mean what I just said, I want us to be lovers again. So the sooner I'm myself again after Clarissa, the better we'll both like it, won't we?"

Luke flushed at this overt suggestion. At the same time, he told himself that he was far more fortunate than most men; the difference in age between Laure—now thirty-three—and himself had in no way affected their happiness. It was certain that Laure's youth, vivacity, and inventive cajolery in adapting herself to the relatively tranquil life of a plantation, after her glamorous life in New Orleans, had been the perfect inspiration to keep him young in outlook and in health, so that they shared all the joys of wedlock.

To hide his embarrassment at her whispered invitation, he straightened and hurriedly declared, "Well, if you are sure that this new doctor is perfectly trustworthy, I'll leave the decision to you, Laure. Do be careful, I beg of you. You know how much you mean to me."

"Yes, and thank you for always showing me just how you feel, dear Luke." She put out a hand to him, which he took, brought to his lips, and fervently kissed. "I'm so very happy with you and with our family."

"And this simple life of a farmer's wife isn't boring to you? Be candid with me, Laure."

She smiled at him again, then shook her head. "I have no regrets at all, I can tell you that honestly. You're the

14

most wonderful husband and lover any woman could pray for, my darling. And if ever I thought you dull and stuffy because you tried to follow in your Grandfather Lucien's footsteps, you've shown time and time again more devotion and fidelity and concern than most husbands would ever do, believe me. I shan't ever forget how you—a man of peace and the highest ideals—fought Henri Cournier in that terrible duel to punish him for having kidnapped little Lucien. And I'll always remember the courage you showed when you ran for the legislature and avenged a slur on my honor during the campaign. Surely that was in the finest tradition of the old swashbucklers."

"Sometimes a man of peace is forced into violence against his will because he wants justice for his dear ones, Laure. Besides"—to relieve the suddenly serious and perhaps overly sentimental theme of their breakfast conversation, he changed to an airy tone—"it's plain to see that Andy Haskins is a far better vote-getter than I ever was. From what his lovely wife, Jessica, has told me about his maiden efforts in the House of Representatives, he's going to make a mark for himself. He could quite easily go to the gubernatorial chair. This state assuredly has need of honest, incorruptible men. Now then, with your permission I'm going to lock myself up with Marius Thornton this afternoon and plan what we're going to grow on Windhaven Plantation this year."

"I'll do my best not to disturb you, and please don't worry about my going for a ride. I'll make sure the weather is cooperating before I leave the house. Oh, and when you see Marius, be sure to tell him I hope his brand-new son Esau is doing well, and that his wife, Clemmie, is the same," Laure brightly urged him.

"I'll be sure to do that, darling. Yes, Marius is very happy that Clemmie's given him a boy this time. Speaking of children, how's Mitzi Sattersfield? She must be expecting her baby fairly soon."

"That's right, my dear. The baby's due in about a month."

"That's wonderful! Well, Dalbert's business is improving by leaps and bounds," Luke smiled, "and if I know him, this new addition to his family will make him work all the harder. As soon as Mitzi's had her baby, I'll send over a nice present to them and the new heir."

"Yes, and maybe next week I'll ride over and have a

15

little visit with Mitzi. I think she'd appreciate it about now."

"That would be fine, dear." Luke smiled broadly. "Now, I'll take my leave of you, Laure darling. I want to spend the rest of this morning writing some letters to James and Arabella in Galveston and to Lucien Edmond and Maxine in Carrizo Springs." He paused a moment, frowning thoughtfully. "All of Lucien Edmond's efforts are put into cattle-raising, Laure. And though I'd normally say that that was a surefire business to give him a very good living, I'm not at all happy with the outlook for our country for this year. Well, I shouldn't be thinking out loud and annoying you with it. I'll see you later, at supper this evening, if not before."

At this moment, Clarabelle Hendry—the brown-haired widow in her early forties whom Luke had recently hired as nurse—entered the dining room and greeted her employers. "Good morning, Mr. Bouchard, Mrs. Bouchard. Celestine is still sleeping, but Clarissa is wide awake and crying—I think she's hungry. Excuse me, sir." She glanced at Luke and blushed. Clearing his throat, Luke nodded cordially to her and left the room.

"Thank you, Mrs. Hendry," Laure said. "Thank goodness I'm still able to nurse her. But, Mrs. Hendry, it might be a good idea if you could look around for a wet nurse, for I don't think I'll be able to do it much longer."

"Of course, Mrs. Bouchard. I think I know someone very reliable. She's a few years younger than I am. Her husband's out of work at the moment, so I'm sure she could use the income."

"Then do please make the arrangements, if you will, Mrs. Hendry."

"Of course I will. Matter of fact, Mr. Mendicott is riding into Montgomery this afternoon, and I'll have him stop over at Elsie Carbury's house and tell her you'd like to see her. Would it be any bother if she brought her children with her when she came to nurse Clarissa?"

"Of course not. We've room enough for them here, and we can put her up for the time—if her husband doesn't object. Well, I leave it to you. You've been so capable and loving to the children, and Luke and I are very grateful to you."

"It's my pleasure, Mrs. Bouchard. You're the nicest

folks I've ever met, and I love your little ones as much as if they were my own."

"Thank you, Mrs. Hendry. That's very sweet of you to say, and the children feel the same way about you."

Marius Thornton, the tall, sturdy black whom Luke Bouchard had rescued from the attack of a group of white racists during the New Orleans riot seven years ago, was now thirty-two and totally devoted to his important post as foreman of Windhaven Plantation. He still retained the youthful enthusiasm and candor that had been so appealing to Luke at their first meeting, but his responsibility and self-discipline in his post of trust had given him a quiet dignity and an awareness of his own competence. Luke's having arranged to liberate his nineteen-year-old mulatto sweetheart, Clementine, from her near-starvation job as a seamstress had enabled the two young lovers to marry and to have a growing family—which further increased Marius Thornton's confidence in himself. During the past year, he had sent away for books on bookkeeping and planting, and assiduously studied them during his free hours. He had even acquired a passable knowledge of French, which enabled him to read in the language, and he had also become conversant not only with Alabama politics, but also with the economic news of the country.

As Luke approached the study, about three in the afternoon, he found Marius waiting outside the door for him and smilingly extended his hand. "How is the newest addition, Marius? My wife told me to be sure to inquire after Clemmie and Esau."

"They couldn't be better, Mr. Luke," Marius grinned as he shook his employer's hand. "I'll tell you something, I'm mighty glad I have another boy. It's good for a man to have sons—I confess I've envied you yours. You know, by the time a man reaches the end of his life, he looks on his sons as successors, to do those things he meant to do and never finished."

"That's my feeling exactly, Marius," Luke chuckled. "Well, now, let's tackle the books and plan for this new year."

"I'm as eager as you are, Mr. Luke. Judging from the winter we're having, and remembering what happened the last couple of years, I'd say we're in for a fine spring and summer. That'll be good for our crops. Might even have a little more rain than we had last year, too."

"Very likely. But I'm not thinking of the weather as much as I am of what's going on in Washington, Marius. There, sit down and make yourself comfortable. Let me pour you some brandy."

"Not too much, Mr. Luke. I want to get out and check those fields before the sun sets. Brandy's a treat for me, but it does go to my head," Marius grinned.

"One snifter won't muddle your judgment." Luke went to the sideboard, poured from a cut-glass decanter, and handed the exquisite, hand-blown Italian glass to his foreman, then poured a liberal measure for himself and went back to the escritoire. "A toast to 1873, Marius. And, specifically, to the good fortune of Windhaven Plantation and all of us who live on its bounty."

"Amen to that, Mr. Luke." Marius raised his snifter and nodded toward Luke, then cautiously sipped, smacked his lips, and smiled. "It's strong and it warms a man right down to where he is, Mr. Luke. Makes me mellow and want to think of the past, and not do any work for the rest of the day—and that's sinful."

Luke chuckled again and shook his head. "I think you can be allowed a good many moments of self-indulgence, Marius, after all you've contributed to Windhaven Plantation. The land is rich, and thanks to your management, it's fertile and it's been allowed to have its rest so that it can produce enough to meet all our needs, plus enough extra to provide a good income for all of us who work here. That's what my grandfather always intended. Once he said to me, 'Treat the land as you would a child of your own family, Luke, and it won't let you down. It'll be as loyal as you are. Waste its resources, and you'll live to regret your selfishness.' That was sound advice then, as it is today."

Luke paused, stared at his snifter, then took a sip from it. After a moment, he went on, "The only problem is that Windhaven Plantation doesn't exist in a vacuum. There's trouble all around us. Though we've come through the worst of the Reconstruction, there are still dreadful abuses—at least in some other Southern states. And now, in Washington, there is conniving and scheming, corruption and a lust for power which, even way down here in Alabama, can change the way we live."

"You mean, Mr. Luke, because President Grant got re-elected?" Marius proffered.

Luke soberly nodded. "That's it exactly. Grant's a bluff, hearty, capable man, and he made a good soldier. As a politician, he's a weakling because he's too friendly. He's surrounded himself with incompetents in the Cabinet, and there are swarms of greedy profiteers converging on him and reminding him that without their help he wouldn't have won a second term. What worries me is that the stubborn determination he showed as a general—doggedly reinforcing his troops until they prevailed by sheer force of arms—hasn't carried over into his enormous job as president. Yes, Marius, I think this year is going to be a crisis for the entire nation, judging by the signs."

"How do you mean that, Mr. Luke?"

"Well, take New York's Tammany Hall. Boss Tweed has just been found guilty of graft and sentenced to twelve years in prison with a fine of twelve thousand dollars. Already there are stories that his prison cell has become a kind of luxurious hotel suite, with fancy meals from Delmonico's and the finest wines and liqueurs and even women. And I suspect they'll find a way to commute his sentence after maybe a year. The public thinks it a big joke—apparently, the more of a scoundrel you are, the more of a national hero you become. That's a very bad sign. It's indicative of the moral weakness of our times, Marius. As my grandfather used to tell me, once you admit the power of evil and give it only token recognition without trying to stamp it out, you lay yourself open to its defeating good. I sincerely pray God that's not going to happen, but I've grave misgivings about this new year." He shrugged and sighed again, then finished his brandy. "Now let's talk about what concerns us most. How many acres are we going to devote to produce and how many to cotton, do you figure, Marius?"

CHAPTER TWO

Luke Bouchard's fears about the economic perils of the new year were greatly intensified a week after his consultation with Marius Thornton. For on February 12, Congress passed the Fourth Coinage Act, by which the silver dollar—with the exception of a heavier trade dollar to be used in the Orient—would be dropped from the list of coins and the gold dollar made the standard unit of value. Most of the economists of the nation proclaimed this legislation to be the "crime of 1873"; but there was worse to follow. Scarcely a week later, a special committee of the House of Representatives reported that Congressmen Oakes Ames and James Brooks were guilty of wrongdoing in the notorious Crédit Mobilier scandal and recommended their expulsion from the House; nevertheless the full House—to its shame—voted merely to censure Ames and Brooks for their conduct.

This was but another sorry chapter in one of the worst scandals in American history. The Crédit Mobilier of America was a fraudulent construction company set up in connection with the building of the Union Pacific Railroad. Through this company, Ames, Brooks, Thomas C. Durant, and others in charge of the Union Pacific Railroad had awarded to themselves lucrative construction contracts that yielded profits ranging from seven million to twenty-three million dollars. To forestall any investigation or interference by Congress, Oakes Ames had sold shares of Crédit Mobilier stock to members of Congress at a fraction of their actual worth. The public had first been made aware of this colossal fraud during Grant's campaign for a second term as president. Thus it was small wonder that Luke was thoroughly disheartened by the forces of corruption that had attached themselves to the Union general during his first term in office, and believed that his second term would only give further leeway to the avid profiteers surrounding Grant.

On the day after he read in the Montgomery *Advertiser* that Ames and Brooks had only been censured, while others connected with the scandal had been virtually absolved of wrongdoing, Luke Bouchard rode over to visit Andy Haskins. The amiable one-armed Tennesseean had been attending the sessions in the state House of Representatives at Montgomery since the middle of January, as Representative of Montgomery County. But this weekend, because the House had taken a ten-day adjournment from its labors, he was back on his little farm and reunited with his lovely wife, Jessica, and their three-month-old son, Horatio, named after Jessica's father.

Cassius Ardmore—the younger of the Ardmore brothers, who were freed blacks working for Andy—saw Luke arrive and hurried up to take his spirited gelding to the stable. Luke greeted him cordially. "How are things on the farm here, Cassius?"

"Jist fine, Mistah Luke, sir," the wiry black grinned. "We all mighty proud of Mistah Andy, now dat he helpin' run de government, you kin depend on dat, Mistah Luke!"

"And you've a perfect right to be, Cassius. How's Burt Coleman feeling these days? I know that he must miss his friend Matt." Luke was referring to Matt Rensler, who had been shot last year during an attack on Andy's property by the Ku Klux Klan.

Cassius Ardmore silently nodded and glanced out toward the spacious fields. Luke's gaze followed, taking in the full extent of Andy's land, which included not only the acreage inherited from Jessica's father, Horatio Bambach, but also the land that once belonged to old Edward Williamson, father of Luke's first wife, Lucy. Luke had deeded the Williamson land to Andy last summer.

After a moment's pause, Cassius turned back to Luke and gave him a reassuring smile. "Well, Mistah Luke, Mistah Coleman, he comin' along jist fine. Jist before de end of last year, Mistah Andy, he hired another white man who come here lookin' for a handout and mebbe a spell of work. Turns out he used to be a corporal in de same outfit with Mistah Coleman. And Mistah Coleman take to him right off, dey be good friends now, workin' all day long and

22

even sharing de same shack where Mistah Matt used to be with Mistah Coleman."

"I'm glad to hear that, Cassius." Luke handed Cassius the reins of his gelding and turned away for a moment. His chance conversation had reminded him all too distressingly of Hugh Entrevois, Mark Bouchard's illegitimate son, who had appeared suddenly in the neighborhood the previous year, ostensibly prepared to make his peace with the Bouchard family. Luke could never forget that he had entrusted Entrevois with the care of Andy's land—the Williamson acreage. If it had not been for that, Matt Rensler would be alive today. Luke wondered if he would ever be free from the memory of his fatal error in judgment.

He was happily drawn from this somber mood when the familiar voice of Andy Haskins hailed him: "By all that's holy, Mr. Luke—it's good to see you out here on this land, because I can't help wanting to thank you every day I'm on it for seeing that Jessica wasn't cheated out of it and for putting me in charge. Yessir, I owe just about everything I've got in life to you, Mr. Luke."

"Not at all, Andy." Luke turned to see the lanky young Tennesseean starting toward him, a hoe in his hand, and laughed with pleasure at the sight. "I wish your constituents could see you now, Andy Haskins," he joked, "because then they'd know they picked a real man of the people! Well now, how does it feel to wear a frock coat and sit with your peers in the House up at Montgomery?"

Andy Haskins made a wry grimace, then chuckled. "I'd just as soon skip the frock coat, Mr. Luke, to tell you the truth. Maybe that's why you see me using this hoe and wearing my work duds. Feels a lot more comfortable, I can tell you for certain. But don't stand out here in the sun, come on in and see little Horatio. Jessica made a pile of biscuits that'll melt in your mouth, specially when you pour honey on 'em. And a good cup of black coffee to wash them down—how does that strike you, Mr. Luke?"

"That strikes me fine, Andy."

"Good. Why, Jessica would scalp me for sure, if I didn't bring you in right away and treat you properly." Andy beamed and added, in a confidential tone: "You know, little Horatio is just the apple of her eye. I wanted her to name him after her father—poor old fellow, with such a hard struggle to hold things together for his daughter and himself. I'll never forget how you took them to your heart,

23

Mr. Luke, and helped them, and helped me meet Jessica. Shucks, time I shut my big mouth and let Jessica do the talking for a spell." He opened the door of the freshly painted frame house and ushered Luke into the kitchen.

Jessica sat in a chair, crooning to the baby. At the sight of Luke she made as if to rise, but he made a gesture to stop her. "No, please don't get up, Mrs. Haskins. Just let me stand here and admire the two of you. That's certainly a fine baby boy!"

"Yes he is, Mr. Bouchard!" Jessica proudly declared as she bent down to kiss Horatio's forehead. "And he's the best baby ever."

"I promised Mr. Luke here a passel of your fine biscuits and honey and good strong coffee," Andy said. "I'll tend Horatio, if you don't mind serving us up."

"Of course I don't. Andy Haskins, I do declare, you don't have to ask me to be hospitable to Mr. Bouchard. Of all the people in this world, and you know it as well as I do, I'm beholden to him." Jessica rose and carefully handed the baby to her beaming husband. "It won't take me a minute, Mr. Bouchard. Just you sit down there at the table and make yourself right comfy."

"Thanks, it's kind of you, Mrs. Haskins." He waited until Jessica had hurried to the kitchen, then turned to Andy. "Right now isn't exactly the time, Andy, but I'd like to ask you your impressions of the House, now that you've had a taste of what state government is like. Maybe after we've had the refreshments I'm looking forward to, we could sit and chat a bit."

"I'd like that fine, Mr. Luke. The fact of the matter is, I've met a few peculiar folks who all of a sudden want to make a big fuss over me."

"My guess is that they're lobbyists, Andy. I'll be very interested in hearing your impressions of them, too. Well now, that looks wonderful!"—this last as Jessica entered with a tray containing a bowl of fluffy biscuits, a little stone crock of honey, a pot of coffee, plates, saucers, cups, and spoons. She set the tray down on the large rectangular table, which served them both as a dining table and as a desk for Andy when he was studying the bills he would be required to vote on when the legislature reconvened.

"There now, Mr. Bouchard, you sit right there, and you, Andy, right next to Mr. Bouchard."

"I do hope you'll join us, Mrs. Haskins?" Luke graciously inquired.

"I mean to, but most of the biscuits and the honey are for you gentlemen. The doctor says I mustn't overeat. And I don't want to get too fat, or Andy won't like me any more."

"Now, Jessica, that's a terrible thing to say." Andy groaned and shook his head as he gave Luke a plaintively appealing look. "Jessica's just fishing for compliments, because you can see she's the most beautiful girl in the county."

"Now you stop that, Andy Haskins!" Jessica blushed as she seated herself, pouring coffee first into the two men's cups and then half a cup for herself. "Don't mind us, Mr. Bouchard, we're just like any young married couple."

"And a great deal happier than most, I can see that already," Luke shrewdly observed, as he took a sip of his coffee and then broke one of the biscuits in two. "A wonderful texture, and it smells delicious." He took a bite, and added, "And it surely is! Andy, this girl is a treasure. You'd better not lose her, because she's beautiful and intelligent, and besides, anyone who can make biscuits like this is worthy of the highest praise."

"Oh, please do stop, Mr. Bouchard, you're just making fun of me!" Jessica blushingly protested.

"Not in the least." Luke helped himself to another biscuit, broke it open, and spooned a liberal amount of honey from the stone crock onto the halves. "I remember eating Mammy Clorinda's biscuits back when I was a boy with Grandfather, and how I learned the trick of being able to eat all the honey I wanted without spilling any on my breeches. I'll admit, though, the method looks a bit hoggish." With this, eyeing the glistening honey that threatened to spill over the rim of the biscuit-half, he swiftly folded it over and crammed it into his mouth, then chewed voraciously, while both Andy and Jessica laughed at his childlike enjoyment.

"I know," Luke chuckled, after he had washed down the biscuit with a long swig of coffee, "*Godey's Lady's Book* would never approve of my manners, but you'll have to admit my method is effective. And that sweet, pure honey just emphasizes the tastiness of your biscuits, Mrs. Haskins. I shan't want any supper tonight—but it'll be worth it."

25

For a time, the two men and Jessica exchanged polite amenities, till at last Jessica tactfully rose and lifted little Horatio out of his bassinet, which she had placed beside her at the table. "I know you two have a great deal to talk over, and besides, it's just about time for Horatio's feeding. So, if you'll excuse me?"

"Reluctantly, Mrs. Haskins." Luke courteously rose to his feet and gave her a courtly bow, which made her flush prettily again.

Once she had gone into the bedroom and closed the door behind her, he seated himself and turned to her husband. "Now then, Andy, suppose you tell me all about these men you encountered in the House—from the beginning."

"Well, sir, just about a week after I took my seat there in the House, when the bell rang at the end of the day, I went out into the hall and one of the pages said that some gentlemen wanted to meet the newly elected representative from Montgomery County."

"I see."

"Of course, I wanted to know what was on their minds—I figured maybe they were some of the constituents who voted for me and of course I'm duty-bound to speak for the people who put me in office."

"You'd naturally feel that way, being the kind of man you are, Andy. Go on," Luke quietly encouraged.

"Thanks for saying that, Mr. Luke. You're sure one to give a man confidence, I'll say that for you," Andy grinned. Then, his face sobering, he went on: "Well, sir, there were four of them. Their leader seemed to be a man who called himself Homer Jenkinson. He told me he'd come to Montgomery just after the war, that he was married and a substantial citizen, living right there in Montgomery. And he said that he and his friends had voted for me, and they wanted to meet me and find out if I knew anything about railroads."

"I begin to smell a rat, Andy. But do go on." Luke hitched his chair up closer to the table and leaned forward.

"Well, Mr. Luke, I told them that railroads were certain to be the lifeline of this growing country. And, of course, everybody knows that during the war the Confederates had to hold on to all the rail lines they could to transport the supplies for their troops in the field."

"Certainly. But I'll wager that wasn't what they had in mind, now, was it?"

Andy ruefully shook his head. "Not hardly, Mr. Luke. It seems this Mr. Jenkinson is behind a bill to lower taxes on some sections of land. This land, as I understand it, will be adjacent to a proposed extension of the railroad tracks of the Alabama and Chattanooga Railroad."

"And there's the rat, sure enough!" Luke grimly averred. "How much do you know about that line, Andy?"

"Enough to know that it's now in receivership, Mr. Luke. There have been a lot of shenanigans surrounding the line, so I said to Mr. Jenkinson that I'd have to look into the matter, and that I wasn't going to give them a yes or a no right away. I also said I didn't know them from Adam—knew nothing about them except that they were better dressed than I."

"Good for you! Now then, can you tell me all that you know about the Alabama and Chattanooga?" Luke earnestly demanded.

Andy leaned back, stared at the ceiling a moment, thoughtfully frowned, and then replied, "Well, now, I've been reading up on the matter, and it's an unsavory story, as I'm sure you're aware. Correct me if I'm wrong, but it seems that the trouble really started about five years ago, when the General Assembly under Governor Smith loosened up the law regarding state endorsement of railroad bonds. The General Assembly amended the law so that railroad bonds could be endorsed in five-mile blocks—after completion of the first twenty miles—and the endorsements were increased from twelve thousand to sixteen thousand dollars a mile. Also, counties and cities were permitted to invest in railroad construction and to levy taxes to cover the obligations they'd have in such an investment. It was all part of a general tendency to pander to the railroad interests in this state."

"Go to the head of the class, Andy. I see you've really done your homework. What else did you learn—and specifically about the Alabama and Chattanooga?"

Again Andy frowned. "Well, there was a man by the name of John C. Stanton who had a lot to do with railroads in this state. It was he who presided over the merger of the old Wills Valley Railroad and the Northeast and Southwest Alabama Railroad, to form the Alabama and Chattanooga. Stanton himself became general superintendent of the newly consolidated line, and his brother D. N. Stanton became vice president. They began construction on a line that was supposed to be 295 miles long, stretching from Chattanooga southwest through Alabama, to Meridian, Mississippi. They hoped to finish by January of 1871, but they never got very far."

"That's right, Andy," Luke interposed, "and I'll tell you, Alabama has had a great deal more trouble and expense out of that venture than ever Charles Douglas will have with the railroads in Texas. But go on. What other information have you gleaned about this ambitious line?"

"Just what you might expect. After reading up on it—from back issues of the *Advertiser* and such like—I went to see one of the other representatives, who has become a friend of mine, old Mr. Dobry, who represents Marion County. He knew a great deal more than I did, naturally, because he's had four terms already. He had a lot to say about the situation, including some unfavorable words for Governor Smith and his role in the matter."

"Smith was a good man in some ways, but he was unfortunately in office at a very bad time, and he alienated everybody, even the members of his own party," Luke replied.

"I gathered that," Andy nodded. "Anyway, Mr. Dobry said that J. C. Stanton got most of the money to build the Alabama and Chattanooga from the sale of the state-endorsed bonds, and that he did a little cheating to get the bonds. For example, the line was given bonds for twenty miles of track which were actually completed by the old Northeast and Southwest Alabama Railroad. Then the line received additional bonds for fifteen miles of track laid down by the Wills Valley Company. Governor Smith was supposed to protect the state against this kind of fraud, and to investigate applications for state aid, but Mr. Dobry said that Governor Smith never used his powers to do any checking."

"That's true, Andy. He let two bond endorsements go through in 1870—endorsements Stanton got by bribing the state legislators. Everyone knew about it, which makes it worse. And I'm afraid Governor Lindsay, Smith's successor, hasn't done much better. He finally acquired the line for the state last year, when it was declared bankrupt—hoping, I guess, to run it or sell it to private enterprise. But then the U.S. Circuit Court stepped in, reversed a lower court decision, and turned the railroad over to receivers for the first mortgage bondholders. Now the receivers are supposed to try and run the line, to see if something can be salvaged from this sorry mess. And that's where we stand right now." Luke paused, sighed, then asked, "So what do this Mr. Jenkinson and his group want from you? Don't they realize that you might be suspicious of anything and everything connected with the railroad?"

"Not from that first meeting, Mr. Luke. Mr. Jenkinson said that the land he was speaking about—the land near that supposed extension of the railroad—would be very attractive to investors, particularly if I sponsored this bill to lower taxes on it. The resulting development, he said, would benefit everyone. I think it's a long shot, myself. I don't think the receivers for the first mortgage bondholders are going to throw good money after bad by attempting to build an extension at this time, and I doubt that either the railroad or the state could wait that long for some resolution to this money muddle. Furthermore, how could this new rail line benefit my own constituents—the people of Montgomery County?"

"You may be a novice to politics, Andy," Luke replied, "but you've got a level head on your shoulders and an honest heart to guide you into thinking straight. Of course, that line wouldn't help Montgomery County. I'll be very interested in seeing just what happens when they come back to you—as I'm sure they will."

"I'll say no, that's what I'll say. What I'd like to see instead is some tax reform for the county and maybe a bill to raise funds for a good hospital. That, and lowering the taxes generally, so that folks who lost almost all they had during the war will have a chance to stand on their own feet," the lanky young Tennesseean retorted.

Luke Bouchard rose from the table and held out his hand to Andy. "Grandfather would have been proud to know a man like you, Andy. I'm luckier than he was, because you're my good friend. And now, as a citizen of this county, I'm grateful to you for being the sort of legislator who can't be corrupted. Believe me, Andy, there are still plenty of loyal citizens in this county who will back you up in trying to achieve those goals you've so admirably set for yourself. God bless you and give you the strength to follow through!"

CHAPTER THREE

Homer Jenkinson scowled as he heard a faint tap at the door of his study. At fifty, he was nearly bald, with an enormous walrus moustache, thick jowls, narrowly set, astigmatic brown eyes, which always seemed to be squinting, and a corpulence that bespoke his predilection for rich food and strong drink. With a muffled oath, he shoved a sheaf of papers to one side and covered them with a copy of the *Advertiser,* then rose and irritatedly called out, "All right, Pru, you may come in now!"

The door was opened to admit an attractive young woman of twenty-four, who approached him with the same submissive attitude a slave might have shown before the war. Her large, soft, blue eyes were downcast, her heart-shaped face wore a constant expression of fearful docility, and her shoulders slumped in a kind of self-dejection. Her glossy, dark-brown hair had been put up in an enormous, old-fashioned bun at the top of her head, which made her look older than she was. She stood beside the desk, nervously twisting her slim fingers and lowering her eyes, as if she feared to meet his.

"Well, what do you want, Pru? You know I didn't want to be disturbed. I'm having a very important meeting in half an hour."

"I—I know that, H-Homer," she quavered in a self-effacing, scarcely audible tone. "I—I just wanted to ask, if you didn't need me—you and your friends—would it be all right if I went to visit Mrs. Parker?"

A contemptuous sneer curved his fleshy mouth as he contemplated her. Without answering her question, he turned to open a fresh box of Havana cigars, took one out, chewed off the end, and spat it into a silver cuspidor. He stuck it into a corner of his mouth and ordered, "You'll light my cigar for me, Pru, if you please."

"Oh, why—yes, of course, Homer d-dear!" she faltered. To do this, she had virtually to bend before him, to open the top side drawer of his spacious oakwood desk and remove a box of lucifers. Straightening up, she struck one of the matches and held the flame to the end of the cigar, while he drew upon it lingeringly, savoring not only the aroma, but also her pose of enforced humility. When the cigar was glowing well, he took a puff and exhaled a ring of smoke above her head and then, turning to the bay window and drawing aside the chintz curtain, he pronounced, "You know perfectly well I don't approve of Mrs. Parker—that stupid old gossip. However, since I want to be left in private with my friends, I suppose you may as well leave the house, Pru. See that you're back in time to start my supper. And tell Mrs. Sedlars that if she doesn't cook any better than she has the last week or two, she's likely to find herself without a situation. I know you would be glad to replace her, my dear."

"As you wish, H-Homer," Prudence Jenkinson stammered, her face coloring hotly. She turned to go, but he put out a hand and touched her shoulder. She stopped short and a convulsive tremor seized her. She turned back to look at him, her eyes wide like those of a startled fawn. "Yes, H-Homer?"

"I should like you to preside over Mrs. Sedlar's feeble efforts; you will remember that, Pru. And I should like a trifle for dessert, as rich as she can make it, do you understand me?"

"Oh yes, Homer—I—I'll see to it. If—if she doesn't know how to make it, I—I think I could do it myself very well to please you."

"Very good, my dear. You may go now."

"Th-thank you, H-Homer. I promise I'll be back in plenty of time to see that your supper's started."

"See that you are," he curtly dismissed her. Prudence turned and went out, softly closing the door, as if afraid of the slightest sound enraging him.

She was not the first woman to be the recipient of Homer Jenkinson's abuse. He had been married at the age of thirty in Trenton, New Jersey, to an introspective, sensitive young woman in her mid-twenties named Anne Morway. Anne was an only child. Her father was a greengrocer whose business was tottering on the brink of collapse. Jenkinson saved Thomas Morway from bankruptcy, and in return had demanded his daughter's hand in marriage. Five years later, because of his shameless philandering and his sadistic treatment of her, she committed suicide by drowning. The coroner attributed her suicide to grief over her father's death from a heart attack the week before.

After the war, Jenkinson, eager to turn the defeat of the South to his own financial gain, came to Montgomery, bringing with him a fortune acquired partly through a legacy and partly through having cheated his younger brother out of the profits of a textile mill they jointly owned. He purchased a sprawling, comfortable frame house at the end of Edgemont Avenue, on the western outskirts of the state capital. Seeking a bank into which to transfer his fortune, he made the acquaintance of elderly William Eullis, who had founded the Montgomery Citizens' Bank and Trust. A quick investigation showed Jenkinson that the bank was in imminent danger of closing its doors forever. What made him decide to perpetuate its existence and to invest a considerable portion of his own capital in the institution was his lust for old Eullis's seventeen-year-old daughter.

William Eullis proved to be as susceptible to an offer of financial salvation as Thomas Morway had been. Prudence, his only child, drawn closer to him by the death of her mother ten years earlier, accepted Jenkinson as her husband out of a sense of dutiful obligation to her adored father. His death from a stroke six months later left her and his bank entirely at her husband's mercy.

Homer Jenkinson had been astute enough to induce Eullis, before his death, to sign a promissory note that virtually gave his son-in-law title to the bank after the old man's demise. Indeed, two weeks after Eullis's funeral, Jenkinson took over the bank and named himself president. By then, to be sure, Prudence was trapped and found herself not so much a wife as a denigrated slave in the house on Edgemont Avenue.

Well-educated and gentle by nature, Prudence had found it difficult from the very outset to submit to her husband's lovemaking. Jenkinson, for his part, had no desire for children, and when she timidly tried to broach the subject, he had coarsely instructed her to see to it that there would be no issue from their union. When she tried to protest, he beat her with a leather strap and bade her say no more about such nonsense.

After this, Prudence's submissiveness turned to revulsion. Jenkinson gloatingly turned this attitude to his own sadistic profit in ways that showed his ruthless contempt for the unfortunate girl. By the end of the first year of their marriage, he had openly taken a handsome quadroon seamstress as his mistress and installed her in a little house only three blocks from his domicile. On more than one occasion, his mistress visited him at the house on Edgemont and, with Prudence's knowledge, shared his bed. Often at breakfast he would salaciously tell his horrified young wife of the quadroon's superior carnal capabilities, comparing her own conjugal shortcomings with the licentious pleasures his mistress afforded him.

More than that, he purposely hired servants who were generally incompetent and had been unemployed for long spells of time, engaging them at low wages and letting them frequently hear his spitefully abusive censure of his wife's failings, both as bedmate and housekeeper.

Deeply religious, Prudence—unlike his first wife—did not contemplate suicide as an escape from her marital prison; instead, resignedly, hopelessly, she submitted, though praying that the man who, as she could plainly now see, had tricked her father out of his bank and condemned her to a life of utter misery would one day be judged and punished by a higher authority.

Back in Trenton, Homer Jenkinson had been an ardent Republican and Unionist. He had come to Alabama with the express purpose of being in the vanguard of Northern carpetbaggers. It did not take him long to study the corrupt machinations of the Alabama and Chattanooga Railroad and to decide that here was an ideal arena for profiteering. By 1868, he had purchased several parcels of land adjacent to the first hundred miles of track and sold them several months later to developers for about five times what they had cost him. Since that time he had on several occasions taken advantage of the confused business affairs of the Alabama and Chattanooga to launch fraudulent schemes that bilked innocent investors. The fact that the railroad was now back in the hands of receivers for the first mortgage bondholders, and that it was their task to attempt to run the road, simply gave him one more opportunity to float one of his cherished flim-flam operations.

34

And he was confident that Governor Lindsay's successor, David P. Lewis, a Unionist who took over the governor's mansion in January 1873, would be no more capable of rooting out corruption in the railroad than his predecessors had been.

To be sure, the present state of the Alabama and Chattanooga hardly augured well for the future success of any speculative venture. With the past record of mismanagement in view, it seemed unlikely that the present receivers of the line would attempt to do anything more than manage it with a bare minimum of expenditure. Nevertheless, Homer Jenkinson had concocted a scheme which, he was confident, would encourage private investors to part with a considerable amount of money on the strength of the railroad's future development.

Jenkinson's plan centered on three tracts of land—the land about which he had spoken to Andy Haskins. These parcels of land were near sections of the railroad in the townships of Brookville, Grant, and Henigar. As yet, the railroad had not extended itself into these areas. The taxes on the land were exceptionally high, a legacy from the last war, and this in itself discouraged any kind of development. Jenkinson proposed to have a bill sponsored by a gullible legislator that would lower the taxes. This done, he and his cronies would proceed to float stock in a corporation organized to buy up the land and hold it for resale to potential future investors. A most attractive and appealing prospectus would be drawn up in which the officers of the corporation would put forward the totally fraudulent claim that they "had a commitment" from the receivers of the Alabama and Chattanooga to extend the railroad into the areas in question, provided that the areas could be shown to be promising regions of development in the future. This "commitment," Jenkinson felt certain, would be sufficient to convince gullible investors that the land was due for a period of booming growth, and that they would be able to resell the land to developers at many times the purchase price. The lower taxes voted by the legislators would keep the cost of holding the land down to a minimum, further increasing the potential profits to shareholders in Jenkinson's corporation.

Once having organized the land-holding firm and received capital from greedy and unsuspecting investors, Jenkinson and his cronies could then skip out of the state with the profits in their pockets. To be sure, before this occurred some individuals might ask detailed questions about the exact extent of the Alabama and Chattanooga's commitment to build more track. To forestall any suspicion, Jenkinson was prepared to go to the receivers for the first mortgage bondholders—two of whom he knew personally—and convince them that some well-heeled land investors were crying out for the track to be built, and that the resulting extension would yield a handsome profit in freight revenues for the beleaguered railroad. He could even hint at the possibility that his own corporation would put up money toward construction of the extension. The receivers could hardly refuse to consider such an offer, but if they did . . . well, then Jenkinson could offer them substantial under-the-table kickbacks for a decision favorable to himself and his partners.

Naturally Jenkinson preferred not to approach the receivers; to do so would merely increase the risk of exposure and scandal, and possibly cut into his own profits and those of his three cronies. No, if all went well, he and his original three partners would leave the state with all their profits intact, and the receivers none the wiser that anything untoward had occurred.

Jenkinson had followed with great interest the 1872 campaign for seats in the state legislature. He had already marked Andy Haskins as an innocent dupe who, doubtless wishing to draw political favor and attention to himself in his debut upon the floor of the House of Representatives, would be eager to sponsor a bill to lower taxes—a bill that, on its face, seemed to promise so much for individual investors, for the troubled Alabama and Chattanooga, and for the people of Alabama.

As he turned back to the sheaf of papers he had pushed aside before his young wife entered the study, the portly carpetbagger leaned back in his stuffed chair and grinned avariciously. He and his friends had already spoken guardedly to a few potential shareholders who had expressed great enthusiasm for the land-holding corporation—an enthusiasm which he well understood as being born out of their own greed. He had little feelings of conscience in the matter: an investor who would buy stock in such an illusory venture would deserve exactly what he would get— nothing. The profits would be channeled into the pockets of Homer Jenkinson and his three associates. It was these three that he was awaiting now, with a nervous impatience shown by the way he kept glancing at his watch.

When the expected knock from the maid came, he sprang to his feet with an alacrity that belied his weight, strode to the door and opened it, a jovial grin replacing the sneer that had been on his lips for Prudence. "Come in, gentlemen, do come in! You're right on time, and I like my friends to be punctual. We've much to talk about, and much to plan!"

The three men were dressed in the height of fashion, with flowered cravats and elegant waistcoats. They held their bowler hats in their right hands as they entered the study.

Homer Jenkinson gestured expansively toward the three chairs drawn up in front of his desk. "Make yourselves comfortable, gentlemen. What do you say to a little brandy to start off our proceedings?"

"I'll not say no to that, Homer," Amos Meredith broadly winked, as he seated himself with a flourish, adjusting his cravat and looking very self-conscious. He was almost fifty, tall and gaunt, with a graying spade beard, and his appearance was appropriate to his profession, which was that of mortician.

Milo Brutus Henson took the chair in the middle, turning to nod to Amos Meredith and then to the man on his right, Judge Albert Siloway. Like his two associates, he had come from the East soon after Appomattox and quickly immersed himself in Alabama affairs with a keen eye to quick profits. Short and dapper, with an elegantly waxed moustache, he was forty-five years old, a bachelor like Amos Meredith and, like the mortician, a frequent patron of Montgomery's most elegant house of ill repute. Ostensibly his profession was that of surveyor, and he had been involved in several shady land deals just before the Civil War in his home town of Cheshire, Connecticut.

Judge Albert Siloway was fifty-nine, white-haired, with a benign face and sanctimonious tone of voice. He was even fatter than Homer Jenkinson, and he had buried two wives and married a third after coming from Pittsburgh to Alabama. Back in Pittsburgh, he had been a judge of the circuit court, and had resigned in order to escape prosecution for accepting bribes in cases against land officers. Currently he resided in Tuscaloosa, where he had won himself a municipal judgeship by making sizable contributions to influential political leaders during the 1870 campaign.

Homer Jenkinson stood behind his desk, beaming at all three of them for a long moment before he walked over to the sideboard near the corner of the room, turned to draw aside the curtain and peer out to make certain that no one was outside watching, and then opened a cut-glass decanter of fine old French brandy and poured our four generous libations in elegant snifters. He came around the desk to serve his cronies, went back to his chair and seated himself with a contented sigh, lifted his snifter to his fleshy mouth and announced, "A toast, gentlemen, to our venture."

The three men chorused their approval of this toast, raised their snifters and sipped their brandy, smacking their lips and pronouncing it first-rate. Jenkinson set his snifter down before him, leaned forward, and intently addressed them. "Now then, all of us remember our first meeting with that persnickety young Haskins. My impression was that he wasn't too favorably inclined to our little venture."

"I'd agree with you, Homer," the judge meditatively scowled. "Might be we've got ourselves a firebrand in the House instead of a nice, easygoing fellow who has brains enough not to stand in the face of progress and a little windfall for himself into the bargain."

"Yes, Judge Siloway, I get your point." Jenkinson nodded, then took another sip of brandy. "But I picked Haskins exactly because he's a newcomer to politics. He can be taught. Oh sure, he's probably eager to make a reputation for himself, make his voters happy with him. And there's a lot of sentimental twaddle that helped him get his seat in the House, like his having lost an arm at Chickamauga. We mustn't underestimate the fact, gentlemen, that these mangy Southerners still have a great deal of pride and patriotism left, and a lot of them still think they should have won the war. So, of course, they'd vote for a disabled veteran, a family man, a fellow who's never had a black mark on his record just because he's never been in politics before. Oh yes, I'm convinced he'll come around."

"Do you have any notions as to how to make him do that, Homer?" Amos Meredith piped up in a reedy voice.

"Well now, that's exactly why I called this meeting, boys." Jenkinson was becoming more affable, after having taken a longer swig of his brandy. "I was thinking that the judge here and I might take a ride out to Haskins's place, pay a social call, as it were, just to get acquainted. The judge here is likely to impress Haskins as a man of great probity. And I'm sure that if he speaks highly of our little venture, Haskins will begin to see the light."

"And if he doesn't?" Milos Brutus Henson anxiously interposed, touching the ends of his waxed moustache and then glancing covertly at his associates.

"Trust me, boys. I tell you I've a few other aces up my sleeve. I'm hoping it won't be necessary to use them. But you can see for yourself that with the shape the state treasury is in, we've got to get this tax bill sponsored and passed in a hurry. Then we can send out the prospectus for our corporation and rake in the gold."

"The only trouble is," Judge Siloway mused aloud as he thoughtfully stroked his double chin, "how can we be sure that a bill introduced by a newcomer like Haskins will win approval in the House? Don't you suppose there are plenty of members who would think twice about any kind of bill introduced by a novice?"

"Why, Judge, I'm surprised at you," Jenkinson reproachfully retorted. "That's where a little education from a man as distinguished as you is going to come in mighty handy. You'll explain to Haskins the great advantages to the state and to the voters themselves, once this bill becomes law. Then he'll be able to convince the rest of the House what a good thing they'll be endorsing. You know, I visited your court a couple of times—I met you three years ago when I had business in Tuscaloosa, as you'll remember. And I like the way you laid down the law and could quote cases from Blackstone. No, I've no fear at all that you won't be able to educate our young friend." He leaned back in his chair again with a smug, self-satisfied look. "As I've said before, gentlemen, it's worth the effort to get Haskins to see the light and think that he's seen it for himself without our help." He shrugged and winked. "If he doesn't, I'll just have to use my aces, that's all. Well now, now that we've settled the business at hand, what's on the agenda for this evening?"

CHAPTER FOUR

"Mr. Haskins, there's a horse and buggy coming; looks like some folks are coming to call on you." Burt Coleman straightened to his six-foot height and dropped his hoe as he turned to Andy, then gestured toward the west in the direction of the frame house. A smart new buggy, drawn by a spirited black gelding, was slowing to a halt in front of the tethering stand Andy had hewn from a live oak tree and solidly planted into the ground. The driver, dapperly attired in frock coat and cravat and a fresh silk shirt, wearing a bowler hat to protect him from the midafternoon sun, descended from the buggy and tied the reins securely. Then he moved back to the buggy to help down his companion, a portly gray-haired man dressed in the sobering black that judges, undertakers, and ministers were wont to wear.

"Dagnabit it, anyway," Andy grumbled under his breath as he flung down his hoe and headed toward the unexpected callers. He stopped to turn back and call to the pleasant-featured southern Alabaman, "I don't expect to be long, Burt. I'll be back to join you on that row and we'll try to get it done before sundown. This is about my last day of work on the farm before I go back to Montgomery and have to dress up and make speeches and such."

"I'd sure like to be there to hear you, Mr. Andy," Burt grinned as he bent to retrieve the hoe and turned back to his work.

"Afternoon to you, Mr. Haskins." Homer Jenkinson advanced and extended his hand, a jovial smile on his fleshy mouth. "You remember Judge Siloway, here—I asked him to come along. You see, Andy—if I may call you that—I thought you'd welcome some legal reassurance on the little matter we were discussing the other day in Montgomery."

"I don't think reassurances would help, Mr. Jenkinson." Andy Haskins tried not to show his irritation, choosing his words with care and maintaining a pleasant smile on his earnest young face. "I've done some boning up on this matter, and I'm extremely dubious about anything even remotely connected with the Alabama and Chattanooga."

"Ah, that's exactly the point I wanted to make to you this afternoon—can you spare the judge and me a few minutes? Perhaps we could go inside. I tell you, the sun shines mighty near the whole year around in this wonderful state of Alabama." Homer Jenkinson was bombastically eloquent as he flung out his arms as if to embrace the entire horizon with a benediction. It was, to be sure, an unseasonably warm day for this early time of year, and there had been surprisingly little rain the last two or three weeks, a fact which had disturbed the young Tennesseean.

Now that Andy was spending so much of his time in Montgomery at the statehouse, he was beginning to feel frustrated in his efforts to expand the farm and develop its crops and profits for all his faithful workers, as well as for his own family. Not, of course, that a man could regulate the weather any more while working in the fields than he could from a seat in the House of Representatives, a good twenty-five miles or more away. But at least when he was out here, toiling alongside Burt Coleman or the Ardmore brothers and sharing their anecdotes and good humor, he felt more of a sense of belonging and of being responsible. He had discovered that he did not miss Windhaven Range at all—of course, quite apart from the friendships he had made there with people like Ramón Hernandez and Joe Duvray and the vaqueros; this land so near Windhaven Plantation had proved a fascinating challenge. He wanted to be as close to it as he could.

He hesitated a moment now, not wanting to offend the lobbyist or the pompous-looking fat judge who stood beside Homer Jenkinson with a fatuous smile on his heavily jowled face. Then he decided that discretion was the better part of valor and that there was no need to be rude: if they had driven all this way from Montgomery, as he surmised they had, the least he could do would be to invite them into the house and offer them a cool drink. He'd listen to what they had to say, but after his recent chat with Luke Bouchard, he was pretty sure of what he was going to reply, no matter what arguments they summoned up to present their case in its most favorable light.

"Of course, Mr. Jenkinson, Judge Siloway. My wife had a baby boy a while back, and she and little Horatio might be sleeping. I'm just mentioning that so we won't disturb her, you understand. If she's not there, I'll see that you both get something tall and cool to drink."

"Now that's mighty neighborly, Mr. Haskins," Judge Siloway boomed in as loud a voice as if he were addressing a full courtroom of spectators from the bench. "You see, Homer boy, the people chose a really fine representative last November. Mr. Haskins is the salt of the earth."

"No two ways about it," Jenkinson admitted as Andy, trying not to show his annoyance, led the way into the little frame house.

He was secretly relieved to find that Jessica had indeed retired with Horatio into the bedroom, where doubtless both were napping. So he turned to Jenkinson and Judge Siloway and invited them into the kitchen. Once they had seated themselves at the old round mahogany table, which blind Horatio Bambach had brought with him when he and Jessica came from Virginia, he went about making them juleps to show that he could be a considerate host. As he worked, he couldn't help noticing that both Jenkinson and the judge were whispering to each other and glancing at him, though he pretended not to notice this.

"There you are, gentlemen. I hope you'll find the drinks satisfactory."

"Aren't you having one yourself to join us, to be convivial, Mr. Haskins?" Judge Siloway anxiously inquired.

"No thanks, Judge. Fact is, I'm anxious to get back to that patch of land Burt Coleman and I've been hoeing down all day long. It's just about got us buffaloed."

"Why, that's a cattleman's expression, that is," Jenkinson grinned triumphantly, as he eyed his portly crony. "Don't tell me you were in that profession once yourself, Mr. Haskins, before you settled down here in Alabama?"

"Well, as it happens, you're right. I was born in Tennessee, I lost an arm at Chickamauga, and Mr. Luke Bouchard—he owns Windhaven Plantation upriver, as you probably know—found a friend of mine and me at the New Orleans docks right after the war. We were trying to

43

make an honest dollar because we didn't have any homes left to go back to."

"A plight that has befallen many of the finest soldiers of our fair Confederacy," Judge Siloway rhetorically observed with a thespian sigh worthy of Edwin Booth himself.

"Yes, you're right about that, Judge," Andy ruefully admitted. "Only Joe Duvray and I were luckier than most. Mr. Bouchard hired us to ride along with him in the wagons he had made to take him and his son Mr. Lucien Edmond out to some good grazing land in Texas, southeast of San Antone. And I worked for a spell on that land—Windhaven Range, it was called. But then I came back here, visiting Tennessee and looking up Mr. Luke, and he gave me a chance to settle down here. Now I'm married and have a family and I'm representing the county—and I'm going to try to do a good, honest job of it, too."

"Of course you will, Andy," Homer Jenkinson purred. He took a sip from the glass and smacked his lips. "That's a splendid julep, Andy, if I may say so. Don't you think so, Judge?"

"Decidedly, Homer, decidedly. Mr. Haskins has many talents, it's plain to see."

"I'll come right to the point, Andy, because I know you're going to be busy, and I know you're going back to Montgomery any day now." Jenkinson leaned forward and intently contemplated the one-armed Tennesseean, an ingratiating smile playing about his mouth. "You see, that's why the judge and I wanted to come see you before you went back into session, so you'd have a clear picture of exactly what it is we're trying to do."

"Let's see if I recall it rightly, Mr. Jenkinson." Andy stood behind his chair, his left hand gripping the back as he stared first at the carpetbagger and then the fat judge. "You want me to sponsor a bill to lower taxes on some land that's not far from the tracks of the Alabama and Chattanooga, isn't that it?"

"Actually, Andy, it's a lot more than that," Jenkinson confided. "You see, this land is in three townships, and their taxes have been excessively high following the late hostilities. Now, the judge and I believe that if we can lower the taxes, we can appeal to speculators who would develop the land, and ultimately to the Alabama and Chattanooga, whose managers will surely want to lay track directly into these areas."

44

"I think I understand, Mr. Jenkinson." Once again, Andy chose his words carefully, deliberately not revealing how much he knew about the railroad and its history. "But those tracts of land you've got in mind, they're not in Montgomery County, are they?"

"No, sir, to be honest with you, they're not. Still in all, as one of the new members of the House of Representatives, it'll be greatly to your credit if you can show not only your constituents here, but the voters throughout the state, that you're concerned with the welfare of the entire state of Alabama. Now, sir, as you know, the South has been in an impoverished condition since the war, and we believe, now that we're citizens here, that our own future, as well as that of every hard-working man in Alabama, depends on improving conditions. Well, sir, developing new lands, extending a railroad line, and bringing goods and supplies and more prosperity to these areas should certainly be a project you could undertake to sponsor."

"But the Alabama and Chattanooga is in receivership, and there isn't any assurance that the receivers will see fit to extend its tracks—at least not until there are more people and more businesses in the areas you have in mind, and that could be years from now."

"That's a mere trifle, my boy." Judge Siloway waved away the young Tennesseean's objection with an almost contemptuous smile. "We've got the investors for the land, and they're influential enough to be able to sway the receivers for the railroad—and even to underwrite the extension of track with, of course, the state's and the receivers' permission. You see, Mr. Haskins, I've heard quite a few cases in my court at Tuscaloosa concerning torts and land values, the transfer of properties, and such matters. Well, sir, I can assure you that where there is good intention and influence and money behind a program such as Mr. Jenkinson and I have the honor of proposing to you, there'll be little legal hesitation—even by the governor himself—to taking up the project once it has been passed by the state legislature."

"But I'm not sure of that, Judge Siloway," Andy protested. "And I don't think either you or Mr. Jenkinson can really guarantee a hundred percent to these investors of yours that any tracks are going to be laid into those areas. As I see it, you'll be out there soliciting funds from private individuals just on the hope that maybe it'll be done. And if

45

it isn't, what happens to the investment made by these individuals?"

"Now, now, Andy, just you leave the financial details to me. I'm an old hand at soliciting funds for a worthy cause," Jenkinson grandiloquently assured him. "And the judge here will validate the legal side of the affair. That should put your mind at rest as to the honesty and integrity of our proposal. Now, Andy, don't you think, in view of all that I've told you and the judge's corroboration of the facts, you could find your way clear to sponsoring our bill?"

Andy Haskins's knuckles whitened as he tightened his grip on the back of the chair. Then he shook his head. "I think you'd better find yourself another boy, Mr. Jenkinson. It's true that I'm new in the House and I don't want to make any mistakes, but it's also true that I've done a little reading up on the past history of this particular railroad line. And I don't like what I see. I don't think the people who voted to put me in office like it much, either. The last few governors have tossed this thing around like a hot potato, and they haven't solved it any. To put it in a nutshell, the Alabama and Chattanooga Railroad is bankrupt, and you can't deny it is. The receivers aren't going to do anything with the line, beyond run it as it now exists."

"But we can assure you that Governor Lewis, once he sees the backing we're going to get for the extension of track, will give the go-ahead sign to the receivers, Andy," Jenkinson eagerly argued.

"But I can't be sure of that, either, and I don't think you can and neither can the judge, with all due respect. I'd like to pass, if I may."

"You're making a bad decision, Andy." Now Jenkinson adopted a paternal, benign tone. "Isn't that your opinion, Judge?"

"Oh, assuredly he is, Homer," Judge Siloway clucked his tongue disapprovingly and shook his head, frowning. "It's a golden opportunity to draw attention to yourself as a junior member of our fine House of Representatives, Andy. And I might add that there will be rewards, quite apart from the spiritual satisfaction of knowing that you had benefited the entire state and the citizens who live in the area of these three towns."

"Rewards, Judge Siloway?" Andy Haskins echoed. "Why don't you spell them out for me? Maybe you mean a little bribe?"

46

"Please, Andy," Jenkinson held up a protesting hand and leaned back in his chair. "That's an ugly word."

"But it's the only word I think you want to use. And it doesn't set well with me, either, I can tell you that right off. I suggest you try to peddle your scheme to somebody else. I don't believe in throwing good money after bad, and that's the long and short of it."

"You're being very shortsighted, Andy. I'm sorry you're taking this view." Homer Jenkinson reached for his glass and drained the rest of it, then set it down with a clatter. "Come on, Judge. Maybe we overestimated Mr. Haskins's patriotism for the sovereign state of Alabama."

"Perhaps we did. After all, he's just told us that he came from Tennessee. That might explain his indifference to a good cause." Judge Siloway rose with some difficulty from his chair. "We must thank you for your hospitality and the refreshments all the same, Mr. Haskins. Good day to you, sir."

"And to you," Andy coolly retorted. He watched them leave the house, and then shook his head and muttered something under his breath. He did not watch them as they got back into the buggy. Otherwise, he would have seen Jenkinson lean over and whisper to Judge Siloway, "He's more of a stubborn mule than I thought, Judge. And he's so goddamned self-righteous it makes me want to puke. I think that boy's got to be taught a lesson. I've got a few ideas on that subject, and we'll discuss them tonight. If you've nothing better to do, why don't you come along with me and let my sweet fancy girl Anna Mae cook you a real Creole supper, gumbo and all?"

"Now I'd like that a lot, Homer. Yessirree, I'd like that a lot. But, of course, you understand, in my official capacity as a judge, I'll pretend I haven't heard what you said about teaching Mr. Haskins a lesson. Though, you understand, off the record, I quite agree with you."

CHAPTER FIVE

Andy Haskins waited until he was certain that his two visitors were well on their way to Montgomery. Then, tiptoeing to the bedroom, he cautiously opened the door and stood there for a moment, rapt with delight at the scene before him. Jessica slept, turned on her side toward little Horatio, cradling him in her arms. Andy shook his head and muttered to himself, "I'm just the luckiest man alive, and I'm so full of it I could burst." Then, closing the door quietly, he hurried out of the house. He had to go to Windhaven Plantation and talk things over with Luke Bouchard. What Homer Jenkinson and Judge Siloway had proposed made his gorge rise.

Before he went to the stable to saddle his horse, he trudged out to the field where Burt Coleman was still working with his hoe. "Burt, I'm damned sorry, believe me. You saw those two fellows who came calling?"

"Sure did, Mr. Andy. What was on their mind?"

"Nothing good, I'll tell you that. They want a little scratch-my-back dealing, and I'm not about to go along with them. And they've got plenty of influence, from all I've heard. Might be some trouble. Look, I'll make it up to you tomorrow—I've got to ride over and see Luke Bouchard. Why don't you rest a spell, Burt? That patch of land is just plain ornery."

"That's the fun of it. Maybe we can turn it into something that'll produce good fruit, if it won't do for cotton." Burt grinned.

"How's your new friend shaping up?" Andy asked, curiously touched by the young Southerner's easygoing optimism, knowing that Burt still thought of his murdered friend, Matt Rensler.

"Just fine, Mr. Andy. Don Elwald's a good man. Quiet, but he does his job."

"I'm glad you're working with me, Burt. I never did get a chance to tell you how you've helped make this farm of mine a really going concern. Look—you see how happy I am with my girl and my son—why don't you think about finding yourself a wife, Burt? You wouldn't be so alone then."

The tall, ingratiating Southerner shuffled his feet embarrassedly and scuffed with the hoe at an imaginary weed. "Shucks, Mr. Andy, not many girls out this way. And I got my work. I'm doing fine, don't you worry about me."

"I know. I felt the same way when I was down in Texas, and even before that, when I was in New Orleans after the war, and there wasn't anything left, and it looked as if the North was going to keep us under its thumb forever. But it happened to me, and it's going to happen to you, you'll see, Burt. Tell you what—next weekend, when I'm up in Montgomery, you saddle a horse and come on up there and I'll see if I can't introduce you to some nice girl."

"Come on, Mr. Andy, I know what you're trying to do. It's decent of you, but I'm fine."

"Just the same, Burt, you're going to come on up. At least, I'll buy you a good dinner. You've got that coming anyway. Now I've got to go see Mr. Bouchard. If you don't mind, take a look in by and by and see if Jessica's fine—you know."

"Sure, Mr. Andy. I'll take care of things."

Andy put out his hand and shook the young Southerner's vigorously. Then, more moved than he cared to show, he turned on his heel and strode off to the stable.

Just before sunset, Andy reined in his gelding in front of the twin-towered, red-brick chateau, tied the reins to a hitching post, and strode purposefully toward the door. He paused a moment at the sight of the heavy bronze knocker, and remembered Luke's explanation of it.

When he had returned to the chateau to begin his new life with his second wife, Laure, Luke Bouchard had a Montgomery blacksmith forge the figure of a bear in bronze, standing upright with paws and claws extended as if to attack, for Luke had never forgotten his grandfather's story of how he slew a she-bear that had killed his horse during the journey to Econchate. Lucien Bouchard had been forced to fight for his life with only a hunting knife, for the flintlock of his musket had been dampened by the rain of the night before. He had stabbed the she-bear to death, and in the process had been wounded and clawed. He had cauterized his wounds and then rubbed the mud of the Alabama River on them to palliate them. Later, Alexander McGillivray, faithful only to his mother's Creek people, had sent a scout after Lucien to capture him and take him to the village of Econchate as a slave. Lucien had had to fight for his life again. He had arrived, nearly fainting, at the village where he was to find his true beloved, the chief's daughter, Dimarte. All this had occurred almost a century ago. Lucien's grandson Luke had commemorated with this knocker the brotherhood of his grandfather with the Creeks, a brotherhood of the bear. That symbol stood for the integrity of a man who had come across an ocean to found a dynasty of those faithful to his credo of honor and truth.

That knocker was now for Andy Haskins a reminder of his own integrity. He reached out his hand to it and struck three times.

Hannah Mendicott opened the door to him and cordially welcomed him. "Come right in, Mr. Andy. Mr. Luke's in the study room. You may as well come right along, I know he'll want to see you."

"Thanks, Hannah. I hope I'm not disturbing him."

"You won't disturb him one bit, Mr. Andy. Miz Laure's out riding, 'n she's got Lucien and Paul on their ponies with her. They ought to be back pretty soon, in time for supper. You know, I'm making fried chicken tonight and biscuits and Indian pudding. I know Mr. Luke would be mighty glad to have you eat with the family. Want me to put on another plate for you?"

"I don't think I'd better, Hannah. Got to get back to my wife and son, you know. But thank you anyhow. And I won't keep Mr. Luke long."

Hannah led the way to the study and knocked gently at the door. Luke's vigorous "Come in!" bade them both enter. Hannah opened the door and then effaced herself as Andy Haskins walked in.

"What a pleasant surprise, Andy! Come in and sit down and make yourself comfortable. Well, you've ridden all the way over from the farm, it must be important. Here, take that comfortable chair right next to the desk." Luke rose and came to shake hands with the young Tennessean. He eyed Andy with interest, as the latter sat down and tried to compose himself and find words to quickly communicate what was troubling him.

Finally, clearing his throat, he began, "You remember those fellows who spoke to me at the statehouse about sponsoring a tax bill? Well, I've had another visit from them. This time it wasn't four men, it was two of them. There was Homer Jenkinson, and he brought with him one of the men I'd seen before—a judge from Tuscaloosa, by the name of Albert Siloway."

"That's very interesting. I'm curious to know what a judge way down in Tuscaloosa has to do with you as representative from Montgomery County."

"I wondered about that some myself, Mr. Luke. Seems as though this Homer Jenkinson fellow brought him along to tell me that it was all on the up and up, this little proposal of his. The two of them still wanted me to sponsor that bill in the House, lowering taxes on three sections of land into which they figure the A and C will lay extra track. Their story was that it would bring business into the area around there and be good for people in general. You and I had discussed all that, so I'd already made up my mind on the matter. But then—and here's the clincher— Jenkinson said that there'd be rewards for everybody, including yours truly. So I came right out and asked him if he was aiming to mean a bribe, and he said he wouldn't use a harsh word like that."

"But that's what he really meant, of course," Luke chuckled humorlessly. "I paid a visit to old Jedidiah Danforth the other day, and he told me what he'd heard about this Homer Jenkinson. He's a carpetbagger for sure. Came here from New Jersey right after the war, bought himself an old house, and has been pretty active in politicking all around the state. You can be sure he doesn't care about Montgomery County or anything else in the entire state except lining his own pockets. And, of course, those of the men who go along with him in this ingenious little scheme. I'm glad you saw through it."

"So am I. I just wanted to come over here and tell you how I'd handled things, Mr. Luke."

"I never had any doubt you'd handle those boys with great skill, Andy. You're a good politician and honest as the day is long, and that's the difference between you and carpetbaggers. Not, mind you, that a few decent ones haven't come to the South and tried their best to give everybody a fair shake. But they're few and far between. And for certain Homer Jenkinson is not one of them."

"Well, I'm glad I stuck to my guns. And as far as I'm concerned, that's the end of the matter."

"I wouldn't be too sure. They might want to put some pressure on you, Andy. That's what happens to a newcomer in politics. Everybody thinks that he's a weak link in the chain and wants to test him. In your case, they hinted at a nice little bribe to make you look the other way and forget your conscience. When they found you don't intend to do that, then they might see what a little forceful persuasion could do in their behalf. But I know what I'm going to do."

"What's that, Mr. Luke?"

"I think it's about time for me to write another letter to the *Advertiser*, Andy. Don't worry, I shan't name any names. But I want the people of this county to be aware of some of the chicanery that's going on in the name of progress. It's plain theft, except that now the carpetbaggers are trying different tactics."

Andy Haskins squinted down hard at the floor, then scratched his head. "Aren't you a little bit afraid, Mr. Luke, that if you write a letter like that, people like this Jenkinson fellow and his friend the judge might go after you?"

"So much the better, Andy," Luke Bouchard steadfastly and quietly responded. "You might call it baiting a trap. If we can get this carpetbagger group to make a few mistakes so that everybody will see what they truly are, we'll very effectively destroy their power to harm. I'm convinced, after studying the results of the election last November, that there are plenty of decent men like you in the House who won't stand for shady deals and swindles. I'm all too familiar with what Boss Tweed did in New York, and we don't want this to happen in Alabama. So, now, Andy, can you stay to supper? Laure would be very happy to see you, and so would Lucien and Paul."

"I'd like to a lot, Mr. Luke, but I'd better not. I want to get back to Jessica and Horatio, you know how it is."

Luke Bouchard came to the one-armed Tennesseean and put an arm around the latter's shoulder. "I know exactly

53

how it is. But as soon as it's convenient for both of you, I want you and Jessica to accept an invitation to have supper with us, and bring the baby too, Andy."

"Thanks, Mr. Luke. I'll tell Jessica. I know she'd like that a lot, and so would I."

After Andy had left the chateau to ride back to his farm, Luke seated himself at the escritoire and, closing his eyes for a moment, pondered on the theme of a letter that would denounce without libel the forces of evil still lurking in a state not yet free from the unscrupulous greed of Northern profiteers.

About half an hour later, Laure, wanting to talk to him, came to the study door, tapped lightly, and then—knowing that he would forgive her intrusion—peeked in. But when she saw him so totally absorbed in the writing of his letter, his head bowed, his face taut with concentration, she smiled knowingly and silently closed the door behind her.

Luke Bouchard's letter to the editor appeared in the issue of March 3. The *Advertiser* printed it verbatim, without any editorial commentary.

It is now nearly eight years since the guns were silenced at Appomattox, yet the South still endures the punitive retaliation of her Northern neighbors, who have sent agents of destruction into all of the seceding states. Today, we in Alabama are still beset by greedy plunderers who seek to fleece our hardworking, impoverished citizens.

Remembering past years, I witnessed the results of last November's election with some hope that prosperity would be restored to our sovereign state and that the depredations of the victorious North would be at an end. But from what I have observed, this hope of mine is not about to be quickly realized. Nor will it ever be, so long as our own legislature does not have the power to suppress the efforts of ruthless Northerners who seek to have bills sponsored that would make their plundering easier. I refer specifically to the case of the Alabama and Chattanooga Railroad. There is no need at this time to repeat the history of this ill-fated venture, save to say that it is presently in receivership. Accordingly, there is little prospect that a sensible administration—which I believe Governor

Lewis's to be—would permit any group of private individuals, no matter how wealthy and influential, to hold out the promise that money could be made by a scheme of investment which involved rail service to communities not now on the map of this line.

It has recently come to my attention that just such a group of conspiring schemers has attempted to bribe a new legislator in the hope of getting him to sponsor a bill to allow tax relief to several areas within the range of the Alabama and Chattanooga, but not now being serviced by it. Even the mere proposal of such a chimerical and implausible scheme suggests not only a contemptuous belief in the gullibility of our citizens and legislators, but also a pattern of unpardonable corruption.

We have already heard of the scandal of Boss Tweed in the state of New York. In the end, even the public revolted against open thievery. We must be ready to do the same. We must all be prepared to repudiate brazen attempts to swindle us.

Even if we observe corruption in the very stronghold of the republic—our nation's capital—we must not let it taint us here in a state that prospered and became great through unity of purpose.

Luke Bouchard

Homer Jenkinson's face was livid as he flung the *Advertiser* to the carpeted floor of his study. He turned to Amos Meredith, Milo Brutus Henson, and Judge Albert Siloway and said in a voice that was choked with anger, "I've heard some talk in town that that young fool of an Andy Haskins was beholden to this nosy, sanctimonious Luke Bouchard. Now it appears they're thick as thieves together. Well, gentlemen, Mr. Bouchard would have made a good lawyer, I'm thinking. He didn't come out at all and name names, and it's just as well for him he didn't. But all of us know whom he meant, don't we?"

"He ought to be tarred and feathered," the undertaker grumbled, eyeing Milo Brutus Henson for approval and getting it in a brusk nod.

"No, that would be too much like the Ku Klux Klan, Amos," Jenkinson declared. "But maybe, since this Bouchard fellow wants to smear us with a little dirt and yet keep his own shirt cuffs clean, we might just try to dig up something about him. Maybe in the digging we'll find something to tie in with Andy Haskins. And then maybe they'll both sing a different tune."

"What do we do about the prospectus, Homer?" Judge Siloway wanted to know.

"We'll go ahead with it, naturally. Do you think I'm going to forget about a money-making scheme that'll get all of us a pile of greenbacks and gold just because of a stupid letter? The idiots who read this paper will see the letter, say to a man that every word is true, then forget all about it. What can they do? No, you go right ahead, Judge. And you boys, Amos and Milo, keep up your end of the good work. Get all the pledges and donations you can. By all means give them receipts—then this Luke Bouchard can't say we're thieves, can he?"

There was a mild titter of laughter from the carpetbagger's three associates.

"Then it's settled. Now you just let me take the next step. And if that doesn't work—" Jenkinson dramatically paused to make sure he had the attention of his listeners, then concluded, "I'll find other ways of silencing trouble-makers like Luke Bouchard and Andy Haskins, see if I don't."

56

CHAPTER SIX

Jedidiah Danforth was celebrating his sixty-fifth birthday on the morning of March 8, though from his irascible mood, one would never have suspected he was secretly touched by the way Emily Cantwell, his housekeeper for the past eighteen years, was fussing over him.

"Drat it, woman!" he testily exclaimed as she filled his cup with steaming, strong coffee from the pot. "You don't have to fuss over me like a mother hen with her chickens, Mrs. Cantwell!"

"Now, Mr. Danforth, why shouldn't I? You're only eight years younger than this century," she began.

"I know that! And there wasn't any need for you to get up so early just to make my breakfast just because it happens to be my birthday. You're getting on in years, too, Mrs. Cantwell, and my birthday isn't so important that you should lose your sleep, especially for a cranky old man."

Emily Cantwell surreptitiously mopped her tear-filled eyes with the hem of her apron and, straightening her shoulders, gave him back good measure. "I must say, Mr. Danforth, age hasn't improved your disposition one little bit. There was a time I can remember when you didn't make sneering remarks about a woman's age. Besides, I'll have you know I'm just fifty-six, and there's nothing wrong with my health, not the way there was with yours last year. Dr. Medbury told me, after you got those fine young men to come help Mr. Lopasuta stand off those awful Ku Klux Klansmen, that you could have had a heart attack, getting excited the way you did."

Jedidiah set down his coffee cup, deliberately wiped his mouth with an embroidered napkin, and glared at his plump, gray-haired housekeeper. "Well, woman, for your information, there's a new doctor looking after me now. And I like this new Dr. Kennery, even if he is a Yankee. At least he's not a carpetbagger. He just carries a black bag, that's all." He permitted himself a mild cackle of laughter at this feeble witticism. Then, seeing that his housekeeper looked downcast, he exclaimed, "Consarn it all, Mrs. Cantwell, don't you know that an old dog's bark is worse than his bite? Thank you for this fine breakfast— though I shouldn't be eating steak of a morning and hominy grits and oatmeal all at one sitting. Just the same, it was mighty tasty. There's nobody in Montgomery who can fix grits and oatmeal the way you can, that's for certain. And besides, you know perfectly well I couldn't have gotten along all these years without you."

"Oh, Mr. Danforth—I didn't mean to make you angry—" Emily Cantwell burst into tears.

With a groan of feigned irritation, the wiry old lawyer got up from his chair and put a comforting arm around her shoulders. "There now, there now," he soothed, "that's a fine way for an old fool like me to start his sixty-fifth birthday. I'm sorry. I didn't mean to rile you up like this. Sometimes I ask myself why you keep on putting up with me."

"Because—because you're the finest man I've ever known, that's why," Emily burst out, and then pressed her tear-stained face against his chest and gave vent to her pent-up emotions while he awkwardly patted her shoulder.

"I know, I know, Mrs. Cantwell. Well, I'll have you know I don't know what I would have done without you all these years, looking after an old fool like me. So that makes us even." Then, reverting to his characteristically sarcastic tone, he exclaimed, "Drat it, woman, stop that crying. You'd think it was my funeral you were attending, not my birthday. Besides, I want to drink my coffee while it's still hot. Hot and strong, just the way I like it. Now you dry your eyes and forget that I said any nasty things to you—for certain I didn't mean them, and you know that."

"Why—yes, s-sir," Emily quavered as she drew two or three deep breaths and forced a faint though tremulous smile to her lips.

He seated himself, sent her a quick smile, then eagerly sipped his coffee. When he finished it, he turned to her again and, in a gentler voice, said, "Tell you what. After a big breakfast like this, I shan't be thinking about food for a good many hours. Why don't you go have yourself a visit with your good friend Clara Moseby?"

"But it's your birthday, Mr. Danforth, and—" again she began.

"We've already gone over that," he barked. "Now leave me be in peace, if you want me to be around on my next birthday for a breakfast just as good as this, which I hope you'll still cook for me."

"Oh, Mr. Danforth, don't talk like that, don't even talk about—well, not being here. You're going to live till the end of the century." Again she tearfully moved toward him, putting out one hand toward him as if, by that gesture, she could halt the inexorable passage of time.

"Then for heaven's sake, Mrs. Cantwell, please stop crying, if you don't want me to think about mournful things. There I go again, only making you feel worse! I suppose that's why I never took me a wife." He grinned sardonically and reached for a cigar. "I don't think any right-minded woman would want to put up with my bad temper. Consarn it, woman, you're making me say things I don't really mean—of course, I didn't mean to imply you weren't right-minded, taking care of me the way you do. And now will you please go over and visit Mrs. Moseby and let me finish my cigar?"

"Yes—yes, Mr. Danforth. I didn't mean to cry. And—and I do hope you'll have the happiest birthday ever. God bless you, Mr. Danforth." She had composed herself by now, and her smile was brighter. She looked affectionately at him and then scolded, "You know you shouldn't smoke too many cigars, Mr. Danforth."

"Mrs. Cantwell, I'll thank you to leave prescriptions to the new young Yankee doctor. I told him what old Dr. Medbury let me have, and he said he didn't see any reason to change that, so long as I did things in moderation. And I'll remind you that this is only my first cigar of the day. Besides which, it's my birthday."

"I—I'll be going, then. God bless you, Mr. Danforth." Emily Cantwell could not trust herself to speak any further, and turned and left the room. Jedidiah Danforth looked after her, then smiled and shook his head, muttering under his breath, "Finest housekeeper in the whole state of Alabama. Pity she lost her husband before the war, and has to waste all her attentions on a stiff-necked old lawyer like me."

When he heard the door close behind her, he chuckled, puffed vigorously at his cigar, and then, reaching for the coffee pot, poured a generous third cup of the still-hot liquid. As he took a first sip, he smacked his lips and declared, "So long as we have real coffee back, I don't figure we exactly lost the war, not hardly." Then he reached for the folded copy of the *Advertiser*, which she had laid on the chair pulled up beside his place at the table, leaned back, and began to peruse it.

He was slight of build, his sparse hair now completely white. His blue eyes were still bright and keen, and there was no failing in his vision, despite his age. However, the illness he had sustained last year had left his face hollow and emphasized the boniness of its structure, particularly the aggressive chin and the prominent cheekbones.

He frowned as he read the front-page news. "Damned carpetbaggers," he growled aloud. "In spite of everything, they're still around to make us remember they won the war. And that idiot in the White House doesn't seem to want to do a thing to stop them, though in his public addresses he keeps saying that he wants the nation to be reunited as we approach our centennial. Pshaw! The man's a fool, surrounded by the worst incompetents possible. The people who govern us aren't one whit better than those thieving carpetbaggers. What's this country coming to, anyway?"

He folded the front page to the back and went on reading. At the bottom of the third page, an item caught his eye and he read it to himself, his lips moving silently, then flung down the paper with a grimace. "The pot calling the kettle black! Here I am giving Washington hell when we're still fumbling around in our own sovereign state. This mess about the Alabama and Chattanooga—when are they ever going to clear that up? The state is still worrying about it, and now we've got a special-interest group of greedy carpetbaggers trying to cloud the issue and line their own pockets. I only wish Luke Bouchard's letter would lead to a legislative investigation and some good, firm action against these Northern crooks!"

His cigar had gone out, and he lit it with an angry imprecation, then puffed great clouds of smoke as he scowled down at the discarded newspaper on the floor.

Somewhat mollified by his energetic rejection of the irritating news it had conveyed, he rose and went over to the window. Drawing aside the curtain, he peered outside and snorted with annoyance. The sky was overcast, and there was no sun to be seen. It was hardly ideal weather for a man's birthday, he decided, and with another disgusted snort, slowly returned to the table, stooped carefully to retrieve the crumpled paper, then seated himself on the overstuffed sofa with its neat antimacassar and leaned back with a sigh of well-being. He hadn't wanted to worry Mrs. Cantwell, and that's why he'd been so quick to rebuke her when she'd shown concern about his age and his health. The fact was, he'd had a few painful twinges in his heart once or twice a day for the last two weeks. That was just old age, nothing more. No sense calling out that whippersnapper of a young Yankee doctor; he'd be sure to tell him the same thing. And it was true: he wasn't drinking or smoking more than old Dr. Medbury had recommended. Well, today could be an exception, to be sure; if a man couldn't have two or three extra cigars on his birthday, then when could he have them, after all?

He smiled wryly as he settled himself and puffed steadily at his cigar, feeling completely satisfied in his enjoyment after having thus justified his action to himself. He closed his eyes and let his mind wander back to the past. He thought about that Comanche apprentice of his, Lopasuta, who had become Luke Bouchard's adopted son. He'd been a strict taskmaster with Lopasuta, but the results had more than rewarded him for his own efforts. By this time, Lopasuta Bouchard was a lawyer to be reckoned with in Montgomery. And he'd had enemies just the way his adoptive father always had—not that they'd be able to put him down any more than they'd been able to stop Luke Bouchard from succeeding. Well, maybe just the once when Luke had run for the job Andy Haskins now held. But there'd been reasons for that, reasons that had had nothing to do with Luke's integrity and decency.

Now he uttered a gloomier sigh, reflecting on the iniquitous corruption that continued in the still-oppressed Southern states and, worst and most dangerous of all, in the nation's capital. He had always pessimistically shared Luke's views that Grant's reelection might well prove to be an economic tragedy for the country.

He tried to think of happier times, and he found himself thinking of Lucien Bouchard, Luke's grandfather. Everybody in Montgomery County and Lowndesboro had heard of Lucien Bouchard and respected him. He had always hoped that he'd get the chance to handle Lucien Bouchard's affairs when he'd been a young lawyer, but in those days, people hadn't used lawyers much. And old Lucien had relied mainly on his bank down in New Orleans to do the things a lawyer did nowadays for a client. That's why Jedidiah had been very glad when Luke Bouchard returned from New Orleans with his wife and retained his services. It had given him a chance to see that the grandson had in every way fulfilled his grandfather's hopes.

Naturally, even as a young man, Jedidiah remembered Lucien's only son, Henry, and what a hellion he'd been, the very opposite of the founder of the Bouchard line. Henry would have made a perfect carpetbagger, he thought to himself with grim humor, and chuckled aloud. Henry's first son was Luke Bouchard. Oh yes, he'd heard about the rumors that had spread around the countryside and how that sweet young wife of Henry's, Dora, had drowned herself in the river not long after Luke had been born. Some said it was because Henry'd been so cruel to her—and from what he remembered of Luke's father, he thought that was pretty accurate. And then there'd been Sybella Mason, daughter of Grover Mason, the lawyer who'd had most of what business there was in Montgomery in those early days long before the war. She'd been Mark's mother, the son Henry favored over Luke, whom he'd considered a milksop.

Jedidiah sighed again, this time nostalgically, leaned back and clasped his bony fingers at the back of his neck. There were a lot of good memories, and some bad. He'd told Emily Cantwell this morning that no woman would have put up with him. That hadn't exactly been the way it was. Way back when he was twenty-three, he'd fallen madly in love with a pretty little Irish girl named Mary Eileen Dugan, a roguish colleen from County Cork, with turned-up nose, gray-green eyes, and a sweet, soft mouth with adorable dimples whenever she smiled. How he'd wanted to marry her! But her father had had other plans for her, which didn't include marriage to a struggling young lawyer who didn't have much more than a bare one-room office and his shingle outside the door and practically no customers. Yes, if it hadn't been for a legacy from his father, who'd sold his plantation just two years before he died, Jedidiah Danforth might not have been able to go on practicing law and getting no clients for the number of years he had before business at last turned his way. Meanwhile, Mary Eileen had gone off to Shreveport and married a young wastrel whose father owned a huge sugarcane plantation. The last he'd heard of her, she'd died giving birth to her second son.

He hadn't found any woman after that who could hold him, and he hadn't tried. He'd wanted all his life to be a lawyer—why, he didn't know then. Today he could tell, reviewing the record of the years, seeing how he'd helped folks, without charging them exorbitant fees and spoiling their lives for them. He'd always tried very patiently to explain the fine points of law to those who weren't educated enough to read, and he'd won cases for them in court against fairly tough lawyers more skilled in courtroom practice then he'd ever been. Yes, it had been a good life, and he could look back on it now and tell himself that the loneliness had been compensated for by the knowledge that he'd worked hard and honestly and done a lot of good for the people of Montgomery. Come to think of it, that was about the best thing a man could have in life: the feeling that you had worked hard to give everyone a fair deal, and that you weren't beholden to anyone for favors.

Now whatever had possessed Mrs. Cantwell to tell him that he was just eight years younger than the century? Following that line of reasoning, he'd arrive at the year 1900 when he was ninety-two! Hmm. He never expected to make that goal, of course, but it certainly would be interesting to witness the turn of the next century. Maybe by then all the carpetbaggers would be long gone, and the South would be on its feet again, industrially and politically. If he got that far along in life, he'd be able to see just how little Lucien and Paul Bouchard made out as grown men and how they'd profited from the legacy of ethics and decency their father was bequeathing to them now, in their childhood. Well, maybe Mrs. Cantwell was smarter than she knew. It had given him some food for thought: certainly one's birthday was a time to look ahead to the future, just as much as to the past. And the future was certainly going to be brighter, a lot brighter, for everybody—especially the Bouchards, if there was any justice in heaven and on earth!

He was startled from his reverie by the sudden, insistent rapping of the front-door knocker. He got to his feet and straightened to his full height of nearly six feet, his face clouded with annoyance. Had Emily Cantwell forgotten something, or had she just come back to make some more speeches about his birthday? No, she wouldn't knock; she had her own key. The knock was heard again. "I'm coming, I'm coming!" he irritatedly called out, as he quickened his footsteps toward the door. When he opened it, he regarded his caller with some surprise, not immediately recognizing him. The man was corpulent, in a black frock coat and flowery cravat, and there was an ingratiating smile on the man's face that didn't set well at all with Jedidiah.

"You're Mr. Danforth, I presume?" the caller asked with an air of expectancy.

"That's right. And who might you be?"

"I'm sorry to disturb you, Mr. Danforth, but I wonder if I might have a few moments of your time. My name's Homer Jenkinson."

"Oh yes. Yes, now I know who you are. Well, if you have to, come on in. I wasn't doing anything special," the white-haired lawyer grudgingly conceded.

"Very kind of you to spare me your valuable time. I appreciate it, sir. And I think," Jenkinson permitted himself a sly little smile, "we may be of mutual benefit to each other."

"That I very much doubt, but I'll listen to what you have to say." Jedidiah tersely gestured toward an upholstered chair opposite the sofa, watched his visitor ostentatiously seat himself, and then resumed his place on the sofa, his eyes intently fixed on his visitor's face.

"I'll come right to the point, Mr. Danforth. I represent an influential group of investors who want to extend industrial development in the state of Alabama."

"That's a highflown way of saying you expect to line your own pockets, I'd guess, Mr. Jenkinson," was the old lawyer's tart retort.

Homer Jenkinson frowned for a moment, but then resumed his ingratiating smile as he leaned forward. In an earnest tone, he tried to mitigate Jedidiah Danforth's hostility. "If you care to examine the record, Mr. Danforth—and as a successful attorney, I should think you'd be willing to examine the cold facts of the matter—I've settled here in Montgomery. I'm married and I own property. I am not, sir, as so many jealous and vindictive persons may have suggested, a thieving carpetbagger."

"That, indeed, would be a a happy change. Pardon me if I'm skeptical. I'm afraid that Alabama, along with the rest of the South, has been flooded with men whose only purpose is to swindle upright citizens."

"Well, sir, you're entitled to your opinion, as I am to mine. Isn't that what a judge would say in court?"

"I suppose that's so. At any rate, get on with your business."

"Certainly. Well, the fact is that my associates and I believe that the future of Alabama lies in the development of its land and industry, and in the extension and regular operation of its railroads. The railroads will bring in needed goods, and they'll be used to transport the goods Alabama produces for its neighbors. All this will mean more income for all those involved and a higher standard of living for every citizen who lives in communities the railroads service."

"I suppose you're referring to the Alabama and Chattanooga, Mr. Jenkinson?" Jedidiah Danforth snapped.

"As a matter of fact, I am. If investors should come along with a way in which the railroad can increase its business and offer its services to new communities, then I'm sure Governor Lewis would be interested. Everyone in Alabama would be glad to see all the outstanding debts of the line paid off and the railroad operating at maximum efficiency."

"I see. And you think that by getting people to invest in some speculative idea, you're going to bring about an economic miracle," was the old lawyer's sarcastic answer.

"Now, now, Mr. Danforth, you're taking a somewhat prematurely dim view of this entire enterprise. You don't even know the details of it. The men with whom I'll be associated are influential citizens, and they've come up with a plan that will effect an extension of service that's bound to benefit the entire state. But you see, Mr. Danforth, there are those who, without understanding the situation, attack it from the very start. I'm referring to the recent letter of a Mr. Luke Bouchard in the *Advertiser*."

"I've always believed in the old adage that if the shoe fits, put it on, Mr. Jenkinson. I'd say Mr. Bouchard expressed himself quite succinctly and accurately."

Once again Homer Jenkinson frowned with annoyance,

but resumed his ingratiating smile. "Well, Mr. Danforth, I'd say that letter's unjust. While it didn't go so far as to name names, it intimated that anyone associated with this project must necessarily be a thieving carpetbagger, which is a phrase that every Southerner seems to use for melodramatic effect whether or not it pertains."

"Oh, but I think in this case it assuredly does pertain, Mr. Jenkinson," the lawyer tartly countered.

"We'll let that pass for the moment, Mr. Danforth. But then, if we're going to allow the reputation of honest and ambitious citizens to be blackened—and I am a citizen, I'll remind you—why, in turn, shouldn't those who are attacked have the privilege of investigating their attackers? I have done a little research into the background of this Luke Bouchard, Mr. Danforth. Isn't it true"—Jenkinson leaned forward, absorbed in the topic—"that he married a woman of ill repute? A woman, Mr. Danforth, who came from a notorious house of ill fame in New Orleans?"

Jedidiah's lips tightened, and his eyes blazed with fury. With an effort, he rose to his feet. Pointing a shaking forefinger at his visitor, he exclaimed in an unsteady, choking voice, "I wish to hear no more from you, sir. You'll do me the favor of leaving this house at once. I think your intimation is absolutely scurrilous. I'd also remind you of the laws of slander. Since I represent Mr. Luke Bouchard, you're on very dangerous ground trying to abuse him to me."

"Not so hasty, please, Mr. Danforth." Jenkinson rose also, lifting a propitiatory hand. "At least let me finish what I was going to say to you. Now, sir, if your client denounces a perfectly honest and intelligent enterprise because of a prejudice against the fact that I was once a Northerner, why don't I have the express right to challenge his integrity on the basis of the facts of his own life?"

"Get out of my house before I lose my temper with you, Mr. Jenkinson! I resent your infamous intimations as any decent man would, and particularly against a client whose honor and integrity are beyond question."

"Your loyalty does you credit. But I suspect you wouldn't be adverse to a handsome retainer. I have come here this morning hoping to engage your services as attorney for our new corporation."

"I wouldn't touch it with a ten-foot pole. That's your answer, Mr. Jenkinson. I imagine you can see your way out by yourself."

66

"Now be sensible, Mr. Danforth." Jenkinson tried a last time, in a wheedling tone accompanied by his most cordial smile. "If you'd be willing to sit down and give me some more facts about Mr. Bouchard's background, I think we could agree upon a very handsome retainer which—"

"Damn your conniving Yankee soul, will you or won't you leave my house this moment? I won't be a party to your dirty little games. And I warn you, if you try to blacken my client's name with your innuendos, I'll use every legal means within my power to block you and to expose you for the liar you are!"

"My, my, Mr. Danforth, those are strong words, they really are. But very well, if you feel that way, I shan't attempt to show you the obvious error in your judgment."

Jedidiah Danforth winced, his face blanching, as a sudden twinge made him grimace with pain. Clenching his fists till the knuckles whitened, striving for self-control, he gasped out, "Get out of my sight! I won't hear another word, and that should be clear enough to you if you understand the king's English. Get out, I told you!"

"Very well, I'm going, I'm going. Don't distress yourself. You're an old man who's lived in the past too long to realize the opportunities for progress in Alabama, I'm afraid. Good day to you." With a contemptuous shrug and a sneer, Homer Jenkinson turned on his heel, walked to the door, let himself out, and then banged it shut by way of showing his annoyance.

Jedidiah closed his eyes and groped for the back of a tall chair placed against the wall beside the old grandfather clock. Then he bowed his head, wincing again as the twinge made itself felt again with greater force. He could hardly breathe. With one hand he tried to open his collar, his face convulsively working as he strove to ease the pain and tension that had seized him.

"D-damned l-liar—the idea, the audacity, the brazen audacity of that man to come here and say—oh my God, oh no—Luke Bouchard—help me—" He tottered, his eyes opening and rolling to the whites, and then he pitched forward and lay still.

Emily Cantwell had lunched with her friend Clara Moseby and spent several hours exchanging nostalgic anecdotes with the affable widow. It was nearly sundown when she reminded herself that she should go back to see if Jedidiah had made any plans for his birthday dinner. The day before she had offered to cook him something special, but he had peremptorily waved aside the idea and remarked that the occasion of a man's birth didn't warrant his stuffing his face to commemorate his having come into this troublesome world.

"You know, Clara," she explained, "he's really the kindliest man on earth, but he doesn't want anybody to know about it. He's so proud; he doesn't like to feel anybody's doing any special favor for him. I can't help admiring and respecting him. Oh yes, there are times when he gets my dander up, but then I know why he does it, and he never means it, not really. And even though he's always been able to cook his own meals when he wants to, I think he'd not be too angry if I fixed him something special. So I'll see you again, maybe next Sunday, Clara."

When she had reached home, she fumbled in her purse, found her key, and let herself into the house, calling out to Jedidiah as she did so. When there was no answer, she called again, then entered the parlor—thinking to herself that she must speak once more to Jedidiah about his cigar-smoking.

A moment later, she was in near hysterics, bending over the old man's inert form; having felt for his pulse, she detected not a sign of life. Her first impulse was to borrow a horse and buggy and ride to Luke Bouchard, but then she remembered that Lopasuta Bouchard lived in a little house nearby. After the Klan had burned Lopasuta's house last year, Jedidiah—who owned several properties in the city—had provided this dwelling for his gifted protégé.

Trying to dry her tears and regain her self-control as best she could, she hurried down the street to where Luke's adopted son lived and hammered at the door with her fist, calling out, "Mr. Lopasuta, please come quick! Something dreadful's happened—Mr. Lopasuta, can you hear me?"

A moment later, the tall young lawyer opened the door and solicitously exclaimed, "Why, whatever's the matter, Mrs. Cantwell?"

"It's Mr. Danforth—he—he's gone! I came back just now—it was his birthday today, you know—and he was lying there on the floor and I felt his pulse and—oh, this is awful, he didn't let on that he was sick at all, he was as spry as ever—and now—and now—" She completely broke down, bursting into wracking sobs, and Lopasuta put an arm around her shoulders and tried his best to comfort her.

Lopasuta was profoundly shaken; nevertheless, he remained composed for Mrs. Cantwell's sake. "There now, Mrs. Cantwell, try to calm yourself. Oh, that kind old man, when I think how he kept after me to study the law, kept telling me what opportunities I could have to help everyone, including my own people—how he arranged for me to be part of the Bouchard family—there now, Mrs. Cantwell. I'll tell you what, you stay here; I'll get a horse and ride over to get Mr. Luke—he'll take care of things."

"Thank you—God—God bless you, Mr. Lopasuta," Emily quavered as she raised her tear-stained face to his.

Three days later, in the little Calvary Cemetery of the First Methodist Church of Montgomery, tall, graying Luke Bouchard delivered the funeral eulogy for his dedicated attorney and long-devoted friend.

"I do not think Jedidiah Danforth would want tears. He died on his sixty-fifth birthday, after a life spent helping others. He was the most unselfish man I've ever known. He sought peace and understanding among all people, and although he was first and foremost a Southerner, he was a man of whom this entire nation should well be proud.

"We lay his mortal remains to rest today, but not his indomitable spirit nor the forthright honesty of his own personal code, which gave him such broad vision and such wonderful humanity and compassion. As a lawyer, he understood—perhaps better than many of us who mourn him—the whims, caprices, and foibles of men in all walks of life. He held the law to be an instrument of justice for the poor as well as for the rich, for the oppressed as well as the powerful. He understood the tragic vulnerability of those less fortunate than himself, in this age of self-interest, bigotry, and prejudice—the sorry legacies of the late Civil War.

"Everywhere in this land, for all those who have suffered at the hands of private, vested interests, there always have been, there always will be, there always must be, men like Jedidiah Danforth. He belongs to that tiny brotherhood of men who battle against evil at all odds and who do not fear for themselves in that conflict. I say, thank God Almighty for such men as he, eternally vigilant and dedicated to the principles of courage and honesty that, nearly a hundred years ago, enabled this young country to throw off tyrannical oppression from across the seas. Jedidiah Danforth will never be gone from us so long as we understand and venerate the spirit of men such as he. He had goodwill in abundance, and it will live long after him to hearten all of us who strive to bring the affairs of our own community, our own state, and our own nation into logical and harmonious order. I weep that I have lost a dear friend; I exult that I was privileged to know him and to be touched by his greatness."

CHAPTER SEVEN

William Darden stood on the eastern edge of his seventy acres, facing a clump of live oak trees. In his right hand, the median and forefingers of which had been shot off by a minié ball at Shiloh, he clutched a tattered prayer book. To protect his bushy, gray-haired, leonine head from the intense mid-March Alabama sun, he wore a faded, broad-brimmed Confederate officer's hat, whose insignia showed that he had been a captain of Georgia infantry in the late rebellion. His face was bronzed by the sun and lined with wrinkles. There was a small wen at the top of his left cheekbone. His lusterless blue eyes had a vacuous, unseeing stare. His thin lips twitched, often moving as if to pronounce words; yet there was no sound from them, as he stood lost in meditation. He was wiry, with long arms, and his shoulders were erect in an instinctive military bearing.

Now forty-six years old, Darden had moved to Montgomery shortly after the end of the Civil War to live with an older sister. When she had died last summer and left him her estate in cash, he had purchased these seventy acres about fifteen miles downriver from the property managed by the newly elected state representative, Andy Haskins.

A stocky, nearly bald man two years younger than Darden now respectfully approached the latter and stood a moment watching him. His name was Jeremy Blodgett, and he had been a corporal in William Darden's Georgia company. After the war, he had voluntarily attached himself to his captain as a kind of manservant, caring for his employer and looking after the little house he and Christine Darden shared. After she died, it had really been Blodgett who had persuaded the former Confederate captain to purchase this farm by the river, because Jeremy believed that

71

it was the only way to save his captain's sanity. He had
sent for his younger brother, Purlie Blodgett, who had
brought his wife and three teenaged sons to help work the
land. He believed that the presence of his brother and the
latter's family might ease the terrible agony that had never
left Darden since that hideous day when, returning to his
home in Hawkinsville, the captain had found his stately
plantation house burned to the ground, his wife insane, and
his daughter dead after violation by a platoon of Sherman's
soldiers.

Kindly neighbors had buried the daughter and committed the wife to an asylum long weeks before Darden, weary
with his march home and the humiliating pain of the Confederacy's defeat, had arrived to see what a shambles had
been made of his life. Jeremy Blodgett had followed him to
that little Georgia town, because the stocky corporal and
his brother lived some twenty-five miles away. Jeremy felt
duty-bound to the captain, because when he had sustained
a bayonet wound in the shoulder at Shiloh, it had been his
captain who had given him first aid, and it had been while
Darden was bending over Jeremy to help him that the errant, nearly spent minié ball had neatly taken off the two
fingers of the captain's right hand.

There were no black workers on the Darden farm, and for
good reason. On that early June day of 1865, when Darden
and his corporal had stood, dazed and incredulous, before
the ruins of what had once been a stately house, a crippled
old man leaning on a cane had come out of a ramshackle
hovel nearby and, in a cackling voice, volunteered, "That
be the Darden house you see there, Cap'n. Terrible thing
those Yankees did, terrible. Burned it down just like you
see it now, that they did. Set on the young girl like a pack
of animals, yessir, and there was two dirty niggers wearing
blue who helped the others with her."

Jeremy Blodgett had turned on the old man with a savage oath and clapped his hand over the latter's mouth,
muttering, "You stupid old fool, that's Cap'n Darden right
there—why'd you want to go and say such a thing? Goddamn your soul to hell!"

He had led his master away, talking as soothingly as he
could, anything to distract William Darden from the dreadful realization that must soon penetrate his mind like a ma-
lignant, growing cancer. He had found a room for the two
of them in a shabby boarding house, seen that Darden ate

something to ease his fatigue, and put him to sleep as he might a baby. And the next day, after making inquiries and learning the full story of what had happened, Jeremy had energetically urged his captain to go visit his only living kin, Christine Darden, in Montgomery.

The ensuing years had deepened the after-effects of the tragedy. With rare and profound understanding, the loyal corporal told Christine to get a little dog so that her brother might have some creature on which to lavish his affection, if only to alleviate the terrible, brooding anguish of his irreparable loss.

Now, as Darden and Jeremy stood together in the afternoon sun, the ex-corporal held the little Scottish terrier under his left arm. It was almost as gray as its master. Over these past years, it had been the friendship of the terrier for Darden that had, many times, drawn him from the long, dark hours of despondent reflection over the annihilation of everything that had been dear to him.

" 'Scuse me, Cap'n," Jeremy respectfully ventured. "Didn't mean to disturb you none, but they's a couple gennelmun come for to see you, Cap'n. I told 'em I'd ask if you wuz receivin' this afternoon, sir."

William Darden slowly turned to face Jeremy, his face expressionless. Convulsively he pressed the tattered prayer book to his heart; then he seemed to notice the little terrier for the first time, and a faint smile creased his tightly compressed, thin mouth. "Blackie—it's Blackie. Goodness, he's getting old, just like me." Then, almost pathetically, his voice trembling, he entreated, "Let me hold him, Corporal Blodgett."

"As you say, Cap'n," Jeremy gave him a cheerful smile: this sign of recognition reassured the faithful ex-corporal that, once again, his master had been drawn out of the miasmic fog of total mental disintegration. "Here you are. He's been whinin' fer you, Cap'n." Gently he took hold of the terrier with both hands and held it toward the now blinking gray-haired man. Darden first thoughtfully eased the prayer book into the pocket of his breeches, and then, a rapt look on his face, cradled the terrier in his arms. He bent to it, and it licked his face and emitted a soft whine.

"Good dog, good Blackie boy." Darden sighed, and then his gaze seemed to sharpen, as he contemplated Jeremy. "Didn't you say something about people? Or was I dreaming again?"

73

"No, Cap'n sir, you wuzn't dreamin', not one bit. You're fine as you ever were, Cap'n. Maybe you didn't hear me—I didn't speak up loud enough, that's what it wuz. Only, right now, those two fellows, mighty important-looking, asked if I'd find out wuz you likely to talk with them this afternoon. That's what it wuz, Cap'n."

"Oh—I see. Why yes, certainly. Shall I go back into the house, Corporal?"

"Whatever's most easy for you, Cap'n. Just tell me."

"Well, it is hot, yes. I think I will walk back to the house. But I'll carry Blackie. He's a little lame in the rear legs, isn't he now?"

"Yes, Cap'n. I'm sorry."

"That's what age does to all of us, Corporal. But we're both old soldiers, aren't we? We can take whatever life has to give. Only, promise me, Corporal, if Blackie doesn't do any better, you and I won't let him suffer, will we?"

"No, we won't, sir, and you can depend on that," Jeremy fervently responded with an emphatic nod. Then, very gently, his left arm around his master's waist, he led the latter back toward the small frame house. He shared it now only with Darden—his brother and the latter's family having built their own cottage on the southern edge of the acreage.

Inside the house, Jeremy gently took hold of the older man's elbow and guided him to a dingy overstuffed chair at one corner of the small living room. Darden nodded his thanks, looked down at the little terrier, and began to stroke it. His eyes were brighter now, his gaze more lucid and comprehending. The stocky ex-corporal glanced at him for a moment, then reassuringly said, "I'll bring them in right now, Cap'n."

He left the house and walked over to the buggy in which Homer Jenkinson and the gaunt undertaker, Amos Meredith, sat, and gestured for them to come into the house. "He'll see you now, he says," he explained.

"It's about time, too," Meredith muttered under his breath, but the corpulent carpetbagger scowled and shook his head, putting a finger to his lips as he got lumberingly down from the buggy, hitched the horses' reins to the tethering post, and preceded his associate into the little house.

"Here they are, Cap'n," Jeremy cheerfully exclaimed. "I'll be outside if you need me."

Homer Jenkinson turned to watch the ex-corporal go outside and close the door behind him, then genially chuckled, "That's a fine, loyal worker you've got there, Mr. Darden."

"Yes. He served in my company. We went through a lot together." Darden's speech was terse and clipped. Now he eyed each of his visitors in turn, his face curious and attentive as he left off stroking the crippled little terrier in his lap.

"I know," Jenkinson soothingly put in, "I went to the trouble of learning something about you, Mr. Darden. That's why Mr. Amos Meredith and I decided to visit you. My name's Homer Jenkinson. I live in Montgomery, as does Mr. Meredith. The two of us, and two other associates of considerable influence, I may add, are engaged in a project that will benefit this sovereign state of Alabama."

"I—I don't understand how I can help you gentlemen," William Darden spoke now with difficulty, and a mystified expression appeared on his face. "I've got just a little farm here, as you can see for yourself; I don't have any influence at all, and the fact is I didn't even vote in the last election."

"That's not important. Believe me, Mr. Darden, I'll try to explain things to you so you'll understand." Jenkinson glanced at the undertaker, who gave him a quick nod, and then went on: "You see, Mr. Darden, Mr. Meredith and I know where to turn for loyal Southerners. You've always been that, sir. We both know about your war record, and we know what happened to you—forgive me for even mentioning it. But the point is, that you have neighbors, who, though they were born and live in the South, are, in my opinion, no better than traitors."

"You must excuse me, gentlemen. The weather's been very hot, and I'm tired. I don't quite understand what you're getting at."

"I'll come to the point, then, and my apologies for tiring you," the carpetbagger effusively declared as he leaned forward from the edge of the couch on which he and Meredith had seated themselves. "Now all of us good Southerners know that the black is an animal. I use the term that our Northern victors give these black scum, but we've always called them niggers, haven't we?"

There was a grimace of pain on William Darden's face, and he closed his eyes and his fingers tightened so convulsively on the body of the little terrier that it squirmed restlessly and emitted a plaintive whine.

75

"Well, sir, the point I'm making is that the newly elected state representative, Mr. Andy Haskins, who lives just upriver from you a few miles, actually pays niggers to work his land, treats them like whites, lets them settle there, and talks to them as if they were his equals. And worst of all, there's Luke Bouchard, who has that big red-brick house that looks like a fancy castle farther upriver near Pintilalla Creek, who talks about having a kind of community where whites and blacks work side by side and are equals and are paid the same wages. Now, sir, I ask you, isn't that treason? It destroys all that the South ever stood for. We fought a terrible war for four years to keep our niggers in their place—but these two men don't care about that. Instead of hiring decent Southern-born white workers, no, they have to go and hobnob with dirty, low, animal niggers."

William Darden started up from his chair, and the little Scotch terrier fell to the floor and began to yowl in pain. The ex-Confederate captain, his fingernails digging into his palms, his mouth agape and twisted, stared first at his two visitors, then down at the terrier, and burst into tears: "Blackie—oh God, what have I done—please don't whine like that, I didn't mean to hurt you, Blackie!"

"Let me get him for you, Mr. Darden," Amos Meredith sympathetically suggested, as he sprang forward and gently lifted the terrier. "Do sit down, sir. We apologize for giving you such a start. But we can see from this exactly how you feel. Yes, you're a true Southerner. That's why we think you can help us pay back these traitors. Imagine, Mr. Darden, one of them is sitting in the House of Representatives of our glorious state of Alabama even at this moment, making the laws that will tell you and your good people here what to do. And you've got white men working side by side with you—that's the way it always should be."

"Yes! Damn those scum—the dirty black scum who killed my poor Evelyn—Christ, I can't ever forget that—but what should I do? I don't know these men you mention—" Darden put out his maimed hand in a questioning gesture, his lips convulsively working, tears starting down his cheeks.

"Look upon Andy Haskins and Luke Bouchard as your natural enemies. After all, Mr. Darden, aren't they as bad as the niggers when they give them free rein and treat them like whites? Ask yourself if that isn't true," Jenkinson glibly pursued. He came to the old man and gently urged him to sit down again, while Meredith lowered the terrier into Darden's lap with a solicitous, "There you are, Mr. Darden, sir. He isn't hurt, he was just scared. He'll be fine, I know he will."

The spasm of agony had passed as swiftly as it had come upon the ex-Confederate captain. His face was again a blank, his eyes unseeing, as both his hands groped for and found the little dog, then began a mechanical stroking of its body back and forth, back and forth.

"We'll go now, Mr. Darden. We didn't mean to upset you. Just think about what we said. Remember, Andy Haskins about fifteen miles upriver from you and then Luke Bouchard in that big, red-brick house. Think about them. Wouldn't you like to punish them with the justice true Southerners give traitors? And now we'll wish you a good afternoon, Mr. Darden." Jenkinson came forward and patted William Darden's shoulder. "It's done us a world of good to talk to a true, valiant Southerner like you, sir. Both Mr. Meredith and I greatly respect you. God bless you for working in this noble cause."

They turned and went out, and Jenkinson jauntily addressed Jeremy Blodgett, who had been standing outside waiting, with a friendly, "Thanks for letting us see him, it was good of you. He's a fine, upstanding man. And just like you, he's a loyal Southerner, even now that the cause is lost. Yes, we need more men like the two of you. A good afternoon to you, sir."

Jeremy turned to stare after them. He squinted, took off his cap and scratched his head, then shook it, replaced the cap, and went back in to see to his employer.

Once they had passed the bend in the river that took them out of sight of the little farmhouse, Jenkinson turned to Meredith and grinned broadly. "It was a stroke of genius, Amos, your hearing a little gossip in town about this poor old lunatic. A very lucky one, too. You know, you could see right off how the word 'nigger' sets him off. And now we've given him something to think about, haven't we? He might just take it in his head to remove these two stubborn opponents to our project from the path of progress, shall we say."

"I don't know." Amos Meredith was suddenly gloomy. "Do you think he might go berserk enough to try to kill them?"

"Shh, you fool, who talked about killing? If an accident like that should happen, we know nothing about it. It's plain to see that he's already on the brink, and a little more will confine him to a lunatic asylum. And of course you can't hang a lunatic if he, shall we say, doles out justice to traitors, now can you? And who's to know what set him off or who gave him the idea to do it, eh?" He nudged Meredith in the ribs, then burst out laughing, as he shook the reins and called impatiently, "Faster, you spavined critter, or I'll take the whip to you!"

CHAPTER EIGHT

It was midnight of the same day on which Homer Jenkinson and Amos Meredith had visited William Darden's little farm. Purlie Blodgett's affable, buxom wife, Grace, had cooked supper for the melancholy ex-Confederate captain and brought it to the house on a tray. Jeremy shared it with him. Seeing that Darden was once again plunged into the passive despondency that characterized his retrogressions into the agonized past, he did his best to cheer up his employer by retelling stories of some of the happier times they had enjoyed together in the army. Once or twice he managed to bring a faint smile to Darden's lips, but the latter scarcely uttered a word throughout the supper. Greatly concerned, Jeremy remained with him, until at last the tall, gray-haired man rose from his chair and docilely went off to his lonely pallet, a mattress made of straw shucks enclosed in a quilt on an iron army cot. Darden had always claimed that he slept best on such a bed, and when he had returned to Montgomery to live with his sister, Jeremy had gone to some trouble to find one for him.

For the next few hours, there was no sound in the house. Outside in the fields crickets chirped and there was the occasional faint call of a night bird seeking its mate. The Alabama River's murmuring sound came from the distance, lulling and soothing.

Waking from his troubled sleep, William Darden slowly sat up, and then plunged his face into his hands as long, muffled sobs shook his wiry body. The little terrier, for which Jeremy had made a bed out of a broken basket, lined with cotton to ease the old dog's arthritic pains, struggled to its feet and limped toward its master, uttering its plaintive whine.

79

Distractedly, Darden put out a hand to stroke the dog's head. It licked his hand, with a soft, affectionate bark. Still in his dazed state of mind, Darden got up from his bed and went toward the kitchen door. Blackie followed, limping much more than he had done earlier in the day. His brown eyes were fixed intently on his master, and he came as close as he dared to his master's feet.

Mechanically, Darden reached for the knob of the door, turned it, and stepped out. He almost stumbled over the first of the two steps that led to the ground, but recovered himself. As he released the door, it swung shut and nearly blocked the path of the little terrier, which, summoning all its strength, lunged forward to evade it and just managed to accompany its master.

The night air was pleasantly cool. A slight wind was blowing from the northwest. Darden lifted his weatherbeaten, haggard face to the cloudless sky. The light of the full moon illumined his stark, anguished features, touched his silently moving lips, made the tears on his cheeks glisten.

He stood there a long moment, as if savoring the smell of the night and the coolness of the air. Then, as if driven by a subconscious purpose, he turned and began a steady walk directly eastward till he had reached the very edge of his acres. The boundary was marked by a twisted, gnarled pine tree. He stood before it, frowning. The terrier, which had lagged behind, now managed to catch up with him, and stood wagging its tail and watching intently to see what he would do.

Near the pine tree there was a pile of dead twigs and small branches. William Darden squatted down, reached his maimed right hand into the pile, and drew out a trowel. He began to dig directly north of the tree. Blackie sniffed the upthrown earth as it fell near him, decided that there was nothing of interest, and carefully lay down, cocking his head and continuing to watch his master with the utmost attention. Sometimes spasmodic twitches passed through the dog's hind legs.

After about fifteen minutes, Darden unearthed a long, narrow wooden crate, which he carefully lifted and set down in front of him. The top was loose, and only a few prods from the point of the trowel sufficed to open it. Inside, covered with an oilskin, was a Whitworth long-range rifle.

Neither William Darden nor Jeremy Blodgett had

owned such a weapon during the war, but when they had begun their long, dreary trek back to Georgia, Darden had found the Whitworth abandoned in a ditch about fifty miles from Appomattox. Renowned for its accuracy, the Whitworth had been the favored weapon of Confederate snipers during the war. Unfortunately for the South, only a small number of these rifles had been imported from England, where they were manufactured, and they had not been put to truly effective use until late in the hostilities. Darden had considered himself lucky to have found the weapon.

After he and Jeremy had arrived at the Darden plantation and learned about the terrible devastation there, Jeremy gently persuaded the dazed captain to entrust him with the weapon. It had been hidden away in Darden's sister's house in Montgomery. Later, Jeremy had brought it along to the farm and hidden it under his own bed in a crate he had made for it.

One evening last week, when Jeremy was away, Darden had found the hiding place of the crate. He had pulled it out, examined its contents, and then hidden it near his own bed. Later that night, after Jeremy had gone to sleep, he had carried the crate out to the pine tree, dug a hole for it, and covered it with earth. But now he was retrieving it. There was ammunition and powder in the crate in leather pouches. Both the rifle and the ammunition were still serviceable, for no moisture had been able to get to them.

Very carefully, glancing around to see if anyone was observing him, the gray-haired man primed and loaded the Whitworth. He then returned the rifle and the extra ammunition to the crate, put it back into its hole in the earth and covered it up.

Blackie had lain quietly, except for occasional whimpers, but now suddenly he seemed to be in greater pain than ever. As Darden turned to go back to the house, he stared down at the little terrier. His gaze was lucid and his face soft with a pitying solicitude for his pet. "You're so old, Blackie. You're in such dreadful pain, aren't you? I don't want you to suffer—not as they did—oh my God, not as they did!" His voice rose to an almost frenzied screech. And then suddenly he was wary, clapping his hand over his mouth as if to silence his own outcry, his eyes dilated as he looked round, fearing that someone had overheard him. But there was only silence in the night.

He began to cry again, softly, almost like a woman. The dog, as if comprehending, came close to him, nudged his leg. Darden squatted down, cupping the terrier's head in his trembling palms. Then he murmured, "You mustn't suffer. It's wrong for there to be suffering on earth. Especially when it's unjust. I must do this, Blackie. I don't want to see you limping like this and getting worse every day. Forgive me—"

As he spoke the last words, his hands slipped round the terrier's throat and swiftly, expertly, he broke the little dog's neck. He laid Blackie near where he had buried the crate, found the trowel again, dug a grave and covered up the dog. He smoothed the ground with his palms so that there would be no trace. Then he put the trowel back under the pile of twigs and little branches and walked back slowly to the house. Now his face was blank and expressionless once again, and he had straightened his shoulders with the proud bearing of an officer who has endured a taxing ordeal and come through it with flying colors. He found his bed, laid himself down upon it, and a moment later was fast asleep.

"I swear, Cap'n, I don't know what happened to Blackie." Jeremy looked worried, twisting his corporal's cap between his long, gnarled fingers. "I wouldn't have thought he wuz the kind to run off, not from you, Cap'n."

"I don't know, Jeremy. When I woke up three mornings ago, all I know is he wasn't there. Well, he was getting old, he'd had a good long life—with less pain than most of us, I reckon." William Darden sat at the little dining table, his shoulders slumped, his face bleak, his right thumb and fourth finger gripping the fork he abstractedly dipped into a plate of stew. "Of course, I'll miss him—but then, I miss my wife and daughter too, you know, Jeremy."

"Yes, Cap'n." The former corporal bowed his head, bit his lips, and crumpled his cap behind his back, ill at ease. Finally, he ventured, "I'll see to getting you a new dog, Cap'n. Like as not, the best way to get over losing one dog is to get another right away. Leastways, that's what my brother Purlie did back in Georgia when his Irish setter got bit by a snake. Yessir, Purlie got himself a young 'un, the same breed, just about a week later."

"What happened to that one, Jeremy?"

Jeremy's face contorted in bitterness. "Some damn Yan-

82

kee trooper shot him when Sherman's boys wuz marching through, Cap'n. From what I heard tell, shot him for no reason at all, just because he wuz running around and barking at them."

"Yes. We've all lost something to the Yankee troops, haven't we, Jeremy? No, don't think about another dog yet. Blackie was good for me. I know why you had me look after him the way you did. You're a good man, Jeremy. Best orderly in the whole Confederate army. If there'd been more like you, we wouldn't have lost to the Yankees."

"No, Cap'n. And there's folks who still don't think we did."

"Yes." Darden dropped his fork onto the plate, retrieved it, and doggedly set about eating his stew for a few minutes. Then, as if gathering his thoughts again, he laid the fork carefully down at the edge of the plate and looked up at his former orderly. "Maybe it'd do me good to go riding for a spell this afternoon, Jeremy. I'd like to see who our neighbors are upriver. Haven't met them yet, heard a lot about them."

"Sure, Cap'n. It's a nice sunny day, but not too hot. Do us both good, for a fact. I guess Purlie can spare me from the fields this one afternoon. Tell you what, Cap'n. You finish your lunch now, and I'll saddle up our horses."

The two men rode upriver, the former Confederate captain on a gentle piebald mare, Jeremy on a black gelding. The sun was warm, but a cool breeze wafted across the Alabama River to temper the heat so that it did not become oppressive. Still concerned that his employer's frightening attacks of deep depression and black moodiness might return because of the loss of Blackie, Jeremy kept up a steady, casual conversation about the happier past, recalling some of the hair-raising escapades in which he had been involved when he had tried to procure a chicken or some fruit to make the monotonous officers' mess more palatable.

"Remember that time, Cap'n, about a month before Shiloh?" he chuckled. "I recollect you and Cap'n Dellison and Lieutenant Carteret wuz saying you'd give a month's pay for a good rabbit stew?"

"Yes. Oh yes. I remember now." Darden seemed to brighten a moment, and nodded as he turned to look at the man riding beside him. But his eyes turned back again along the river trail, and now they narrowed with a peculiar anticipation and intensity which made Jeremy frown.

Hastily, so as not to let this pleasantly nostalgic mood slip away, Jeremy proffered, "Well, but you don't know how I managed to get those two rabbits, now, do you, Cap'n? It wuz when you wuz commanding Company B, Georgia Volunteers. Well, sir, I moseyed over to old Big-Belly Jones—he wuz the mess sergeant with Company A, I don't know if you recall—and it seems he'd got hisself three rabbits and a coon over at a farm. Seems an old man and his boy had gone out huntin' the day before and bagged those critters, and when they saw us Johnny Rebs make our camp not far from their shack, the boy trotted over to Jones and made him a present. Said it wuz his patriotic duty, that's what he said, Cap'n."

He waited a moment, till at last William Darden slowly turned to look at him, his eyes again lusterless, almost unseeing. But then there was the slow nod of recognition which reassured his corporal. "Yes. That was a very good thing. There were a lot of fine, decent people in the war on both sides. I know that. But then there were others—" He fell silent again, brooding, and his maimed hand convulsively tightened on the reins of the piebald mare.

"Sure there wuz, Cap'n, and most of them wuz on our side." Jeremy again hurried to divert his employer's attention from yet more painful memories. "Anyhow, I knew exactly where Big-Belly would be hidin' the rabbits 'n the coon, so I told him I'd seen a flock of mallard ducks a-settin' on a little creek about half a mile away. You know, Cap'n, he wuz always braggin' 'bout what a crack shot he wuz. I knew he'd take the bait, and he sure did." Jeremy slapped his thigh and burst into reminiscent laughter. "Well, Cap'n, nothin' would do but that he would have to take his Henry and traipse after those mallards. All I did, I just went into the mess tent, appropriated the spoils of war, and beat it back to our tent. That's why you had such a good supper that night."

"Yes. That was very clever of you, Jeremy. But—but didn't the sergeant suspect who stole his fodder?" Once again, Darden turned to look at his former corporal, and this time his face was attentive.

With a sigh of relief, Jeremy chuckled. "Oh, I'm sure he guessed who it wuz, but he couldn't prove it. You see, I beat Corporal Tomlinson, Jones's right-hand man, in poker three nights running, and he owed me good. I told him, I

84

did, if he'd say he saw some scrawny private get into that tent and steal those rabbits 'n that coon, I'd fergit what he owed me. Sure enough, he did. Man, those wuz the days, wuzn't they, Cap'n?"

"They were indeed, Jeremy. Yes, they were happy days. We didn't know then what we know now—" Suddenly a spasm of anguish twisted Darden's gaunt face, and he bowed his head and began to sob. Alarmed, Jeremy leaned over, jerked on the reins of the piebald mare with a hoarse "Whoa!" while at the same time halting his own mount. "I didn't mean to stir you up like that, Cap'n. Honest to God I didn't. I ought to be horsewhipped. Please, Cap'n. Look there—" His voice rose in bluff encouragement, as he pointed toward the nearby frame house of Andy Haskins. "There are both your neighbors, Mr. Luke Bouchard and Mr. Haskins. Mr. Bouchard's the one just getting down from that gray gelding, and Haskins is the one who lost his right arm at Chickamauga."

William Darden straightened in his saddle and leaned forward, his eyes again intent and narrowed. "Yes. I see them, Jeremy. I see them very well. And this is Mr. Haskins's farm, I take it."

"Sure is, Cap'n. Mr. Bouchard's place is upriver a mite. Big red-brick house with two towers. Way I heard it, his daddy built it for his daddy in turn, who came from France a long time ago and lived in just such a house over there. It's sort of a landmark around here, Cap'n."

"Yes, I understand that. It's good to have tradition, something to cling to, like a strong family, Jeremy. And happy memories that go back for generation after generation—he's been mighty lucky, this Luke Bouchard." His face hardened. "So at least his daddy was born here in Alabama?"

"That's right, Cap'n. But his granddaddy, like I said, came from France, though he settled here with the Injuns, the story goes. And they gave him the land and then Mr. Lucien Bouchard's son built him that house of his before he died. Now what I heard tell wuz that the Yankees burned the house right at the end of the war, so Mr. Luke Bouchard took the family off to New Orleans, and then on to Texas. But he came back and married a New Orleans gal and he settled down here after the house had been rebuilt just like it wuz before." As he finished, Jeremy bit his lip and shook his head, furious with himself. He realized only too well how easily this talk of united family life could crumble the dam of Darden's distraught mind and let out the bitter flow of despair and implacable hate. So once again, more exuberantly than was necessary, he added, "Why don't we just go up there and say hello to them, Cap'n? After all, it's only right, they're neighbors of ours, don't you think?"

"No. Thank you anyway, Jeremy. I'm not up to it this afternoon. I feel very tired all of a sudden. And I miss Blackie so. Let's ride on back. The air's pleasant, and I like the sound of the water. It goes on down winding its way to Mobile, where once the bales of cotton were on the docks and there was money in everyone's pocket and people were happy. Let's go back home, Jeremy.

CHAPTER NINE

"Good to see you, Andy." Luke Bouchard advanced to shake the young Tennesseean's hand and clap him on the back in accolade. "I paid a visit to the House chambers day before yesterday, and I heard your speech about resisting taxes that would benefit special interests. Keep it up, lay it on strong as you please, Andy. Maybe you'll help flush those skulking carpetbagger hyenas out of their lair and make them show themselves for what they really are."

"I already know who they are, Mr. Luke." Andy gave him a crooked grin as he led him into the house where Jessica was knitting a sweater for baby Horatio.

"I declare, Mrs. Haskins," he amiably greeted her, "seeing you knit that sweater for little Horatio brings back some wonderful memories of Mother Sybella—peace to her dear, brave soul. And I must say, you're lovelier than ever—Andy's a very lucky man."

"Don't I know it, Mr. Luke!" Andy grinned from ear to ear and eyed Jessica, who blushed vividly and turned all her attention back to her knitting.

"When do you go back into session, Andy?"

"Next Wednesday, Mr. Luke. Seems like my colleagues like to vote themselves little vacations every now and then, instead of minding their business and cleaning it all up."

"Yes, that's politics for you, Andy. You're getting a good, first-hand lesson. And the *Advertiser* is on your side. They quoted some of that speech of yours in this morning's issue. Yes, fine work. By the way, I've two pieces of news for you. The first is, Mitzi and Dalbert are parents again. It happened last night, and Mitzi has a fine, bouncing baby boy she and Dalbert have named David. That's three boys, and that's certainly the way to carry on the line. Dalbert is proud to bursting."

"I'm glad for Dalbert and I know how he feels," Andy replied. "Shucks, I reckon when it comes to feeling really good, I thank God for my Jessica and our little Horatio."

Jessica glanced up from her knitting and sent him a loving glance, then swiftly went back to her work. Luke observed this and his smile broadened. "There's nothing like being a father for the first time. And you deserve every bit of your good fortune, Andy. Well now, the second piece of news I have concerns you, too. Now that poor old Jedidiah's gone to his final reward, I've asked Lopasuta to represent the Bouchards' legal affairs, and he's agreed."

"That's just fine, Mr. Luke! Now there's a fellow who's done wonders, but then again, it's thanks to you. I wouldn't have believed that an Injun could come up here to Montgomery and get himself admitted to the bar and stand in court and defend blacks and poor folks and come away a winner, but he's done it."

"That's because he's got a good, keen mind and he's dedicated, just the way you are. Yes, it's a heartening story, because it shows that in this country, the premise of our forefathers, when they drew up that Declaration of Independence to proclaim that all men were free and equal, can still hold true and not be just empty words." In a more casual tone, he added, "I had to persuade that adopted son of mine to take Jedidiah's place. I told him it was only right, because Jedidiah had taught him the law and shown by his own life how the law can be on the side of those who need it most, if it's properly practiced." ˙

"I agree with you, Mr. Luke."

"Mrs. Cantwell has shown Lopasuta where old Jedidiah kept all his files—some of them he had in his house, you see. And he's been studying them, bringing himself up to date on what's happening over at Windhaven Plantation, as well as on this Williamson acreage which is now yours and Jessica's. Fortunately, because Jedidiah was so conscientious, there won't be any unforeseen problems about the title of any of the acreage, nor will there be any unpaid taxes that will suddenly crop up to plague us. He wrote everything down in the ledger books."

"Do you think he can do anything about Homer Jenkinson and that fat judge from Tuscaloosa—what was his name—oh yes, Siloway, Mr. Luke?" Andy anxiously asked.

"I mean, in case they try to stir up any trouble for either you or me."

"I think he can do a great deal," Luke slowly replied. "Naturally, I told him everything I knew about the men who approached you and what they had in mind. He's also studying up on the history of the Alabama and Chattanooga Railroad, and he's already seen for himself what happened to some of the questionable bond issues. He agrees with my own layman's opinion that if these men asked you to favor lower taxes on properties around the line at a time when the entire railroad is in receivership with the state government standing by, there's obviously deception and fraud in view."

Andy Haskins' solemnly nodded. "I've sounded out a couple of more fellows in the House, Mr. Luke, old-timers who sure know more about Alabama than I do, and that's exactly what they think. You can depend on it, I'm not going to let Jenkinson and his friends pressure me. But what else do you figure they can do? They've already offered me that bribe to sponsor their crooked little scheme."

"I hope they'll take your no for an answer and my letter in the *Advertiser* as a checkmate of their plans, and just retire gracefully. Only, knowing how greedy they are, especially Jenkinson, I imagine they'll try to influence other legislators in whatever way they can. And of course, they're petty and vindictive men—they might attempt some reprisals against us. I'd be prepared for just about anything."

"Do you think they might turn the Ku Klux Klan against you and me, Mr. Luke?" Andy purposely lowered his voice almost to a whisper, glancing quickly over at Jessica, who was preoccupied with her knitting.

Luke moved closer to him, shook his head, and murmured, "I doubt it very much. Jenkinson's obviously a Republican, as practically all of the carpetbaggers are. Besides, the Klan is now officially outlawed, and for certain it wouldn't come to the aid of a Northern swindler bent on taking money out of Alabama for his own profit. No, I'm not afraid of that at all." He raised his voice to conventional speaking tone. "We'll just keep our eyes and ears open from now on, Andy."

"That we will, Mr. Luke. Say now, it's getting late, and I know Jessica'd like it a lot if you'd stay to supper with us."

At this, his wife looked up, eagerly nodded, and put in, "Oh yes, Mr. Bouchard, please do!"

"Well," Luke wryly responded, "I'm going to be a little selfish and accept your invitation. The fact is, Laure—once she heard about Mitzi's new baby—took Hannah and some baked goods and went right over to Lowndesboro. She told me I'd have to fend for myself, so far as meals were concerned, until she returned on Sunday. So I'm a bachelor again, and I'd certainly appreciate one of your wonderful home-cooked meals."

William Darden had seemed so calm and even cheerful on their return to the little house that Jeremy had been greatly cheered. And when the gray-haired officer had yawned and said that he wanted to go to sleep early because the horseback ride had tired him, the devoted orderly stayed a moment or two to make certain that he had fallen asleep, and then went off to spend the rest of the evening with his brother Purlie.

It was about nine o'clock that night when Darden opened his eyes and got up from his cot, fully dressed save for his broad-brimmed hat with its military insignia. He hurried out to the pine tree, glancing across the fields to the cottage where the two Blodgett brothers were. Seeing no sign of anyone about, he groped for the trowel and quickly dug up the case that contained the loaded Whitworth. He buried the empty crate and hurried off to the rickety little stable in back of the frame house, saddled his piebald mare, and rode off into the night.

He headed upriver, kicking the mare's belly with his heels to urge it to swifter gait, till he reached the outskirts of Andy Haskins's acreage. Tethering the mare's reins to the low-hanging branch of an old cypress tree, he crouched like an infantryman, grasping the rifle with both hands and obscuring himself till he was within range of the frame house. He could see the light of the oil lamp in the living-room window. He sucked in his breath and lay flat on his belly and waited.

Jessica Haskins had given Luke Bouchard and Andy a veritable feast, with roast chicken, sweet yams, garden greens, and a sugar-sweetened rhubarb pie, topped off with good strong black coffee from Dalbert Sattersfield's general store. Little Horatio had long before been put into his crib and was soundly sleeping, and over their coffee Luke,

90

Andy, and Jessica talked of domestic pleasantries. For Luke and Andy both, it was an enjoyable time of relaxation and warm neighborliness; it delighted Luke at his age to chat genially about his two little sons and to feel himself on equal terms with Andy, who was reveling in being a father for the first time.

"It's one of the finest dinners I've ever eaten, Mrs. Haskins, and it was good of you—though you shouldn't have gone to all that trouble," he complimented her.

"No such thing, Mr. Bouchard," she smilingly flung back at him. "I'll admit that a part of it was in your honor, but most of it was to show how proud I am of Andy's being so useful in our government here. You should know, Mr. Bouchard, that it flatters a wife a lot when her husband's doing so well, because when everybody says what a smart man he is, it reflects back on how smart he was to pick a wife who could be a helpmate to him."

"You've got a very good point there, Mrs. Haskins, and of course, I couldn't agree more wholeheartedly," Luke genially laughed, as he rose to stretch his limbs. "With your permission, I'll go for a little stroll by the river. The moon's out and the air's still nicely cool. Besides, I need some exercise to work off the weight I've put on after a supper like this."

"I'll go with you, Mr. Luke," Andy proffered.

"No, you show what a well-trained husband you are by helping your wife with the dishes. Besides, I'm in a certain mood tonight. I'd like to go down by the river and think back to how things used to be, when Grandfather came along this way so many years ago looking for Econchate."

"Sure. I understand, Mr. Luke. Jessica, I'll do the dishes myself. You just go in and see if Horatio's nice and comfy." Andy bent to kiss Jessica on the cheek, then whispered, "That was a scrumptious meal, honey. You're going to get me started thinking about my weight, too, if you keep that up. But it was so good, maybe I ought to invite Mr. Luke over here every night."

"Get along with you and do those dishes like Mr. Bouchard said," Jessica laughed, and then, locking her arms around his neck, drew him down for a very loving, wifely kiss.

Luke Bouchard turned back at the door to smile at the happy couple, sighed, and then let himself out into the night. The moon had gone behind a straggling cloud, and he breathed in the pleasantly cool night air. There was the smell of the river, which eternally suggested the fertility of the fields it helped irrigate, the profusion of trees and flowers and shrubs which, as they had done for so many generations in the past, now lent an unforgettable beauty to the upriver trail Lucien Bouchard had seen and taken toward his destiny.

Luke walked slowly down toward the river, looking northward. How often he had seen the river and thought of the trail and of the harrowing difficulties his grandfather had endured in seeking a new life in a strange new land. Tonight, wonderfully at peace with his own family and his commune of loyal workers who were much more than employees to him, he could savor all the more his memories of the old days, as well as the glowing delight young Andy Haskins and his sweet Jessica were taking in the start of their own new life together, already blessed by their first-born.

He thought, too, of his own very human frailties, of the errors of judgment of which he had been guilty over the years since he was a boy dogging his grandfather's footsteps, eager to hear once again the by-now legendary story of his journey from the little province of Normandy to the wilds of the New World. Luke had made far more errors, he believed, than old Lucien Bouchard had in his entire life, and his was not yet done. He raised his eyes to the gentle night sky and prayed silently that he would err no more.

Then he turned and walked resolutely forward toward the bank of the Alabama River, as the moon emerged from behind a cloud to illuminate his path. Suddenly, from the top of a live oak tree, a screech owl fluttered its wings and hooted at him. As he turned to look in the direction of that sound, there was a sharp crack of a rifle and he heard the bullet whiz by his head. He uttered a startled gasp, turned to his left, and saw a shadowy figure far distant rise from the ground, run toward a horse, mount it, and ride off downriver.

Almost immediately, Andy emerged from the house and came running toward him. "My God, Mr. Luke, what was that? Sounded like a rifle, and I ought to know from Chickamauga, I heard plenty of them popping that hellish day!"

"It was a rifle, all right," Luke Bouchard grimly said. "The man who fired it rode off downriver."

"Who do you suppose it could be?" Andy turned, then uttered a most uncharacteristic oath. "Goddammit, it frightened Jessica—I'd like to get my hands on that bastard, whoever he is!" Turning to his wife, who had followed him in alarm, he soothed, "It's all right, nobody was hurt, honey. You go back, everything's fine."

"But it was a shot, Andy—and someone tried to kill Mr. Bouchard—oh my God, why would anyone want to do that? He's the kindest man—oh Andy! Somebody out there hiding with a gun, trying to kill him—or—or, if you'd gone out—" She put her arms around him, pressed her face against his chest, and burst into hysterical sobs.

He stroked her head, murmuring words of endearment, trying to urge her back into the house. "Mr. Luke, I don't like this one bit. You know what I'm thinking—and it's an ugly thought."

"I can guess. You think Jenkinson may be mixed up in this."

"That's exactly it. There isn't any proof, but if I see that damned Yankee carpetbagger once more—excuse me, Jessica honey—I'll cut his guts out, so help me! Now, now, honey, it's all over now, nobody's hurt. Let's you and me go back in the house. Come on, Mr. Luke. I've got a Spencer carbine loaded and ready in the closet. If anybody tries this little trick again tonight, we'll both be ready for him."

The piebald mare was lathered with sweat and foam as William Darden galloped up to the little stable, led the faltering horse into its stall, unsaddled it, and removed the reins and bit. He was about to leave the stable when he realized that he should give the animal a rubdown. This accomplished, he took the Whitworth and went out to the pine tree. Digging up the crate, he replaced the weapon in it, then buried the crate again. He glanced toward the house, hoping that Jeremy had not yet returned; when he saw the faint light he had left burning, he relaxed a bit, knowing that his friend must still be away. Then he hurried toward the house, where he stretched out on his bed and fell fast asleep.

CHAPTER TEN

Old Elmore Hancock, the venerable Speaker of the House from Autauga County, rapped his gavel for order, stalling as the vociferous shouts and catcalls from opposing Democratic members threatened to disrupt the proceedings. Once again he brought his gavel down as hard as he could, swearing under his breath, until at last a semblance of order was restored.

The Alabama House of Representatives was an unruly and contentious body this year, partly because neither the Democrats nor the Republicans held an effective working majority of the seats. In the election of November 1872, the Democrats had won a majority of the seats in both houses of the General Assembly, but the Republicans had contested the returns and refused to meet with the Democrats. They were spurred on in this action by the United States senator from Alabama, Senator Spencer, who was seeking reelection by the General Assembly and could not obtain his goal if the Republicans did not have a majority of the seats in the Legislature. The two party organizations met separately—the Republicans at the federal courthouse, the Democrats at the state capitol—and the stalemate might have continued indefinitely had not David Lewis (recently elected Republican governor) and other Republicans appealed to President Grant to help resolve the dispute. A compromise was finally worked out, and grudging peace was restored between the two parties. The peace, however, was superficial. The fact of the matter was that the two houses of the General Assembly, as finally constituted, were so evenly divided between Democrats and Republicans that legislative action was stymied, and nothing could be done about such urgent issues as the near-bankruptcy of the state government—an insolvency caused in large measure by the scandalous financial affairs of the Alabama and Chattanooga Railroad.

It was that railroad which the House members were now discussing in the most heated manner. Speaker Elmore Hancock once again rapped his gavel with all his strength and called out, "The members of this House will come to order. We shall hear from Representative Haskins of Montgomery County. *If* you please, gentlemen! Let us remember that we are all gentlemen here, and that we have legislative business to attend to. Bickering will not solve our difficulties."

"Neither will you damned Republicans!" an unidentified and disgruntled Democrat cupped his pudgy hands to his mouth and bawled, and a snicker of appreciative mirth was heard as the young Tennesseean got to his feet and cleared his throat. Earnestly he turned to contemplate his colleagues, some of whom began to applaud, while others openly hissed.

"I rise to a point of order, Mr. Speaker," Andy Haskins declared in a firm voice. "When we broke off at the last session, there was a lot of talk about the Alabama and Chattanooga. You have copies of the record just as I do, so I'm not going to drone on and tell you history you're all too familiar with. Instead, I'm going to tell you about something that happened to me just last week. Some gentlemen who shall be nameless came to me asking me to sponsor a bill that would lower taxes in certain sections of this fair state of ours. Their explanation was that lower taxes would spur growth in those areas and in turn bring revenue to the Alabama and Chattanooga."

"Sure, and fill somebody else's pockets in the process!" a fellow Republican called out amid mingled laughter and jeers.

"Exactly!" Andy put his left palm on the rostrum of his desk to steady himself, took another deep breath, cleared his throat again, and resumed, "Ever since the war ended, people in this state and a lot of other Southern states have been talking a lot about scalawags and carpetbaggers. These terms aren't meant kindly, we know that. But on the other hand, gentlemen, I see many among you who are scalawags or carpetbaggers, yet whose motives I don't question as regards honesty and interest in the voters who put you in office."

96

Once again, mingled applause and catcalls greeted this statement. Ignoring the reaction, Andy waited for a moment of silence and then went on. "Now we all know that the Alabama and Chattanooga was declared bankrupt, taken over by the last governor of this state, and finally put into receivership for the bondholders who had backed the first mortgages on the enterprise. In light of that history, I think all of us should look with great suspicion on any proposals put to us by outsiders who have no understanding of the problems of this state. We should view with skepticism any scheme which promises prosperity for our state and its citizens and just ignores the plain facts. Any fool plan which claims to offer an easy way to help the railroad by extending its track is, at this stage of the game, not only unrealistic as hell, but also as close as anything I've seen these days to an outright swindle."

"Hear, hear!" Two middle-aged members chorused their approval, while a third rose from his seat, cursed profanely, and walked out of the chamber.

"I'm not going to take much more of your time; I'm a junior member, and I know I'm on probation before all of you. Maybe I haven't yet mastered all of the parliamentary procedures I need to know in order to say things properly before you, but I've got to say this: when someone offers me a bribe which I refuse, and when a friend of mine is nearly shot on my own property a while later, I'm bound to suspect—unless I'm a jackass, which I'm not—that there is some connection between the two episodes. Furthermore, I'd say that the person or persons responsible for such bribery and violence ought to be driven out of our state forever. That's all I have to say." He sat down, flushed and trembling with excitement, while the applause drowned out the unhappy murmurings and grumbles of a few members.

After the House had adjourned for lunch, several of his colleagues came up to Andy to congratulate him on his stand for honesty and proper representation of his constituents, adding that they, to a man, would oppose any plan that smacked of self-interest, particularly any measure that tended to permit unscrupulous Northerners to defraud the citizens of Alabama.

One of the men who did not congratulate the Tennesseean was Lance Remerswald, once a realtor in Baltimore who had married a Montgomery girl shortly before the Civil War, established a thriving business as a land agent in

97

Montgomery County, and had, with Andy Haskins, been elected last November. Lance Remerswald had already been approached by Homer Jenkinson and his three associates and had agreed to do what he could to further their measure if it could be brought before the House of Representatives, though he had declined to sponsor it himself for various personal reasons.

He sent a venomous glance at Andy, who stood chatting with his friendly colleagues, and hurried out of the state capitol building to a little lunchroom across the street. When the buxom, affable waitress approached him to take his order, he winked at her and muttered, "Get word to Amos that Andy Haskins is up to his old tricks. He'll know what that means, Della."

"Sure, honey. Now whatcha you gonna have this noon? We got some real tasty spareribs 'n grits. Joe's in the kitchen now fixin' 'em pipin' hot."

Remerswald speculatively eyed her and gave her a knowing grin. He was forty-five, florid of face and bulky of stature, an inveterate tippler and womanizer, though he professed the utmost reverence for and fidelity toward his far younger wife. Glancing around to make sure that none of the other customers in the lunchroom could overhear the conversation, he vouchsafed, "I'd rather have you served up piping hot any time, sweetheart. When can we get together?"

The waitress simpered, pretended to blush, and turned away. Then she whispered, "You know where my place is, Lance honey. Whyn't you drop around any time from five on—I'll be off then and go straight home." Then aloud, for the benefit of the other customers, she exclaimed, "I'll get your ribs 'n grits right away, honey."

Andy Haskins came down the steps of the capitol building and self-consciously grinned as he was welcomed by Luke Bouchard and the latter's twenty-five-year-old adopted son, Lopasuta. The latter, as tall as Luke himself, coppery-skinned, with strong, resolute features, had by now been accepted by most of the Montgomery citizenry, who had read of his legal exploits in the *Advertiser*. More than that, his staunch championing of the poor and oppressed freed blacks had won him a devoted loyalty in the black community. Those whom he had aided, who could not otherwise have afforded legal counsel, had told their friends and neighbors what he had done for them, repeating parts of his speeches before the court. On more than one occasion, Lopasuta had won for his clients cases against white carpetbaggers who had sought to fleece the poor blacks by contracting with them for labor and then refusing to pay for it on the grounds that the work had been unsatisfactory.

Lopasuta had come to Montgomery in May of 1870. His departure from the Comanche stronghold of Sangrodo, across the border of the Rio Grande, had come about as the result of the visit of Djamba and his wife, Celia, to the stronghold to visit their daughter, Prissy, who had married the Comanche brave, Jicinte. Sangrodo had told Djamba of a young brave whose mother had been a Mexican girl; Lopasuta's Comanche father had captured her in a raid. As the only daughter of a *rico*, Lopasuta's mother had learned to speak English fluently; after her capture, she had fallen in love with her Comanche husband and willingly adopted the ways of his people; nevertheless, she had taught her son to speak and write both Spanish and English. Lopasuta thirsted for knowledge, and after Djamba had met him and heard him speak eloquently of wishing to acquire more education, he had returned to Windhaven Range and told Lucien Edmond Bouchard of this meeting. In turn, Lucien Edmond had written to his father, Luke, who had visited old Jedidiah Danforth and proposed that the young Comanche study law with the attorney. Lopasuta had come to Alabama, passed his bar examination, and been admitted to practice. Luke had adopted him as a son of whom he was as proud as he was of his own offspring.

"That was a great speech, Andy!" Luke exclaimed as he shook hands with the fledgling politican. "You roused a storm of indignation, I can tell you that, judging by the response in the House. And those who happen to be on the side of the thieving rogues who tried to bribe you and then get someone to frighten you and me off by gunfire have been served very appropriate notice."

"Yes," Lopasuta gravely agreed, "it may very well force their hand, and if they commit a stupid mistake where there are witnesses to observe it, then I shall be able to proceed against them legally. I can assure you, Mr. Haskins, that legal punishment can very often be much more effective than a sound thrashing, because it will hold them up to the light of investigation and every citizen will know about their infamous acts."

"Shucks, Lopasuta," Andy's self-conscious grin grew broader, "I'm mighty flattered by your calling me Mr. Haskins, but by now we're friends enough so's Andy's just fine with me. But about what you just said, there's times when a good thrashing is a lot more satisfactory than a lot of legal palaver, isn't that so, Mr. Luke?"

"Possibly so—but Andy, boy, turnabout is fair play." Luke gave him an affectionate nudge in the ribs. "If you want Lopasuta to call you just plain Andy, by the same token it's high time you started calling me just plain Luke."

"Shucks—well, I'll tell you straight off, I guess it's a matter of ingrained habit. But since you ask me to, I'll try to remember. But say now, I'd like it mighty fine, Lopasuta, and you too, Mr.—I mean, Luke—if you'd both ride down and have supper with Jessica and me tonight. We're going to adjourn about three o'clock this afternoon, so I'll have plenty of time to get home and freshen up and help Jessica fix something special. I think she said she'd pick snap beans, and you ought to taste them the way she fixes them with herbs and a little butter."

"I accept already," Luke Bouchard laughingly assented. "Laure has been spending a lot of time with Mitzi, and I sometimes think she's more excited about Mitzi's latest son than she is about her staid old graybeard of a husband. I know she'll be over at Mitzi's again tonight, and after that last supper I had with you, Andy, my mouth's watering already. Lopasuta, you've a treat in store for you."

"Thank you, Andy," the young Comanche lawyer responded, "I thank you for your kind invitation. My father has told me what a wonderful cook your wife is, and besides, I'm eager to pay my respects to her. I've met her several times when she's come to town with you, and I look forward to a much longer visit with her this evening. You are very fortunate to have so gracious and lovely a wife."

"You're right there, Lopasuta," Andy energetically nodded. "Say, it's about time a strapping young fellow like you started thinking about finding himself a nice girl and settling down. That's what Mr.—I mean, Luke—always kept telling me. And you see that I took his advice."

Lopasuta's smile vanished and he looked somberly thoughtful. "You forget that I am a Comanche. It would not be easy in Montgomery to find a wife, Andy. There are still many people here who look upon me as they would upon a black because my skin has a different color from theirs."

"Probably so," Andy countered, "but the way I figure it, your people were here a lot longer than any of us, which sort of makes you blue-blooded aristocracy. I mean, I used to read in school about the folks who came over on the *Mayflower* and founded this country. The fact is, that if the Indians hadn't been friendly in that neck of the woods where they landed, this country might never have gotten started."

"That's the way my grandfather and I have always felt, Andy," Luke put in. "But it will be a long while before prejudice and bigotry based on fearful ignorance of the difference of one person from another can be eliminated in this nation. All the same, I agree with what you said about Lopasuta's thinking about marrying a fine, unbiased girl who would admire him for his achievements, respect him for his honesty and decency, and love him simply as a man. There's no law in this state that I know of which would prevent such a marriage if such a girl and Lopasuta were to declare their intentions."

"That is true enough, Mr. Bouchard." Lopasuta could barely bring himself to address his adoptive father by the latter's first name, despite Luke's repeated urgings. "Yet even though it is legally possible, I must think also that, if by some chance I were to meet a girl that I loved and she were white, there would be difficulties for her—perhaps difficulties so great that I myself would not want her to endure them for my sake. And, too, I do not think that a well-bred girl from here would want to live with me in Mexico in the stronghold of my chief, if one day I return. I have already kept my vow to Sangrodo that I would bring honor to the tribe and stand for justice; one day I may be able to speak for his people as I do now for those who need me in Montgomery."

"Lucien Edmond has just written me a letter telling me that Catayuna and Sangrodo are happy and taking joy in bringing up their little girl, Consuela, who must be about three months old by now. Theirs is a peaceful life in the stronghold, and Sangrodo was very wise in realizing that for you, Lopasuta, with your keen mind, an agricultural life would be, in one sense, a prison for you."

"Yes, it is true," the Comanche lawyer soberly admitted.

"That is why I feel my responsibility weighing heavily upon me, because there is Comanche blood in my veins and I must always be worthy of it." Then, earnestly, turning to Luke he added, "When you next write to Lucien Edmond, will you ask him to send my warmest greetings to Sangrodo and his Catayuna? I, too, shall write soon. Sangrodo is truly a good man, and fortunate in his mate. She has become the beloved woman of the tribe, and they love and respect her for her courage and kindness and for the happiness she has given my chief."

Jeremy Blodgett was busy hoeing the weeds out of a patch of ground in which he intended to plant melons and sweet yams, and his brother Purlie, passively smoking a corncob pipe and giving directions to his three sturdy sons nearby, was chatting with him. Purlie's wife was in the kitchen of their cottage preparing supper for all six of them. It was a Friday evening late in March. There had been a welcome, moderate rain that night before, which, in Purlie's view, would accelerate the growth of crops.

"How's Cap'n these days?" he inquired, taking his corncob pipe out of his mouth, lowering it to knock the bowl against his boot and empty it, then stuffing it into the pocket of his work trousers.

"It's a funny thing, Purlie." The former orderly stopped his weeding and leaned forward with both hands gripping the top of the hoe to support himself as he faced his brother. "I thought he'd be fair down in the dumps for losing Blackie, but he took it real strong, the cap'n did. Since then, he's been what you might say real cheerful. No trouble with him at all, not hardly."

"It's a terrible thing," Purlie commiseratingly sighed and shook his head. "One of the best officers in the whole damn Confederate army, had to come home like that and find out what happened to his house 'n family. Turned his mind; probab'ly won't ever be back to what he wuz before the war."

"None of us will, for that matter, Purlie. But it's kinder this way, I figger. You know, lots of folks, if they wuzn't kin, would have clapped him right into a place for loonies. But I couldn't let that happen to the cap'n, Purlie, I jist couldn't. Not after he saved my life at Shiloh. I'd of bled to death for certain, if he hadn't got that bandage around my shoulder after that damned Yank stuck his bayonet into me. And, mind you, Purlie, with two fingers of his'n shot away and all, he still kept on tending to me till he was sure the bleeding wuz stopped as best he could. Surgeon said the tourniquet he put on saved my life; he did that, Purlie." Jeremy hawked and spat and shook his head. "Nope, right then and there I said to myself I wuz the cap'n's man as long as he'd want me around. That's the way it's gonna be, Purlie.

"Anyhow, you've gotta admit, Purlie, we're doin' better here than we could of back in Georgia. This land's real good, not ruined by cotton and tobacco like so much of the land down there. We'll always be able to eat off this land, Purlie, and you can bring up your kids a proper way. It's not an exciting life, you might say, but it'll do for a long spell, I'm thinking."

"Yup, Jeremy, you're right about that. As for me, I wouldn't want to see the cap'n get stuck in some madhouse with nobody to look after him or care what happened to him. At least this way, he figures he's got kinfolk looking after him, and that's us. My boys and I and my missus are glad to do it for his sake, as well as for yours, Jeremy."

"I'm mighty grateful. Having you here has been good for the cap'n, and that's no lie."

Purlie took a pouch out of his pocket, filled the pipe with tobacco, lit it, and drew on it till it was going. "Way the sun's setting, looks like we might have a tech of storm again tonight. Hope we don't have too much rain after planting all the seeds we did the last couple of days, Jeremy."

"Well, we've planted them deep enough, and if the rain isn't too hard, they'll make do. You have to start with good land, though, and I tell you, when the cap'n's sister died and left him that money last year, it was a Godsend to find this land up for sale and to get it so cheap. There's enough left, I figger, to take care of the cap'n's needs a good long while. That way, he won't have any worries. Just have to keep him from those bad spells when he remembers coming back from Appomattox, that's all," Jeremy gloomily declared. Then, straightening, he began to ply his hoe with an emphatic vigor that spoke more than words about his anxiety for his employer.

"Well, I'll go see how the missus is doin', Jeremy. Supper'll be on purty soon, I reckon. Mebbe you'd best come along and take something back for the cap'n and see he's comfortable. I feel like playing me a little rummy tonight—you in the mood for that, Jeremy?"

"Sure. I got to get back that fifty cents you won off me last time, Purlie. I feel lucky tonight, so you'd better have your loose change ready for me."

"It'll be ready. All you have to do is win it, Jeremy. Come along now. I think the missus has got some nice tasty pork meat cookin', and there's corn pone and yams, and she's got some brown betty left from last night I reckon the cap'n'd fancy."

"That was a mighty fine supper, Jeremy. Thank you." William Darden pushed away the empty bowl of brown betty and sat back in his chair. Jeremy had tried to make this supper kind of a special occasion, though it was partly for himself that he was celebrating, in seeing his employer's unusually cheerful demeanor. And there was no doubt about it: Darden had eaten with great relish, and made several flowery compliments about Purlie's wife's cooking which would please her a good deal, Jeremy was certain.

"Our pleasure, Cap'n. Wait till I tell her how you went for that brown betty of hers—'course, I'm mighty partial to it myself, truth to tell." He chuckled reminiscently, reached for the dishes, and took them into Darden's little kitchen. They would be cleaned later. When he returned, he was affable, almost wheedling. "Wonder if you'd mind, Cap'n, if I'd stay for a spell over at my brother's and play some rummy? He's been boastin' how he beats me all the time, but tonight I'm going to show him what's what."

"Of course. You go right ahead, Jeremy. My gracious, you spend nearly all of your time when you're not working out there in the fields catering to me. I'm not an invalid, you know." There was a flash of spirit in Darden's usually lusterless blue eyes. His shoulders had noticeably stiffened and he held himself proudly. "You know, I've been thinking. I've made you work just about like a slave, Jeremy. And you've certainly got a right to simple pleasures. No, you go right ahead. I can take care of myself." Then he yawned, putting his hand to his mouth. "You see, this wonderful supper you brought me has made me sleepy. I'm going to sleep well tonight, for sure. Why, I shouldn't be surprised if I didn't open my eyes till nigh unto noon tomorrow."

"You're sure you don't need me, Cap'n?" He stood look-

104

ing at his employer intently, half-reassured, not yet quite certain that he was not being overly selfish in wanting to play cards with his brother.

"Jeremy, you go, and that's an order! You're not to bother about me tonight. I'll be just fine. And be sure you convey my appreciation to Purlie's wife. I can't think when I've had a better supper, and that's the gospel truth."

"Thank you, Cap'n. Good night to you, then."

"And to you, Jeremy."

Darden rose from the chair, made his way slowly toward his hard bed, and stretched out on it, wearing only a torn shirt and old, faded trousers. Jeremy watched him, then nodded as if satisfied and left the house.

Darden lay there for about ten minutes, his hands clasped behind his head, his eyes closed, a faint smile on his lips. There was the ticking of an old grandfather's clock, rhythmic, inexorable. He seemed to listen to it, turning his face in its direction. Then, about a quarter of an hour later, he sat up with a start, rose, and went to the window which faced the cottage at the other end of the fields. He could see the faint light in the window; the fields between the two houses were empty and touched by moonlight. Dusk had already settled, and there was a stillness and a peacefulness on the countryside. In the distance was the gentle sound of the river.

The tall, gray-haired man let himself out by the back door and hurried purposefully toward the pine tree. As he squatted down to retrieve the trowel, he repeatedly glanced over toward Purlie's cottage. Then he began to dig till he had unearthed the crate and taken out the Whitworth, which he loaded. This time he took with him the pouch containing gunpowder and balls, stuffing five balls into the pouch to be sure to have sufficient ammunition. He replaced the rest in the crate and covered it over with earth.

Then, thrusting the pouch into the pocket of his faded trousers and gripping the stock of the rifle with his maimed right hand, he hurried to the stable and saddled the piebald mare. Barefooted, his shoulders straight, he turned her toward the road upriver. His eyes glowed with an alacrity and eagerness he had rarely displayed since that dreadful day of homecoming.

The tall young Comanche lawyer ruefully patted his stomach and sighed with contentment. "It's good that I do not have such wonderful food to eat each night, or I should look like one of the old grandfathers of the tribe around the campfire who gorges himself because he knows he will not have to go on the hunt the next day. Mrs. Haskins, it was delicious, and it has been a pleasure for me to enjoy your company and that of Mr. Haskins this evening."

Jessica Haskins dimpled and blushingly responded, "You're quite welcome, and thank you, Mr. Bouchard. And I'll tell you something, there isn't a woman alive who wouldn't be flattered when a nice man like you appreciates her cooking."

"There, you see, Lopasuta," Luke chuckled, "that's something to be remembered when you go courting a young lady. Always praise her cooking, it's the surest way to her heart."

"Go along with you, Mr. Bouchard," Jessica laughingly responded. Andy beamed with prideful pleasure. It had been a warm, companionable evening. For once, the three men had eschewed politics as a topic of conversation, and dwelt rather on the simple pleasures of home life, on the weather and its likely effect on the crops, and on what was happening in town that might be of interest to a young, gracious wife who rarely visited there.

"I think, Lopasuta, we'd best be riding back to the chateau. It's getting late, and we don't want to keep Mrs. Haskins up when she has a baby to attend to."

"Why no, Mr. Bouchard," Jessica protested, "Horatio's just fine. He's sleeping sound as you please, and it's really not late, only about nine-thirty."

"Just the same," Luke firmly avowed, "Lopasuta hasn't been over to my house for quite some time, and besides, I'd like to have a talk with him about some legal matters. Then, he'll sleep the night, and we'll go into Montgomery in the morning. Of course, I'm reluctant to tear myself away from such lovely company and from my good friend, Andy, but we don't want to wear out our welcome." He smiled and made her a courtly little bow to evidence his sincerity. "But I'm hoping, and I know Lopasuta is too, that you'll invite us to supper again, Mrs. Haskins."

"You don't need an invitation, not ever, Mr. Bouchard, and you know it," Jessica teased him. "Well, I'll say good-night then, so I can look in on Horatio."

As she disappeared into the bedroom, Andy accompanied Luke and Lopasuta to the door and opened it ahead of

106

them. "It was good to have you both here," he earnestly told them. "Land of Goshen, an evening like this makes me forget how riled up I can get in the House. It's good for a man's soul every now and again to relax—what's that expression you used, Luke?"

"To relax in the bosom of one's family, Andy. Yes, I know just what you mean. I've that same feeling when I'm with Laure and the children," Luke nodded.

"Well, our horses have been very patient," Luke observed as he moved forward ahead of Lopasuta and Andy toward his gelding.

Suddenly, the crisp report of a rifle sounded, and Luke staggered with a cry, clapping a hand to his left shoulder. Andy Haskins swore aloud, whirled and saw a shadowy form about a hundred yards to the south, and gave chase. Lopasuta followed, easily outrunning Andy, seized the assailant around the waist and flung him to the ground.

"That's good, Lopasuta, hold him like that! I'll just get that rifle—it's a Whitworth. Luke, you're hurt!" Andy called as he turned back to look anxiously at his tall, gray-haired friend.

"It's not bad, Andy. Who is it?" Luke Bouchard's face was strained as, keeping one hand pressed against the bleeding wound, he came toward the two men. Andy had lifted the Whitworth, inspected it to make certain that it had not been reloaded, and bent over the man who lay on the ground, Lopasuta still leaning beside him and pinning his arms to his sides with both his strong, wiry hands.

"Who are you? Why did you try to shoot Mr. Bouchard, answer me that?" Andy angrily demanded.

"Let me go—I had to. And you too—you're Andy Haskins, aren't you?" the man gasped as he struggled to free himself of the young Comanche's grip.

"Yes, I am. But I don't know you."

"My name is Darden. I was a captain in the First Georgia. I've land downriver from you, Haskins."

"That's right, I've heard about a little farm down there, but I've never been there. But that doesn't explain why you took a shot at Mr. Luke. Now I want an answer, and I want it fast!" Andy indignantly ordered.

"Let him get up, Lopasuta," Luke said as he gritted his teeth against the throbbing pain of the wound. His sudden movement forward toward his horse and then a momentary halting of his step had prevented the shot from striking his heart: the ball had instead nicked the upper part of his shoulder. The wound was bleeding profusely, but it was not serious.

Lopasuta helped Darden to his feet but stood beside him, gripping the former officer's left hand in his right and eyeing him warily to make certain that there would be no further attack upon Luke or Andy.

"Yes, I meant to kill you," Darden suddenly said, his face twisting and darkening as a sudden black, unreasoning mood took hold of him. "You and that Haskins, you're traitors to our South, the South we fought and died for. You've let niggers come to live with you, work for you, treating them like equals—the black, filthy scum that murdered my poor daughter, that drove my wife insane."

"My God, what are you saying?" Luke gasped. "Why is my treatment of my fellow black workers an accusation against me? What is this about your—"

"They told me," Darden broke in. "My wife, my daughter, if you'd seen them, you'd know why I want to kill you both." Darden's voice was hollow and shaking, and he tried to jerk his wrist loose from Lopasuta's grip.

"Luke, I'm going to bind that shoulder up for you. You'll bleed to death if you keep standing there. Lopasuta, you keep a good grip on that lunatic," Andy fiercely exclaimed. He flung the rifle out toward the river bank, then hurried to Luke Bouchard, tearing a strip off his shirt as he did so. He quickly bound the bleeding wound with the improvised bandage, knotted it, and then went back to confront William Darden. "Who told you that Mr. Luke and I treated niggers as free and equal? Tell me!" he hotly urged.

"They came to see me. Mr. Jenkinson told me all about you two," Darden responded. Then suddenly he began to cry like a child, bowing his head and sinking down on his knees as Lopasuta, astounded, released his grip. "My little girl, my wife—all gone, the house burned to the ground, that man telling me that if I'd come to see the Darden place, it wasn't any use. And he said that niggers, niggers wearing blue, forced my poor girl and then—oh God, oh God, and you're the ones that treat animals like that the way you would folks of your own color—traitors—traitors to the South—both of you—I wanted to kill you—I wish I had—oh God, won't there ever be any peace for William Darden?"

He sank forward on the ground, his hands covering his tear-stained face, his shoulders convulsively jerking.

"Who's that coming? I hear a horse galloping hard." Andy turned.

Jeremy rode up into the clearing before the little frame house, sweating, his face contorted with anguish. He dismounted quickly, and ran to his employer. "There now, there now, Cap'n, it'll be all right. Don't take on like that, Cap'n." Slowly, he looked up at Luke and Andy and Lopasuta, who were compassionately regarding him.

"He can't help it, he just can't. I did the best I could, I always tried, God knows."

"I think I understand," Luke hoarsely murmured. "He came back from the war to find he'd lost everything."

"That's right. The house burned, and then an old man coming out and almost like it wuz a joke telling him that his wife tried to stop those goddamn Yankees who were forcing his daughter—and they were niggers who helped do it—I took him away to his sister in Montgomery, you see. I got him a dog—it ran away some weeks ago, God knows where—and then, when his sister died and left him a little money, I bought this place downriver from you, Mr. Haskins, so there'd be something for him to turn his mind away from all he'd lost," Jeremy's voice broke and he could not hide his tears.

"Just before you rode in, he was telling us that a fellow by the name of Homer Jenkinson told him about Luke and me treating niggers the way we would white folks."

"I don't rightly know what he told the cap'n, Mr. Haskins, but I know he and another fellow did come calling. I asked the cap'n if it'd be all right, and he said he'd talk to them."

"It's very plain now," Luke reflectively declared. "Somehow Jenkinson must have found out about this poor man's tragedy and preyed on his hatred for blacks."

"Yes," Lopasuta spoke up, "and probably hoped that the unfortunate man would take the law into his own hands and look upon both Andy and my adopted father as those in some way responsible for his own misfortunes. It was a cruel, terrible thing to do, a criminal thing to do."

"But there's really no proof," Luke mused aloud. "Poor Mr. Darden's mind is gone, and you, as a lawyer, know that in a court of law his testimony wouldn't be taken seriously.

109

We can guess, all of us, that Jenkinson and his friends used Mr. Darden as the unreasoning instrument of his contemptible plot to threaten you, Andy, into sponsoring his bill. But, as I say, we can't prove it."

"What can we do with him?" Andy gestured toward Darden, who lay motionless on the ground, his face still covered with his hands, his sobs almost inaudible.

Jeremy knelt again, patting Darden's shoulder, speaking soothingly to him, "Come on, Cap'n. That ground's moist from the night air, you know it is. You'll catch your death. Come on, I'll take you home, Cap'n. Please, Cap'n. It's all over now. I thought I'd hidden that Whitworth real good—" He looked up at the three men watching, shook his head, and, fighting back his tears, averred, "Before God, I thought I hid that Whitworth. It wuz a salvaged gun, and the cap'n here wuz always a pretty good shot. Thank God he didn't kill anybody—I'd have had it on my conscience all the rest of my life. I can't say anything to you; if you want to send him to jail, you're within your rights. But he's broken by all this, he's never been right, not since that day when we got back to Georgia—"

"Don't worry, we won't press charges," Luke Bouchard softly interposed. "There's a house near Tuscaloosa that'll take good care of him. I have a friend there. I'll write a letter and see if we can't find a home for your captain. And you can be with him if you want. I know there are cases like that—"

"That's mighty kind of you, Mr. Bouchard. I'm beholden to you. He saved my life, you know, the cap'n did. He lost those two fingers on his good right hand trying to bandage me up, and I had to take care of him. I wuz his orderly in the company. It'd only be right if I went along with him to see that nobody treats him badly."

"Of course. You take him home now. I'll get this letter off tomorrow to my friend in Tuscaloosa, and I'll let you know when we can make arrangements. Don't worry. I bear him no malice," Luke declared.

Jeremy stared almost blindly at the tall, gray-haired man. "God will bless you, Mr. Bouchard. I'm awful sorry. I can't say more. Somehow, I just had a feeling things weren't right. He ate a good supper. He said he wuz sleepy. And now I remember he had us ride on down here to see your place, Mr. Haskins. Poor Cap'n, he wuz figgerin' something like this all the time, and I couldn't guess it. It wuz my fault—"

"You mustn't think that. No, it wasn't your fault. You're a good man. If you like, we'll help you take him home with you."

"No, I thank you kindly. I'll manage fine," Jeremy hoarsely said.

Lopasuta and Andy Haskins came forward, and gently lifted the still-sobbing ex-Confederate officer to his feet. Jeremy Blodgett put an arm around his shoulders, murmuring, "It's fine, Cap'n. I'm awful tired and so are you. We'd best go home and get some sleep, don't you think? Come along. I saw where you tethered your horse. We'll ride back together. Reminds me of that time we went scouting to see if we could tell how many troops those damn Yankees were putting up against us."

They watched Jeremy lead the broken, dazed William Darden away. A few minutes later, there was the soft sound of horses' hooves receding. And again the night was still.

CHAPTER ELEVEN

Luke did not ride back to the red-brick chateau after William Darden's shot had nicked his shoulder. Instead, he and Lopasuta rode into Montgomery and called on Abel Kennery, the new doctor. The wound, as Luke anticipated, was diagnosed as superficial. The energetic, earnest doctor praised Andy's hasty first-aid efforts and declared that the improvised bandage had prevented a rather serious loss of blood. But he advised Luke not to travel at all for at least forty-eight hours, so Luke sent a courier to the chateau to tell Laure that he and Lopasuta were staying the night in Montgomery and not to worry about him. He added that he had legal business to transact in town and would return within the next few days.

During the next two days and nights, while Luke recuperated in the little house where his adopted son resided, he and the ambitious young tribesman were drawn closer together than ever. They talked endlessly, sharing their profoundest feelings about tolerance, justice, and the superiority of selfless work over the wish to surpass one's neighbor in possessions, social prestige, and egotistical accomplishments.

More than ever, Luke Bouchard, in the twilight of his life, knew that he had made no mistake when, out of impulse and grateful remembrance of his grandfather's alliance with the Creeks, he had made it possible for a deserving young man with Indian blood in his veins to come to Alabama and to achieve stature among citizens who ordinarily looked askance at anyone of another race, creed, or color. It was not yet the millenium of which old Lucien Bouchard had so long dreamed; but it was a creditable beginning. And when Luke left Lopasuta's house, it was with a sense of understanding the full meaning of how the lives of even aliens and strangers can be entwined, if one opens one's mind and heart to those whose basic motivation is the same as one's own.

On the third night, when he returned to the red-brick chateau, it was to receive a passionately eager welcome from his golden-haired wife, Laure. He recounted all the circumstances surrounding his shoulder wound, asking her forgiveness for having kept the truth from her until he could return home to explain in person. She forgave him readily, exclaiming tearfully how grateful she was that he was not more seriously hurt.

After dinner, Luke excused himself to retire to his study and write some letters. Later, to his delight—a delight that seemed to strip away the years and send him back once more into the halcyon days of his youth—Laure came silently into his study without knocking. She reached over his shoulder to take the pen out of his hand and lay it down, and then she bent to him, cupped his face in her hands, and kissed him lingeringly on the mouth, whispering, "I need you, I want you, my love. Come to me now."

He let her take him by the hand, his eyes wide with ecstasy. He followed her to their bedroom, and there all pain from his wound was forgotten as he trembled to the touch of her fingers, the urgency of her kisses. Once again they were reunited in a loving hunger which was total assuagement. Gently, eagerly, in the soft darkness of the night, they communed, learning each other anew, pledging each to the other a sacrament of devotion and desire that knew no difference in years and that welded them in harmonious fidelity.

Ten days after Darden's deranged attempt on Luke's life, Luke and Andy Haskins rode over to the little farm and conferred with Jeremy Blodgett. Luke had written a letter to his friend in Tuscaloosa, who had replied that arrangements could be made at once for the confinement of the ex-Confederate captain to an excellent private sanitarium. In his original letter, Luke had intimated that he would contribute a given amount per year so that the unfortunate Georgian would be given additional creature comforts and treated with the utmost concern. Luke had clearly pointed out that, in the treatment of this man, it would be well to avoid any references to blacks, since this

114

was an incendiary stimulus that had tragically changed Darden's morbid depression into an overpowering, unreasoning, homicidal fury.

A few days later, Jeremy Blodgett and his brother Purlie, flanking the gray-haired officer, rode down to Tuscaloosa and saw to it that their employer was cordially received and given a pleasant room where he might find at last some peace of mind, free of the goading and ruthless abuse of men like Homer Jenkinson and his evil colleagues.

Young Lopasuta Bouchard had handled the legal details in having Darden committed to the Tuscaloosa institution. At Luke's request, Lopasuta drew up a contract between Andy and Burt Coleman, naming Burt as foreman of the four hundred acres that had once belonged to Edward Williamson. The contract stipulated a salary of four hundred dollars per annum and authorized Burt to hire black and white workers who would assist him in the development of this acreage. The genial Southerner was overjoyed at this unexpected promotion. His only request was that he be allowed to take with him, as assistant foreman, his new friend Don Elwald, a thirty-six-year-old Mississippian widower who, like so many other Confederate soldiers, had come back to his native town to find his house and family gone. Both Andy and Luke were satisfied with this condition, and Burt and his friend at once took up their new duties.

Luke was also satisfied with the progress of Windhaven Plantation itself, which, in spite of both the nation's and the state's growing economic apprehensiveness, was showing heartening signs of prosperity that augured well for the future of Luke's farsighted and surely unorthodox commune. One example of this was the transformation of Buford Phelps. He had come arrogantly to Windhaven Plantation as an emissary of the Freedmen's Bureau, and then had been convinced of the value of Luke's communal farm, as an enterprise where both white and black men would work as brothers. He had quit his job with the Bureau to stay and work at Windhaven.

Buford was still working on Luke's land when Hugh Entrevois had suddenly appeared and been introduced as Dalbert Sattersfield's helper in the store in Lowndesboro. Entrevois had turned out to be the illegitimate son of Mark Bouchard and Louisette Entrevois's half sister Rosa; he had black blood in his veins. Luke had given him the post of foreman of the four hundred acres of Williamson land; Buford Phelps took Entrevois's place as clerk in the Sattersfield store.

In helping Hugh Entrevois, Luke had been motivated by the gnawing fear that he had acted selfishly against Mark, all those years ago, and deprived him of his rightful legacy—even though he had generously given Mark a third of the gold old Lucien had put away in a reliable Scottish bank. To make up for any wrong he might have done Mark, Luke had magnanimously placed his trust in Mark's son, but the latter had turned out to be the leader of the ruthless Ku Klux Klan, seeking to avenge on the name of Bouchard the taint of his rejection.

But that was over and done with, and Luke had buried his ghosts last December, when, as was his wont on the birthday of his beloved grandfather, he had climbed to the towering bluff that overlooked the Alabama River, confessed his impractical idealism, and sworn that henceforth he would more vigilantly defend Windhaven Plantation, Windhaven Range, and all those other outposts where members of the Bouchard clan now dwelt.

As a result of her visits to Mitzi Sattersfield, Laure talked a great deal not only of the latter's adorable little baby, David, but also of Dalbert's effusive praise of the work of Buford Phelps. The latter had made many suggestions for bringing new patrons into the general store, even for merchandising staples in a way that would increase a householder's expenditures for necessary goods. He had, indeed, acquitted himself so well and shown such eagerness to serve that even those hidebound white citizens of Lowndesboro grudgingly admitted that "This nigger treats you the way people ought to be treated and gives you an honest bargain every time you come in to buy things you need."

One of Dalbert's best customers was a fifty-year-old widow who, with her thirty-year-old son, was managing a farm of some two hundred acres downriver from Lowndesboro. The widow's housekeeper was a young mulatto girl named Dulcie Martin. She had been the widow's personal maid before the war. Now twenty-five, Dulcie had taken over the housekeeping post with a bona fide contract and specified wages—a stipulation prescribed by the victorious Northern army of occupation. However, there was not the least animosity between employer and employee, since Mrs.

116

Abigail Martin had always been extremely fond of the alert girl and even encouraged her to learn how to read and write.

Dulcie Martin had been entrusted with the task of purchasing foodstuffs for the farm and, quite naturally, she was a frequent caller at Dalbert's store. Buford Phelps had frequently waited upon the young mulatto woman; they had become friends, and now, as Laure smilingly informed her husband, it appeared that Buford Phelps and Dulcie were going to be married. The happy couple would move into a little cottage down the street from the store. And this was still another proof to Luke Bouchard of the wholesome influence Windhaven Plantation exerted upon all who worked its fertile land.

Shortly after the end of the first week in April, Luke summoned Burt Coleman to confer with him and Marius Thornton in drawing up plans for the guided overseership of the Williamson acreage. At the time that Hugh Entrevois had taken over as foreman, there had been fifteen black and eleven white workers, experienced carpenters, blacksmiths, stablemen, and field hands. Last summer, fifty acres had been set aside for growing yams, beans, okra, and cabbage, as well as melons and some field corn. Another twenty acres, the most fertile of the entire plot, had been planted with cotton. Several of the workers had constructed pens for hogs and cattle, and Luke had lent the Creole two thousand dollars to buy five sows and a boar, eight heifers and a bull, and a dozen horses.

That investment had more than doubled itself, despite the treachery of Hugh Entrevois. Even at the low price of eleven cents a pound, the baled cotton had brought in nearly two thousand dollars, and the sale of produce to stores in Montgomery and Lowndesboro had yielded an amount almost equal to that figure. Thus, Luke Bouchard's investment had not been wasted, and in this year of 1873, with pleasant weather ahead for the rest of the summer, the forecast Burt Coleman had already given old Lucien's dedicated grandson was indeed optimistic.

Last year, when Jedidiah Danforth had arranged for the transfer of title of those four hundred acres to Andy Haskins, he had indicated to Luke that ownership of the land could eventually pass to Luke himself if he so desired it, thus nearly doubling the acreage old Lucien Bouchard had been given by the Creeks. But it was not possession *per se*

117

that pleased Luke: it was the knowledge that at last his ruthless father's plans to exploit that land and to gouge its owners into debt would be totally negated. As in the case of Windhaven Plantation itself, a commune could be established on the four hundred acres wherein both white and black freed workers under contract would prosper. Thus, Luke felt that he had fulfilled his pledge to his dead grandfather and that even the malevolent intervention of Hugh Entrevois had not hampered him in the long view from keeping that pledge. Meanwhile, to be sure, he had no selfish interest in acquiring the land for the land's sake: so long as it was worked by an honest, loyal man like Andy Haskins and was now under the supervision of the equally dedicated Burt Coleman, its yield would be a valuable safeguard against the economic depression he pessimistically foresaw. Moreover, he had already determined to allow Andy to keep permanent title to the acreage. Perhaps one day his children and Andy's would be partners in a joint enterprise which at last would formally join the two men's property.

By occupying his mind with the simple, eternal task of caring for the land, Luke managed to cast aside his troubling thoughts about not only the nation's growing indebtedness, but also the devious machinations of men like Homer Jenkinson who had been ruthless enough to employ poor William Darden as the tool of their vindictive reprisal. To be sure, the attacks made on his life and Andy Haskins's had served to sharpen his wits and keep him vigilant. But the weeks after William Darden's attack came and went without incident, and it was Luke's fervent hope that these men of ill-will had learned their lesson from their failures and would at last realize that their fraudulent scheme had no hope of success.

Ten days had passed since the April 14 decision by the Supreme Court in the Slaughter-House cases, that the Fourteenth Amendment did not give the federal government complete jurisdiction over the entire domain of civil rights. This unexpected interpretation of the controversial amendment, in effect, returned some power to the states, and it gave many Southerners hope that at last justice would be tempered with mercy so far as the vindictive North was concerned. At first Luke joined with his neighbors in experiencing a surge of optimism at the news of the high-court decision. If this interpretation of the amendment meant that Southerners could at last rely on the dictates of their own sovereign state judicial courts, then perhaps the punitive tactics of men like Thaddeus Stevens were at last coming to an end, and the South might spring like the phoenix from the ashes of defeat. But in time Luke, who by now had added pragmatism to his innate idealism, understood that such optimism was premature. The South was far from free of her troubles, and any rebirth Luke had perceived was occurring only on his own property. And he was realistic enough to see that, if only the Bouchards and their workers here and on Windhaven Range triumphed against crisis, while the rest of the South and the nation was beset by the disasters he secretly feared, then it was truly no renascence at all.

All the same, there was no denying the satisfaction of seeing crops planted, black and white men working side by side in a cheerful and purposeful fraternity, enjoying the simplest things of life with a particular relish just because they were substantially pleasing. Just as his grandfather had done before him in the fields of Yves-sur-lac, Luke, during this month of April, often spent an hour every morning or afternoon wielding a hoe alongside Dan Munroe or Hughie Mendicott; often he leaned on the hoe, damp with sweat, while Hannah hurried out with a pitcher of cool lemonade. To drink that refreshing liquid after honest labor was in itself a pleasure. Such simple, good things served to banish, if only for a time, the thought of that ugly conspiracy Homer Jenkinson and his conniving associates had devised and into which they had drawn the unfortunate Darden.

When Luke had told Laure about Darden, she had shown deep compassion for the poor ex-captain, and this attitude, in its turn, had drawn them closer together than ever. Indeed, if Luke Bouchard could have selfishly isolated himself from the rest of the world, he would have been content with the serene and joyous love and companionship he could enjoy in this twilight of his life. And when, one afternoon in late April, he received a letter via the *Alabama Belle* (now manned by a heavily moustachioed middle-aged man who had replaced venerable old Horace Tenby, now deceased) from Lucien Edmond in Carrizo Springs describing with great enthusiasm how he, Ramón Hernandez, and Joe Duvray were busy interbreed-

119

ing their cattle and making plans for the coming year, he was gratified to know that at least all was right with the world of the Bouchards.

Once again, the House of Representatives had voted for a brief adjournment this last Thursday in April, and Andy Haskins, after convivially chatting with his colleagues and wishing them a pleasant weekend, had gone to the stable on DeLancey Street, ordered his bay to be saddled, and prepared to ride back to Jessica and little Horatio. It was a pleasant, cool day, and Andy always enjoyed the long, leisurely ride along the river trail. The bay was intelligent and spirited, and it seemed to sense his every mood.

This afternoon he was in high spirits. The Speaker of the House, nearly seventy-two and a man of staunch dignity and unshakable moral fiber, had gone out of his way to compliment him on his speeches and his candid denunciation of corruption. "You have a gift for words, Mr. Haskins," old Elmore Hancock had solemnly said, "but then, anyone can have that. What counts is that they come out of your heart, and you're sincere. I'm an old man, Mr. Haskins, and I cast my vote for Henry Clay, I did, sir, and I've watched Alabama turn from cotton to just about ragpicking since we lost that war which oughtn't to have happened. But I still think we're going to make it, in spite of the North and in spite of the skulking rats who sneak down here to line their nests. And as long as there are men like you to point them out and try to exterminate them, then I say, there's hope, Mr. Haskins."

Andy felt good about that, though he modestly discounted what he had done. Anyone could make a few speeches, and it had been Luke who had really put his finger on the heart of the matter. Come to think of it, it wasn't such a bad thing, taking a cue from a man like Mr. Luke Bouchard. You couldn't go wrong if you backed the horses he was backing—that's what they used to say about a man in Tennessee who stood for fair play and the right of things. Yes, he had a feeling that Luke would be respected in just about any state of this union, yes, even Pennsylvania, where that hateful old reprobate Thaddeus Stevens had come from.

As he rode at a leisurely trot, he saw a young couple walking down by the river, sparking. The boy had taken the girl by the shoulders and he was kissing her. He turned to look at Andy and grinned and waved a hand, and Andy waved back with an answering grin. It was good to see that. The war hadn't stopped everything, not the good, loving feeling decent people had when they meant something to each other. The way he and Jessica did now, with little Horatio to make them all the happier for their loving. What a wonderful girl Jessica was! There was such a well of gratitude and happiness rising up in him that he shook his head and reprimanded himself for being so sentimental. Yet, at the same time, he thought he ought to make more fuss over Jessica, like bringing her a bouquet of flowers, just for no reason at all except that he was mighty happy with her.

He broke his journey to stop at the old Williamson farm and confer with Burt Coleman. The two men walked out over the fields. Andy liked what he saw. Burt's new friend had given him an incentive and also a solace. Still in his joyous mood, Andy hoped that one day this hard-working Southerner would find a girl just as he had done, one who would channel his life into loving accomplishment. And once again, he had to reprimand himself inwardly for the mawkishly sentimental thoughts he was thinking all this pleasant afternoon.

It was twilight when he rode at last up to the little white frame house, unsaddled the bay, and went in to find Jessica preparing supper, with Horatio fast asleep nearby in his bassinet. He took her by the hips, lifted her up, and whirled her around, to her laughing protest: "I declare, Andy Haskins, is that what you learned in the House of Representatives?"

"No, ma'am, not likely." He set her down on her feet and kissed her heartily. Her arms went round him and she kissed him back with considerable interest, and he laughed aloud from the sheer jubilation of feeling alive and feeling loved. "No, ma'am, I guess I had that cooped up in me all this time till I met you, Jessica honey."

"Well, I don't believe it at all, but it certainly sounds very nice. And I'll accept it just this once," she teasingly murmured, as she kissed him again. Then, very primly, "And now, if you expect any supper tonight, you'd best take yourself and freshen yourself up and just wait till I call you."

"Your devoted servant, ma'am." He executed a mock bow and Jessica giggled. Blowing her a kiss, he walked off

121

to the living room, flung himself into an easy chair, and closed his eyes. He was smiling. At this moment, nothing could have reminded him of the ingratiating visit Homer Jenkinson and that fat judge from Tuscaloosa had paid him. After an enjoyable supper topped off with apple turnovers, which Jessica had baked to a piping-hot sweetness, he would assuredly have agreed with Voltaire's Dr. Pangloss, who had blithely assured Candide that this was the very best of all possible worlds.

Indeed, he was so contented with life that he insisted on helping Jessica with the dishes. She gave him the role of wiper. He held a towel in his left hand while she passed each dish to him, holding it while he assiduously dried it. Her eyes were warm with affection, knowing how much it meant to him to show that his handicap in no way hampered him. Privately, she told herself that even if he had no arms at all, he would still be the dearest man any girl could want. And when they were finished, he drew her to him and kissed her very lingeringly and whispered, "Honey, it chokes me up inside just thinking what you mean to me. I'm so darned lucky I have to pinch myself every now and again to make sure I'm not dreaming."

Her head against his chest, she was about to confide her own ardent happiness when there was a peremptory knock at the door. Andy straightened, scowling. "What the devil? I sure wasn't looking for any visitors this weekend, I can tell you, Jessica!"

"Now don't you swear, Andy Haskins. You just go see who it is and I'll look in on Horatio. Besides, the sooner you get rid of whoever it is, the sooner you can get back to kissing me properly—that is, of course, if you still want to."

Andy groaned aloud and gave her a reproachful look as he strode to the door. When he opened it, he was confronted by a thin little man in a black frock coat, who had obviously ridden hard. The man promptly inquired, "Be you Mr. Andy Haskins?" and having received a nod of affirmation, handed Andy an envelope sealed with sealing wax and hurried back out to his horse.

Wonderingly, Andy closed the door and opened the letter. Jessica hurried to him, her eyes wide with concern. "What's the matter, Andy?"

"Shucks, it's from one of my constituents, I guess you'd say. Seems as how he wants me to meet him in Montgomery tomorrow, shortly after noon, about something very important. He says here he's contributed a lot to the campaign that got me elected."

"What's his name, dear? Do I know him?"

"I don't know him myself, Jessica honey. It's Edward Tholfson. He says here he's a Republican Unionist and he likes the cut of my jib, that's why he voted for me and spent some money getting folks to cast their ballots my way last November."

Jessica's face fell. "Are you going to meet him? I was so looking forward to having you home here this nice long weekend, Andy dear."

Andy scratched his head, his frown deepening. "You know I'd like nothing better, honey. But this might be important. And if I'm beholden to him, I want to see just how far he thinks I am. You know, come to think of it, those fellows who came calling some weeks back wanting me to sponsor a bill that would make money for them and skin the voters might be connected with this Tholfson fellow. And that's another reason I'd better go check him out, just in case there's a little conspiracy here to get me to see things their way."

"But if that's true, Andy," Jessica doubtfully put in, "mightn't it be dangerous to go there and meet this man you've never seen before? They might be up to something."

"That's it exactly. The more I think about it, the funnier it is that this fellow never came forward during the campaign or afterwards to let me know who he was, but all of a sudden he wants to see me about something important. And that's after they took that shot at Mr. Luke and me— leastways, we're pretty sure they as much as pulled the trigger even if that poor fellow Darden was the one who had held the rifle." His face hardened with resolution. "You see, Jessica, I've got to go. If there's anything fishy about this, I'll be able to tell Mr. Luke and Lopasuta, and then we can really get them and expose them for the crooks they are. And that'll end their troublemaking for sure. All the same, I hate to be away from you. I was counting on the weekend, too."

She came to him, her eyes tender, her voice soft. "You'll do what you have to do, Andy dear. You're a fine, honest man, and I'd just as soon everybody in this state knows about it the way I do. We'll have lots of time together just by ourselves, and I'll keep telling myself that so I won't

123

miss you so much. But take care of yourself now, my darling."

He put his left arm around her shoulders, drawing her to him, and gave himself up to the sweet, trusting gentleness of her kiss.

Then, with a boyish chuckle, he murmured, "Well anyhow, honey, tonight's Thursday, and it won't take long to ride into Montgomery to meet him tomorrow noon the way he wants. We'll still have time to spend together this weekend, and I mean to make the most of it. Now you come here and finish what you started."

Blushing, Jessica embraced him, and then, hand in hand, they walked toward their conjugal chamber.

CHAPTER TWELVE

Edward Tholfson's note had requested that Andy meet him about one o'clock Friday afternoon, in Tholfson's suite at the Excelsior, Montgomery's finest hotel. On that day, Andy rode into town about twelve-thirty and stabled his horse, ordering the proprietor to see that his bay got an extra ration of oats. Then, self-consciously brushing off his frock coat with his left palm and glancing unhappily at his newly shined shoes, which were much too tight, he headed for the Excelsior.

When he inquired at the desk for Edward Tholfson's suite, the plump little clerk gave him directions, commenting on Mr. Tholfson's generosity as a patron of the hotel. He had, it seemed, given the clerk a sizable tip to be on the lookout for Andy and to have him ushered up to the suite just as soon as he arrived. To earn that tip, the clerk insisted—much to Andy's embarrassment—on leaving his counter and escorting the one-armed Tennesseean up the steps to the top floor, then leading him to the very back of the hallway at the right and discreetly knocking three times. "Come right in, Mr. Haskins!" a hearty baritone voice bawled out. "You're right on time, sir!"

"There you are, Mr. Haskins," the clerk ostentatiously declared. "By the way, Mr. Haskins, I was told to tell you that Mr. Tholfson will have a small collation in your honor served in about half an hour. I trust it will be satisfactory."

"Thanks." Andy gave the fluttering little clerk a nervous smile and half-nod, then turned the knob of the door and opened it. The room he entered was part of a large and well-appointed suite, brightly lighted by windows on the north side. A stout, black-haired man with sideburns and goatee stood in the middle of the room, facing Andy, a beaming smile on his heavily-jowled face, his hand already extended. "Good of you to come, Mr. Haskins. I'm Edward Tholfson," he introduced himself.

"Glad to meet you, Mr. Tholfson. I have to admit your name isn't familiar to me—" Andy tentatively began.

"You mustn't fret about that at all, Mr. Haskins," Tholfson genially reassured him. "Make yourself comfortable on that sofa, sir. Yes siree, it's a real pleasure to meet a man young in politics but already with a decided future. I picked you as a winner right off, first I knew about your campaign. That, Mr. Haskins, is why I went out of my way to contribute so that enough voters would get the message and send you to our fine House of Representatives."

Unused to so much high-sounding, loudly voiced praise, Andy uneasily fingered his tight collar, made his way over to the sofa, and sat down. In a somewhat warily attentive attitude, he waited for his host to discuss the matter at hand. However, Tholfson was not inclined to do this at once.

"I was in the gallery when you made your first speech in the House, Mr. Haskins. I must say, sir, you fulfilled all my expectations and more."

"It's good of you to say that. I just tried to come out with what I felt, that's all anybody can do," Andy modestly parried the florid accolade.

"You see—" Tholfson was obviously in a reflective mood and also enjoyed the sound of his own resonant voice— "you've no idea how hard it is these days, Mr. Haskins, to find a loyal Southerner who upholds the best, the most honorable traditions of the true old South. When you had finished that speech, sir, I knew that my judgment had been correct in backing you. Why, I may say, Mr. Haskins, I shouldn't be surprised if one day you run for governor and are elected."

Again, Andy plucked at his oppressively tight collar. He was perspiring now, not only from the horseback ride into Montgomery, but also from this tête-à-tête. "Well," he guardedly replied, "I guess you might say I am a true Southerner, because I was born in Tennessee."

"Exactly!" Tholfson boomed with a grin which revealed unpleasantly yellowed teeth. He took out a monogrammed lace handkerchief, daintily mopped his forehead and cheeks and then patted his plump mouth. "And now that the North seems at last to be easing up on us long-

126

suffering Southerners, Mr. Haskins, I may say I think there's every hope that one day all of us will call you Governor Haskins and be proud to do so."

By this time, all Andy could think of was that he had wasted what had promised to be an idyllic weekend with Jessica to come here and listen to needless and embarrassing rhetoric. So he put in, "Excuse me, Mr. Tholfson, but I'd really like to get to the point with you. I don't know why you wanted to see me; it's awfully nice of you to say all these fine things about what I've done—but I really haven't done much at all yet."

"There, you see, Mr. Haskins," Tholfson beamed, "you're only confirming, sir, your essential modesty, which is what makes you such a potentially great legislator. I do hope, sir, that you'll join in the collation I've had prepared in your honor. At that time, I sincerely promise you, Mr. Haskins, to use your own words, that I'll come directly to the point."

"All right, then, I guess I could eat something," Andy confessed with a noncommittal shrug. He was thinking of Jessica's biscuits and honey, her batter-fried chicken and her mouthwatering pies. He watched Tholfson rise, go to the door and open it, draw out of his pocket a little silver handbell, and ring it loudly. A few moments later, a black porter, nearly bald, with a semicircle of white hair around the edge of his skull, shuffled toward the occupant of the suite and received the order to bring the lunch, which had been ordered from a restaurant adjacent to the hotel. "Yassuh, right away, Mr. Tholfson, suh." He bobbed his head and went back down the hallway.

"It will be here shortly, Mr. Haskins. I took pains to order what I thought you might enjoy. The finest corn-fed beefsteak money can buy, and sweet yams—you Southerners dote on sweet yams, I'm told."

"You Southerners?" Andy picked this up at once. "You mean you're not one yourself, Mr. Tholfson?"

"Excuse me, that was only a figure of speech," Edward Tholfson hastily amended. "I'll have you know, sir, I've been living in a suburb of Montgomery since 1866. And, I confess it without shame, I was a Democrat until I saw the light. After the elections of 1868 and 1870, I realized that the only hope for our Alabama was on the Republican side, to which I now loyally contribute. And, sir, I always stood for the Union, indivisible and inseparable. Originally, to be sure, I was born in Cleveland, but I had friends here, and, you understand, there was a pretty girl—well, you know how those things are."

Andy shrugged, not wanting to make any comments. He was becoming more and more annoyed at Tholfson's empty speechmaking.

There was a knock at the door, and Tholfson rose and strode to it, exclaiming, "Here's our lunch, Mr. Haskins. We can be more at our ease. Don't you agree, it's always easier to discuss serious matters during the conviviality of breaking bread together?"

"I—I guess so," Andy mumbled, again easing his tight collar. His host admitted the black porter who wheeled in a tray and, with a flourish meant to be both impressive and deferential, whisked off the silver tops of the chafing dishes. "Thank you, George." Tholfson took out a greenback and handed it to the man. "Don't forget the bottle of Kentucky bourbon."

"Nossuh, ah'll bring it in directly, suh."

Closing the door, Edward Tholfson seated himself beside Andy, for there was a small table in front of the sofa, and the porter had pushed the tray up beside it. "Allow me to serve you, sir," he told Andy.

Reluctantly, Andy Haskins accepted a plate and began to eat. The beefsteak, as it turned out, was tender and extremely palatable, as Tholfson had promised, and Andy found himself eating it with gusto. The sweet yams and the rice, which the cook had prepared exactly the way Andy liked them, greatly added to his enjoyment. He was therefore in a more tolerant mood.

"I know, Mr. Haskins, you must be asking yourself why I wanted this meeting with you. First of all, to meet you socially and to have you to myself so that I could better appreciate the qualities of the man whose campaign I helped sponsor."

"That's kind of you to say."

"Nothing kind about it, sir, just truthful. Yes, I was a major contributor to the gallant cause you espoused and which won your election to your present high status in our fine state government. But I would ask only, Mr. Haskins, that you spend a little time studying the past history of this great state."

"I've tried to do my best in that regard, Mr. Tholfson."

Andy gave him a congenial smile, then attacked the rest of his beefsteak again.

"Just so, sir. If you do, you will see that the Civil War, brought upon us by these wicked, conniving Yankees, brought to ruin all our efforts at independence. Now today, when it seems that the North is at last beginning to forget its determination to crush the conquered South into the dust under its heel, there is a chance for us to catch up on the progress which has been thwarted during this time of so-called Reconstruction."

"Could you get to the point, if I may be bold enough to ask, Mr. Tholfson? I still don't see how I can be of service to you," Andy frowningly ventured.

Tholfson had managed to cut his beefsteak and down it while continuing his political harangue. He now patted his mouth with his napkin and went on, "Well, Andy, you see, what I'm heading up to is that, with the help of railroads, mining, and agriculture, there is a good chance that Alabama can rally and come out of the economic chaos which the Northerners visited upon us and which has so beset us for the past eight years."

Though his host had thus far said nothing of substance, he had also said nothing that contradicted Andy's own political views. Everyone knew that Reconstruction had been the main deterrent to Southern recovery after Appomattox, so Andy was in agreement with Tholfson on that count. Yet one nagging little fact kept bothering Andy: Tholfson had made that slip in which he had referred to "you Southerners," and then had revealed that he had originally come from Cleveland. That would make him a carpetbagger, despite the number of years he had lived in Alabama and been active in its politics.

Andy was about to say something even more pointed following this sudden reflection on his host's as yet unstated interest in him when there was another knock at the door.

"That's our whiskey, Mr. Haskins. The finest Kentucky bourbon that money can buy. I'd like you to join me in a toast to the future of Alabama and to your own inevitable rise to a post of great responsibility in our government here," Edward Tholfson expansively declared as he hurriedly rose and went to the door.

Again taking out his wallet, he tipped the black porter and took the bottle and two glasses from the latter's tray. Then, noticing that Andy had gone back to finishing his meal, he made an obscure gesture and the porter nodded. When the latter had closed the door, Tholfson returned and, setting the glasses down on the side of the table, proceeded to open the bottle. Slowly he poured out a full measure in each glass, till Andy held up a protesting hand. "Whoa there, I'm not much of a drinking man, Mr. Tholfson."

"I want you to have the full bouquet of this magnificent bourbon, Mr. Haskins. Pouring practically a full glass gives you that heavenly aroma—ambrosia of the gods itself, veritably, Mr. Haskins," his host rhetorically declaimed.

Outside, there was a sudden loud noise, and an angry voice was raised in indignation. "You goddamned nigger, why don't you look where you're going? You almost ran plumb into me, hitting me with that tray. Why I've half a mind to—" Then was heard the black porter's apologetic, fearful voice: "Didn't mean to, suh—mah 'pologies, suh. Don't hit me, suh, please. Kin ah do anythin' to make it up to you, suh?"

"No, you stupid nigger, just stay out of my way the next time, hear?" the loud, angry voice retorted; then there was the sound of heavy footsteps retreating down the hall.

Startled by this violent commotion, Andy had jumped up and gone to the door. He opened it and peered out, to reassure himself that no harm had come to the unfortunate porter and the disturbance was at an end. Meanwhile, Tholfson jerked a little phial out of the pocket of his vest, opened it, leaned over, and tilted its contents into the one-armed Tennesseean's glass, then swiftly pocketed the empty phial and leaned back with a smug little smile.

"I'll admit, sir, the help in this hotel isn't all it might be. But that's because you've got freed niggers now and you have to have contracts with them, and they know it and take advantage of you. Old George there is a good man, but he ought to be put out to pasture. A little slow on the uptake, if you follow my meaning, Mr. Haskins. But now to our toast. And let me add to it that I want to toast you and your lovely wife and family, and to wish you long years as a respected member of the House, which will pass good laws for the well-being of the people of our entire state."

Andy Haskins reached for his glass and took a sip. Edward Tholfson grinned at him, lifted his glass, then downed a sizable gulp of it. "Superb bourbon, don't you think, Mr.

Haskins. Why, sir, you've hardly touched your glass. Surely you aren't going to be standoffish on such a toast which regards yourself and your wife and baby, are you?"

Thus cajoled, Andy could hardly be ungracious. He drank about a third of the bourbon, coughed and choked, set the glass down, and finally regained self-control. "It's got the kick of a mule, Mr. Tholfson. Yes, I told you, I'm not a drinking man. And that's my limit right there, I can tell you straight off."

"Of course, of course," Tholfson purred. "I've had George go for some strong black coffee. And you have to try the special pecan pie—that little restaurant does wonders with it."

"I *would* like some coffee," Andy ruefully admitted. Suddenly it seemed to him that his collar was tighter, hotter, and sweatier than ever, and he tried to ease it by inserting his left forefinger inside the collar and moving it this way and that.

"I trust you noticed, Mr. Haskins," Tholfson shifted himself a little closer to his guest on the sofa, "I had them fix you a specially tender beefsteak. I know you're a proud man, and I know how heroically you lost your arm at Chickamauga—that was one of the facts in your campaign which drew so many loyal Southerners to you, sir. I'd heard that you were remarkably adept with just the one hand—still in all, I wanted to be sure that the beefsteak was easy to cut. It was, wasn't it?"

Jessica had always tactfully managed in preparing his meals to cut the meat and fowl servings to make them easier for him to manage. This afternoon, however, had presented something of a quandary. Andy had solved it by gripping the handle of his fork with his teeth, setting the tines into the beefsteak, then cutting the meat swiftly into convenient strips with the sharp knife held in his left hand. He had been grateful to Edward Tholfson for not having watched while he performed this rather cumbersome maneuver. However, when his host now directly referred to the steak, Andy could not help flushing self-consciously. "It was fine, Mr. Tholfson. I'm beholden to you. Now why don't we get on with—" Suddenly there seemed to be a ringing in his ears, and black spots danced before his eyes. He felt faint, and again he tried to loosen his collar.

"Why, whatever's the matter, Mr. Haskins?" his host's voice registered genuine alarm.

131

"Don't know—all of a sudden—weak as a kitten—I don't know what's come over me—I wish that George of yours would hurry up with the coffee—" Suddenly Andy's head bowed forward, and he lapsed into unconsciousness.

Edward Tholfson grinned wolfishly. He rose swiftly, with an alacrity which belied his stoutness, hurried to the door, put two fingers to his mouth, and emitted a long mournful whistle.

At the other end of the hallway, a door opened and the black porter emerged, followed by a tall, blond young woman. She wore a red calico dress, gauzy black net stockings, and high-button shoes, and she glanced nervously about as she and the porter came quickly toward the suite.

"Good girl, Judy! You know what you're supposed to do?"

"Sure. Mr. Jenkinson told me." Her gaze swept over the lolling figure of Andy Haskins. "This is the mark? Who is he?"

"It's no matter to you who he is. Let's just say this is going to help Mr. Jenkinson and his friends a great deal. That's why you've already had half your pay in advance so you won't flub your part in the deal."

"Don't worry. But I expect to get the rest of the money when you've finished. Can we get it over with quickly?"

"Such scruples, my dear," Tholfson sneered as his eyes appraisingly swept the tall young woman from head to toe. "All right, George, go get that picture-taker, Felix. I've given our friend here a pretty strong dose, he ought to be under for a good long time. Tell Felix I'll need two or three pictures, just to make sure everybody can see what's happening, understand me?"

"Yassuh, ah sho does! Be back in a jiffy, Mr. Tholfson, suh!"

"Might as well peel down, Judy girl," Tholfson instructed the young blonde. "Get in the mood, so to speak. As for the rest of your money, just as soon as Felix takes the pictures, you'll get what you were promised."

The young woman shrugged, then calmly took off her dress, and stood in a thin, revealing camisole that fell to mid-thigh. Her black net stockings were rolled around elastic garters. One could see the nacreous tint of her smooth skin at the deep cleft of her bosom and just where the camisole left off and the stocking tops began.

"Hmm, Homer has good taste, I'll say that for him.

Sweetie, when you've finished, if you've got nothing else scheduled tonight, maybe you and I could have a little party? I can be just as generous as Homer, as you'll find," Tholfson ingratiatingly proposed.

Once again the tall blonde shrugged. "Makes no difference to me so long as I get paid."

"That's the way I like to hear a girl talk. Homer tells me you've been very accommodating to him and his friends. You didn't make a mistake when you came to Montgomery from that cruddy little town of Tensaw, Judy girl. There's plenty of money up here, as you've already found out. That boyfriend of yours—what was his name, oh yes, David Fales—he was smart telling you where to head for. And if you're a good girl and keep your mouth shut, Homer and I and the rest of our friends can take pretty good care of you so you won't have to worry where the next greenback's coming from. All right, here's Felix." A young, sallow-faced, red-haired man entered with a large camera, an unwieldy tripod, and a set of glass photographic plates.

"Set everything up right here, Felix," Tholfson said. "I want you to get a picture as close up as you can, so there's no mistaking our friend here. He won't give you any trouble, he passed out like a light."

"I can see that, Mr. Tholfson," the red-haired man sniggered as he set up the camera and readied his plates for exposure. From time to time he disappeared beneath a cloth covering that hung from the bank of the camera and which served to block out the light so that the photographer could adjust the focus of his lens. Once or twice he paused in his work to allow his eyes to sweep appreciatively over the blond young woman as she now carefully seated herself on Andy Haskin's lap, circling his neck with her left arm, while with her right she gripped his left wrist and drew his limp hand to the full globe of one gently swelling breast, keeping it pressed against her.

"How's this, Mr. Tholfson?" she volunteered.

"Couldn't be better. I swear, Judy Branshaw, you know your trade, even if you've only been in it a few months."

"I know. There wasn't much else left for me after that fine Southern gentleman Mr. Fales got through with me," she countered with a sarcastic smile.

"Wait a minute before you start to take that picture, Felix. Let's see if I can get his eyes open. I don't want anyone to think he passed out, not while he had such a hot

133

little filly as our Judy here right on top of him," Tholfson coarsely guffawed. Going over to the couch, he pried open Andy's eyelids with his thumb, but when he straightened, they closed again. "Damn it to hell! Well, no help for it, Felix. You'll just have to do the best you can. That's why I want a couple of shots. And you, Judy, we'll change the pose after Felix takes this first one."

"Just tell me what to do and I'll do it, Mr. Tholfson." Judith Branshaw drew Andy Haskins's hand up more tightly against her breast, leaned closer to him. "How's this?"

"Even better, my dear," the politico exulted. "Now don't move a muscle, and be sure to hold Haskins steady. That's right—you can take the picture now, Felix."

With this the photographer, who had been busy focusing the camera and inserting a plate, now removed the cap covering the lens in order to expose the plate. Judith held both Andy and herself motionless, and in just a few seconds Felix replaced the lens cap and the picture was finished. With a sigh of relief, Judith stirred restlessly, and Tholfson came forward.

"And now, Judy," he said rather coarsely, "if you don't mind, why not pull that camisole of yours up just a little— you've beautiful legs, you know."

"Thank you. My pleasure," she sarcastically retorted as she released Andy's hand and jerked the hem of the camisole to her upper thighs, then crossed her legs and seductively twisted her right foot this way and that.

Felix had inserted a new negative plate and was busy focusing. When all was in readiness, he removed the lens cap, and soon the second picture was done.

"Just one more now, and then you can get back to your studio and develop the plates, Felix. And remember, I want to see the pictures just as soon as they're ready, and you'll get paid once I see them," Tholfson instructed.

"That's fine, sir. It's a pleasure to do business with a man who knows what he wants and is willing to pay for it," the photographer cynically remarked.

"Tell you what, Judy honey," Edward Tholfson now proposed. "Leave his arm free there, so everybody can see he's only got one arm. They can't mistake Andy Haskins if they see that picture. And, Judy, why don't you sort of hold his face with both hands and give him a nice, hot kiss. Don't hide his face altogether, but you know what I mean—good

134

girl!" The politico gleefully rubbed his hands as he watched the young blond woman execute his orders.

When the third plate had been exposed, the photographer disappeared with his equipment, the black porter following him down the hallway. Tholfson turned to the blonde, took out his wallet, and handed her two greenbacks. "That's the rest of your money. As you see, there's a little bonus for a job well done, honey. Now about tonight. I'll be checking out directly—we'll leave Mr. Haskins here to sleep it off. But I've got a place on Mason Street, on the corner of Eberhard. There's a big willow tree in front of it—you can't mistake it. Maybe you could manage to be there about eight o'clock tonight? I've got some good drinking whiskey and some fine French wine that came in from New Orleans the other day, Judy girl. And since I'm not a married man like our friend here, I won't have to chase you out—you can sleep the night and I've got a nice four-poster bed. How does that sound?"

"I'll take the whiskey. It'll get me drunk faster so I won't have to remember what I'm doing," Judith said as she smoothed down the camisole and put her red calico dress back on. Then she looked down at the somnolent one-armed Tennesseean. "He looks like a nice guy. How did he come to get mixed up with Mr. Jenkinson?"

Edward Tholfson's face hardened. He took a step forward and backhanded her across the cheek. "Maybe you didn't learn your lesson when you were back in Tensaw, honey," he said harshly. "Your fellow down there wrote me you had a lot of spunk and you could take punishment. But just a piece of advice—if you're going to get along here in Montgomery, Judy girl, you'll try not to show that spunk when it's a matter that doesn't concern you. Otherwise, you might get a lot worse than you did in Tensaw."

She faced him a moment, thoughtfully rubbing the red mark his blow had left on her pale cheek. "Just as I thought: David had it all planned from the very start," she said, half-aloud to herself. Then, with another sarcastic shrug, she said "I'll be at your place at eight. You won't have any trouble with me, Mr. Tholfson. Just have plenty of that whiskey ready."

CHAPTER THIRTEEN

"Wake up, suh! You jist gotta wake up, mistah! Mistah Tholfson, he done gib up dis room—you been sleepin' like a daid man!"

The urgent, reedy voice of the old hotel porter drew Andy Haskins out of the black fog of drugged sleep, and the porter's prodding his shoulder made him blink his eyes and look blankly around him. "Whazzat? Who—where—" His voice was thick, and his mouth felt as if it were crammed with cotton. His head throbbed ferociously, and he put his left hand up to his forehead, leaned back against the sofa, and closed his eyes again.

"Man, you cain't go back to sleep, you jist *cain't*, mistah," the porter plaintively declared. "Mistah Elton—he de manager ob dis hotel—he says I gotta git you up 'n out right now, mistah!" Then, pleadingly, he again shook Andy Haskins by the shoulder and repeated, "You jist gotta, mistah!"

Wanly, Andy opened his eyes and tried to stand up, but he found himself weak in the knees and had to sink back on the sofa. He put a hand to his head, for he had a splitting headache and felt nauseated. But the hovering presence of the porter recalled him to necessity: falteringly, he held out his hand and, in a hollow voice, said, "Help me up, please."

"I's sho'nuff glad to do dat, mistah. Here you be, nice 'n easy now, up you goes!"

Andy rose to his feet, tottering, his insides churning. He looked dazedly around the room, and then remembered where he had been and why. That drink—that drink of bourbon whiskey—he'd passed out like a light right afterwards. Something was very wrong—and how long had he been sleeping, anyway? "What time is it?" he asked.

"Mistah, it be well past noon, and this be Sattiday." The porter was querulous with anxiety now and kept glancing toward the door. "Kin you stand 'n walk all right, mistah?"

"I—I've got to try, that's for sure. Saturday noon—Jessica—I've got to get home—" Andy rubbed his face and felt the stubble. Then he grimaced as a wave of nausea seized him again, and he quickly sank back down on the sofa, much to the porter's consternation.

"But you cain't do dat, didn't I tell you, mistah? You have to git up. Mr. Elton he say Mr. Tholfson's room gonna be rented to some preachah from Natchez, 'n I has tuh clean up dis here place real quick 'foah he come in."

"All right, George, you've done your bit, you can go now. We'll get Mr. Haskins out of here." An oily voice broke into Andy Haskins's groping consciousness. He turned his head with an effort, and then he forced himself to rise, using all his wavering strength. It was Homer Jenkinson, and Edward Tholfson was with him. Both men were broadly grinning.

"Well now, Mr. Haskins, what a pleasure to find you here," Jenkinson smirkingly began. "Guess you'll be wanting your horse, and we're here to put you on it and help you get back home where you want to be. But there's something we'd like you to see first, before you go."

"What are you talking about, Jenkinson? Don't tell me you're in cahoots with Mr. Tholfson here." Andy took a few tentative steps, found that he could manage, then took several deep breaths and confronted the two carpetbaggers. "Well, if you've got something to show me, make it quick. I'm going back home, but I don't need your help, not hardly, thanks just the same."

"I'm not so sure about that, Mr. Haskins." Jenkinson was holding something behind his back. Now he made an ostentatious flourish and held up a photograph between his thumbs and forefingers so that Andy could see it plainly. "Mr. Representative, you sure had yourself a time last night. Judy was telling us what a hellion you can be once you relax and forget your political duties."

Andy swore an unprintable oath. "Now I get it all. You, Mr. Tholfson, or that porter of yours, put something in my bourbon. I passed out, and then you took this picture."

"Correction, Mr. Haskins," Jenkinson smoothly intervened. "Who said anything about your passing out? No one could tell that from looking at this picture. Aren't I correct, Edward?"

"That's right, Homer. The focus is good, but not perfect, and no one could say for sure that he wasn't awake and having a high old time."

"You see, Andy? I'd prefer to be on a first-name basis with you. Because, you see, I think we're going to be good friends from now on. There's been an unfortunate misunderstanding in the past, I'll admit, but by now I believe you're ready to see the light of day. Particularly if this picture should find itself into the hands of the editor of the *Advertiser*. I wonder what your lovely wife would think of a little story in the newspaper, based on the clear evidence here of your exploits? And what about your constituents who voted for you because you're supposedly a morally upright fellow?"

Andy clenched his fist and ground his teeth, fighting to control the impulse to smash Jenkinson's grinning face. "I've done absolutely nothing like that and you both know it," he doggedly retorted. "The *Advertiser*'s a fair paper; I don't think it'll print that trumped-up story without hearing my side first."

"I'm not so sure about that, Andy boy." Edward Tholfson was genial. "But whether it's printed or not, I don't think you're going to find it very easy to explain all this to your dear wife. You see, I first off plan to make sure that she has a copy all her own."

Andy could no longer control his rage at the shabby trick that had been played upon him. With all his strength, he smashed his balled fist into Tholfson's jeering mouth. The stout carpetbagger yelled with pain, stumbled backwards, and went down hard on the carpeted floor. He struggled to his feet, nursing a swollen lip and a broken tooth, and bleeding profusely.

"That was extremely unwise and very foolish of you, Andy," Jenkinson reproved him, much as a schoolteacher might rebuke a disorderly boy in his classroom. "You shouldn't show such hostility. I'll give you a last chance to reconsider. All you have to do is to endorse this bill about which we've already talked, as you well remember. There'll be a bonus in it for you, needless to say."

"Do you want a punch in the face too, Mr. Jenkinson?

Get out of my way. I'm going back home. And you can do your damnedest with that filthy picture, so far as I'm concerned. You won't make me try to rob the voters of this state no matter what kind of bribe or threat you offer, and that's my last word on the subject." He kept his fist clenched and turned on Tholfson, who was groaning and trying to stem the flow of blood from his mouth with his lace-monogrammed handkerchief. The stout carpetbagger stumbled backwards with a cry of alarm. "Don't you hit me again, don't you dare! I'll have the law on you for this—you've broken one of my teeth—"

"I'll break all the rest in your dirty, lying mouth if you say anything about my wife again—and that goes for you too, Mr. Jenkinson. Now I'm getting out of here, and neither of you had better try to stop me!"

"So you see, Lopasuta, they really suckered me. I never thought I'd live to see the day when two city slickers like that could hornswoggle a good old Tennessee boy," Andy Haskins glumly told the young Comanche lawyer. After saddling his horse and paying his bill at the stable, he had ridden to Lopasuta's frame house and explained what had happened.

"I don't think they're going to get anywhere with their blackmailing scheme, Mr. Haskins—er, Andy. First off, you've won yourself a reputation already for honesty and being a good loyal family man. Besides, the editor of the *Advertiser* isn't especially fond of carpetbaggers. Furthermore, I know where he lives, and I'll pay a call on him before supper this evening. I'll just tell him that if he should print any kind of story based on the flimsy evidence of that photograph, he'll find himself facing a suit for libel. Don't worry, Andy, nothing will come of it."

"I'm fair relieved to hear you tell me that, Lopasuta. Whew! I feel better already, though my stomach feels the way it did after rounding up cows after a stampede." The one-armed Tennesseean took another deep breath and passed his hand over his forehead. "But it's a nice cool afternoon, and that ride upriver ought to help clear the last of that drugged bourbon out of me. If you've got any strong black coffee, though, I'd appreciate a cup right now."

"Of course. Sit down there and rest, Andy, I'll get it for you. I'll have one with you, and as soon as you've gone, I'll ride over to the editor's house, I promise you."

Lopasuta excused himself, went into the tiny kitchen, and brought back two cups of steaming coffee, blended with chicory in the New Orleans fashion.

Andy Haskins felt better after he had downed nearly half of the coffee at a gulp. "I'm mighty grateful for the advice and for the coffee, I can tell you. You know, it's a good comfortable feeling to know that Luke's affairs are going to be handled right and proper, even with old Jedidiah gone. You're a good lawyer, Lopasuta. Well, I'd better start home before Jessica really gets worried about me. I'm going to have to tell her all about this—those dirty scum, to try to involve her!" He walked toward the door, then turned back. "I'll tell you one thing, you're never going to have to get me out of another scrape like this one. Next time somebody wants me to come into town and have lunch, I'm going to say no."

"Don't blame yourself, Andy. They're unscrupulous men, and the way they tried to turn that unfortunate Mr. Darden into a weapon of assassination shows just how far they'll go. I'm going to try to spike their guns once and for all, you can be certain of it. Now give my very best to Mrs. Haskins."

"I know you'd never do a thing like that, Andy." Jessica sat beside her husband on the sofa in the living room of their little house. He was leaning forward, his face hard and drawn, his elbow on his left knee and his palm pressing against his chin. He had looked at her all through his narrative of the "luncheon in his honor," but now, the thought of the vileness of Jenkinson's blackmail as it would involve this loyal, sweet young woman who meant as much as life itself to him had sent a gnawing rage through him.

"I ought to have smashed them both, not just Tholfson," he growled.

There were tears in Jessica's eyes. Very gently, very softly, she cupped his face in her hands and forced him to turn to her. "Now you listen here, Andy Haskins," she said firmly. "I love you and I trust you, and if that awful man Mr. Jenkinson comes around here with that picture, you can be sure I'll tell him a thing or two." She flared up indignantly, her eyes sparkling with anger. "I might just take my broom to him and lambaste him a few good ones."

Andy burst out laughing and put his arm around his wife. "Honey, I don't deserve a prize like you!" Her face

141

was radiant as their lips met, and Andy knew that with Jessica standing by him, he was more than a match for the wiliest and most ruthless of carpetbaggers.

The one-armed Tennesseean was out in the fields with the Ardmore brothers when Jenkinson's buggy drove up to the little frame house. The carpetbagger was accompanied by Edward Tholfson, whose mouth was still swollen from the altercation at the hotel.

Jessica had heard the sound of the buggy. She opened the door and came out to confront the two carpetbaggers. Just as she had promised Andy, she had a broom in her hands and she glared defiantly at both men as they got out of the buggy and advanced toward her.

"You just scat, do you hear me?" she indignantly exclaimed. "Andy's told me all about what you did, and I think it's contemptible and filthy! I know my husband, and he wouldn't consort with a creature you hired to blacken him like this."

"Now then, Mrs. Haskins," Edward Tholfson wheedled, "we don't want to argue with you or get you angry, ma'am. But there could be a great deal of scandal if this story were released to the newspaper. And it's not as if we'd asked your husband to do anything wrong, truly it isn't. This bill—"

"I don't propose to listen to another word of your contemptible lies. You must be Mr. Tholfson. I see my husband marked you so I could recognize you," Jessica triumphantly declared, brandishing the broom and taking a step closer to the two carpetbaggers. Tholfson recoiled and started back for the buggy. "That's right, you're afraid of a woman, which just proves what yellow-livered skunks both of you are. Now you'll oblige me by getting off our property—or else I'll have the law on you. And we've got some good strong workers here who know how to use a gun, if you don't think this broom can fetch you a few good licks!"

"Come on, Homer," Tholfson nervously exclaimed. "We'll drive over to the *Advertiser* office." Then, raising his voice toward the defiant young woman, he called, "All right, Mrs. Haskins, but just you wait till this gets printed. Then you and your husband will change your tune."

But when they returned to Montgomery and entered the newspaper office, the elderly editor coldly informed them that his newspaper would not be a party to such an obvious

142

falsehood and blackmail, and concluded by saying, "Mr. Lopasuta Bouchard has already called on me, gentlemen, and advised me of the particulars in this matter. I think he has in mind bringing a suit for vicious libel and slander against the both of you and your associates, at the very least demanding a public apology. My advice to you is to destroy that photograph and any other such you may have. And personally, I'll tell you, I've got no use for scheming Yankee carpetbaggers who, when they can't openly steal what they want, have to resort to dirty lying scandal like yours. You'll do me the courtesy of getting out of my office before the air's contaminated, *gentlemen*!"

On the following Wednesday afternoon, Lopasuta Bouchard tied his horse to a tethering rail opposite the Jenkinson house, walked up the stairs, and rapped the knocker three sonorous times. Homer Jenkinson himself opened the door, then scowled and made as if to close it, but the strong young Comanche pushed his way inside. "Not so fast, Mr. Jenkinson," he exclaimed. "You're aware that I know about your scheme to involve Representative Haskins in a scandal you contrived. Your evidence, if I may dignify it by calling it that, sir, is laughable, and no court in Alabama would accept it, particularly after the testimony of George Bannister."

"George Bannister?" Homer Jenkinson wonderingly echoed.

"Precisely. That's the hotel porter you bribed. I had a little talk with him this morning, and he told me everything."

"Why, that goddamned nigger! He was paid—" Jenkinson blurted out, then turned livid with rage and confusion.

"Of course he was. But at least he has more of a sense of decency than you and your colleagues, Mr. Jenkinson. I've already been over to see Mr. Tholfson. He's written out an apology at my dictation and signed it. And he's agreed to leave town. I might suggest, sir, that you do the same. Otherwise, I shall bring suit against you, and I'll win it. I'm not interested in damages, but I *am* interested in getting a man like you out of this town so that he can't do any more harm to decent citizens."

"Now you see here—" Jenkinson tried to bluster.

"No, *you* listen to me, Mr. Jenkinson. If it's scandal you want, there's enough in your own life which, if disclosed, would serve to discredit you in this town once and for all."

"I don't know what you're getting at! I'm a busy man, I—"

"I'm referring to a Miss Judith Branshaw. George Bannister told me where she was living, and I had a chat with her also. I found out about the cruel, wretched way she was treated in her home town of Tensaw by a man who, it seems, had certain alliances with you and your cowardly group of crooked profiteers. She is willing to turn state's evidence against you, Mr. Jenkinson, and against all of your associates, if I file suit and it comes to court."

"That *slut*!" In his fury, Jenkinson did not notice that his cowed young wife Prudence was listening at the hallway door, which was slightly ajar.

"That's what David Fales made of her, before he sent her on to you to be used as a tool. Unhappily, her cruel treatment led her temporarily to want vengeance against what she termed 'fine Southern gentlemen.' But though she was party to this monstrous blackmail scheme of yours the other night, she felt a great compassion and contrition when she saw Mr. Haskins for the first time. She realized that he wasn't to be compared with David Fales or you, sir."

"You—you—" Homer Jenkinson sputtered.

"Miss Branshaw is beyond your attempts at reprisal, sir. She is beginning a new life, living under an assumed name in another state." Lopasuta did not add that he and Luke had seen to it that Judith found employment in a bank in New Orleans, and had given her enough money for transportation and living expenses until she could earn enough to support herself. "Your infidelities with Miss Branshaw," he went on, "together with your compelling her to service such colleagues of yours as Mr. Tholfson and the disreputable Judge Siloway, would also not set well in a court of law. Nor, I might add, would your notorious liaison with your mulatto mistress. Quite a number of this woman's neighbors, Mr. Jenkinson, have seen you visit her openly and would be willing to testify as to those visits. I do not think your own wife would care to have such unsavory domestic matters aired in court."

"Damn you to hell, what do you expect me to do?" Jenkinson almost shouted, clenching his fists.

"You'll prepare a letter to the *Advertiser* retracting everything that you've said against Representative Haskins

144

and apologizing to him for attempting to involve him in your wretched schemes. By the way, I've said nothing about how you and your friends exploited poor William Darden. The only reason I do not charge all of you with attempted murder is that his testimony would not stand up sufficiently, although he did tell Representative Haskins that it was you who told him that niggers, to use your own expression, worked side by side with both Representative Haskins and Mr. Luke Bouchard, who is also my client. You knew of his tragedy and what an obsession he had against the blacks because of what had happened to his daughter, Mr. Jenkinson. But, as I say, he could not testify against you because he is totally deranged. You can look back on that as an after-effect of your contemptible handiwork, Mr. Jenkinson." Lopasuta turned on his heel and walked to the door to let himself out. Then he turned back and said, "If by Friday afternoon your letter of retraction and apology is not in the hands of the editor of the *Advertiser*, be assured, sir, that I shall formally proceed to the suit for libel and slander on Monday morning. That is all I have to say to you, Mr. Jenkinson."

Homer Jenkinson stood, unable to speak, his face mottled with the fury that was consuming him. Behind him, the hallway door had closed. He turned at last and bawled out, "Prudence! Prudence, come in here! Do you hear me, you stupid bitch! Come in here!"

Receiving no answer, he strode to the hallway door, flung it open and called out again for his young wife. "What the devil's the matter with you, Prudence? Listen, you'd best start packing. I'm going to sell this house and move. I'm sure you'll be glad of that, so show some life for a change. Will you answer me, you bitch? Of all the women I could have married—where are you, anyway?"

"In the kitchen, Homer!" he heard her call out.

There was a crooked grin on his mouth as he strode purposefully toward the kitchen. Why didn't she come when he called? It was time she got a taste of the strap again. He'd been much too soft with her lately, and she was taking advantage of him. And as for that Haskins—well, never mind him; there was always some other member of the House who'd go along with him and wouldn't give him the trouble Haskins had. Besides, he was sick and tired of Montgomery anyway. But if he ever got his hands on that long-legged blond bitch, by God, he'd make her sorry for the way she'd gone over to the enemy camp, he would for certain.

"Prudence?" he called as he stepped into the kitchen.

Prudence had long performed the chores of scullery maid, cook, and servant to her sadistic and parsimonious husband. Only last week, Jenkinson had ordered her to make soap at home instead of purchasing it. Accordingly, when Jenkinson came looking for her, she was boiling the ingredients—potash and animal fats—on the kitchen stove. And as he entered the room, she lifted the kettle and dashed its contents into his face, causing him to stumble back screaming in maddened agony.

When she went for a doctor, Prudence explained that she had stumbled when Homer struck her, and that the contents of the pot had spattered into his face in a way that she could not prevent. The next afternoon, when she visited Homer in the little hospital on Eberhard Street, her solicitousness caused the nurses to dab their eyes to hide their tears, as they watched and listened to her trying to console her blind husband.

Now she sat at his bedside, her face serene, her eyes gentle as she bent to him and murmured, "I'm so sorry, Homer dear. I know it's dreadful to be blind, a fine strong man like you in the prime of life. But I'll look after you. I'll devote myself to taking care of you the rest of my days. I promise I will, Homer dear."

Edward Tholfson had already arranged to sell his house, pocketed his savings, and gone to Atlanta. A year later, he would be so deeply involved in Georgia politics that he would be challenged to a duel by a patriotically overzealous Democrat and would cough out his life with a bullet in the lungs.

CHAPTER FOURTEEN

When Lucien Edmond Bouchard, Luke's oldest son, had written from Carrizo Springs in April, describing his plans for Windhaven Range during the coming year, he had already given serious thought to the idea of not going on another trail drive this spring. Last year, when he and his vaqueros had driven his herd to the Santa Fe Railroad in Newton, he had managed to sell 2,928 head of cattle at the disappointingly low price of only ten dollars a head—a price that hardly seemed to recompense them for all the suffering they had endured at the hands of Jack Martin and Benito Tonsado's bushwackers. Then, too, Lucien Edmond, like all cattlemen, still carried in his mind the stories he'd heard of the bloody shootout at Perry Tuttle's saloon in Newton, which had left the marshal and eight other men dead or wounded. He had no desire to return to that unruly town.

There were, to be sure, factors that made a trail drive to Kansas still worth considering. The Kansas Pacific Railroad had pushed westward to Ellsworth, which lay on the flat, treeless banks of the Smoky Hill River. The town had managed to divert some herds from Newton last year, and this year promised to be bigger than ever. By February, agents for Joseph McCoy, the famous cattle buyer, were already riding south to Texas to urge the cattlemen to bring their herds to the new market. Likewise, the Santa Fe line now ran as far south as Wichita, and already that town was becoming a boom town. Lucien Edmond carefully weighed both towns as a possible destination this year, for he predicted that each would be determined to attract the lion's share of the cattleman's business by offering ample facilities for the cattle and cowboys, as well as buyers willing to pay fair prices. But in the end, the proprietor of Windhaven Range became discouraged with the Kansas markets, owing partly to some news sent to him by Dr. Ben Wilson.

The young Quaker doctor was now living in Wichita with his Sioux wife, Elone, little Tisinqua (her daughter by her first husband, a Kiowa), and Bartholomew, Ben's firstborn by Elone. Thomas and Sybella Wilson, the two children whom Ben's first wife, Fleurette, had given him, were also with them, residing in the house Jacob Hartmann, the town's Quaker pastor, had found for the Wilson family.

The Wilsons and the Hartmanns were very close. Ben had first met Jacob a little more than three years earlier, when Ben was living with the outcast Creeks on their reservation in Indian Territory. From time to time he had come into Wichita to pick up supplies for the Creeks from the general store Jacob owned. After Ben and Elone moved to Wichita, Jacob's kindly, devoted wife, Tabitha, often helped Elone with the children on those occasions when Ben was absent on his rounds. Meanwhile, much to Ben's satisfaction, the *mico* Emataba and his people were under the supervision of an honest, dedicated Indian agent named Douglas Larrimer, who had arranged for a doctor stationed at a nearby army post to visit the reservation regularly. Thus, Ben, who had spent so much time serving the Creeks, now was at ease in his mind about their welfare; he felt free to devote himself to his family and to their new life in Wichita, in the bosom of Jacob Hartmann's Quaker fellowship.

The Quaker community in the town was quite large, and its members often met together not only to share their spiritual concerns but also to discuss news of the day—in particular anything that might affect the common welfare of every one of them in this rugged cow town. Thus it was that Pastor Hartmann, after the Quaker meeting on the last Sunday in February, came over to Ben Wilson.

"I have something to tell you, Ben, after everyone has left the meeting. It would not be seemly to talk of worldly concerns in our little meeting house. But I think it is news that will concern your good friend, Mr. Lucien Edmond Bouchard, of whom you have told me so much and who, had he ever taken up our faith, would surely have been as welcome among us for his honesty and goodness as you are."

Half an hour later, Jacob opened the door of his general store and Ben Wilson, Elone, and the four children followed. Tabitha Hartmann bustled about, offering the children candy and, to the delight of Tisinqua and Sybella, giving them presents of rag dolls she herself had made. Meanwhile, the Quaker doctor went into the office at the back of the store. There Jacob Hartmann declared, "Yesterday, a man rode into Wichita and came to my store for supplies. He told me that he is a member of the Kansas legislature, and that the members are going to push the tick quarantine westward and southward. That means, he explained, it would be illegal to drive Texas cattle not only to Abilene—which as you know is just about deserted—but very soon to both Newton and Ellsworth. Perhaps even Wichita will be affected in the future."

"That indeed is news which would concern Lucien Edmond Bouchard," Ben excitedly declared. "I should write to him and tell him this news. I've heard that Joseph McCoy's riders are going to Texas now to ask ranchers to take their herds to Ellsworth—but it would be a long drive, and if what this man tells you is the truth, the herd would be turned away. It would then be more vulnerable to outlaws who might try to seize the herd and take it elsewhere for their own profit. There could be bloodshed—just as occurred last year when Lucien Edmond drove his cattle to Newton."

"Exactly. But now, with the talk of Newton and Ellsworth being closed soon, and with the Santa Fe branch in Wichita, those ranchers still willing to risk the long drive may all bring their herds here, for the next few years at least." Jacob Hartmann shook his head and thoughtfully tugged at his beard. "Wichita is becoming a boom town. It has many advantages for the grazing of cattle, and if more and more cattle come here this year, I fear greatly that there will be many more cowboys and guns. There will be lawlessness and bloodshed. We must pray that the peacefulness we have known thus far in our Quaker community is not menaced by this danger."

"The people of Wichita will have to elect a good marshal, then, with deputies who can suppress rowdyism and the disorder that comes with strong drink."

"Alas, Ben, you and I know that we already have many saloons in Wichita, and already men quarrel and draw their guns over trivial matters once they are under the in-

149

fluence. Therefore, as a body of citizens who believe in a God of peace and love and who abhor violence, we must urge the influential men in this town to appoint courageous lawmen. But let us not think such gloomy thoughts on such a bright Sunday. Your children are very well, and your Elone has studied our faith and is sincere in it. She speaks English very well, Ben."

"And she has taught me how to speak her Sioux tongue and also the Kiowa, and of course I already know the Creek. Such knowledge may be of advantage if I am called upon to help the sick and the needy in the reservations, just as I was with the Creeks where I found her."

"There again a gloomy thought assails me, Ben. Our government seems determined to kill the buffalo and make it almost impossible for Indian tribes to hunt and to sustain themselves. It is part of a plan, I fear, to drive them off the land till they have nowhere else to go but these pitiful reservations, where they are herded in like animals and treated even more contemptuously." Again Jacob shook his head. "They who were first upon this land, Ben, have become the disinherited. In a sense, they are being persecuted as were our Quaker forebears with George Fox in England. The difference is that they have few spokesmen in high places who can help their cause. They are called bloodthirsty savages only because they seek to defend their land and their lives. It is a lesson God sends us to teach us humility."

"A lesson which, alas, too few heed, Jacob. We shall pray for them, and for peace in Wichita. But now, let's go back to the children. They're very fond of you, Jacob, and it was very kind of your dear wife to give Sybella and Tisinqua the dolls, and candy to all the children."

Jacob Hartmann beamed and patted Dr. Ben Wilson on the back as he led him back into the store. "Alas, God did not see fit to bless us with children, Ben, and perhaps that's why Tabitha and I are so drawn to yours."

"Thank you, Jacob, you have been a good friend and spiritual counselor for Elone and me as we have begun our new lives. I pray I shall always be worthy of my new responsibilities. Oh, one thing more—do you know any riders who might be heading for Texas? If so, I'll send Lucien Edmond Bouchard word of what you have just told me. He may want to change his plans."

"Yes, as a matter of fact, Jack McCready, who rides for

150

Joseph McCoy, leaves tomorrow for the southeastern part of Texas. He's staying at the Noblach Hotel."

"That's good. I'll write the letter and go see him this evening. And again, God bless you for your kindness to my family and to me." The two men fervently shook hands, and then Ben took little Bartholomew in one arm and held out a hand to Tisinqua, while Elone eagerly took the hands of Thomas and Sybella. It was plain that these two already loved their Indian stepmother, and the doctor watched them leave the store with her, eagerly chatting over how kind their Aunt Tabitha had been to them. Sturdy young Thomas volunteered, "Mama, we didn't forget to thank her for the candy, either!"

Ben chuckled, glanced back at both Jacob and his wife, wished them a happy Sunday, and rejoined his family on the heavy planking that formed the sidewalk of Wichita's main street.

In spite of the extension of the Santa Fe line and the influx of cattlemen that was the inevitable result, Ben Wilson had a presentiment that the boom in Wichita could not last long. Though he naturally did not have the economic insight of Luke Bouchard and Lucien Edmond, he nonetheless sensed that some economic change was in the wind. Last year, some seventy thousand head of cattle had come up the trail to take advantage of the new Santa Fe branch, and this year—the first full year of operation—was bound to be better; but there were some who said that future years might see a decline. Already many people had begun to doubt whether there would be anything—even this year— to equal the six hundred thousand head that had crowded into the Abilene market in 1873.

The busiest place of all in Wichita was the land office, for there were more and more farmers coming in and settling around the outskirts of town, scattering their dugouts, soddies, and log huts all along the streams and over the high, grassy tableland. There was no great concern about Indian raids, since most of the Indian attacks were far to the southwest, and most of these were directed not against farmers, but against buffalo hunters and thieves who stole horses and cattle from the reservations.

In some ways, Ben Wilson thought, Wichita would last as a settlement long after the cattle drives had ended. There was well-established trade to the Indian Territory

151

and huge government contracts for Indian goods, with plenty of stealthy profits along the way for those agents and suppliers involved. There were dance halls, a variety theater, a beer garden with a band, a hall that housed from a hundred to a hundred and fifty players of keno, bawdy houses that boasted twenty and even thirty women apiece, as well as several churches.

And even if Dr. Wilson had known nothing about the process of cattle raising and the arduous task of marketing the beef once it was ready to be sold, he had learned from Jacob Hartmann's close contacts with cattlemen, agents, and legislators that the growing numbers of settlers and farmers all around Wichita must surely, one day soon, cut off this Kansas mecca for cattle. Besides, the men in the cattle business who had run Abilene, Newton, and Ellsworth had learned their lesson: a town can't exist on seasonal business alone. Hence, soon his new home of Wichita would exist on varied enterprises and industry, on farming and trading. In a sense, it would be more akin to Pittsburgh, and with the Quaker community to hearten him and the new friends he had made in it, he could be content. There was his practice, and best of all, there was Elone, who was again with child and would have her baby sometime this June.

It had not always been easy, those first days in Wichita, even with the joy of having his family reunited. There were always those who cast slurs upon Elone and himself when the two of them walked down the street to Jacob Hartmann's store. That had happened at the very beginning, and he had tried to ignore the obscene catcalls and the scurrilous remarks hooted out after him and Elone by drunken cowboys lounging against the front of the dance hall or the saloon. What hurt him most was the proud, dignified silence Elone observed—for, of course, she understood English well by now—when such ugly incidents occurred. She would turn away from her assailants, giving him a swift, loving glance, as if to reassure him that she did not at all mind these verbal attacks so long as he was there beside her to assure her that she was loved and protected. Sometimes he clenched his fists till the knuckles were whitened, and engaged her in random conversation simply to deafen his ears and to harden his soul against the vicious epithets called after them. He knew himself to have a temper; he had shown it with Matthias Stillman, the corrupt Indian agent, when he had tried to rape Elone back at the Creek reservation. He had shown it again last year on the journey to Wichita, when he had beaten a bushwhacker nearly unconscious, after Elone had shot and killed the bushwhacker's partner. But his religion forbade violence, and he knew that he must try to turn the other cheek, though there were times when such humility rankled.

Yet he had made friends among even the cowboys and the merchants. Shortly before Christmas, there had been a drunken altercation in one of the boisterous saloons along the main street of Wichita. One of the bartenders had run to his house, knocked on the door, and urgently demanded that he come to try to save the life of Dallas Masterson, who used to ride point for the big Glossop outfit in the Panhandle. Masterson, a wiry, wry-humored man in his early forties, had fallen prey to the temptation of Wichita's gambling halls. After he had ridden his boss's herd to market last summer, he had taken his pay and told Hiram Glossop that he was done with riding point and would try his luck at the wheel, at faro and keno.

Dallas Masterson was admired throughout the Kansas territory for his raw courage and bravado. It was almost legendary, the story of how, six years earlier, he had taken two thousand head of cattle along the Chisholm Trail to Abilene with only twenty riders in the outfit, fought off a gang of cattle rustlers twice the size, been wounded in an attack by Kiowa Apaches who had stampeded the herd. He and his dozen remaining men had driven the Indians off with heavy losses, then spent a week retrieving the stampeded herd and brought them into Abilene. Some said that he had become a cowboy a decade ago after a girl had broken his heart in New Orleans, where he had been a blackjack dealer. That might well have explained his sudden desire to return to the gambling halls of Wichita and to pursue his livelihood there.

Dr. Wilson followed the bartender to the saloon to find the former cowhand in critical condition from a bullet near his lung. Improvising as he had to, using a table as surgical table, dosing Masterson with enough whiskey to numb the pain, sterilizing his instruments in boiling water—a procedure he had learned in Pittsburgh and which few doctors at the time employed—he had extracted the bullet, stopped the bleeding, then used an ordinary needle and heavy thread for sutures. Miraculously, within ten days Masterson was sitting at the faro table as house dealer. That same night, although Ben did not know it, someone in his cups made the jesting remark that the Quaker doctor was a squaw man, probably because no white woman would take a liking to his homely face. Masterson politely excused himself to the patrons at the table, walked over to the bar, and felled the foul-mouthed drunkard with a blow of his fist that broke the latter's nose. Then he turned and said sibilantly, "Nobody'd better downgrade the doc when I'm around to hear it, savvy? That's enough said," and went back to his table.

"Pastor Hartmann is a good man, Elone." Ben turned to his young wife with a questioning smile, eager to see her response. Ever since he had first met her at Emataba's pitifully neglected village, he had never ceased to marvel at the exquisite mobility of her face, the expressiveness of her eyes and lips, which conveyed so much that there often was no need for words between them.

It warmed his heart with a secret, joyous delight when she swiftly turned to him, her eyes glowing, and murmured, "He loves the children. A man who loves children is blessed by the Great Spirit, and He can surely read the hearts of men."

"That is very true, my Elone," Ben agreed. "Are you content here in Wichita?"

"So long as I am with you, my husband, I should be content anywhere. Even back there in the village of Emataba where first we met," Elone confided.

"It is good of you to say this, my dear one." It was strange, he thought to himself, how often this gentle young girl declared her grateful love for him, and each time she did so, he felt tears sting his eyes. It caused him to think of his first wife, Fleurette, but it was not only her memory that brought tears: it was the profoundly religious conviction that a kind and understanding Creator had assuaged his tragic bereavement by directing his footsteps to the Creek reservation, there to find the gentle Elone. She herself, an outcast, had come to Emataba's village through two acts of violence: first, her ruthless abduction by a Kiowa chieftain, and then the bushwacker massacre of his tribe, which had forced her to flee with Tisinqua to take refuge with the Creeks.

To Ben, their coming together was a miraculous reaffirmation of the Divinity in which he so unswervingly believed, and even now he looked up at the gray February sky and murmured a silent prayer of grateful thanks for the blessed bounty of Elone and the children she had given him, the child she would bear him this summer.

"Yet it is noisy here, Elone, and there are guns and there are people who look at you because you have Indian blood—this does not disturb you?"

"No, my husband." She smilingly shook her head, glancing down at the two children who clung to her hands, happily sucking away at the pieces of horehound candy Tabitha Hartmann had given them. "When I was a little girl in the village of the Aiyuta Sioux, my father and mother taught me about the Great Spirit to whom one prays for strength. Now that I am your wife, I have learned your faith, of the gentle Great Spirit you call God. And thus, I have twice within my heart the knowledge that I am being watched over and protected—and here on earth you are with me to make me feel safe, to make me feel loved. No woman could ask more, were she white or black or any other color of the peoples of this world, my husband."

"How clearly you understand, how beautifully you say these simple truths all men should know!" he admiringly responded. "And yet there are so many of my own people who are blind to these truths, Elone. While I lived with Emataba and his people, I had reason to learn the difference. These Indians who came first to this land and who dwelt upon it and lived from it without spoiling it seemed to be closer to that Great Spirit my people and I call God than many of us, for all of our knowledge. Perhaps there is a great message here, a universal truth—" he sighed heavily, shook his head, "—but what I see of the way our government still treats the Indian tribes, they do not listen to the message, they refuse to understand this universal truth. And one day, Elone, perhaps even in my own lifetime, the tribes that once hunted the plains for buffalo and deer and who lived in friendship upon the land they cultivated for their own needs will disappear and be forgotten. I pray it will not be so, but I am not hopeful that it will be otherwise."

"I think of that sometimes too, my husband. I think of Emataba and the old ones in his village, who with each new year go to join their forefathers and are forgotten. Their names are no longer spoken. And when they are all gone and there is no one to remember their names, it may be as you fear. I, too, pray it will not be so."

They were about two blocks away from their house when suddenly, from across the muddy street which a rainstorm last week had turned nearly into a quagmire, a man bawled out in a loud, jeering voice, "There goes the squaw-man doc—and his injun wife's got a big belly from him. 'S'matter, Doc, can't you find yerself a white gal who'll let you poke her?'"

Dr. Ben Wilson stiffened, his face flaming with a sudden irrational rage. He turned to look across the street, and saw a fat man in a bowler hat, with graying sideburns, leaning against the outer wall of a saloon, his thumbs hooked into his vest.

"Yeah, Doc, I'm talkin' 'bout you! Wanta do something about it?"

"Be careful, my dear one!" Elone gasped, "he has a gun!"

The fat man had suddenly drawn a silver-mounted pistol out of a holster attached to his belt, and brandished it. Elone, her eyes wide and dark with fear, shrank back, drawing Thomas and Sybella behind her, trying to efface herself.

But before Ben could reply to this insulting taunt, a tall gray-bearded man came out of the saloon, turned to stare at the fat man, then glanced across the street. Whirling, he struck the pistol out of the fat man's hand and then dealt him a right uppercut to the jaw, which made the latter sprawl flat on his back on the planked sidewalk. "You bastard, what was that for?" the fat man gasped as he stumbled to his feet.

His assailant, for answer, applied right and left uppercuts to his belly and sent him floundering into the muddy street. Then, staring down at his agonized, crestfallen opponent, he barked, "I don't ever want to hear you talk to the doc and his wife like that again, mister! Yeah, I used to think the same thing about the doc there myself—till he cured me of scarlet fever when I like to have died. You'd better not ever open your yap again about him when I'm around!"

Then, cupping his hands to his mouth, he called to Ben, "He won't bother you none again. You remember me, don't you, Doc? I'm Dave Haggerson. Wichita needs you, Doc. Don't you let a fat pig like that chase you out, you hear?"

"Thank you, friend. Yes, I remember you. God bless you

and give you long years," Ben called. He turned then to Elone. "Come, my dearest. We can go home. You see, I have had my answer. This is truly our home now. We are accepted and loved by strangers. When we help others, we assuredly help ourselves, and the dear Lord sees to it."

CHAPTER FIFTEEN

On the very Sunday in February when Dr. Ben Wilson determined to send a letter to Lucien Edmond Bouchard, Luke's oldest son conferred with his brother-in-law, Ramón Hernandez, and Joe Duvray and Eddie Gentry, to get their views on the disposition of their combined cattle herd this summer.

When Eddie Gentry returned from the Newton drive last summer, he had brought back with him a lovely young Mexican girl, Maria Elena Romero, who had been virtually sold by her father to the Newton saloon owner Jim Bradshaw. Bradshaw had intended to make her a prostitute. Eddie had borrowed in advance against his wages from Lucien Edmond Bouchard to purchase Maria Elena's freedom. But Jim Bradshaw drew a gun on him as he was going down the stairs with the frightened girl. At her call of warning, Eddie turned, fired, and killed the saloon owner, though he himself had been slightly wounded. And on the return journey to Windhaven Range, Eddie had fallen desperately in love with this lovely, black-haired waif . . . a consolation after his fiancée, Polly Behting, had been killed in Chicago in the heroic act of trying to save a little child from an oncoming carriage.

Eddie Gentry had been at Corpus Christi when, four years ago after Fleurette's untimely death from diphtheria, Ben Wilson had brought little Thomas and Sybella to visit Fleurette's wonderful old mother, Sybella. Because Eddie had shown courage and steadfastness, the Quaker doctor had recommended that Lucien Edmond hire him as a cowhand.

Soon after Christmas last year, Eddie had married Maria Elena, and Lucien Edmond had given him fifty acres of good grazing land beyond Joe Duvray's acreage as a wedding present. With the help of many of the vaqueros, Eddie had built a little house for himself and his lovely Mexican bride. And now, somewhat to his own awe, Eddie found himself sitting in on this important conference which would decide what was to be done this year with the cattle of Windhaven Range.

"First off, Joe, Ramón, Eddie," Lucien Edmond began, "I want you to know that I'm not going to make the final decision. We're all in this together now as partners. By combining all our acreage, we intend to turn Windhaven Range into one of the largest cattle ranches in all of Texas. There's no ego involved. No, that's not important at all. All of us are partners now. And by banding together, just as we extend our boundaries to an overall limit which includes the acreage of each one of us, we can stand very strong against attack, whether it be from bandits or rustlers or bushwhackers."

"I agree with you, Lucien Edmond," the handsome young Mexican smilingly declared. "It's true that the last few years we've marketed the herds and gotten a good price. Last summer wasn't too good, as we all know: ten dollars a head for just under three thousand cattle doesn't match our record of previous years. After we paid the men, each of us taking a share of profit according to the agreement we'd arrived at before starting the drive, there wasn't much left. Not enough capital to buy what we need—more Brahmas, as well as some good Herefords and maybe even a few Durhams."

"I know what you're leading up to, Ramón," Lucien Edmond thoughtfully replied. "You're thinking that we should hold back our herd and develop it again this year. Last year we held back five thousand head, and if we continued in this way for several years, we would have a really big herd by the time the market swings upward again—as I know it must in a few years. But, coming back to the question of a drive this year: I wouldn't want to sell more than a thousand or fifteen hundred at most—those are the animals we really must sell this year—and for ten dollars a head or maybe even less this summer, I'm beginning to wonder if a drive would be worth it."

"I don't think so, Mr. Bouchard," Joe Duvray spoke up. "Me, I'd rather aim at a closer market. Why couldn't we sell some beef to the army posts?"

160

"That's not a bad idea," Lucien Edmond thoughtfully reflected as he stroked his chin. "I'd like to investigate that before I pass final judgment on it, Joe. But it's certainly worth thinking about. I think right now, in the next week or so, our vaqueros ought to go and make sure that all the boundary markers are up. If any strangers come calling, they'll see just one huge ranch, and the boundary markers will be for the total acreage of all us partners. That way, anybody who wants to tackle us will realize that he'll have to bite off a great deal more than he could possibly chew, unless he's got an army of gunmen to come against us. And that's not very likely."

"We could put some of the vaqueros to work on the bunkhouse and on your own house, Lucien Edmond. It could stand some painting and maybe we should even add an extra room or two," Ramón twitted his brother-in-law with an amiable grin. "Seems to me your new daughter will want a room to herself when she starts growing up."

"Yes," Lucien Edmond chuckled, "our newest was born as a kind of Christmas present to us both. And she looks like her mother, which means that in about eighteen years or so, if I'm still around to watch over her, I'll be fending off suitors right and left. But then, that's what a father's for, isn't it, Ramón?"

"That's true, *mi amigo*," Ramón assented. "So then we'll put some of the vaqueros to work doing useful things, and also we could use more horses. Even if we just take a *remuda* to an army post, it's a good idea to have fresh horses, well trained. And that reminds me—last week, when I was riding out just northeast of here about ten miles, I thought I saw a herd of wild mustangs. If they're still in the neighborhood, I'd like to go after a few of them."

"That's a very good idea. I tell you what I'll do," Lucien Edmond concluded. "There's a new commander now—you remember how Captain George Munson was in command there some years back and took his troops to massacre Sangrodo's stronghold when Sangrodo and his braves were out hunting. A rider from Uvalde on his way to Austin stopped over here last week for provisions, and told me that they've got quite a good-sized contingent of soldiers over there now. Well, it seems to me they could certainly use good fresh beef. And I've always heard that army quartermasters pay top prices for top quality. Yes, I'll send Simata out there tomorrow. Well, gentlemen, I think we're all of a mind that we'll hold off a bit before we make any elaborate plans for a big drive. We'll consolidate, we'll keep on interbreeding, and we'll strengthen and remodel and paint our properties so we can take pleasure in them—and for sure our womenfolk will share that pleasure. And now I'm inviting you all to supper, with your wives and children, of course. Maybelle Belcher has been wanting to cook a feast for some time now, and tonight's just as good a time as any."

Three weeks later, the courier delivered Dr. Ben Wilson's letter to Lucien Edmond Bouchard, who put him up for the night in the bunkhouse with the vaqueros and, seeing that his horse was nearly foundering, made him a present of one of the docile mustang geldings Ramón Hernandez had trained for the *remuda*. After reading the letter, he went in to visit his lovely chestnut-haired wife, Maxine, who was nursing their daughter, little Gloria. He stood watching with rapt delight at this tender maternal scene, and Maxine looked up at him and anxiously inquired, "Is it good news, Lucien Edmond darling?"

"In one sense, very much so, Maxine. I've a feeling I'll be able to spend much of this summer with you and our children. Ben Wilson's just written me that he's heard that the Kansas legislature is considering extending the quarantine line because the settlers are worried about fever ticks which Texas longhorns bring. That sounds so familiar. It reminds me of the days right after the Civil War when many cattlemen tried to get to Sedalia and were driven off by angry citizens. Often their herds were stolen and illegally sold. A lot of ranchers in those days were lucky to get away with their lives. I've been thinking all along that perhaps I shouldn't drive our cattle all the way to Kansas, and Ben's letter just about convinces me, even though the quarantine doesn't extend as far south and west as Wichita at present."

"That *is* good news, dearest. I feel like a widow every time you go off on one of those three-month cattle drives. Worst of all, I'm always so worried about what might happen to you and the men, what with bandits and Indians and rustlers and the like."

"God has been very good to us thus far, Maxine. I thank Him always in our little chapel. First, for giving you to me back in Alabama, and then for our family and the love we

162

have, and finally for all of the people who work with us here on Windhaven Range."

"I thank Him, too, for my husband and my children," she softly added, sending him a look of intense devotion and love.

He came to her and kissed her, then glanced down at Gloria. "I can see already that she has all her mother's beauty. As I was telling Ramón, it won't be long before I'll have to decide which suitors are the right ones for her."

"If she meets a man like her father, darling, you'll not have to worry," Maxine smilingly told him.

Three days after Ben Wilson's letter had arrived, Simata returned with news that would make Lucien Edmond Bouchard decide to forego the arduous, dangerous drive to the Kansas market.

Now in his early thirties, Simata was a Kiowa. His father had been a tribal chief and his mother a comely black. He had met Luke Bouchard in New Orleans nearly eight years earlier, when old Lucien's grandson had brought the family there to prepare for the journey that would lead them to Windhaven Range. Luke had protected Simata during the terrible time of the race riots in New Orleans, and the tall, handsome scout had dedicated his life to the Bouchard family, just as had Joe Duvray and Andy Haskins, whom Luke had met on a New Orleans wharf at about the same time. Luke often said that he believed in the Biblical adage of casting one's bread upon the waters so that it might be returned a hundredfold. Assuredly, what these three men he found in New Orleans had contributed to the success of the Bouchards was inestimable; above all, they were loyal, steadfast friends, and as much members of the Bouchard family as those related by blood—so Luke and his son Lucien Edmond had always felt.

"I rode first to Fort Inge," the Kiowa scout reported, "and there I talked with the new commander, Major Dana Creston. He is a good man, Mr. Lucien Edmond. He received me as if I had been a white-eyes, truly. And one of his men told me, as I was ready to leave, that he was sent to Fort Inge because in Washington they did not like what he said about the way the Indians were treated out here."

"I should like to meet Major Creston, and we shall give him a good price for what beef he buys," Lucien Edmond averred.

"After that, as Major Creston said I should do, I rode

southwest to Fort Duncan, which is at Eagle Pass. There, too, the soldiers would be glad to have good beef. There are not so many soldiers there as at Fort Inge, however."

"Thank you for this helpful information, Simata. I'm very pleased with what you've learned. Yes, I think that we might very well manage this year without a Kansas drive. If we could make more than one trip, and sell, say, five to seven hundred head to Fort Inge over a period of twelve months, and perhaps three to five hundred to Fort Duncan, we'd be doing well. On each trip, we'd cover perhaps a hundred or a hundred and fifty miles and easily be back within a few weeks. Our supply costs would be drastically cut, and even if we had to take a lower price than ten dollars a head, we'd still come out with a tidy little profit."

"I would be glad to ride with you when you go to the forts, Mr. Lucien Edmond," Simata volunteered.

"I want you to. Things are peaceful around this part of the country right now, and if we take cattle only that short distance this summer, we shan't need too many vaqueros. That way, we'll have plenty of men to guard Windhaven Range in the event there should be any unforeseen trouble. Altogether, I'm not at all displeased with the way things are going to turn out, Simata. I see you're smiling—does that mean you approve?"

Simata had permitted himself a faint smile after Lucien Edmond's remark about selling cattle to the army forts, but now it vanished and he stood stiffly, just as a scout might, reporting to a commander with whom he was on only the most impersonal of terms. Lucien Edmond, noticing this sudden change of demeanor, teasingly persisted: "Come now, Simata, you don't often smile, and that's why I noticed it just now. Did something happen on your long journey? Something you want to see again—wait, could it be you've found a pretty *muchacha* who looked on you with favor?"

"It's true, Mr. Lucien Edmond," Simata abashedly confessed. "At Fort Duncan, there was a Kiowa Apache woman who helps the cook. She is paid wages, too. The commander there, like Major Creston, does not believe in looking upon Indians as bloodthirsty enemies. Her name is Najalda, which means in my tongue Sky at Daybreak. Her parents were killed in a battle against Comanches, and a soldier found her in the burning village and took her to a little town near the fort. She was brought up by good peo-

164

ple; they taught her English, had her baptized in the Christian faith. When they died last year, she went to the fort and the commander there gave her work."

"Well, I'll confess that I've been hoping that you'd find a wife before long, Simata. I've always felt a man can't really be happy or channel his life in a clearcut direction unless he has a wife to inspire him, work with him, and share his dreams. But living out here in this isolated part of the country, there hasn't been much chance for you to meet someone you could care for. So I promise you that we'll certainly work out our drive so that at least I call on the commander at Fort Duncan, even if I don't sell him any beef. In that way, you can see your Najalda."

"You are a very kind man, Mr. Lucien Edmond." And now Simata was smiling broadly and shared Lucien Edmond's hearty laugh.

In mid-April, Lucien Edmond Bouchard dispatched a dozen vaqueros and two hundred head of yearlings, with Eddie Gentry as trail boss, to ride to Forts Inge and Duncan. Simata rode ahead as scout. Eddie was instructed to deliver a hundred head to each fort, to obtain a fair price, but not to argue over it. It was, as Lucien Edmond explained, a trial run. "If the army shows an interest in regular buying," he said, "it may very well be that we can count on a steady turnover of our cattle through the year. In the long run, as I'm sure you'll see, Eddie, that may turn out to be more profitable than taking a single huge herd to a Kansas market."

About three days after Eddie Gentry, the vaqueros, and Simata had ridden off, Ramón Hernandez came back late in the afternoon from working in the corral with several new mustangs he was breaking in and training for the *remuda*. He was alarmed to find that his beautiful dark-haired wife, Mara, and their youngest child, Edward, now eight months old, were flushed and hot with fever. Mara had put little Edward into his crib, and was in the act of putting a damp cloth on his forehead to break the fever as Ramón entered the bedroom. As she straightened, she swayed, put a hand to her head, and then sank down on her knees with a soft groan.

"*¿Querida, qué pasa?*" he anxiously cried as he hurried to her and gently lifted her to her feet, then drew her to the edge of the bed, where they both sat down.

"I—I don't know, Ramón," she faltered, her voice faint and weak. "I felt strange this morning when I woke up, and then Edward seemed to be hot and restless, and just now I felt dizzy."

"But what can it be?" he demanded, alarmed. "Is it from food, perhaps?"

"No—I—I don't think so, Ramón dear. All I can remember is that yesterday morning I went for a walk by the creek. There were lots of mosquitoes, and I think one bit me. Maybe one bit little Edward too. Could it be from that?"

"*Dios*, I hope not, *querida*!" he gasped. "But one thing's sure, we must have a doctor to see you both. But there's none around here."

"I—I'll be all right, if I rest a little. I'm sure Edward will feel better by tonight."

"I won't take that chance, not with you two. And the other children—I'll have Maybelle Belcher look after them so that if this thing is contagious, they won't come down with it, too." He felt her forehead and bit his lips with anxiety. "Yes, you do have a fever. I do not know what it can be. It is true that the creek is stagnant this time of year; perhaps the mosquitoes carried some poison in their bite—I am not a *médico*, but I know that we must have one and as quickly as possible." Suddenly he brightened. "I will ride to Wichita and bring back Dr. Ben Wilson. He will cure you." Then, scowling with growing apprehension, "But it will take long weeks to ride all the way to Wichita and as many for him to return here—I've a better idea! I'll ride to San Antonio and send a telegram to Wichita for him to come as quickly as he can, my dear one. He is the only doctor I can truly trust in a situation like this. Maybelle will look after you and so will Maxine and Felicidad. Oh, I pray the good *Señor Dios* you will not grow worse until Dr. Wilson can come here to cure you and the *niño*!"

He hurried to the ranch house and informed Lucien Edmond of the plight of his wife and younger son, then hurried to the Belchers. Maybelle at once went over to the house to tend to Mara and Edward, while Ramón mounted a black mustang stallion, not yet fully broken in, but on which he could count for the swiftest ride to the telegraph office a hundred twenty miles from Carrizo Springs.

Hardly stopping to eat or to sleep, he came into San Antonio on the third morning, hurried to the telegraph office

166

and, his voice breaking with strain and exhaustion, told the elderly telegrapher what he required. A few minutes later, as he leaned forward on the counter and drew breath upon breath, he heard the clicking of the telegraph key, closed his eyes, and silently prayed.

He told the telegrapher that he would go to a hotel for some much-needed sleep and return in several hours to see if there was a reply. Then, after stabling his horse, he engaged a room, flung himself down on the bed, and fell fast asleep. When he woke in the early afternoon, he hurried back to the telegrapher's office, and there found a message from Dr. Ben Wilson.

Am leaving today for Windhaven Range. Symptoms you describe may be blackwater fever: days of fever, then intervals of chills before next fever period. Advise you to use cinchona bark as treatment. Bark supplies quinine to counteract blood parasites. Try to obtain from doctor in San Antonio, or there may be cinchona trees near Windhaven Range. I will try to get some from Emataba. Small pieces of bark should be used as tablets, chewed but not swallowed. Use sparingly; too much can be poisonous.

Dr. Ben Wilson

Ramón fervently thanked the old telegrapher, paid for the telegram, and added a substantial bonus. He then visited several doctors, but was unable to obtain the remedy the Quaker doctor had suggested. After paying his bill at the hotel and then the stable, he spurred the black stallion back to Windhaven Range.

Subsisting on jerky and water from his canteen, and allowing only a few hours of rest for himself and his sturdy mount, he rode up to the stockade late in the evening of the third day. Hurrying to his house, he found Felicidad and Maybelle there caring for his wife and little one. Mara lay in bed, the prey of a recurrent bout of fever, perspiring, her teeth chattering, almost delirious, as she murmured, "Ramón—*querido*—the little one—I am so sick—thank God you're back—my husband—poor little Edward, I am so afraid for him—"

He turned questioningly to Maybelle Belcher, who was trying to ease Mara by placing another pillow under her shoulders and pressing a cloth dipped in cool well water

167

onto her flushed face. "Has she been like this since I left, Maybelle?" he hoarsely demanded.

"No, Ramón, she's had spells of chills and then this fever. And Felicidad's been looking after Edward—he's been the same way, poor little fellow."

"Felicidad," he turned to Lucas's attractive young wife, "I sent a telegram to Dr. Ben Wilson in Wichita. He told me to try to get cinchona bark and to make them chew it. Just a little. It has quinine, and that will drive away the fever. I could not find any in San Antonio."

"Pero sí," Felicidad eagerly responded. "I know there is such a tree to the north of the creek. I will go there now and get the bark."

"God bless you, Felicidad!" Ramón gasped. Then he sank down on his knees, reached for his wife's hand, kissed it, and murmured soothingly, "I am here now, *mi corazón,* everything will be all right now, you will see. Rest, and Felicidad will get some medicine that will help you till Dr. Ben Wilson gets here."

Then he went to the crib where Edward lay, crying fitfully, his face flushed, beads of sweat on his tiny forehead. Agonized, Ramón clasped his hands in prayer and his lips moved as he looked upwards, invoking the divine power to intercede for his helpless little son.

While Felicidad hurried out to the creek, Maybelle heated some chicken broth. "You'd best have a bowl yourself, Ramón, you look ready to drop," she declared. Then, her face lined with concern, she murmured, "I hope it isn't the river fever they have in New Orleans in the summer."

"But how could it be? Do not even think that, Maybelle. *El Señor Dios* could not be so cruel to my sweet Mara and little Edward. We are here in the country, where there is only the sweet grass and the open air, not the rats and the garbage and the filth of a city like New Orleans. How could they become so sick? And if this bark does not work—may the holy saints watch over us—it will take Dr. Ben Wilson nearly three weeks to ride here from Wichita, it is at least seven hundred miles! I must go to the chapel and pray."

"Not till you have a bowl of broth, and that's an order, Ramón," Maybelle firmly insisted. "It won't do Mara and Edward any good if you drop in your tracks from the way you've ridden to San Antonio and back, probably without sleep and almost no food, worrying every minute of the time. Now you sit down at the table and I'll get the soup for you. I'm sure God has heard your prayers, Ramón, and Felicidad and I and Lucien Edmond and Maxine and all the vaqueros have been praying, too."

Distraught, the young Mexican burst into tears which Maybelle pretended not to notice as she ladled out the soup and set it before him, together with some freshly baked biscuits.

Felicidad had found the cinchona tree and cut off a few small pieces of bark; she returned to the house and came into the kitchen as Ramón was finishing his meal.

"This is what *el señor médico* wishes," she eagerly announced.

"Not too much, he said in his telegram," Ramón urged. "Little bits for them to chew. Felicidad, give it to Edward, but please be careful."

"Of course, I will, Señor Hernandez," she assured him.

"Now you go to the chapel and pray and I'll attend to Mara, Ramón," Maybelle solicitously urged.

Mara grimaced at the bitter taste of the bark, but managed to chew it till it was pulp. "Don't swallow it, whatever you do," Maybelle anxiously ordered, and retrieved it from the trembling lips of Ramón's wife.

Felicidad chewed a bit of the bark herself, to loosen its juices, then wrapped the morsel in one layer of a loosely woven coth. The cloth would prevent any fragment of the bark from coming loose and being swallowed. She then introduced the cloth and bark between Edward's lips. The baby promptly spat it out, but Felicidad determinedly repeated the process until she was sure that Edward had sucked some of the beneficial juices.

When Ramón returned from the chapel, his face drawn and haggard, Maybelle assured him that both his wife and little son had successfully taken the prescribed medicine. "*Bueno, muchas gracias,*" he hoarsely gasped. "I will sleep here in this room on a blanket, so I can be near my wife and child. I have prayed, Maybelle, and you pray also. If anything happens to them, I will have no zest for life, I will be a lost soul."

"Now don't you start talking like that, you know better, Ramón," Maybelle scolded him, but softened her harsh words by gently touching his shoulder. "In the morning, when you've had a good sleep, things will be better. And Felicidad will go and get some more bark in the morning."

169

"Of course, I will, Señor Hernandez," Felicidad emphatically nodded.

On this late April morning, the sky was cloudless and the sun mercilessly beat down. There had been little rain in Carrizo Springs, but the bountiful water from the underground well, together with irrigation from the Nueces River, fortunately was sufficient to meet the needs of the Bouchards and their workers.

Mara Hernandez and her baby Edward seemed to have improved in their battle against the fever; Mara could talk more coherently, and the chills seemed less overwhelming. Ramón, who had slept all night long on a pallet flung down on the floor beside his wife's bed, was quick to see the improvement, and gave silent thanks as he hurried out to the kitchen and helped Maybelle Belcher prepare a simple breakfast for his wife. He contented himself with a cup of coffee and a piece of melon, and took a tray in to Mara. Her eyes seemed less dilated and glassy from the fever; she put out a hand to touch his arm and he trembled with an inexpressible joy at this fortuitous sign. Edward, too, seemed less restless, and was sleeping, although fitfully.

"Thank the good God you're almost well, *querida*," he murmured as he stroked her hair and looked lovingly at her. Then, glancing over at the crib where little Edward lay, he added, "My prayers have been heard. And Dr. Ben Wilson is on the way. He is a good, kind man, and I have a feeling that he will cure both of you and that this illness will pass and you will be stronger than ever, *mi corazón.*"

"You're so dear to me, Ramón," Mara whispered, groping for his hand. Her voice was wan and weak, but he could feel the pressure of her fingers and he thrilled to it. "How lucky I was that you rode after me that day, after I'd insulted you because you were Mexican. I'm so happy you taught me how much I really needed you."

"It is not a question of victory of one or the other, my dear one," he murmured. "*El Señor Dios* tested both of us, and saw that we needed each other. That is all that counts. And now that I have you, I'll never let you go; we shall have long years together and many more children."

He chuckled with gratified relief to see a faint blush suffuse her pale cheeks at this suggestion. She closed her eyes and lay back on the pillows, but he could still feel the pressure of her fingers against his hand. "That's good;

170

sleep, my dear one. Felicidad has gone out to get more of the cinchona bark. It will keep you and the *niño* protected until our good friend can come from Wichita."

He heard her faint sign of acquiescence, then he turned as he heard Maybelle entering the room, bustling with encouragement and good humor.

"It would do you good to get outdoors and do some work with the horses, Ramón," she jocularly bade him. "I'm here now, and you know yourself that a woman can take better care of a woman than any man."

"I won't argue with you, Maybelle." He laughed more heartily than he had in weeks. "You yourself radiate health, and so I know that it will be contagious for my beloved *esposa* and my youngest son. And you're right, it would do me good to break in some rebellious horses just to make sure that I haven't lost my ability."

"That's the way for a man to talk. Now skedaddle, and for your information, Henry is looking after your other children, and so are Timmy and Connie." Maybelle was referring to Henry Belcher's two children by his first marriage. "I declare, those young ones are sprouting up so fast I hardly recognize them one year from another, and I've already told Henry that he oughtn't be surprised if in a couple of years he becomes a grandfather." Maybelle patted him on the shoulder and summarily dismissed him with a toss of the head. He laughed aloud again, the weight of his concern greatly lifted by her exuberant optimism.

Felicidad had hurried out to the corral, where her sturdy husband, Lucas, was busying himself working with the mustangs. She carried little Celia with her left arm, hugging the eight-month-old baby against her firm young bosom, while James—named after Lucas's heroic father, Djamba, and now two and a half years old—clung to her other hand and toddled after her, looking up at his attractive young Mexican mother and prattling words that only she could understand.

Lucas waved to her from the corral, and she nodded gaily and gestured with her head that she was going toward the creek. The cinchona tree was to the southeast. She had a small paring knife in the pocket of her skirt.

When she reached the tree, she carefully set Celia down and let go of James's hand, then cried out with joy to see that her *aplomado* falcon, Coraje, was swooping overhead. How thoughtful it was of Lucas to free the falcon, which she had cared for ever since they had found it fallen from a tree as a young bird with a broken wing. Now it constantly circled over her wherever she went, perching nearby and uttering its shrill little cry to tell her that it had not forgotten her. Nor had Felicidad forgotten, in her turn, how aptly this savage bird of prey had been named. When the two bushwhackers, Marve Fenstrom and Jake Ellison, had invaded the ranchhouse nearly four years ago while the vaqueros, Ramón, and Lucien Edmond had been on their way to Abilene with their herd, she had brought Coraje out of his cage, seized a carbine, and, entering the living room where the two ruffians were holding Maxine and old Sybella Bouchard Forsden at bay, tossed the carbine to Maxine and flung Coraje into Marve Fenstrom's face. Sybella had been slightly wounded, but the two bushwhackers had been killed. Truly, Coraje had earned his rightful place on Windhaven Range!

"Mi halcón querido," she called, waving her hand to the blue-colored falcon perching on a branch of a nearby pecan tree, "it's good of you to come wish us all a good morning. Now you watch there while I cut some bark so that Mara Bouchard and her *niño* Edward will soon be well, do you understand, Coraje?"

The falcon flapped its wings and uttered a shrill caw, as if it truly understood what its young mistress had said to it. Felicidad giggled happily. *"Bueno,* Coraje! You grow more intelligent each year. Truly, one day Lucas and I will have to have a serious talk with you. It is time you found a mate. You have earned your freedom many times over, Coraje. You are loyal and brave and you have watched over us all. *Muchas gracias,* Coraje!"

She glanced quickly at little Celia, named after Lucas's mother, that strikingly handsome young mulatto girl whom Henry Bouchard, so many years ago, had purchased from Pierre Lourat and secretly brought to Windhaven to be his concubine. His wife, Sybella—then young and high-mindedly determined to make her dissolute husband recognize her as an equal—had demanded that Henry set Celia free. He had refused, saying that Celia was his slave; later, when his teenaged son Mark had crept into the bedroom where he had secreted the girl and had been the first to possess her, Henry and his son had come to blows. Finally, Sybella had herself manumitted Celia, and when Henry

172

had attempted to exercise his rights as master, she had taken a pistol and broken into the bedroom where he was lying with Celia. This wifely defiance, so stunningly unexpected, had given Henry Bouchard a fatal heart attack.

Two years ago, Sybella had died on the very same day that Djamba—who had once been a king of the Mandingo tribe in Africa—had also died, in saving his own son, Lucas. It had been Sybella's express wish that Djamba and Celia should wed, and it seemed fitting now that the daughter of their son Lucas should be named after the child's grandmother, whose destiny had been so intertwined with the early saga of the Bouchards.

The baby clapped her hands, looking about wonderingly, and Felicidad laughed joyously as she herself moved toward the cinchona tree. Assiduously, she cut small pieces of bark and put them into the pocket of her skirt, all her attention given to her task. She did not see that James had impatiently wandered off toward the creek; when she looked up again, he was almost at the bank of the creek and she uttered a horrified cry as she saw a small brown snake crawling toward the little boy.

"Oh, *mi Dios*, save him, oh, what have I done—" she hysterically cried, paralyzed with fear.

But suddenly the falcon, its bright yellow eyes gleaming, sprang into the air from the branch on which it perched, and swooped down toward the bank of the creek. Its sharp beak struck the head of the poisonous snake, and as it ascended, Felicidad, astonished, speechless, could see the serpent wriggling in the clutch of Coraje's beak.

Sobbing wildly, she ran to her little boy and clutched him to her bosom, weeping, almost incoherent in her gratitude.

James could not understand the reason for such excitement. He seemed to frown, then pointed upward to the sky where Coraje soared, and petulantly declared, "See bird with snake? Bird take pretty snake away from little James. Bad bird. Snake pretty!"

"Oh my darling, my *niño*, Coraje has saved you! Just as he saved the señoras Maxine and Sybella," Felicidad tremulously exclaimed, as she hugged and kissed the little boy. Then, turning back, she ran to the little girl still sitting clapping her hands and looking up into the sky while Coraje circled, the inert body of the reptile tightly clutched

173

in its beak. "Celia, sweetheart, *mi querida*, now we'll go back home. You have been such a good girl, I will make you something very nice this evening, you'll see."

Tears unrestrainedly streamed down her face. Lucas came running from the corral, having heard his young wife's frightened cry when first their little son had spied the deadly snake. "Felicidad, honey, what is it? What made you cry out like that?"

"God is so good." She turned to him, her eyes blinded by her tears. "He has given me you and our two lovely children. And He has given us Coraje, who protects us even when I am stupid and do not watch as I should. Oh, *mi amor*, hold me very close, but what you should really do is whip me for being so forgetful of the two I love best next to you. It was a snake, Lucas, *mi esposo querido*, and if it had not been for Coraje, I could not have faced you— forgive your stupid little wife."

"Now, now, honey, it's all right. Of course, I won't whip you. I'm the one who ought to be whipped for not coming out and helping you. There always are snakes near that creek, and I know it as well as you do. Now, don't carry on so. That's right, cry it out." He put his arms around her and drew her to him, and they kissed in a fervent pledge of their trust and love.

CHAPTER SIXTEEN

The improvised quinine treatments, which Felicidad and Maybelle repeated daily through the next week, taking care not to give either Mara or little Edward too much of the bitter alkaloid substance, served to break their fever. By the first week of May, both Ramón's spirited wife and the baby had greatly improved, though Mara remained listless and pale after her bout with the mysterious fever. Edward, too, seemed to have suffered some aftereffects in his noticeable irritability and uneven eating habits, which greatly worried Mara. During this period, Ramón was constantly with his wife, assuring her that Dr. Ben Wilson would soon be at Windhaven Range. And this prediction came true when, scarcely eighteen days after he had replied to Ramón's anguished telegram, the Quaker doctor rode up to the gate of the stockade. He was escorted by two young braves from Emataba's village. The *mico* had sent them to guarantee the safety of this gentle man who refused to carry a weapon across the lawless plains.

Ben had spent two brief hours at the Creek reservation. When he explained to Emataba his need for cinchona bark, the *mico* gave him an ample supply of it, for, of course, such a remedy was known to the Creeks; they had brought large quantities of it with them when they had been forcibly transplanted from their original home in Alabama to this desolate section of Indian Territory. The Quaker doctor was heartened to see that there was no illness among Emataba's people, and that they were content with the new army doctor, who made monthly calls and gave thorough examinations to the elderly and ailing. Best of all, there was no want of food: Douglas Larrimer had kept his promise and was as dedicated as Ben himself in caring for these dispossessed native Americans.

Emataba replaced the Quaker doctor's weary gelding with a fine mustang mare one of his braves had captured and tamed. In return, Ben had brought a large package of candy from Jacob Hartmann's store to be distributed among the children of the village. There were tears in his eyes as he stood with the tall *mico*—visibly aging and drawn with the cares of his people—and greeted the villagers who hurried up to him, recognizing him as the man who had been their beloved shaman. Unlike so many white-eyes they had known, he had taken an Indian wife whom he respected and loved as deeply as if she, too, had been a white-eyes.

He had ridden on, with two of the strongest young braves of Emataba's village alongside him, inwardly rejoicing at this proof that his work had not been in vain. A great peace had come over him, and the soul of his first wife, Fleurette, seemed to communicate with him as he rode south. It was as if she were watching over him now— as in fact it seemed to him that she had always done, ever since she had been taken from him. Ben even thought sometimes that perhaps—since surely she was among the angels—she had interceded long ago to let him meet Elone so that his life might be completed and fulfilled. In an almost mystical way, he felt that Elone and little Tisinqua had been miraculously sent to him for the renewal of his life, so completely dedicated to medicine and to the service of those who needed his ability to heal, to ease, and to comfort.

Ramón and Lucien Edmond joyously welcomed him, and saw to it that the two young Creeks were quartered in the bunkhouse, their horses stabled and fed, and they themselves served an appetizing repast. Ben went at once with Ramón to the latter's house and entered the room in which Mara lay in bed, propped up on two pillows. Maybelle Belcher was solicitously making certain that Ramón's black-haired wife finished all of the good chicken broth she had just made that morning.

"Ben, how good it is to see you!" Mara exclaimed, sitting upright, her eyes brightening.

"It's good to see you too, Mara. The quinine helped, thank God. It was all I could think of. It's hard for a doctor to diagnose from long distance, but when I received

176

Ramón's telegram and he told me of the fever, I was sure that this bark would help, and so it has. But now, Mara, you have to get your strength back. I'm going to talk to Maybelle and Felicidad, I'll examine little Edward, and we'll try to get you both back on your feet."

"To think you've ridden all this long way—Fleurette was very lucky to have a man like you, Ben," Mara faintly said with a wan smile.

"I was blessed to meet her, and I feel almost as if I were a Bouchard, Mara. The lesson that all of you have shown is one of abiding love and faith and loyalty. Though you are Catholic, Mara, the creed that guides you is not so far removed from my own Quaker faith. But now, drink up all that broth, it'll be good for you, and I'll go see Edward."

Felicidad had put Edward's crib into the adjoining room; she entered his room now and for a time sat watching the sleeping child. The baby's color had improved, but there were little restless movements and faint querulous sounds, which told the Quaker doctor that the child had not yet totally shaken off the fever. His face became taut and he concentrated on his work. He took Edward's pulse, put his hand on the baby's forehead, examined the back of the child's ears, and was satisfied that there were no swollen glands.

He turned to Felicidad. "Of course, the child doesn't nurse any longer with Mara, Felicidad."

"No, Señor Ben." She shook her head.

"It's as well. I think her milk might be tainted from the fever. I suppose you've been feeding the baby some broth and, as you did with the bark, chewing a bit of meat and perhaps vegetables and then putting the morsels between the baby's lips?"

"*Pero sí*, Señor Ben!" the attractive young Mexican girl eagerly nodded assent.

"Good! Now, since the fever has broken, though his pulse is not so strong as I'd like it, give him quinine just every other day just before the sun sets. You see, I've found that, when people have fevers, they come on strongly at night, even though during the day the patients seem perfectly normal."

"I will remember, Señor Ben."

"Thank you, Felicidad. Eventually, with Mara, the poison of this fever—which I am convinced was conveyed by the mosquito bites Ramón mentioned in his telegram—will pass. With a baby so young, however, it's not quite so easy. I shall stay here until I am sure that Edward is completely cured. And I hope that you can help me."

"I will do all I can, you need not ask that, Señor Ben."

"Lucas is lucky to have a *mujer* like you, Felicidad." He smiled gently at her, as she blushed and lowered her eyes in self-effacing modesty. "Since Edward won't nurse with Mara, I'd be inclined to suggest you give the baby a little milk. There are cows here on Windhaven Range, and there should be plenty of milk."

"*Pero sí*, there is milk for my little James." She blushed again and lowered her eyes. "But I still feed Celia myself—you understand, Señor Ben."

"Of course. That's good. We know this fever isn't contagious, because you've been with Mara and Edward for quite some time now, and there's no sign. Yes, decidedly, it must have been those mosquitoes. I've always had the conviction that insects or animals could transmit diseases to humans, although my colleagues in Pittsburgh used to laugh at my ideas as being wildly radical." For a moment, he closed his eyes, thinking of Benjamin Hardesty, the ironworks mogul who once had him discharged from his post at the Pittsburgh hospital because he had wished to offer a clinic for the poor. What an irony of life it was that, when Benjamin Hardesty had been near death, he had sent for Ben and driven away his own fawning physician. Ben had operated on Hardesty to prevent strangulation in the windpipe from the attack of diphtheria that had seized the industrialist. The same disease had stricken his gentle Fleurette, and God had willed that she should die and Benjamin Hardesty live; there was an eternal reason for the will of our dear Lord, and now he did not question it. With Elone and the children she had given him, and Thomas and Sybella, he was once again completed, purposefully channeled toward the life that had been originally intended for him when he had first wanted to study medicine.

When he opened his eyes, he saw Felicidad looking at him with a compassionate concern that deeply touched him. He turned back to the child in the crib, again felt Edward's pulse and passed his palm over the baby's forehead. "I think a little exercise every day, in great moderation, would be helpful. Perhaps Edward can be put down on the carpet and allowed to crawl a little. It would be good for him. It would sweat out the poison, and it would develop his muscles, which have been weakened by this feverish attack," he pronounced at last.

"That is very easy, Señor Ben. I will do whatever you tell me. I love the Señora Mara and her children."

"And Dolores, Ramón, and Jaime are well?" he pursued.

"Oh yes, very well, Señor Ben! Maybelle and her family are looking after them."

"It was very good to isolate them—I hadn't thought of that when I first got Ramón's telegram. And even though I think now that this fever is not contagious, but caused by the bite of the mosquitoes near the creek, it's still a good idea to keep them away from Mara and little Edward." He rose, smoothing back the unruly lick of hair from his forehead, and Felicidad smiled at him. She could understand why the *indios* respected him. He was a good, true man, a man like her own blessed Lucas. How fortunate she had been, she thought now, recalling how she, an orphan, had very nearly become the *criatura* of the owner of a *posada* in Nuevo Laredo. The vaquero Vittorio Salencár had seen her weeping, had learned her story, and had brought her back to Windhaven Range to be employed by old Sybella Bouchard Forsden in the kitchen. Then Lucas had fallen in love with her, and now she was a wife and mother, knowing herself loved, and happy to have given her strong young husband children.

"I'm going to the chapel to pray now, Felicidad," Ben softly told her.

"*Sí*, Señor Ben, *comprendo*." Her eyes were luminous as she fixed his homely face with an instant gaze. "Pray also for Lucas and me and our *niños*."

"Of course, I will. *Hasta la vista*, Felicidad!"

Certain that all was well within the Hernandez house and thankful that his suggested remedy for the fever had saved both Mara and her youngest child, the Quaker doctor went out toward the creek south of the Bouchard ranch house. He walked slowly, and his hands were clasped in prayer. He stood at last before the oak tree in which Felicidad had found her *aplomado* falcon, Coraje. There was a marker there, to signify the last earthly resting place of Sybella Bouchard Forsden. Tears came to his eyes as he read the inscription. The marker gave only the birth and death dates, and her name, with the simple phrase: *Loved by all, God rest her soul.*

He thought how appropriate it was that this young Mexican orphan Felicidad had herself proposed Sybella's burial place. That valiant white-haired woman who had learned how to use a Spencer carbine and herself had defended Windhaven Range during bandit attacks would have understood the symbolism. It was proof again that the eternal cycle of life went on and that grief was replaced by an abiding love and faith in restoration and fulfillment.

He knelt down now and said a prayer for Sybella, paying homage to her courage and her indomitable optimism and integrity, qualities she had imparted to the young red-haired girl who had been his gentle, loyal first wife.

When he rose, he turned to look out at the vast fields of Windhaven Range, and from a distance he could hear the cattle lowing. The sun was bright in the sky, and there was a soft murmur of the creek. Truly these things were timeless; truly the very goodness of God and the richness of His earth would survive all wounds, all hatreds, and all evils. Even in death there was life, he knew it well, having found Elone and Tisinqua in that dejected little village of Creeks who had once ruled the South.

He thought of his boyhood back in Pittsburgh. Now he was thirty-nine years old, yet he had greater zest for life than he had ever before known. That was Fleurette's legacy to him, born of the love and the steadfast devotion each had shown the other. In transmitting this same devotion to Elone, he was paying tribute to the memory of Fleurette Bouchard. And so it would be always, until his last breath, and he thanked God that he understood it and was enraptured by it.

He turned toward the north and thought of Wichita and the contrast between that bustling, noisy town and the serene, almost primitive peacefulness of Windhaven Range. That was his home now. And in a few weeks more, he would be a father. He would go to the chapel now and pray that it would be a boy, because he wanted to name it after kindly Jacob Hartmann. There again was the hand of God; He had directed Ben to that good man, a leader of his own faith in that rawboned town out on the plains, when he had gone there to buy supplies for the impoverished Creeks. It was always the same; everywhere Ben could see the singular miracles of God's design wrought in his own insignificant life.

As never before, he felt himself an integral part of the

Bouchard clan. He had come to Windhaven Range and met Lucien Bouchard, Luke's oldest son, and only this morning the latter had mentioned that last month he had sent off a telegram congratulating his father, Luke, on the latter's fifty-seventh birthday. And Luke Bouchard, at an age which many considered advanced, had revitalized his legendary grandfather's dream of a commune where all men would be equal and work side by side in harmony. Luke had lost his wife, just as he, Ben Wilson, had; and in return, he had been given Laure and children by her. Was this, too, not yet another proof of the eternal vigilance and justice and goodness of our dear Lord?

His heart was too full to be content with merely thinking these thoughts. So he went to the chapel, which Friar Bartoloméo Alicante had dedicated. It stood southeast of the bunkhouse where the vaqueros were quartered, framed by two large oak trees. The vaqueros had lovingly painted it white only a few weeks ago to make it seem shining and new, and its doors were always open to those who sought the comfort of prayer.

It was empty now, and he went to the front row of pews and prayed silently for a long moment. In his prayers were thanks for the bounty of the Bouchards, for the kindly way they had welcomed him and little Thomas and Sybella when he had come from Pittsburgh, agonized by the loss of Fleurette, feeling nothing inside save anger and grief. Yes, he confessed contritely, there had even been moments when he had railed against God's own justice in taking her life but sparing Benjamin Hardesty. Had that affliction and sorrow been a trial imposed upon him to test his faith? He could see now that it had been, and he was at peace with himself because he understood it. Fleurette was at peace too, and surely wherever she was in heaven, she saw how in his love for Elone he was rekindling that never-to-be-forgotten love he had pledged to her and fulfilled in the relatively short span they had been together.

He wept again, unashamedly. It was a purge, a kind of spiritual catharsis. There was no anguish in it, only a joyous knowledge of his own redemption and the reaffirmation of a strong belief in the peaceful, unselfish friendship for all mankind, which was the very core of the Quaker faith. He would never again question that faith, not after that Sunday in Wichita when one of his patients had defended him against the scurrilous slurs of a drunken cowhand. He was needed, even if the acclamation of the un-sentimental people of Wichita never went beyond grudging acceptance. He would serve them as he had served the Creeks. And because people of all kinds, all faiths, all be-liefs mattered to him, he would never question by what standards they lived, but judge them only in their very hu-man need for the medical services he could render. That would be his duty and his inspiration.

He left the chapel, his shoulders straight and a smile on his homely, earnest face. As he turned to look at the chapel, he idly wondered what had happened to Friar Bar-toloméo, that jovial, dedicated man of God who had been an outcast from Santa Fe because the rich had inveighed against him to the Bishop of Madrid, spitefully accusing him of catering more to the poor and to the Indians than to the elite of the town.

Over two hundred years ago, George Fox, who had founded the Society of Friends, had turned from organized religion to a direct, personal relationship with God through the "Inward Light" of Christ. He had been persecuted and imprisoned, mocked, abused, and scorned. Fox had be-lieved that every man upon this earth is involved with his neighbor, and each should turn to the other in friendship; then there could be no wars, nor suspicions, nor enmities. It was a lesson the world had not yet accepted; but for Dr. Ben Wilson on this sunny May day in Carrizo Springs, it was a magnificently satisfying truth, which would con-stantly give him the strength to continue on the path that had been chosen for him.

CHAPTER SEVENTEEN

Ten days after the Quaker doctor's arrival at Windhaven Range, Eddie Gentry, Simata, and the vaqueros who had driven the small herd to the two army forts rode back. Nacio Lorcas, whose hard work and cheerful acceptance of the most menial tasks assigned to him had led Joe Duvray to promote him to assistant foreman on the latter's ranch, had gone along as one of the point riders. Indeed, this sturdy, always affable vaquero had impressed Ramón Hernandez in his work with the horses, and still more so when, after he had learned that Ramón's wife and baby were ill with fever, he volunteered to ride to San Antonio to bring back a doctor. Ramón had pondered this possibility briefly but had decided in the end to go himself. He had wanted to avoid choosing a doctor at random in San Antonio, and he had been eager to send the telegram to Ben and to receive the reply with instructions at the earliest possible moment.

Eddie Gentry went at once to Lucien Edmond's study, where the latter was working on his accounts, to report the success of the cattle sales.

"Both the commanders were happy to get the beef and they want lots more, Mr. Lucien Edmond," he declared. "The prices weren't anything like Newton, but at least we made some money for you, and we didn't have the cost of supplies or the wear and tear on the *remuda* and on the men too, for that matter."

"That's what I'd calculated, Eddie. Well now, how much did you bring back?"

Eddie took out a leather pouch into which he had put the greenbacks the quartermasters at Forts Duncan and Inge had given him in payment. "Well, we picked up seven-fifty a head at Fort Duncan, and eight dollars at

Fort Inge. The commander there has a taste for prime quality beef, he says, and he'd like maybe two or three hundred more head before September and even more by the end of the year."

"We'll be glad to furnish that. And if we can sell to both forts on a regular basis, Eddie, it might turn out to be a better deal than the three-months' drive to Kansas, only to find when we got there that either the quarantine had been extended still farther, or else the bottom had dropped out of the market entirely."

"Do you really think that might happen, Mr. Lucien Edmond?" Eddie anxiously asked.

"Well, all I can tell you is that when Ben Wilson sent us this letter about the quarantine, he mentioned some talk about prices, too. And my father wrote me from Alabama, about the near-bankruptcy of his state because of the railroad scandal and about some of the things that are going on in Washington. I wouldn't be surprised to see prices drop all over the country. The last time I was in San Antonio at our bank, the president himself told me that he was pulling in his horns on loans to ranchers and raising his interest on loans to people who were building stores and houses and the like." Lucien Edmond frowned and shook his head. "It's a troubled time, Eddie. We're eight years past a war that ruined the South and made the North the dominant economic power, and three years away from celebrating the centennial of this vast new country, but things aren't going smoothly yet. I think Father was very right when he predicted that if Grant was reelected, we'd have a flock of new carpetbaggers who wouldn't just concentrate on the South, but would try to swindle wherever they found good pickings. That's the way I'm beginning to feel, too. But anyhow, I'm glad you delivered the herd and made a good contact for us at those forts." Then he leaned back in his chair and grinned. "Did Simata see his new girl?"

"He sure did, Mr. Lucien Edmond," Eddie slapped his thigh and guffawed. "That Najalda at Fort Duncan—she's a looker, all right. Taller than most Apache girls, I hear tell, and thick black hair in a braid, flashing eyes, but real soft when she powwowed with Simata." He winked broadly. "I've a hunch that Simata will be wanting to ride with us every time we take cattle to Fort Duncan, and he'll be disappointed when he hears that we probably don't go back there till next month."

184

"Well, for that matter," Lucien Edmond good-naturedly remarked, "since we're going to have an easy summer of it doing odd jobs and going on with our cross-breeding and waiting to see which way the market jumps, you can tell him for me I've no objection if he takes a week or two off as a kind of vacation and goes riding out to court his Indian girl. Tell him that faint heart ne'er won fair lady."

"I'll do just that, Mr. Lucien Edmond. Now, if you'll excuse me, I want to get back to Maria Elena."

"I think you're going to have a very pleasant surprise when you do, Eddie."

"Oh? What's that, Mr. Lucien Edmond?"

"Well, I really shouldn't be the one to tell you, but it seems that Maria Elena told Felicidad and she told my wife, Maxine, who told me. It appears that you're going to be a father before the end of the year."

Eddie emitted a low whistle, then flung down his sombrero on the floor and let out a rebel yell. "Excuse me, Mr. Lucien Edmond," he said abashedly as he stooped to retrieve the sombrero, "but I just had to do it. Darn it all, if I'd known that, I'd have tried to bring her back a present or something."

"I think right now she'd much rather have you, Eddie. And it couldn't happen to a better man. You deserve all the happiness you get and then some, for what you've done for us here on Windhaven Range."

"Shucks, Mr. Lucien Edmond, you ought to chew me out now and then instead of saying such nice things about me all the time. I'll get slack and lazy if you keep doing that."

"No you won't, that's not Eddie Gentry. But wait—speaking of presents, I sent some of the vaqueros to San Antonio last month to bring back supplies and I had them shop for a few little things for Maxine, one of which I haven't given her yet. It's a lace shawl, Eddie, and now that I think of it, a lovely Mexican girl like Maria Elena might just take a greater fancy to it than Maxine. Besides, I've something special in mind for her for our next anniversary, anyway. I'll get it for you—it's in the drawer of my desk, wrapped and waiting."

He leaned forward to open the lower drawer of his sturdy desk, took out a parcel, and handed it to the delighted cowboy. "With my compliments to Maria Elena, but you tell her it's from you, Eddie, and that you got it when you were out on this drive. A little white lie like that won't hurt at all, and the recording angels aren't likely to give you a bad mark in their books. Now get off with you!"

In this month of May 1873, there was little news from Washington, and nothing of the gathering economic crisis. The Montgomery *Advertiser*, as well as the San Antonio *Express-News*, reported that on May 1 the government had inaugurated the one-cent postal card for the use of mailed messages, but there was little other news of interest. At home, however, the news was all good. The third week of May found Mara Hernandez and little Edward fully recovered from the wasting, prolonged fever that had beset them. Dr. Ben Wilson had been busy during the period of recuperation; doggedly, realizing the greater potential danger to a nine-month-old baby, he had administered all the therapeutic care he knew, calling upon his memory of his early training in the handling of infants and young children. It was essential that Edward regain his strength so that the ravages of the fever would not linger and affect any of his vital organs.

At last, with Edward recovered, it was time for the Quaker doctor to return on the long journey back to Wichita and his beloved Elone. He thought now on this bright, sunny morning that she would be delivering her child, if she had not already done so.

The two young braves who had accompanied him from Wichita had already made many friends among the vaqueros. They themselves had been overjoyed to be allowed to break in some of the newly captured wild mustangs, since they were expert horsemen as their fathers before them. For them, these weeks during which Ben waited to make absolutely certain that his patients had completely recovered were an unexpected bounty. They knew that when he returned north they must accompany him back to the isolated village on the barren plains of Indian Territory.

At last, on the Thursday of the third week in May, Dr. Ben Wilson said his farewells. Early that morning, he went to the chapel and prayed earnestly in his gratitude for his humble skills as a doctor and in a joyous thanksgiving for the manifold blessings of his new life. And he prayed also for the souls of his dead wife, Fleurette, and her valiant mother, Sybella, and for all the Bouchards. For these good people assuredly were a bulwark against the lawless, the corrupt, the cynical profiteers who thought only of material gain and scorned the decency of human life.

He breakfasted with Lucien Edmond and Maxine, affectionately said his farewells to their children, to Maybelle and Henry Belcher and Henry's grown children, Timmy and Connie. Timmy was now twenty, and Connie had become a lovely young woman at eighteen. They had not lacked for schooling all these years, for Maybelle had insisted very strictly on sitting at their lessons with them. As she had confided to her doting husband, "Henry, it's a good thing I had an education when I was a girl back in Alabama, or I swear those two strapping youngsters of yours could never have gotten proper book learning. And one of these days, you mark my words, Henry Belcher, we're going to have to scout around and see that they get married to nice, decent folks. They've a right to their own lives, and if we keep them cooped up on this ranch, they'll never get to meet anyone, they'll never have a choice."

Ben rode over to Joe Duvray's house to say goodbye to Joe and Margaret and their little son, Robert. He had shaken hands with Eddie Gentry and, at the latter's request, had examined Maria Elena. He turned to Eddie and smiled reassuringly. "Your wife is a strong, healthy girl, and I foresee she's going to have no trouble. You'll have many sons and daughters, and the best thing of all is that you love each other and belong to each other because of what you've been through."

Lucien Edmond had given the Quaker doctor a buggy and had the vaqueros load it with supplies, some of which were his personal gifts to Emataba and the villagers. Ramón had attached two well-trained mustang geldings to the buggy, his present to the Quaker doctor. And each of the Creek braves who were to escort Dr. Ben Wilson home were given hunting knives for themselves and blankets, shells, and strings of beads for their wives.

Ben got into the buggy and waved goodbye to Lucien Edmond, who had come out to see him off, along with Maxine and their two eldest children, Carla and Hugo. The two Creeks sat astride mustang geldings also, which Lucien Edmond had instructed Ramón to give them as their own. They were overwhelmed by the generosity of this white-eyes, and they murmured to each other that truly the white-eyes shaman had been sent by the Great Spirit to teach them that there were others like himself who could be true friends to their people.

A last farewell, and Ben called to the geldings as he flicked the reins to begin the journey. But just then Maxine, shading her eyes with one hand against the fierce sun, called out, "Lucien Edmond, someone is riding toward us from Joe's ranch. He's on a mule!"

Ben halted the horses, stood up in the buggy, and turned to stare at the lone rider. Some of the vaqueros, attracted by Maxine's cry, had come out of the bunkhouse and, saddling their horses, ridden out to intercept the stranger. When they reached him, they doffed their sombreros and bowed their heads and cried out, "It is the good Friar Bartoloméo!"

"But what has happened to you—you are hurt, *padre!*" one of the newest vaqueros anxiously exclaimed.

The brown-robed Franciscan was a stout jovial man, now nearly sixty. Four years ago, when he had first come to Windhaven Range after having been driven out of Santa Fe by the arrogant *ricos*, he had had a white circular fringe of hair around the top of his bald pate. Now that hair was gone, and there were ugly patches of a coarse, black substance clinging to his scalp. His jowls and his cheeks had large blisters and bits of the black substance still clung to them. But his pale blue eyes still shone with that zest for life and that indomitable humor which had won the hearts of all of the vaqueros whom he had accompanied on the cattle drive to Abilene four years earlier. He had stayed at Emataba's village while they had driven their cattle on to market, and then returned with them when they had come back to Windhaven Range. There, he had blessed the chapel the workers had built to honor him and to give thanks to God for their freedom and their prosperity, which they enjoyed as workers for a *patrón* like Lucien Edmond Bouchard.

"It is nothing, my son," Friar Bartoloméo Alicante sighed deeply. "It looks worse than it is. You do not know how happy I am to see you all again. You"—he called out to one of the men who had come to meet him—"were you not among the vaqueros when we rode with the cattle that time four years ago?"

The middle-aged, black-bearded vaquero grinned and nodded, delighted by this recognition after four years. "*Es verdad, padre.* My name is Benito Contraro. I remember you well—how you ate with us and prayed with us and even sang with us. Those were good days."

"They were indeed, my son. But you, *hombre*," turning to the tall, wiry vaquero in his late twenties who rode at his left side, "you're new to this ranch, aren't you?"

"*Sí, padre.* My name is Miguel Sandoso. It was the Señor Ramón Hernandez who engaged me early last year. But everyone has told me so much about you that I recognized you—though I do not like to see you this way—what happened to you, *mi padre*?"

"It is a long story and it has been a very long journey," Friar Bartoloméo sighed. "And my old bones have been rudely shaken by this obstinate burro. Still, we must not revile the good creature. The mother of our dear Lord and Savior rode upon an ass when her husband took her to Bethlehem."

"Yes, so my own mother taught me." Miguel Sandoso crossed himself. "Never fear, *padre*, they will give you good food and look after you, and instead of this old burro, the *patrón* will give you a fresh horse."

"And *padre*," Benito Contraro joined in, "there is someone here who knows you and was just now about to leave the hacienda when we saw you coming. You know him too—it is Dr. Ben Wilson."

"That man of good faith! Assuredly I know him and of his works. What a fortunate day that our paths should cross again!"

The friar and the vaqueros had by this time nearly reached the main house, and the burro at last determined to go no farther. With an indignant bray, it stopped dead in its tracks. Miguel swore at it in Spanish, and then, crossing himself, begged pardon of the Franciscan friar. "I did not hear you, my son," the latter said, with a twinkle in his eyes. "But you have forgotten so soon what your mother taught you. For shame, *amigo*. After all, the poor beast has come many long miles with a fat old man astride him. He has done better than I'd thought possible, and if it were not for him, I should not be here. Nor indeed, if it had not been for those friendly Comanches who rescued me, but that is another story. If you will help me down, I will pray for you!"

"Of a certainty, *padre*." Both vaqueros hastened to the burro and gently lifted the plump old Franciscan friar down.

Ben had leaped down from the buggy and strode over to the friar. "Friar Bartoloméo, I'm glad I tarried in making my farewells long enough to see you—but, my God, what has happened to you? Who has done this?"

"I ask only a cup of water, my son, and it will loosen my tongue. Alas, neither my burro nor I have had much water the last hours of our ride here."

Lucien Edmond spoke up. "Miguel, Benito, take the burro to the well and see that it drinks its fill, then stable it down and give it plenty of oats and hay. Here, Friar Bartoloméo, lean on me, I'll help you into the house. Maxine, would you get Friar Bartoloméo a cool glass of our sweet well water? And some biscuits and honey—I'm sure you haven't eaten—but not too much, because in an hour or two it'll be time for dinner."

The old man put his arm around Lucien Edmond's sturdy shoulders and limped slowly up the steps and into the living room of the hacienda where he eased himself down onto the sofa with a great sigh of relief, closing his eyes and leaning back.

Maxine quickly returned from the kitchen with a cup of cool well water and a plate of biscuits and honey, seated herself beside the friar, and solicitously saw that he drank the water and ate most of one biscuit, liberally smeared with the wild honey Felicidad and Lucas had garnered from a hive in a rotted tree stump near the creek.

"Thank you, my daughter, a thousand thanks. I feel my strength returning," he exclaimed gratefully.

"And now, what happened to you, Friar Bartoloméo?" Lucien Edmond leaned forward, his face taut with anxiety.

Ben, who had come into the house, rose from his chair and came over to inspect the abrasions and the marks of what apparently was tar on the friar's plump face and on his raw scalp. "I have some ointment which will heal those chafings and bruises, Friar Bartoloméo," he proffered. "If you will allow me, it will ease your pain."

"Thank you, my son. But before I tell you how I came to be here, I'm anxious to know about you, Dr. Wilson. You had become the shaman of the Creek village, as I recall."

"That's true. And then a young Sioux girl by the name of Elone and her baby girl, Tisinqua, found refuge in that village, Friar Bartoloméo. Now, thanks to God's kind mercy, we are married and living in Wichita, and she has

190

given me a son I named Bartholomew—after you, Friar Bartoloméo."

"I am deeply touched, my son. I am only an insignificant servant of our dear Lord, but to think that you would remember me in naming your son—it makes my few pains vanish and makes me humbly contrite to know how merciful He has been to me."

Ben smiled, then left the room briefly. When he returned, he had some salve, which he began to apply gently to the friar's bruises and cuts.

"Does the ointment help, Friar Bartoloméo?" the Quaker doctor asked. "I think in time it will help dissolve some of the hardened particles of what seems to be tar—"

"And so it was, my son. Oh yes, I feel a thousand times better. Bless you. But you shouldn't fuss over a garrulous old man like me. As I arrived, I saw that you were ready to leave—you'll want to get home to your wife and your children. Yes, I remember—your first wife had died in Pittsburgh and you came here to visit her mother and to be consoled in your grief. And you brought—my memory does not yet fail me even if my old body does—you brought Thomas and Sybella with you—"

"Your memory is ever green, Friar Bartoloméo!" Ben exclaimed admiringly, and then went on to tell the friar about the Creeks, Douglas Larrimer, and his own new life in Wichita with his growing family.

"Blessed are the ways of our dear Lord," Friar Bartoloméo said, when Ben had finished. "It was He who set you on this new course in life."

"Amen, and I have been to the chapel early this morning to thank Him."

"You are a Quaker, my son, and I am a Catholic. But when I saw your work in that village of Emataba's, I knew the eternal truth that men of good will and good faith everywhere must know: that there is but one true God, and He watches over all of us, if only we have the compassion and the humility to accept His blessed doctrines."

"Amen to that, Friar Bartoloméo," Lucien Edmond Bouchard solemnly avowed. "But who dared abuse a man of the cloth in such a fashion? Indeed, whoever did this to you must have been godless."

"I'm not one to judge, my son. But those who did it call themselves Comancheros—or rather, that is how they are known throughout Texas. You see, after I had left the

191

Creek camp, I told you that I would go to live among Indian tribes and to do what good I could, having seen the example of Dr. Wilson here. And so I did indeed. My journey took me to a village near Big Spring, where Penateka Comanches dwelt. They were not warlike, though they did hunt the buffalo. There were buffalo hunters who came from the north to kill for the hides and to leave the rotting carcasses on the fields where they lay—the food which these Indians needed to sustain themselves."

"This I know," Lucien Edmond interrupted. "I believe it to be the government's policy in making it more and more difficult for Indian tribes to survive in the southwest, forcing them to leave their land in search of new buffalo herds. And, if this is continued, there will one day be no buffalo herds and the Indians will have nowhere to live except on reservations."

"Exactly so, my son," the elderly friar rejoined. "But such wanton killing for the sake of gain and the waste of nourishing meat that would feed many is assuredly a sin. Yet I speak of the Comancheros. They are, from what I have learned, renegade whites who band together and who sell strong spirits and firearms to the Indians, to Comanches and the Kiowa Apaches and to the Apache tribes farther to the west beyond Texas. But the evil they do is not measured alone in terms of their greed, my son. They prey upon white settlers, and they dress themselves like Comanches, killing and robbing, and abusing the unfortunate women who fall captive to them. They do this so that the Comanche tribes will be blamed for these depradations upon the settlers, and so army troops are sent out against the Comanches. In the village where I resided for many months, their chief, Durado, which is their name for avenger, said that fifteen of his braves were shot down by soldiers while they were on a hunting party seeking the very buffalo the hunters had killed and driven off." Friar Bartoloméo lifted his eyes and sighed deeply.

"But the Texas Rangers would know the truth about the Comancheros," Lucien Edmond interposed.

"True, my son, but this land is so vast and there are only a handful of Rangers; you cannot expect them to patrol all the boundaries of Texas. They try to help the settlers, they pursue thieves and murderers as best they can. But they have not yet caught the Comancheros. But now you ask what happened to me—and this is what took place. About

192

a month ago, I had gone with one of the young braves of Durado's tribe in search of medicinal herbs to heal the sick. As we were picking these, our horses grazing peacefully beyond us, three men rode up, heavily armed, to inquire what I was doing with the Comanches. I had nothing to hide and no reason to lie, my son, and I therefore told them that I was administering to the spiritual needs of these good people. The leader of these three men, a tall ruffian with a straggly black beard and cruel eyes and mouth, laughed and told me that I was a meddler and that my loose tongue would make trouble between them and the Comanches with whom they traded."

"But why would they accuse you of such a thing, Friar Bartoloméo?" Dr. Ben Wilson perplexedly asked.

"It is true that I talk more than I should, my son," the elderly friar whimsically responded, "and you see, when Durado had told me of the killing of his braves by the soldiers, I said that perhaps it was the result of what the Comancheros had done and that these innocent men were being punished for the evil others had committed. It is true that Durado himself at times did business with the Comancheros—and perhaps, without meaning to harm me, he told them of my presence in his village."

"But if that is true, then you were betrayed by the very people you sought to help, Friar Bartoloméo," Lucien Edmond indignantly declared.

"Oh no, my son, I do not think that of the Penatekas, though I think that Durado had already come to see that the men he traded with were not honest. Some of the rifles that had been sold to him were worthless, and the ammunition was defective also. It may have been that he spoke in hasty anger. No, my son, he was a good man, and if he sought the aid of the Comancheros, it was only because he was afraid for his people, that the soldiers would drive them away from their hunting grounds. Often I spoke with him late at night over the campfire, urging him to find a new stronghold, perhaps farther to the west where the soldiers might not look for him and where, if there was plentiful meat, he would not have to depend upon the Comancheros. But at any rate, two weeks ago this same man who had told me to leave the tribe came back with ten of his band. Durado himself had gone hunting with a party of his warriors, and the old men and the old women could not be expected to help me. The desperadoes took me and they rode me on a horse with my hands tied behind me for many miles till they came to a scrub tree. There they bound me to it and scourged me, yes, even as our dear Lord was scourged. I bore this without complaint, for it is well that all men suffer that they may know the trials of Job and thus have their faith strengthened within their hearts. But then, after the scourging, they made a fire and they put tar and feathers upon me, Comanche feathers, and the leader joked and said that, since I loved the Indians so much, it was only right that I should wear their garb. Then they tied me to a cactus tree and left me to die, as the leader said."

"How horrible!" Maxine gasped, twisting her hands in her lap, her eyes widely fixed on the elderly friar's face.

"My daughter, I prayed to Him to give me strength for this ordeal and He heard me. Some hours after they had left me, Durado returned and one of his braves found me. They tended my hurts, and they gave me this burro, for they could not spare horses. I told Durado that I could only bring harm upon him and his people by remaining there and that I would set forth upon my journey as a kind of penance. And, as you see, my daughter, He who watches over even the tiniest sparrow that falls watched over me and brought me safely to you good people. I give Him thanks and I pray that He will reward you for your kindness to me."

"But where will you go now, Friar Bartoloméo?" Lucien Edmond inquired.

"I have no parish save the wilderness, my son. And no parishioners save those who are in need and whom I may encounter along my way. He will guide me, as He has all of my life, I know. And I pray your indulgence—in the morning, when I am stronger, I should like to say a mass of thanksgiving in that chapel which your vaqueros built and which I was privileged to dedicate."

"All of us here will attend your mass, Friar Bartoloméo."

The portly old man nodded and smiled. "Do you know, my son, I have been thinking, and just now when you asked me where I might go, suddenly a thought has come to me. You recall how often you spoke to me of the Comanche chief Sangrodo. You told me how, after he gave battle against that army officer who cruelly killed the

194

peaceful people of his village, he and the rest of his tribe went across the Rio Grande and settled in Mexico."

"That's true, Friar Bartoloméo. And all this time he has lived in peace. His people till the land and his men, whose wives were slaughtered by that Captain Munson and his men, have married Mexican women and had children and thus begun new families who are Christian."

"It is a courageous thing for a man like that to have done. He was never a sinner, from what you have told me of him. And what he does now in a sense pursues the course our blessed St. Francis of Assisi ordained for us to live by. Truly I should like to see him again and to observe how the people of his village live and how they accustom themselves to a life that surely no Comanches ever pursued before."

"And that is also true, Friar Bartoloméo. Something even better than this has happened. My father, Luke Bouchard, has adopted a young brave from Sangrodo's tribe, named Lopasuta. Lopasuta studied to become a lawyer and now practices in Montgomery near where my father and his family live. He aids the oppressed and the needy."

"Truly this Sangrodo is a man of great wisdom and gentleness. Now I know more than ever that this is where I shall go when I leave here, my son."

"You will be welcome, Friar Bartoloméo," Dr. Ben Wilson softly put in.

"I told you all once how I began my life as the wastrel son of a wealthy merchant in Madrid. I fell in love with an innocent, God-fearing girl, and our banns had been read. Then there came into our lives a swaggering captain of a ship, who met the girl to whom I was promised and so regaled her with stories of his adventures that she yielded to his lusts. Then, learning how she had been duped and debauched, she took her own life and thus risked the peril of eternal damnation."

"I remember that," Lucien Edmond softly murmured, crossing himself.

"I swore an oath of vengeance. I challenged this captain to a duel, and I killed him. The duel took place in observance of all the rules sanctioned by law. Yet when he lay dead at my feet, I knew that I had committed murder before Him and that I was worse than this man who had taken only his carnal pleasure of an innocent girl. My father had died a week before that duel. So, like St. Francis, I gave my legacy to the poor and I took monastic vows. Thus you see, my son, I have devoted all of my life from that time forth to helping the lowly and the oppressed. Only thus can I redeem my own soul from the perdition that awaited me when I took human life even in the spirit of what I believed to be holy vengeance."

"God surely forgave you long ago for that understandable act of violence, Friar Bartoloméo," Ben murmured.

"I cannot be certain of that, my son. I know only that I have not forgiven myself. And that is why adversity strengthens me. Yes, I will go to the stronghold of Sangrodo, and these good people will give me renewed strength, that I may continue my mission."

"We will talk of this tomorrow, after the mass, Friar Bartoloméo," Lucien Edmond said. "And I will send four of my men with you to escort you safely to Sangrodo's stronghold. They will take with them twenty head of cattle as my gift."

Friar Bartoloméo Alicante crossed himself, closed his eyes, and murmured a silent prayer. Then he said in a stronger, clearer voice, "Already I have forgotten my suffering. Your compassion and goodness show me that there are still many in this world who live by the teachings of our dear Lord." He turned to Ben. "You are returning to Wichita—you must be eager to see your dear wife and the new child she has borne."

"I will stay for your mass tomorrow, Friar Bartoloméo. But now, as a doctor, I prescribe that you lie down and rest. And when I leave tomorrow I will give you the rest of this ointment, which you should apply daily."

Friar Bartoloméo sighed and nodded. "I think I shall follow your orders, my son. Now I am beginning to feel tired, truly. But also I feel that the weight in my heart has been lifted. For this, I thank all of you."

CHAPTER EIGHTEEN

Kitante, Sangrodo's son by his dead first wife, had begun to chafe against the monotony of the peaceful life in his father's Mexican stronghold near what had once been the little village of Miero. Now eighteen, he envied the brave Lopasuta, who had left the stronghold several years ago and gone to live in Alabama. Sangrodo had told him of Lopasuta's acceptance among the white-eyes as one who spoke before the judges of the white-eyes, and how Lopasuta had been adopted as a son by the man they had named *Taiboo Nimaihkana*, "the white-eyes one who is called."

Kitante would never forget the *Taiboo Nimaihkana*. Eight years ago, when he had been jeered at by the son of a war lieutenant, Kitante had stolen his father's horse and ridden off in anger, resolved to prove by counting coup against an enemy that he was already a brave warrior. The horse had thrown him and he had been bitten by a rattlesnake. If the *Taiboo Nimaihkana* had not found him and taken him to his hacienda, he would not be alive today. Yet, remembering that, Kitante was the more restless to prove that he was truly the son of the great chief of this Comanche tribe.

They, the People, who had never known either a master or defeat by the white-eyes soldiers, had come across the border to Mexico and, instead of hunting and raiding as had been their wont, had settled down to the peaceful agricultural life of the peon. There was no future to it, Kitante reasoned. If he were truly the first son of the chief—that was true, for his little half-brother, Inokanti, had not seen more than four summers and Inokanti was the child of the beloved woman Catayuna—then surely he, Kitante, must prove to the braves his right to be named chief when Sangrodo was called by the Great Spirit. To be sure, that would be a long time off, yet all the same he was restless because he had done no deeds of valor.

Kitante remembered how the *Taiboo Nimaihkana* and the Kiowa scout Simata had helped his father on that terrible day seven years ago, when the white-eyes Captain George Munson had taken his soldiers and raided the stronghold while his father had been out hunting with the braves. He remembered how Catayuna, though wounded in the shoulder, had ridden like the strongest brave to find Sangrodo and the warriors. They had taken a vow of vengeance, and the *Taiboo Nimaihkana* and Simata had told them how to lead the white-eyes troops into the Canyon of Death. There, Sangrodo avenged the slaughter of the old ones and the children. Ha, that had been a day to remember; it would be long sung in the chants and the stories at the campfire.

Sangrodo had hated Catayuna at first. When she had been brought to the stronghold as a slave—Catayuna Arvilas, the wife of the *alcalde* of a Mexican village, who had killed many peaceful Comanches and sold their scalps to the Mexican government—he had wanted to see her suffer after watching her husband die by the ordeal of the ants. But Catayuna had shown herself so courageous, so defiant in the face of torture, that in his grudging respect for courage Sangrodo had spared her life and then impulsively freed her from slavery.

Now they were inseparable; now she was his second mother, and he, Kitante, respected her because of what she had done. And there was more: five summers ago, after the *bandido* Carlos Macaras had attacked the hacienda of the *Taiboo Nimaihkana* and his son, he and one of his *bandidos* attacked the stronghold, carried off a young Mexican squaw of one of the warriors, and tried to kill Kitante himself. It had been Catayuna who had struck away the rifle of the *jefe de bandidos* and then gutted him with her scalping knife, even though she had lost the child she bore in her belly when the *bandido* had cruelly driven the butt of his rifle against her. And because of this, there was not a brave, not an old one in the stronghold who did not revere her as one of the People, as the beloved woman, and as Sangrodo's squaw—as brave as any warrior because she had counted such a coup as only a chief himself might make. Yes, he, Kitante, respected and loved her, and it was

198

not so much that she was his second mother, as that they were friends and could communicate with each other.

She understood his restlessness better than anyone, better than even his father, Sangrodo. And she continued to counsel him: "The time will come, Kitante. You are still young. You are not yet ready to be chief, and your father is not yet ready to give you his place. That will happen only when he has gone to the Great Spirit, and then the elders will vote on who is to replace him. When that time does come, you must prove yourself worthy. Because he has counseled us all to be patient and to live in peace, you must show that you are as able to take orders as to give them."

Ho, yes, that was true. But it did not help to relieve the inevitable sameness of the hot days here in this little Mexican village, even though he could amuse himself with his friends racing their horses, shooting at marks with their bows and arrows, and hurling their lances at a target. This was but play, not preparation for a young man who was the son of the chief and should one day be chief himself!

Surely he had done his best. He managed to spend some time each day playing with his little brother, Inokanti. Why, he had even amused him by cutting reeds from the river and fashioning them into animals, or into flutes with little holes along the sides. He had given these toys to Inokanti and also to their sister, Miquerda, who was now two years old. Catayuna was with child again, as she had proudly told him a few days ago.

Last fall, Catayuna had once again proved herself to be as courageous as any Comanche brave. One of the men who had been with Carlos Macaras had joined another group of *bandidos* and had told them that there would be treasure here in the little stronghold. The *bandidos* had attacked the stronghold and kidnapped Catayuna, taking her into the woods. The son of the *Taiboo Nimaihkana*, called Lucien Edmond, and his vaqueros had joined Sangrodo and his braves in fighting the *bandidos*. When one of the *bandidos* was about to kill a vaquero with his rifle, Catayuna had clawed at his face and blinded him. Sangrodo had killed the *mejicano* who had led all the *bandidos* to the stronghold. In honor of the son of the *Taiboo Nimaihkana*, Sangrodo had performed the ceremony of blood brotherhood.

But the remembrance of all these heroic deeds only anguished Kitante more. His father said to him, "If you wish

199

to prove your young manhood, there are women in the stronghold who have lost their men and who will instruct you and ease your needs—that is the way of a man, and do not be ashamed of it."

Kitante pondered this, recalling also that certain of the younger women who were not yet married had likewise given him to understand that they would be eager to mate with him. But as yet there was no one on whom his heart was set, no woman he wanted. So he replied to Sangrodo, "It is not that, my father, it is the chance to show the stronghold that I am worthy to be your oldest son, to walk in your footsteps."

Sangrodo stared at him with that stern look which always boded a scolding that hurt him more than any thrashing could have done, and said at last, "I have learned much from the white-eyes since first we met the great *Taiboo Nimaihkana* and he saved your life, Kitante. What I have learned is that we live in peace and that we need not do battle each new day to prove our courage. Aye, it was as he had predicted, too many white-eyes have come to this land where we once were free and hunted the buffalo, and they spring up like the blades of grass. And if some are mowed down, more take their place. The days of warfare between the Comanche and the white-eyes are over forever—at least so they will be for the tribe as long as I shall lead it. And, if one day you, Kitante, take my place and the elders proclaim you chief of the Wanderers, you must swear to me that you will not try to go back to the old days when we counted coup over enemies. We are happy here, even if the way is strange and new to us who once lived by the lance, the bow, and the arrow. Remember that and be patient. The good chief of a tribe is not one who wishes war for the sake of counting coup and bringing back plunder, Kitante; he is the one who stands against the restless young braves—such as you yourself are now—because he knows the outcome of war, and how many names will never be spoken again, and how many widows will smear their foreheads with ashes and weep."

Yes, it was all very well for Sangrodo to tell him this, but it did not still the ache in his heart, the longing to show all his friends, even the elders, that he was worthy of respect, not because he was the son of Sangrodo, but because he was a Comanche who had brought honor to his people. And when he thought this, then momentarily he almost hated Catayuna because she, a mere squaw, had shown at least three times greater bravery than any warrior . . . greater than he till now had ever dreamed of! Then, of course, came the feeling of shame that he should so hate the one who had made his father happy in this strange new stronghold of theirs, where each day saw the growing and the harvesting of crops, not the battles and the ceremonial dances that celebrated great victories.

It was a warm May evening, and the moon was rising high in the sky. Kitante had shared the evening meal with Sangrodo and Catayuna, and he had been morose when his father had tried to draw him out. Catayuna had sent her husband an entreating look, and the Comanche chief understood well what was in her heart: he, too, had once been as young, as impatient, and as lonely. Tonight, therefore, he would not talk of the duties a son owed to his father; he would let Kitante struggle within himself until at last the Great Spirit should send him a sign that would tell him what was meant for him. Yes, that was the best way.

So Sangrodo talked gently of the old days, just after the death of his first wife, and Kitante, half listening, reluctantly understood, from the words his father spoke to Catayuna, that he had always been loved. That comforted him somewhat.

When at last Sangrodo and Catayuna went into their tepee, Kitante wished them both a night of happy dreams, and then disconsolately walked out to the end of the stronghold. It was peaceful. Kitante could see the fields where the braves and the women tilled the soil and planted seeds. Here in Mexico the land was rich and the sun warm. Corn grew in stately rows, the stalks almost as high as Kitante's head.

He saw a young girl come out of a tepee at the very end of the village. She looked at him for a moment, her dark eyes showing admiration. Then her mother called to her angrily, and with a soft giggle she disappeared back into the tepee. Kitante sighed. It was Mitiswa, whose rites of young womanhood would soon be celebrated. But he had no great fondness for her; she was too young, still almost a child, and besides she would make a lazy squaw. Her mother was constantly berating her for not keeping the fire lit when it was time to cook the evening meal, for not bringing enough water, and for many other things a dutiful squaw must do.

He turned to the corral and remembered as if he were plunged back into his boyhood days again how he had ridden off on his father's horse and, for an inescapable moment, thought himself as powerful as a chief who would lead the braves in raids against the hated Mexicans. Alas, they were no longer hated; they were now part of the tribe, and in the papooses and the sturdy little children one saw the mixed blood of *mejicano* and Comanche.

He did not wish to sleep. Suddenly and impulsively he entered the corral and chose a black mustang, which snorted and pawed the earth with its front hoof as he approached it. With a soft, eager laugh, he stroked its head and spoke to it, took a thong from his belt and wound it round the mustang's neck, and led it out of the corral, closing it so that the other horses would not run off.

"We shall ride tonight, black one," he told the mustang. "There is a need in me, and I see the same in you. So we shall share the night and see what lies beyond our stronghold. Come now, ho!" With a bound, he sprang astride the black mustang and headed it toward the east.

Carmencita Caldera could not bear to sit near her father and his new wife any longer. She was sixteen, with the swelling bosom and hips of a beautiful young woman, her skin a warm olive, her eyes a lustrous brown, and her mouth ripely curved. But her face was sullen tonight and her eyes downcast, save for the stealthy, hateful glances she sent toward her father and his young wife, Juana, who was only four years older than Carmencita.

Until five months ago, she and her father, Jorge Caldera, and her mother, Marta, had lived in Sabinas. Her father, a stocky man in his mid-forties, had worked for many years as a blacksmith employed by a rich old landholder who boasted that his forebears had come from Castile and had the blood of *hidalgos* in their veins. Then one day her mother had suddenly and mysteriously sickened. The old woman who was both midwife, and as some said, *bruja*—witch—had said that it was a sickness deep within the belly that could not be cured. She had brought potions to Marta, but they had not worked. Carmencita had been agonized, for her mother had been kind to her and often had defended her against her father's angry rages when he had drunk too much tequila, and when he boasted that one day he would turn *bandido* and be a free man instead of the servile dog of some accursed old *patrón*.

And then, one night, to Carmencita's horror and stupefaction, her father came into their little *jacal* and roughly told her, "Girl, a priest is with your mother. She is not much longer for this world, and there is nothing you and I can do to save her. We're going now. It will be a new life, you'll see, Carmencita, it will be better for all of us. I won't have to bow my head and bend my back over a forge for a fat old fool who doesn't pay me enough wages to keep us all in food and shelter. Come, pack your things and we'll be off."

She had wept and pleaded with him not to desert her mother, not while she yet lived. He had struck her across the face and cursed her, saying, "I am your father, girl, you'll obey me. Your mother is dead, or will be before dawn. Now must I thrash you before you understand? Come with me!"

She had never seen her father like that before. But then she had seen a holstered pistol strapped to his belt; his eyes were wild and glowing, and his mouth wore a crooked grin that made her tremble. And so, fighting back her tears, she mutely packed what few possessions she had and joined her father outside to find that he had saddled three horses, one of which was tethered to his own.

They rode all night and at dawn Jorge Caldera stopped at a small village. He dismounted, put two fingers to his mouth, and emitted a shrill whistle. A few moments later, this woman, Juana, came running out of a little hut and flung herself into his arms. Carmencita sat on her horse, her mouth agape, dazed, not comprehending what this meant.

Then her father lifted Juana onto the horse behind him, freed it and gave Juana the reins, and exclaimed, "Now we ride to find a priest, *querida!*"

An hour later, Caldera halted his mount again in front of a little church which stood fronting the dusty roadway marking an even smaller village. He helped Juana down and they went into the rectory behind the church. Carmencita could not believe what she then saw. A priest came out, his eyes blinking with sleep, his hands raised above his head, and her father trained his pistol on him and ordered him into the church.

Ten minutes later, when her father emerged, it was with

Juana on his arm, clinging to him, looking at him in a way that made Carmencita turn away with shame and agony. Then Jorge Caldera joyously called, "Carmencita, girl, say good morning to your new mother, Juana! And now we ride to our new home, where we shall meet some good *compañeros* of mine!"

On that terrible morning Carmencita found herself confronted with a young stepmother before she was even sure that her ailing mother was dead. And then there followed three days and nights of riding, till they came to a tiny village near the border. There she learned what her father had planned for so long: not only to marry this insolent young woman who treated her with contempt, but to give up the honest toil of a blacksmith to become the *jefe* of a band of some twenty outlaws.

Most of the outlaws were peons who had fled their masters' service; several of them had even killed the *patrones* to whom they had been bound by contract. One of these men frightened Carmencita merely by looking at her, a man whom her father greeted as Manuel Regado. He was a surly man of forty, with a short black beard and a scar above his right cheekbone; he wore both a pistol and a knife strapped to his belt. He was, Jorge Caldera curtly informed her, the second in command, a true friend whom he had known for several years and who had helped recruit the others. It was not long before she learned that Manuel Regado had killed at least six men and openly boasted about his crimes. Whenever he looked at her, she felt her flesh crawl; she saw the sneering, covetous look in his eyes and she was afraid.

This little village was about a dozen miles to the west of Miero. Like Miero, it had been abandoned years before when a group of poor settlers and their wives and children had lost their crops two years in a row because of a grasshopper plague. They had moved farther southeast, and few soldiers ever patrolled this desolate region.

During these past few months, Carmencita had seen her father and his men frequently ride out and come back two or three days later; then she had been forced to serve them food and tequila to celebrate their plundering of a distant village. They brought back gold, silver, even some crucifixes stolen from a church they had razed to the ground. And some of them brought back young women whom they forced into "wedlock" in drunken mock-marriages over which one of her father's henchmen, Eduardo Santarla, a lean, saturnine man in his late forties, officiated. He had once been a monk in Durango, but had renounced his vows and run off with the priest's young housekeeper, abandoned her a year later, and then taken his fill of loot and women as he chose, till he joined her father's band.

Carmencita spent many hours late at night weeping and praying, praying not only for her father's redemption but for the salvation of her own soul—and her own safety. There was not a man in the *bandido* camp who did not openly lust for her, but they were controlled by her father and his lieutenant, Manuel Regado. And what she feared most was that one day, if Juana continued to taunt and upbraid her and to treat her like the lowliest *criatura,* her father would marry her off to his evil henchmen.

On this May evening, she had docilely served supper to her father and his woman—she could not bring herself to call Juana *madre*. She had pretended not to notice while Juana openly leaned against her father, an arm around his waist, sometimes whispering to him and making him burst into bawdy laughter at some of her licentious observations. Carmencita could feel a slow rage begin to swell inside her, and she flushed hotly and was the more wretchedly angry at herself for letting Juana see how such shameless flaunting tortured her. She had already learned that Juana was coarse-mouthed, as much as any two-peso *puta* in Durango or Monterrey might have been; conversely, her new step-mother, observing at the very outset the resentment the younger girl bore, had gone out of her way to make explicit sexual comments on Carmencita's modesty which, according to her, hardly went hand in hand with the girl's mature physique.

At the end of the meal, when Carmencita served coffee and then poured tequila into the clay bowls her father and Juana held out to her, Juana taunted her by eyeing her up and down and remarking, loud enough for some of the men around the campfire to hear, *"Pobre muchachita,* you watch your father and me all the time—oh, do not think I don't see you with those great cow's eyes of yours stealing secret looks! I know what it is, you are envious, you are wishing for a *novio* to take you into the bushes."

Her father, instead of defending her against this wicked slander, tilted back his head and burst into a guffaw of acquiescent laughter, saying, "Now then, my little dove, there's time enough for Carmencita. And when the time comes, I have in my band many strong men with *cojones* to wed her properly. Let her be for now, Juana *querida!*" And he pulled Juana to him and gave her a long, lecherous kiss, which made the men call out with lewd approval.

It was too much. Carmencita effaced herself, and then fortunately her father desired to call some of his men into a conference. They were doubtless planning a raid on some unsuspecting nearby village. She had to get away from the camp, she could not bear any longer to watch how Juana gloatingly showed off the domination she had over her father, nor abide those scandalous references to her own chastity. She almost wept, remembering how her beloved mother, Marta, had praised her for her modesty and shyness and told her that one day a good man would value such qualities far above the beauty of her body.

As the fires dwindled and her father drank more and more tequila, she could hear the excited voices of the men about him as they plotted their next campaign. Juana had gone into the *jacal,* and that was good. Now she could leave the camp, walk out where the trees and the flowers and the night birds were, feel clean again, away from this intolerable prison. What crushed her most was the awareness that her father seemed no longer to respect her, nor even to want to protect her from the malicious sallies of that woman. She was, for all intents and purposes, abandoned, virtually an orphan, and there were twenty *bandidos* to menace her chastity.

She walked westward, taking a narrow pathway that led through a clump of trees, turned about twenty yards northward to avoid clumps of brambles and mesquite, and came at last to a wider clearing. The moon was high now, and it lighted the way. She did not fear the loneliness and the darkness, or the trees and the bushes which cast weird shadows along her path; she feared far more what she had left behind her.

A few yards ahead of her, a large iguana scurried across the narrow pathway. The sight brought a brief smile to Carmencita's lips. But it was swiftly replaced by a look of brooding discontent. In happier days, when her father had been content with his life as a blacksmith, he had hunted iguanas, and her mother had made savory stews and baked dishes from the giant lizards. In those days, her father, though never really demonstrative toward her, had at least touched her hair from time to time, or made some jesting comment to her mother that their little one would one day become a *mujer linda* with many *novios* coming to their *jacal* to ask permission to court her. But now all this had vanished. She had even begun to wonder for how many years her father had dreamed of becoming a *jefe de bandidos*; how long he had been planning to desert her mother. No, it was assuredly that woman, that contemptible Juana, little more than a *puta* the way she displayed her affection for Carmencita's father in front of all of those coarse ruffians. Juana certainly must have been the one who had lured him away from her mother and herself, perhaps even the one who had insinuated that he could win her and have *mucho dinero* if he would change his life. And now there was no turning back. She could never go back to Sabinas again. Perhaps she should run away, put many miles between her and this forsaken little village and go to a church to beg sanctuary from some kindly old *padre*.

She suddenly burst into sobs and covered her face with her hands, her shoulders heaving as she fought to control this anguished outburst. Then she heard the sound of a horse's hooves. They halted. At first she did not look up, so anguished was she still, but when she did lift her eyes at last, blinking through hot tears, she saw a tall, handsome, coppery-skinned young man, so dark that he looked *mejicano*. He was astride a black mustang, which snorted and tossed its head as he firmly drew on the thong reins to curb its skittishness.

"Why do you cry, *pequeña?*" His voice was gentle.

"Who—who are you, señor?" she quavered.

"I am Kitante, son of Sangrodo, chief of the Wanderers. We are Comanche. But you—why do you come out so far into this forest by yourself? It could be dangerous. There are snakes, there are *jabalíes*."

"I—I don't care! I wish I were dead—I don't ever want to go back to them—" she burst out. And then, realizing that she was revealing her innermost secrets to a stranger, she put a hand to her mouth and abashedly looked down at the ground.

Kitante dismounted, stroked the head of his black mustang, and spoke to it softly till it quieted. "That is good. Stay here now. Do not run away. You are strong, you will protect us both from the night."

"You—you are *indio*?" Carmencita faltered.

"*Pero sí*. But you have not yet told me your name."

"It is Carmencita Caldera."

"*Es un nombre lindo*—like you, Carmencita."

She blushed at this unexpected praise, put her hands behind her back, and twisted her fingers, as she continued to stare down at the ground. Kitante smiled gently. "But why do you wish you were dead? That is a strange thing for one so young and so lovely to say."

"But you don't know—oh, *Dios*, I must tell someone—I have had it in my heart for so long, I think I shall die of the sorrow of it!" she burst out.

"But you must not talk of dying. Come, tell me. When one has sorrow, it is the better for sharing it with someone else."

"You—you are very kind, señor. I—I wanted to go to a church and to confess to the *padre*. Oh, how I wish I could kill her!" Now Carmencita's head rose. Her dark eyes were wide and angry, and her lips twisted as she spat out the words.

"Truly, this is a mystery." Kitante soothingly chuckled. "First you wish to die, now you wish to kill someone. And who is this 'her' whom you wish to kill?"

"It is Juana. You see, we lived in Sabinas, and my father was a blacksmith there. My mother and he and I were happy. And then, not even a year ago, when my mother fell ill and was dying, my father made me leave the *jacal* where we had lived and told me that my mother would die at any moment. He did not even send for a priest to hear her last words—"

"Do not weep, *linda*. Tell me." For the girl had burst into uncontrollable sobs again, and Kitante impulsively stepped close to her and put an arm around her shoulders. She did not draw away, but instead pressed her tearful face against his chest and went on, between sobs, "He made me ride with him. We came to a village and he whistled, and then Juana came out to meet him. She—she is young, perhaps four years older than I am—and then—oh it is too horrible to tell, *es un sacrilegio*!" Once again, she could not halt her sobs, and Kitante awkwardly put both arms around her, to hold her to him till the spasm had passed.

"Tell me, *pobrecita*," he gently urged.

"You are kind, Señor Kitante. Yes—I must tell you—

you are the only one who has been kind to me in all this time—my father and this Juana, they rode with me to a little church farther on, and there my father made a priest come marry them, and he forced the priest at the point of a *pistola* to perform this unholy sacrament."

"I know, I understand now why you have such hatred in your heart, Carmencita. And this *madrastra*, this step-mother, is cruel to you?"

"You do not know how cruel she can be! She hates me, she mocks me!" Carmencita passionately burst out. "When she is with my father, she flaunts herself before all the men of the camp—they are all *bandidos* there, Señor Kitante, and I am afraid of them. Especially my father's lieutenant, Manuel Regado. It is my dreadful fear that Juana will urge my father to give me to that cruel, hateful man—he is a murderer many times, and when he looks at me, I feel ashamed and dirty!"

"*Pobrecita, pobrecita*, I wish I could help you, I wish I could free you from that—but I did not know that there was a camp of *bandidos* so near our stronghold. It is something I must tell my father, Sangrodo. It is possible that these *bandidos* may try to attack us. Just the same—"

Perplexed by this dilemma, and stirred by the beauty of the young girl who clung to him, still weeping, Kitante suddenly whirled. From a thick clump of mesquite fifty yards away, a wild *jabalí* came charging, its tusks gleaming in the moonlight.

With a cry of alarm, he pushed Carmencita to one side, calling out, "*¡Cuidado, cuidado!*" And then, crouching, he drew his hunting knife and moved forward to intercept the *jabalí*, whose angry, reddened eyes had perceived the young girl beside him. It veered to charge her.

"Aiyee, ho, ho, *jabalí*!" he cried, brandishing the knife and moving to his left so that Carmencita was behind him.

With an angry snort of rage, the wild boar dashed at him, and Kitante agilely stepped to one side and then drove his sharp knife into the *jabalí*'s side. With a wild bellow of pain, the beast turned and lunged with its tusks at Kitante's left leg, gouging his calf. But the young Comanche unflinchingly ignored the pain of the wound and, catching the boar's ear with his left hand, plunged the knife repeatedly into the *jabalí*'s side and belly till at last the beast kicked in its death throes and lay still.

"Señor Kitante, you are hurt! Oh, you have saved my life—how brave you were—truly *el Señor Dios* sent you to save me!" she cried as she ran to him.

"It is only a scratch, Carmencita," he reassured her.

"But it's bleeding badly—wait, I will bind the wound!" she exclaimed.

She tore a piece of her yellow cotton skirt and wrapped it tightly around the wound. Fortunately, it was only a superficial cut, for the tusk had not gouged deeply. Then, staring wide-eyed at the body of the dead boar, she flung her arms around him: "You were so brave, Señor Kitante! Heaven sent you to me when I was so desperate, so unhappy—and now you have saved my life too!"

He held her for a moment, then began to tremble, for in spite of his wound he was beginning to feel the onrush of desire. For the first time he felt himself truly drawn to a woman. The comely young girls and the widows who had eyed him in the stronghold had never stirred him so. As Carmencita clung to him, he felt the heaving swell of her young bosom against his chest and was shaken by the storm of emotion that assailed him. His right hand stroked her long black hair, which fell nearly to her waist, and when she lifted her tear-stained face to his, he impulsively kissed her. Then, aware of his impetuosity, he released her and stammered, "F-forgive me, *pequeña*. I—I had no right—it was unworthy to take such advantage of you."

Carmencita found herself trembling. Like the young Comanche, she was innocent of physical desire; yet because of her own terror at the sight of the sharp-tusked *jabalí* and Kitante's bravery and gentleness, she had felt her maidenly restraint slipping away. Now, blushing, face downcast, she in turn stammered, "But no, Kitante, you did not take advantage—it is what I feel inside—for you—because you are so strong and have saved my life, I feel for you a new thing I have never known before—"

He tried to be very mature and almost stern, as his father Sangrodo would surely be. Straightening, he told her, "Carmencita, this new feeling, if it is love—you must not feel it for me out of gratitude. Our hearts must speak straight and true. And I think they do. If this new thing between us—if it is love—then we have the right to choose each other, even though in the stronghold of my father, a man and a woman are pledged from a young age. Yes, if it should go well between the two who seem to have decided on each other, they can go before the shaman—who is like your *padre*, Carmencita—and he mingles their blood so that they become one. Now—" he kept his eyes away from her, trying to speak impersonally, though every fibre of his being yearned to embrace and console her, to accept this wondrous gift of love which he sensed she was ready to offer, "—now, as I mean to say, if that is the way it will be for us, dear Carmencita, that is the way it must be done. Know that I desire you, for you are sweet and gentle and lovely, and I know how much you suffer where you are. But I would not take advantage of you here, and we should not touch each other again till the ceremony, which my father will order to take place . . . once I tell him that I wish us to be as one."

Her face was suffused with color at this suggestion. She averted her eyes from his as she quavered, "Can it be that, though we have not known each other for very long, you wish this to happen for us, K-Kitante?"

"Yes, with all my heart!" He turned to her, his eyes eager; he had to hold himself in check lest he grasp her and kiss her, for the temptation was great.

Her face was radiant as she moved to him. A hand on his shoulder, she murmured, "Oh, Kitante, dear kind Kitante, I wish that too, with all of my heart and soul. No man has ever been so kind to me, so gentle—" And with this, her eyes filmed with sudden tears, and she gasped and put her arms round him, bowing her head against his chest as she uneasily confided, "But, oh, *querido*, I do not know how it can be done. My father is now *el jefe de los bandidos*. I'm sure he wouldn't let me marry an *indio*—he'd rather have me wed that cruel, hateful man, Manuel Regado—and I would rather die! Oh, Kitante, if you speak true words when you say you wish our blood to mingle in the union of your people—the union which for me as *católica* is marriage—what is to be done for us?"

"I do not know, *querida*. I will talk with my father. He is a wise man. He has been our chief for many moons and all of us do willingly what he bids us do. But if I can, I promise to take you to his stronghold and there to have the shaman make us one—if you are sure that you wish it so, *querida*."

"With all my heart and soul, Kitante! We are both young, but if I were yours, it would be a new life. But my father—he has so changed, I do not dare tell him about

211

you, about us, Kitante. I do not know what would happen if I did."

"I must think on this. It is a matter that concerns our lives together, *linda*." Kitante's face was grave. "Now you had best go back to your village. I will ride back to talk with my father about what can be done. But know this, Carmencita—I want you, and I would be proud to have our blood mingled by the shaman. Yet, since it has come upon us both so quickly, we who have been strangers until now, it is wise to think many times about what we should do."

"Yes, Kitante. You are right. It shows me how good you are, a true *hombre*, for you could have taken me now and I—" She bowed her head. "I could not have, would not have stopped you, if you had wished it, truly."

"You are very sweet, Carmencita. There will be time for us when all is decided in the right way. And now go back quickly, and say nothing. Perhaps my father will show me the way to find you again and to bring you to our stronghold."

"Oh yes, I pray for this with all my heart, Kitante!" She was smiling radiantly as she put her arms around him and kissed him. Then she turned and hastened back to the camp of the bandits.

CHAPTER NINETEEN

The men of her father's band had gone back to their *ja-cales*, most of them drunk from the tequila they had imbibed. But as Carmencita entered the little village, her heart sank to see Juana standing in front of her father's hut, hands on her hips, her lips compressed, her eyes narrowed and angry.

"You little *puta*, where have you been all this time? Your father asked for you, and I did not know what to tell him. You ran off into the woods, shameless one! Ah, and your skirt, it is torn—truly you are a *puta*! You do not even deserve to be married to one of our good men!" Then, turning and leaning toward the open door of the *jacal*, she called shrilly, "Jorge, *amorcito*, it is Carmencita. She favors us by returning. Come outside and scold this wicked little slut—and just look at her skirt!"

Jorge Caldera emerged, yawning, wearing only his breeches. He was half-sodden with drink, and his black beard and sideburns, tinged with gray, were tousled and matted. His nose was hawklike, his mouth thin and cruel, as he fixed his daughter with a baleful glare. "What's this now, Carmencita? Where have you been all this time? And your best skirt—have you been lying in the bushes with some *gringo*, perhaps?"

"No, *mi padre*, I've done nothing wrong! I—I tore my skirt on a bramble, that is all. I—I went for a walk—the men were noisy and they were drinking, and I did not like the way they looked at me—" Carmencita nervously improvised.

"Do you hear her lies, Jorge? This little one needs the strap. You have been too gentle with her in the past, but we shall change all that, shan't we, *mi corazón*?"

213

Caldera scratched his hairy belly, hiccuped, then nodded. "It's true, she's hated me all this time. And she's not shown you respect, you, my proper wife."

"That's a lie, *mi padre!*" Carmencita indignantly cried. "My dear mother was not yet dead, you were not even sure that she would die, when you came to the village and whistled for that woman—and then you forced a priest with your *pistola* to marry you both—it is sacrilege, I say! I will never call her mother, *never*, though you whip me to death!"

"I shan't whip you to death, you little *puta*," Juana cruelly smirked, "but only just enough to teach you manners. And it will do no harm for the men to see how a wayward, stupid young girl who knows nothing is taught to obey her parents! Jorge, get me the strap, and then hold Carmencita's hands."

"You shan't, you shan't, I won't let you—" Carmencita began, but Juana had already seized her wrist and dealt the girl a resounding slap across her cheek with the flat of her right hand.

Hysterically, Carmencita tried to free herself, incoherently crying and imploring her father not to abandon her to Juana's spite. But Caldera emerged from the *jacal* with a leather strap and then pitilessly seized his daughter's wrists as he tossed the strap to Juana.

"*¡Bueno!*" the young woman hissed. "Now I am going to teach you a lesson. And if one does not work, there will be many more, depend on it." Then, stationing herself behind Carmencita, she called, "Hold her tightly, Jorge, I do not wish her to escape what is her due!"

With this, brandishing the strap high, she slashed it with all her might across Carmencita's hips. The shame, the ignominy of this public whipping, drew an agonized cry from the unhappy young girl, who dragged wildly at her father's hands but could not break his hold of her.

Roused by the noise, the other men emerged one by one from their *jacales*, and stood mocking and jeering, calling encouragements to Juana. "Lay it on well, Señora Juana! Make her dance, eh?" And from one, a short, corpulent man who had killed his *patrón* and raped his daughter before fleeing to join Jorge Caldera's band, "The strap is best on the naked flesh, Señora Juana!"

"No—stop—oh *Dios*, you horrible woman, aiii! You are hurting me! *Mi padre*, how can you let her do this to me? I

214

swear by the Holy Virgin I have done nothing wrong—aahhh! Oh, *piedad*, not before them—please—it hurts me—no more, I beg of you!"

"That's right, beg, you *puta!*" Juana, her eyes blazing with sadistic joy, flogged Carmencita pitilessly, the thick strap biting against the girl's shoulders and back, her hips and thighs. Twisting, crouching, writhing, vainly trying to escape the furious assault of the strap on her soft flesh, Carmencita at last tearfully broke down and implored mercy.

Implacably, Juana continued to rain blows on the helpless girl. At last, her soul annihilated by this public degradation and her flesh feverishly burning from the stinging cuts of the strap, Carmencita sagged in her father's grasp as he roughly ordered, *"¡Basta!"*

Panting, Juana lowered the strap, her ripe bosom exultantly heaving, and licked her lips with sensual gratification. "Very well, *amorcito*. I think for once she has had enough. But you, Carmencita, let me catch you being disrespectful to your father or to me again, or before these men, and I swear to you that you will taste the strap again—yes, girl, again and again until you are properly docile and humble! Now go to your room and go to sleep. Try not to cry too loudly to disturb your father and me—it is a night for love, *no es verdad*, Jorge, *mi corazón?*"

Carmencita had sunk down to the ground and now slowly, painfully, straightened, with a grimace and a cry of pain. She heard—buzzing in her ears through her feverish suffering—the ribald, lewd guffaws and remarks of the bandits who had enjoyed her martyrdom. She limped unsteadily back into the *jacal* and went into her little room, flung herself down on her face, and burst into heartrending sobs.

She was hardly conscious that Juana and her father had entered the *jacal* and gone to their bed in the larger part of the wide hut; she did not hear the sounds of their kisses and their hoarse murmurs of lustful consummation.

When Carmencita Caldera awoke the next morning, she made up her mind to run away forever. Last night, if her father had shown the slightest concern for her, she might perhaps have been able to come to reluctant terms with this agonizing situation which made her little more than Juana's slave and the imminent prey of a man like Manuel Regado.

215

For now, she was thoroughly convinced, it would not be long before Juana persuaded her father to give her to that horrible *bandido*, that swaggering murderer.

No, there was no hope for her so long as she remained with the camp of bandits. Now her father had utterly destroyed her respect for his authority. It would be absolutely futile to plead with him, to urge him to let her lead her own life, to wed anyone, much less the tall young Comanche who had saved her from the *jabalí*.

It would be very dangerous to try to leave the camp again, and it must be planned very carefully, she knew. She must let her father and Juana think that last night's whipping had completely humbled her. She must be cowed, even repentant, to convince them that she had accepted her lot. Only then would they relax their vigilance.

So, in the morning, fighting back the revulsion that swelled in her when she saw her father and Juana seated on their rude bed, lasciviously fondling and embracing each other, she lowered her eyes and meekly asked, "Excuse me, *mi padre*, Juana, shall I bring breakfast for you? I see that Felipe Gonzalez has already lit the fires under the cooking pot for the men."

"Well now, Carmencita," Juana preened herself, an arm around Jorge Caldera's shoulders, arching her right breast against the thin shift that covered her opulent nudity, "this respect becomes you much more. You see, Jorge *amorcito*, it is as I told you, a good whipping always teaches a rebellious girl her place before her father and mother." Then, frowning at the trembling young girl, she snapped, "Yes, of course, stupid one! Can't you see we're ready? Bring it at once! And one more thing, girl—your father wishes you to call me *madre*. I hope it will not be too long before you give up this disrespectful stubbornness of yours and obey his wishes, as a good daughter always should."

Carmencita bit her lips and sent her father a frantically imploring glance. To her consternation, he vigorously nodded and growled, "It's as Juana says. You know yourself, girl, we were married by the *padre*. Therefore, Juana has the right to be addressed so. See that you do this, if you don't want another good dose of the strap."

Carmencita could not suppress the tears that sprang to her eyes. This was the final blow. It was as if her father was dead for her; now truly she was little better than a cast-off orphan—and that would mean she was meant to be the *criatura*, even the *puta*, of Manuel Regado.

"I—I pr-promise I will try, *mi padre*." Her voice broke as she forced herself to mouth these self-effacing words. And then, born out of her desperate ingenuity, she added, "I—I beg your pardon for last night. I was disobedient. I am sorry, and I will try to please you both."

"Now that's being sensible, Carmencita," her father averred, giving Juana a hug and then bending his head and applying a loud smacking kiss against the young woman's ample bosom. "And that's enough talk now. Bring our breakfast and quickly, *comprendes*?"

"At once, *mi padre*." She bowed her head, turned, and left the *jacal*. As she walked toward the little clearing beyond the huts of the *bandidos* to the cooking pots where all the meals were prepared, she winced at the dull, throbbing pain from the whipping. She forced herself to walk as casually as she could, though the twinges made her grimace. Some of the men had come out of their huts, yawning and stretching, and they called to her, "*Hola, muchachita*, are you going to be a good girl now?" And, "Perhaps one night you'll dance with us, Carmencita, *no es verdad*? Last night you entertained us very well with your dance of the strap!"

There were guffaws and whispers which came to her ears after these taunting sallies, and Carmencita tried not to hear them, but her cheeks were burning as she approached Felipe Gonzales and timidly quavered, "*Señor, por favor, mi padre y mi m-madre* have ordered me to bring their breakfast. Will you be so kind, Señor Gonzalez?"

"Certainly, *muchachita*." The squat, thickly-bearded Mexican made her a mock bow, doffing his sombrero, which drew another heartless chorus of laughter from the watching *bandidos*. "There is chili and coffee and tortillas. I will prepare them for our *jefe* and his *mujer*. And take care you do not spill anything, *pequeña*, or perhaps we'll see you dance again, eh?"

Shame burned Carmencita's cheeks at this cruel allusion to her public disgrace last night, but she again meekly replied, "I shall be very careful, Señor Gonzales. *Muchas gracias*."

"*De nada, muchachita*. Here you are, the bowls of chili. Walk as if you were walking on eggs. You know what

217

might happen if you spill a single drop, *no es verdad?*" he added with a salacious guffaw.

She took hold of the two clay bowls into which the burly cook had ladled chili and carefully walked back to her father's *jacal*. Behind her, there was a buzz of lascivious conversation. She could well guess what they were saying about her, how they were speculating on what would happen to her. Worst of all, Manuel Regado came out of the *jacal* opposite her father's and jestingly called out, "When you've finished serving our *jefe* and his *mujer linda*, it would be kind of you to bring me my *desayuno* too. I will even give you a kiss for doing so, little one!"

She shuddered, and it was all she could do to keep the bowls steady in her trembling hands. But she managed, entered the *jacal* and, bowing her head, set the bowls down on an empty packing crate which served as a table and which had once contained powder and bullets which the *bandidos* had stolen. As she straightened, she stammered, "I'll bring the coffee and the tortillas directly, *mi padre, mi m-madre.*"

"Oh yes, this girl is learning very well, Jorge," Juana gloated. "Didn't I tell you she would? Now be quick about the rest, girl!"

Carmencita obeyed, and then at last was permitted to have her own breakfast, which she took into her little room in the *jacal* and half-heartedly ate. All the while, she began to plan what she must do and how it could best be done. She would leave the camp after midnight, when she was sure that everyone was asleep. But it would not be tonight, that would be too soon. She would let two or three days pass, until all of them thought that she was resigned to her fate. Tears blinded her, and she covered her face with her hands and silently prayed that her dead mother would forgive the sacrilege she had just committed in bestowing upon Juana the name of *madre*.

So, for the next three days, she went about her chores, drawing water in wooden buckets from a nearby little creek, bringing kindling wood for the cooking pots, ignoring the ogling stares and lecherous remarks of the men who appraised her and coveted her.

On the third morning, however, a new tribulation awaited her. As she brought her father and Juana their breakfast, Jorge coldly declared, "I wish you to bring Manuel Regado his *desayuno* this morning, Carmencita. I may

218

tell you that he has asked me for permission to be your *novio*. You will show that you accept him by bringing him food. It is an old custom and a very good one. One day, when you become his *mujer*, you will do everything for him."

"*Mi padre*—surely you don't mean—" Carmencita began, her voice choking in her throat.

"I *do* mean, girl! Now no more of that stubbornness of yours, *comprendes*? I'm your father, and you're to do what I tell you. Otherwise, there'll be a reckoning, and you know very well what it will be. Now go do it, as I've told you."

"But—but I don't love him—he's too old and besides— oh please, *mi padre*, not Manuel Regado!" Carmencita tearfully implored.

Her father rose from the bed on which he was sitting with Juana, his face dark with anger. "I swear to you, girl, if you keep me from my breakfast with this nonsense of yours, I'll thrash you till the skin's flayed from your bottom, and that's my promise! Go do what I've said at once!"

There was no help for it. Scarcely able to see for her tears, Carmencita stumbled out to the cooking pot, and brought the bowl of chili, the coffee, and the tortillas to Manuel Regado, who stood in the doorway of his *jacal*, grinning and showing his decaying, yellow teeth, stroking his beard and eyeing her from head to toe.

"Now that is very sweet of you, *pequeña*," he drawled as he stepped aside to let her enter the *jacal*. "We shall make a fine pair, the two of us. You'll see, Carmencita. You'll have no reason to complain of me as a husband."

As she set down his food and the coffee and turned to leave, he put a hand on her hip and sniggered, "You're made for *niños*, and you'll give me many of them once we're married, *no es verdad, linda*?"

"Please, Señor R-Regado, I—I must draw water from the creek."

"To be sure, Carmencita!" He made her a bow like a cavalier's, bending low, sweeping his sombrero to one side. "Such diligence is a very good sign. It tells me that you are the woman for me—though, of course, I've already known that for some time. And one thing more, little one. Your father has given me permission to call upon you so that I may become your *novio* and, before too much longer, your husband. That should please you, eh?"

She shuddered violently and, through gritted teeth,

219

forced herself to murmur, "I shall do what my father asks of me. And now I must go."

When she went to the creek with two buckets, she told herself that tonight must be the time. It was intolerable to think of that horrible man as her husband. He had dared to touch her as he might touch a *puta*; he had even spoken of her having his *niños. Holy Virgin, do not let it happen, I pray unto you with all my soul!* She lifted her eyes to the bright May sky, but once again she was blinded with tears.

CHAPTER TWENTY

It was after midnight. Carmencita had overheard her father remark to Felipe Gonzalez, at suppertime, that three days hence they would ride against the village of Coalixa, fifty miles to the southwest. It was said that the *alcalde* there had hoarded many silver pesos in a chest buried in his garden. Also, he was a doddering old man married to a flirtatious young girl no older than Juana; there were also other girls in the village and it was high time that all these loyal men had *criaturas* to serve their needs.

Then her father had said something else which had made her blood run cold. They would have a great fiesta when they returned from Coalixa, and Manuel Regado and Carmencita would be married. And if Carmencita thought that her senses had betrayed her, and that perhaps she had misunderstood her father's words to Felipe Gonzalez, he boastingly confirmed this only an hour later, after he had finished his supper. "Girl, we ride to Coalixa in a few days. I shall try to find you a proper dress for your wedding to Manuel Regado. We shall bring back a priest, so that it will be done properly. Then you'll have no reason to complain, and when it's done, you'll obey Manuel as you would me, do you understand me?"

Mutely she had nodded, gone back to her little chamber, and flung herself down on her bed to weep and pray. With this had come the unswerving resolve to leave tonight, to flee to Kitante. The *indios* were brave fighters, and surely they would defend her against these dreadful *bandidos*. There would be bloodshed, and she prayed the Holy Virgin to pardon her this terrible transgression against her own father, one that might cost the lives of men. And yet she could not submit to the fate her father planned for her, she could not!

Her father and Juana had come back to the *jacal* late tonight, after the plans had been made for the attack. Both of them had drunk too much tequila, and they were laughing boisterously, kissing and fondling each other. She had tried not to listen to the sounds that followed. It almost seemed to her that the two of them were purposely more shameless than before, as a way of showing her the life she would be expected to lead with the bearded rogue they had chosen for her. The thought was sickening, and yet in a sense she was almost grateful to them. Even as she put her hands over her ears to drown out the sounds of their kissings and obscene exhortations, the slaps of hands on naked flesh and the coarse laughter of their animalistic mating, she strengthened her determination to make an end of her enforced servility—yes, even if it meant an end to her own life. Then, aghast that she should even contemplate such a dire alternative, she crossed herself, prayed, and fell asleep.

When she awoke, it was just two hours before dawn. There was absolute silence throughout the camp. The moon was obscured by thick, slowly drifting clouds, and no one would see or hear her go. Cautiously, she got out of her bed, still clothed in her blouse and skirt, tiptoed to the door of the *jacal*, and opened it to peer out into the night. There was not a sound, and no sight of any of the *bandidos*. Taking a deep breath, she tiptoed out of the *jacal* and made her way toward the forest, toward the narrow pathway that led to the west, to the stronghold of the young Comanche who had befriended her.

There were two things Carmencita took with her, both of them precious reminders of her dead mother. One was a little wooden crucifix, which a mendicant friar had given to Marta Caldera a decade before, blessing it and her little daughter in return for food Marta had given him. Marta Caldera told Carmencita, "This little crucifix is blessed, my daughter. A worthy *padre* gave it to me, and prayed for your happiness when you should become a woman. Keep it, let it bring you luck, and when you are troubled, hold it and pray to the dear *Señor Dios*." The other memento was a small red and yellow *rebozo*, or shawl, which Marta Caldera had knitted just a year before she died.

As she made her way out of the camp, Carmencita wrapped the *rebozo* around her slim shoulders and tightly

222

clasped the little crucifix in her right hand, praying to the Holy Virgin to protect her in her flight. Once beyond the clearing of the camp, she disappeared into the forest and found the pathway. She began to run, for she knew that it was a long journey. If any of the *bandidos* discovered she was missing, they would mount their horses and easily overtake her. She must go as swiftly as she could, to be as close to the stronghold of Señor Kitante as possible before any of them wakened.

She had gone about two miles when she suddenly stopped with a terrified gasp. She had heard an angry squeal in a thicket of mesquite off to her left, and she remembered the ferocious *jabalí* the young Comanche had killed. She moved to her right and crouched behind a gnarled cottonwood tree. The squeal was repeated, closer this time, and she held her breath as she saw a large *jabalí* break through the mesquite, its beady little eyes searching this way and that, till at last with a snort it trotted off toward the *bandido* camp.

She waited a few minutes, her heart beating wildly with terror, and then she began to run again. In her distraction, she did not notice that the loosely tied shawl, which had brushed against an overhanging branch of the cottonwood, had fluttered to the ground behind her and lay plainly in view on the narrow path.

On the preceding afternoon, Friar Bartoloméo Alicante and the four Windhaven Range vaqueros who were escorting him had ridden into the Comanche stronghold. There the elderly, jovial friar had been welcomed by Sangrodo, who gave orders that a feast be held to honor this beloved shaman of the white-eyes and the four brave men who had ridden all this way to guard him. After they had eaten, Sangrodo filled a calumet with tobacco, puffed at it, and handed it to the friar, who responded in kind. "You do me much honor, *padre*," Sangrodo said. "Long before I met you, there were runners among the tribes who brought word of your courage and kindness and how you lived among the *indios* of the plains. Be sure that you are welcome here, *padre*. You say that you wish to live with us and to help us. And I say that this is a good thing. You can help teach the children, you can bring contentment to the hearts of some of my young braves who are dissatisfied with the peaceful life we lead here in our new home, and you can comfort the sick and the old. But you see for yourself how far we are from any neighbors. I have often thought that we are as isolated here as we should have been if the white-eyes troops had captured us and sent us to a reservation in the way they have driven so many other tribes."

"If your people have need of me, Sangrodo, that will be my reward, and there will be no loneliness for any of us," Friar Bartoloméo smilingly responded. "Because I am growing old and my weary body becomes too heavy for a poor burro or even a sturdy horse, I will say selfishly that it will be good to live here with your people and to teach the children how to read and write. I have heard how the young brave Lopasuta, who sought wisdom, found a home and a calling. Well, it may be that I shall find other pupils as apt as he who will do equal credit to your people, Sangrodo."

The Comanche chief smiled and nodded, and once again passed the calumet to the friar. They looked at each other with an understanding and trust between them that needed no further words.

Carmencita halted, out of breath, glancing back wildly to see if anyone pursued her. She did not know how far she had come, but already she was exhausted. Bowing her head, she took hold of the branch of a cottonwood tree. Suddenly there was a whirring of wings and an angry hooting as a screech owl, disturbed by the movement of the branch, soared overhead to the top of a tree. She uttered a startled cry, looked back again, and then stumbled onward. As she put a hand to her throat, she realized that she had lost her *rebozo*. But there was no time to think of it now, and certainly it would be foolish to retrace her steps and find it. Nonetheless, she mourned its loss; it was one of the last links that bound her to her beloved dead mother. The crucifix was in her left hand, and she opened her palm and stared at it, then kissed it and murmured a prayer for the soul of Marta Caldera.

The first faint rays of dawn appeared in the eastern sky. A faint purple and red glow began to illuminate the dark blue of the sky, touching the thick, slow-moving clouds as if with a painter's brush.

She did not know how much farther she could go on. The muscles of her legs were stiff with fatigue, and the sudden irrational fear that she might not find the Comanche camp now assailed her. Once again she paused to regain her breath, to ease the pains in her lungs and leg muscles. Once again, she opened her left hand and kissed the cross, then raised her eyes to the slowly brightening sky to pray for strength and courage.

Manuel Regado had not drunk too much tequila at the celebration that anticipated their victorious raid against the village. After all, he would be riding as *teniente*—lieutenant—to the *jefe*, and would be giving many of the orders, so it was as well not to cloud his head with too much drink. Besides, the thought of his oncoming nuptials with that tasty *muchachita* kept him from deep slumber. He lay on his pallet, arms pillowing his head, grinning lecherously at the erotic images that danced through his mind. He'd teach her how to service him, that fancy girl who gave herself such airs. Oh, he knew very well that she was afraid of him and hated him: that would make his conquest of her all the sweeter. Nor had he forgotten how aroused he had been to watch her cowering under Juana's strap. He put his hand to the glossy black leather belt round his middle, with its silver buckle, and chuckled lewdly to himself. He would take that to bed with him on their wedding night, *seguramente*.

As he speculated on his sadistic pleasures, he suddenly scowled. Ever since that whipping, she'd been very docile—too docile—and that was suspicious. And the way she had spoken to him—so humbly, as if she were already prepared to accept him as her *hombre*. Perhaps, yes, just perhaps this had been a little game of hers. Perhaps she would try to run away. *Por Dios*, perhaps this very night!

He must make sure of her. When he came back after the raid with all the plunder, he would want Carmencita ready for him, he would want her to marry him that very night.

He sat up abruptly, slipped on his boots, and strode across the way to the *jacal* of Jorge and Juana Caldera. Very carefully he opened the door and peered inside. He could see the *jefe* and his woman lying entwined, she turned toward him and one arm flung over his face. The *jefe* was snoring. Manuel Regado laughed silently, and then turned toward Carmencita's chamber. But there was no one in her bed—by all the saints, the *puta* had run away!

He went out quietly, then hurried to the corral. Saddling

his horse, he rode to the edge of the clearing. There he found the narrow path to the west, and guessing that Carmencita had probably taken it, he followed it. His eyes were cruel and narrowed as he spurred his horse on, his lips twisted with a vicious anticipation. He'd teach her to run away from him. If he found her, he'd take her then and there, and then bring her back with her wrists thonged behind her back and tell her father and Juana what she'd done. He'd watch while they gave her the strap, and then he'd see to it that she was locked up under guard while he rode off with the men. And by the week's end, by all the saints, and by the devil too, if need be, she'd be his *mujer* for good!

Mercilessly spurring his horse, he rode at breakneck speed down the path. Then suddenly he reined in the snorting mustang, for he had seen the *rebozo*. He dismounted and retrieved it, stuffed it into the pocket of his breeches, and rode on. She could not have gone too far afoot. And the forest would frighten her. Ah, well, he'd see that she was really frightened this time, in such a way that she'd never try to run away again. Besides, he fancied himself as *muy macho*, and he had had many woman who had told him that he was. Once she felt his *cojones*, she'd forget all her silly notions. And if she didn't, there was his belt to assure her total obedience to his will.

Carmencita had come within a mile of the Comanche stronghold. Her footsteps were flagging; she was gasping for breath and drenched in sweat. Again she paused, her head bowed, as with both hands she grasped the sturdy branch of a tall juniper tree. The crucifix fell from her palm, and she sobbed aloud as she saw it lying in the dirt at her feet. She sank down to her knees to retrieve it, passionately kissing it, and she wept again for her dead mother, for all the agony she had endured since that unforgettable night five months ago.

At last, she stumbled to her feet, tears glistening on her flushed cheeks, and went on. And then her heart nearly stopped as she heard the thundering of a horse's hooves behind her, and as she glanced back over her shoulder, she saw the bearded rider, crouching over the neck of his mustang, brandishing her *rebozo*.

"¡Dios, ayúdame por piedad!" she hoarsely cried. She tried to run, but tripped and went down to her knees. And then the horseman was upon her. With a vicious oath, he

226

reined in the mustang, leaped down and seized her by the armpits, dragged her to her feet, and grinned at her.

"Good morning, Carmencita. You've led me a merry chase, you tricky little *puta!*"

"S-Señor R-Regado, I beg of you—let me go—I can't bear it—I hate my father—and—and that woman Juana—oh have pity, Señor Regado! She hates me too, as my father does—let me go, they'll never see me again—let me live my life—have mercy on me!"

"Why, so I shall, *pequeña*," he wolfishly grinned, his eyes devouring her. "Now there is many a man who, if you played a trick on him like this when he was betrothed to you, would consign you to the devil. But not I, Manuel Regado. You see, Carmencita, I've wanted you ever since your father brought you to our camp. We'll be married on the night when I come back with the men from our raid. They'll sing my praises, because of the booty I'll bring back, the silver, the gold, the jewels, the women for the others—and you for me, *linda!*"

"Oh no—let me go—I don't want you—I'm too young—I've never been with a man—you'll have all the women you want—please, I shall pray for you always—do this one kindness and let me escape them forever!" she sobbed.

Kitante, too, had spent a sleepless night. He could forget neither Carmencita's beauty nor her poignant anguish. He had of course told his father about the *bandido* camp, but he had not been able to bring himself to mention Carmencita. He would, in time. It was inhuman to keep a young girl like that against her will in a camp of *bandidos*, and what her father had done in deserting her dying mother to take that young woman as his new wife was an act that no Comanche brave, not even a coward, would have dreamed of doing.

He had hoped that she might come again to see him, late at night, just as they had met that first time. For the last few nights, indeed, he had gone riding on his mustang, back to where they had met; he had waited, listening to the sounds of the night, hoping that she would come.

Now he felt ill at ease, and he could not explain why. On a sudden impulse, he left the tepee and went to the corral to get his mustang. Then he turned it toward the east and down the path.

* * *

"But you see, Carmencita, I don't want other women, I want you. The other women will go to my *amigos*, my *compañeros*." Again Regado grinned, baring his teeth as she shrank back, helpless in his grip. His eyes lecherously traced the swell of her bosom. "Besides, once you're my *mujer*, your father and Juana won't bother you. It will be I who will teach you what's right, and what pleases me, little one. You'll do your best, I know. And now, since you've given me all this trouble, it's only fair that you give me a little reward for having found you before you could have done something very foolish."

"What—what do you mean, S-Señor Regado?" she faintly quavered.

"Why, I mean to give you a little taste of what is in store for you, as my *mujer*. Then, you see, on the night when the priest comes, we'll be properly married and that will make twice. It will be more lasting that way, little one."

"No—I beg of you—have pity on me—I don't want you, I don't want to be your woman, not even your wife, not even in the Holy Church—in the name of the sweet Virgin, the Holy Mother, take pity on me, let me go—*oh no!*" Her voice rose to a shriek as, with a brutal laugh, he put his hands to the top of her blouse and ripped it, baring her to the waist.

"Ah, now there's something a husband can appreciate, *linda!*" he leered. He cupped her firm, round breasts with his sinewy fingers, and leaned forward to kiss her piteously trembling mouth. She shrieked again, and with her remaining strength struck at him with the little wooden crucifix. With a savage oath, he tore it from her and flung it into a clump of mesquite. Then he forced her down on the ground so brutally that she was stunned, and began to loosen his breeches as he towered above her, uttering a sinister chuckle as he watched her cringe and try to cover her nakedness with her soft, trembling little hands.

"I'd have preferred a softer bed, little one," he gloatingly confided, savoring her helplessness, her shame, her terror. "But you'll see, a girl's first time is the most exciting one of all. And once you feel me in you, *pequeña*, you'll want me in your bed every night and maybe even in the morning before breakfast, *no es verdad?*" Tilting back his head, he burst into salacious laughter.

She began to whimper, her eyes enormous, glazed with abysmal revulsion as he bared himself. She tried to rise, but

228

she could not. She was paralyzed. Her lips moved in soundless, jumbled prayer.

"And now let's see the rest of you, *pequeña*. Don't be shy; when a girl's married to a man, it's only natural for her to show him all she has to offer. I like what I've seen so far, and I'm sure I'll enjoy the rest."

He was about to kneel down to rip off her skirt, when suddenly he heard a noise. He looked up—and swore a violent oath, for bearing down on him from the west was a rider—a tall, slim young Comanche, naked save for breeches and moccasins. He reached for his pistol, cocked it, and pulled the trigger; but Kitante made his mustang swerve and the bullet whizzed harmlessly past. Straightening in the saddle, the young Comanche drew his hunting knife from his belt and flung it with unerring aim. It buried itself in Regado's chest. The outlaw stiffened, his eyes rolling in their sockets. The pistol dropped from his nerveless hand, and with an unfinished oath on his lips, he pitched forward and lay still.

Kitante leaped off his horse and ran to Carmencita. "I thank the great Spirit that I came in time!" he gasped. Then, retrieving her tattered blouse, he handed it to her, averting his eyes as he said, "Cover yourself, *pobrecita*. I'll take you to my father's stronghold. There you'll be safe."

CHAPTER TWENTY-ONE

Kitante helped Carmencita mount up behind him, bidding her lock her arms round his middle, and rode back to his father's stronghold. She sobbed softly, but the feel of Kitante's wiry young body and the gentleness in his voice as he sought to soothe her fears reassured her. And for him it was inexpressibly thrilling to feel her body pressed against his and to know that she entrusted herself to him. At this moment, there was not a warrior in the Comanche camp, no matter how many coups he had counted over enemies, to whom Sangrodo's stalwart young son felt inferior.

It was a radiant morning, and the air was soft and warm. Already the squaws were out preparing the cooking fires for their men. Most of them were Mexican, for the Comanche squaws of many of these braves had been mercilessly slaughtered when Captain George Munson and his troops from Fort Inge had raided the Texas stronghold years ago. When Sangrodo had brought his people across the border to settle, the Mexican girls of the nearby villages had learned that his braves were not bent on raids, but eager to live in peace. And so there had been many alliances, and now many young children of mingled Mexican and Comanche blood were growing to adulthood in this isolated stronghold.

Catayuna had come out of Sangrodo's tepee to prepare the morning meal. She saw Kitante riding in with the young Mexican girl behind him. Her eyes widened with surprise, and then she could not help smiling. It was time this eager, impatient young man had something more important to think about than helping till the fields. She saw Kitante dismount and gently help Carmencita down. She came to them, a finger to her lips. "He's still asleep. You ride back as from a battle, Kitante." Her lips curved into a whimsical smile. "And is this part of your booty?"

"No, beloved woman. This is Carmencita. She ran away from the village where the *bandidos* are staying. Her father is their *jefe*. He took himself a *mujer* not much older than she, and would mate Carmencita with the worst of his men."

Catayuna's eyes fixed on Kitante's hunting knife, and saw the blood on it. She gasped, "And you killed him when he came after her, is that not so, Kitante?"

"It is so, beloved woman. I had to. I could not stand by and see such a man abuse this girl. And there is more—before all of the *bandidos*; her father held her while the woman who calls herself 'mother' to Carmencita whipped her with a strap. It was not to be borne, and I would be no Comanche man if I had not tried to help her."

Catayuna smiled gently and touched his shoulder. "You *are* Comanche, you are your father's son. No, no man worthy of the name would have stood by and let so young a girl suffer. But what will you do now, Kitante?"

"Yes, Kitante, what will you do now?" came Sangrodo's gruff voice, as he emerged from the tepee.

"My father!"

"I heard what you said to Catayuna. Girl, come forward to me. Tell me if what I have heard is true."

Carmencita had covered herself as best she could with the ripped blouse, and with an arm pressed tight against her bosom, she blushingly approached the tall Comanche chief. "It is true what your son says, señor," she stammered, and then poured out her whole sad story, interrupting herself occasionally with sobs. "Please, señor," she concluded, "please, I beg of you, do not send me back to them!"

Sangrodo turned to his beloved woman, saw her compassionate gaze, then frowned and slowly shook his head. "My son, you well know that we have given up the old life across the Rio Grande. The Great Spirit willed it so when that *yanqui* captain rode into our peaceful village and killed the old, the squaws, the children. We took our vengeance, yes, but we knew what would befall us if we stayed there free on our land. And so we came here and we chose the way of peace."

"But, my father—" Kitante began, with an imploring

look at Carmencita, who had begun to weep softly, one hand over her eyes.

"I will speak, my son," Sangrodo firmly interposed. "In the old days, we rode among the *mejicanos* to pay them back for their crimes against our people. We took their women to make them slaves or squaws." He glanced at Catayuna, who lowered her eyes, and then, straightening her shoulders, looked up again and smiled proudly at him. His lips curved in a faint smile of understanding. "But today, Kitante, in our new life, we court these *mujeres mejicanas* to become our squaws, we do not steal them." His voice grew harsher. "If you keep this girl, my son, it will lead to the shedding of blood between those people who are now our countrymen, since many of their women now live in our village."

"But they are *bandidos*, my father!" Kitante indignantly protested. "And theirs is not a village but a stronghold, from which they go forth to raid and kill and take booty. Do you wish this gentle girl, Carmencita, to go back to live with such evil ones?"

"There is the honorable way, Kitante. You will take her back, you will speak with a straight tongue to her father and explain what has happened. And if, as I now think, my son, seeing how you look upon her, you desire her as your squaw, then you must ask her father for permission to make her your woman. With us now is the white-eyes shaman, Friar Bartoloméo. If her father gives consent, Kitante, then he will make the two of you one, after our own ritual of the mingling of blood which is the law of our ancient people. I have spoken, as your chief, as your father. This you must do, my son."

Though he had consumed a good deal of tequila the night before, Jorge Caldera woke at dawn, sat up and blinked his eyes, then ran his hand over Juana's bare shoulder and slyly cupped her full breast. She did not stir, and he yawned again, then eased himself out of their rude bed and stretched his limbs. Today was the day of preparation for the raid. Manuel Regado had instructed the men as to their duties, but he as *jefe* could still improvise new ideas to gain them greater plunder.

And, too, today would be one day nearer to Carmencita's wedding day. He chuckled to himself, walked to the narrow little door of her chamber, pushed it open, and then let out an empty oath. "¡*Caramba!* The girl's gone!" Then, turning, he bawled, "Juana, wake up! Wake up, I say! Carmencita's run away. The spiteful little slut, to vex me so when there's so much to be done today! Oh, but she'll pay for this! Wake up, Juana!"

The young woman groaned, drawn from her half-drunken torpor by the loud anger in his voice, and abruptly sat up. "¿*Qué pasa, mi amor?*" she mumbled.

"Are you deaf, woman? I told you, Carmencita's run away!"

"We should have tied her up in her room—or sent her over to Manuel," Juana shrilly declared, shaking a forefinger at him. "I told you, you've been too gentle with that stubborn one!"

"What's done is done, Juana. Now, when I want to plan for this raid and make sure that all goes well, I must waste time hunting her down. I'll go find Manuel, he's the man to find her, since it's his future wife he'll be hunting!" Then, gruffly, as he strode out of the *jacal,* he ordered, "Get me some *desayuno,* and quickly, woman!"

Juana made a face behind his back, and grumbled to herself. "Just you wait, Carmencita, just you wait! I'll have you peeled down raw, you nasty little baggage, I'll thrash you till the skin's off your bottom, and then we'll see if you'll try this trick again!" Then, tugging on her blouse and skirt, she hurried out to the cooking pot.

When Jorge Caldera called out for his lieutenant and there was no answer, he entered the *jacal* and found it empty. Now really concerned, he came out and, cupping his hands to his mouth, cried out, "¡*Hombres, vengan despiértense!*"

As some of the bandits appeared in the doors of their huts, he furiously gestured to them. Fifteen of them at once gathered around him, and he quickly explained that both his daughter and Manuel Regado were missing. "Three of you with me, to the west. You others, ride to the east, north, and south. See if you can find their trail."

Felipe Gonzales, sniggered and proffered, "*Jefe,* perhaps Manuel wished to enjoy his wedding night a few days in advance, *no es verdad?*" His remark was greeted by a murmur of lewd laughter from the others.

The men mounted their horses and rode, as bidden. Caldera was visibly irritated. Leaning to one side, he shouted to Felipe Gonzales, "If Manuel went after Carmencita, that's one thing. But if I find he's amusing himself with her when he should be back at the camp preparing for our raid, I'll nail his ears to the door of my jacal!"

"Mi jefe," Gonzalez pointed ahead, "there's something lying in the path there. The body of a man!"

"¡Diablos! ¡Adelante, compañeros!" he shouted as he spurred his mustang forward.

He dismounted, hurried to the inert body, and swore a violent oath. "¡Por los cojones del diablo! It's Manuel—he's been knifed—but how could Carmencita have done such a thing?"

"And where is she now, mi jefe?" Gonzalez shook his head as he stared down at the lifeless body of the bearded lieutenant of the bandit band. "Look there, hoofprints to the west!"

"We'll follow them and see where they lead us, Felipe! ¡Pronto!" Caldera sprang into his saddle and spurred his horse on toward the Comanche stronghold, Gonzalez and the other two bandits closely following him.

They came out of the woods into the clearing. Then, to the west, Caldero spied the Comanche stronghold. He rose in his saddle and uttered an astonished gasp: "¡Caramba, los indios! I did not know they were so near us, Felipe."

"Nor I, mi jefe," the stocky Mexican averred. Then he pointed excitedly toward the village: "Look there—isn't that Carmencita? And that tall gray-haired indio, he must be their jefe!"

"By all the saints, it's my daughter, you've sharp eyes, Felipe! But there are too many indios for us. We'll ride back to our village and bring the men with their weapons." Caldera grimly chuckled. "It may be that we shall find greater treasures in this camp of accursed indios than in the village—and if we take them by surprise, we'll still have time to attack the village, too, before the week's over."

They turned their horses' heads and galloped back to their camp, where they found all the bandidos returned from their search of the countryside. A quarter of an hour later, all of the men, fully armed, rode out with Jorge Caldera at their head.

Carmencita began to sob piteously after Sangrodo's solemn order to Kitante to take her back. Catayuna, deeply moved, put an arm around the young girl's shoulders and tried to console her. "Do not cry, querida. First, you'll rest

235

and have *desayuno* with us. Then Kitante will take you back. And several of our braves will ride with you so that there will be no danger. Kitante will explain to your father, and the good God who knows all sorrows has heard your prayers—He will answer them, Carmencita. Have courage!"

She drew the weeping girl away toward a nearby tepee, urging her to lie down and rest while she prepared food for her. Meanwhile, Friar Bartoloméo had wakened and emerged from the tepee in which he had been quartered, and the four Windhaven Range vaqueros followed him as he walked toward Sangrodo.

The jovial old friar had seen Carmencita's distress and Catayuna's attempt at consolation, and gently asked, "Why does that young girl weep, Sangrodo?"

"Because Kitante saved her from an evil man, a *bandido*, one of a band whose stronghold is to the east of us. He wishes to make this girl his squaw. I have told him that he must take her back, and if he is truly resolved to share his tepee with her, he must ask her father's permission. This is the way it has been done among our forebears. Now all the more, since we live in peace, as you well know, we go back to the old, the good, the honorable ways."

"Your way is not so different from ours, Sangrodo," the friar responded. "And if it is God's will they be wed, I myself will unite them."

"I pray to the Great Spirit," Sangrodo gloomily avowed, "that there will be no battle between the *bandidos* and my braves. And also that, when my son goes to their camp, they respect his courage and his honor and do not draw their weapons because he is an *indio*."

"I pray this also, Sangrodo. The shedding of blood is banned by one of our Ten Commandments," the friar solemnly responded.

"For us, the will of the Great Spirit is handed down to us by our ancestors, in stories around the campfire; then each man goes to his secret place and there speaks to the Great Spirit for guidance."

"In this also, we are like brothers, Sangrodo," the friar smiled.

Nacio Lorcas, one of the vaqueros who had accompanied the friar, overheard this conversation in Spanish and, seeing that Friar Bartoloméo had concluded it, came up and whispered, "Do you think the bandits of whom you speak may ride in upon us and attack us? I will tell my *compañeros* to have their weapons ready. And the *señor patrón* himself told me, before I rode with you, that he had given the *jefe* of the *indios* guns like ours so that they could defend themselves."

"I understand that it is wise to prepare for the worst, my son." The portly friar turned to him and touched his shoulder. "But it is not for you or for me, either, to tell Sangrodo that he should use those weapons. It is because he is *jefe* here and we are his guests that we let him decide what is to be done. You and I can only pray that there will be no bloodshed." And then, compassionately, stroking his double chin, he mused aloud, "Kitante is such a fine young man, and that Carmencita is sweet and gentle, and I am sure she is chaste. I shall pray that they may be united in wedlock and that their lives will be happy and long."

"Amen to that, *mi padre*," Nacio Lorcas bowed his head and crossed himself.

The vaquero turned to his companion, Octavio Negras, and whispered, "There will be trouble, Octavio. Do not let the *jefe* of the *indios* see you, but get your Spencer and have it ready."

Octavio Negras, a plump, genial vaquero, nodded and moved over to his horse, which was tethered to a wooden bar at the Comanche corral. The Spencer repeating carbine was attached to his mustang in a leather sling. Glancing warily about, he drew the weapon out and held it behind his back, fixing the pathway toward the stronghold with an apprehensive look.

It was not very long before there was heard, in the east, the thrumming of horses' hooves. An electrifying aura ran through the Comanche stronghold. Friar Bartoloméo rapidly crossed himself and, his eyes turned toward the sky, prayed for a peaceful solution to this confrontation. Sangrodo stood before his tepee, arms folded across his chest, his face impassive, while Kitante stared beseechingly at him.

The bandits reined in their horses. Jorge Caldera, carrying an old Belgian musket, dismounted from his mustang and warily approached the gate of the Comanche camp. Tied to the musket was a white scarf, the symbol of a truce.

"I am Jorge Caldera, *jefe*, and I come to claim my daughter, Carmencita!" he loudly shouted.

237

"I hear you, *jefe de bandidos*," Sangrodo cupped his hands to his mouth and called back. "We live here in peace, we seek no quarrel with you. My son Kitante was about to take your daughter back to your camp, and would parley with you to ask that you let her go."

"I have pledged her to my lieutenant, whom I find dead upon the trail which leads to your stronghold!" Caldera angrily called back. "I am her father, and thus I alone order what she shall or shall not do. It was my wish that she marry my *teniente*, Manuel Regado, but he has been slain by one of you."

"By my son Kitante," Sangrodo solemnly retorted, as he moved slowly toward the gate of the stronghold.

His eyes fixed on the mounted bandits, armed and surly, glowering at him, and he glanced back at Kitante and proud Catayuna. Then, facing Jorge Caldera, he called again, "We seek no quarrel, *jefe*. But your daughter was followed by a man of your band who sought to abuse her. My son could not let this be, and in fair fight killed him."

Felipe Gonzalez leaned toward Carmencita's father and whispered, "They are better armed than we are, *mi jefe*. There are more of them, and if there is a battle, we shall be destroyed. Think well what you do."

"I do not need you to tell me this, Felipe Gonzalez," Caldera angrily hissed back. "They have new guns, we are no match for them. But I cannot lose face—my daughter stands there, and Manuel Regado lies dead."

"Then let me challenge this boy who boasts of having saved her, *mi jefe*," Gonzalez murmured. "Perhaps he took Manuel by surprise, but he will not take me. You know well that I am the best of all in your camp with the *cuchillo*."

"That is true, Felipe. You have faced many men and bested them." He pondered a moment, then cupped his hands and called to Sangrodo. "If it is true that this weakling son of yours has somehow killed my *teniente*, Manuel Regado, and if it is also true that he has thought himself man enough to take my daughter as his *mujer*, then I ask that you settle this by a duel to the death between my new *teniente*, Felipe Gonzalez, and this untried boy."

"Do not let them fight, Sangrodo," Catayuna passionately whispered.

But Sangrodo, his face still taut, standing erect with arms folded across his chest, the eyes of all his braves upon

238

him now, looked at his son appraisingly. Kitante stiffened, straightening his shoulders and regarding his father with an earnest, determined look.

The graying chief of the Comanche Wanderers was satisfied. He put his hands to his mouth and called to Jorge Caldera, "So be it. This is the way it was in the ancient days, one man against the other. And it is better so, for we bear you no hatred. I, Sangrodo, *jefe* of the People, the Wanderers, accept your challenge in the name of my son Kitante. He will fight against the man you choose. If he wins, you will agree that your *hija* may remain with us and become his *mujer*."

"I do so agree, chief of the Comanches!" Caldera angrily cried back. "And if Felipe Gonzalez, who shall fight against your son, defeats him, I have your promise that you'll return my daughter to me. And that will be an end of it."

"To this I pledge my word, as chief of my people," Sangrodo proudly retorted.

Friar Bartoloméo Alicante crossed himself and hastily murmured to the tall Comanche leader, "Your son is only a boy, and he will fight that *bandido* in whose face I read evil and cruelty. That one has killed many, and your son has little chance against him. Be wise, Sangrodo, and do not agree to this uneven duel. There is surely a way to deal with these men in parley."

"It is true that he is young, but he is my son. He is Comanche. I will stake all upon his honor and his courage. Without this, his mother bore him in vain," was Sangrodo's solemn reply. And then, with a compassionate glance at the anguished friar, he cried, "It shall be done. You will send the man who will fight my son into my stronghold. You have my word that it will be a fair fight."

"And you have mine that we shall let the matter be decided by the outcome," Caldera called back. Then, leaning toward the stout Mexican, he muttered, "If you win, Felipe, I will give you Carmencita as your *mujer*."

Gonzalez grinned lasciviously. "I will cut him to ribbons, *mi jefe*. I have had no *mujer* for many years, but I shall win your Carmencita as my own. And she will be obedient to me, I pledge this to you."

"*Bueno*, Felipe! You will fight with the *cuchillo*, and there is no one else in Mexico more skillful with it. I have confidence in you, *mi teniente.*" Caldera grinned crookedly.

Friar Bartoloméo made a last attempt to appeal to the bandit leader's reason. Holding up his right hand and advancing to the entry of the stronghold, he exclaimed, "*Hombres,* in the name of Him who died upon the cross to save us all, I beg of you to observe His holy ordinance against taking human life. What will you prove if your champion kills this young *indio*? Only that he is the stronger, the older, hence more experienced in the use of a weapon. And it is against all Christian teachings to let this unfortunate girl be the prize for the winner. Can this not be disputed peacefully? Will you not let the girl herself plead for her freedoom?"

"Priest," Jorge Caldera harshly retorted, "do not try me too far! For long years I sweated over a forge as a blacksmith while a fat old *patrón* grew rich from my labors and gave me scarcely enough pesos to feed my wife and child and myself. What I have now I have earned by my wits, without being a slave to any man and least of all to a priest. Would you have me abandon my daughter to a savage and ride away with my men, disgraced, because as her father, I did not demand her return to my household?"

"But the girl is young, innocent, and she abhors the life you have made her lead, Jorge Caldera," the friar earnestly countered.

"Take care, priest." Caldera's face was livid with anger. "I do not need your sermons this fine morning. Now, a last time, this is what I propose to you: this *indio* meets Felipe in the *lucha a muerte.* If the boy wins, my men and I will observe the fair outcome and return to our camp—then let him take Carmencita, for he will have won her. But if Felipe wins, as he is certain to, then it is he who will be Carmencita's *esposo.* In either case, priest, you see that we observe your Christian teaching in not attacking and taking back my daughter by force of arms! There now. Decide quickly; my men and I are impatient. We have other business to attend to this day."

Carmencita, who had risen from the pallet in the tepee at the first sound of her father's voice, ran toward the slim young Comanche and sobbingly entreated, "No, Señor Kitante, he will kill you! I would not have you die for me. Not after what you have done to save me—oh, my father, I will go back with you of my own free will if only you'll promise not to marry me to any of your cruel men! Have pity on me, *mi padre!*"

Jorge Caldera uttered a mocking laugh. "No, girl, you've tried me too far this time. Say to yourself that it was you who brought about the death of my faithful *teniente* Manuel. He would have been a proper *esposo* for you, *muchachita*. He would have known how to deal with your childish obstinacies and your haughty airs. Do not forget, you are only the daughter of a blacksmith who was once a peon. I have no patience for a girl who would play at being *duquesa!*" Then, his voice hardening, he exclaimed, "Enough of this! The *lucha a muerte*, or I shall give the signal to open fire on all of you. If your women are killed as well as your men, it is your own doing."

Kitante gently disengaged Carmencita's clinging arms and strode forward. "I am ready to fight your Felipe Gonzalez. It will be between the two of us, that is to be understood."

"To be sure, my fine cockerel," Caldera guffawed, slapping his thigh and turning back to wink at his men, who joined in his mocking laughter. "You have my word that there will be no blood shed other than your own. You'd best say your goodbyes now to my daughter, *indio*. You won't have time for them once Felipe cuts out your tripes!"

Catayuna, standing beside Sangrodo, grasped his arm and whispered, but the tall Comanche chief shook his head. "It is his right, beloved woman. What he does shows great courage. Let us pray to the Great Spirit to give him cunning and strength against his enemy."

Felipe Gonzalez dismounted and tethered his horse to the branch of a nearby tree. He swaggeringly advanced, drawing out his sharp knife from his belt and brandishing it as he bared his teeth in a ferocious grin of anticipated triumph.

The bandit's weapon was a Bowie knife. Perceiving it, Sangrodo now held up his hand and called, "*Señor jefe*, my son has accepted your challenge. But if this fight is to be fair, the weapons must be equal between these two men. We have no such knife among us. Your man's is broader and longer by far."

Caldera was about to answer angrily when Gonzalez turned back, shook his head, and boastfully exclaimed, "It matters not to me what kind of *cuchillo* be used; I will kill him anyway, *mi jefe!*"

241

"Very well," Carmencita's father gruffly conceded, "let the circle be drawn and two knives of equal length and breadth given to Felipe and the *indio*! And you," pointing toward Sangrodo, "as *jefe* of the *indios*, will draw the circle of honor. You know the custom."

"I know it well," Sangrodo gravely replied. "When I was no more than Kitante's age, I fought just such a duel against a *mejicano* like yourself." With great dignity, his face impassive, he took a piece of firewood from the cord neatly arranged near the tepee, advanced to the broad clearing just in front of the entrance to the stronghold, and traced upon the sun-baked earth a circle some twelve feet in diameter. Nacio Lorcas and Octavio came forward with their hunting knives and held them up in the air before Carmencita's father, who tersely nodded his approval that they were indeed of equal length and breadth. At Caldera's sign, Nacio handed his knife to Kitante, while Octavio offered his to the smirking Gonzalez.

"You'd best instruct your son as to the rules, *jefe* of the *indios*," Carmencita's father sarcastically drawled. "He seems too young to have ever fought such a duel before. And do not leave out the most important rule of all, that if he steps outside the circle, he is dishonored, and Felipe has the right to kill him then and there."

Catayuna suppressed a cry of anguish, her hand at her mouth. But Sangrodo approached his son and said, "It is as he says, Kitante. Yet if your opponent steps outside of the circle, then he, in turn, must await your blow. The chances are equal. The Great Spirit will decide."

"I will not disgrace you, my father," Kitante said, as he stiffened, his head erect, his eyes filled with a look of determined pride.

"Please, my father," Carmencita entreated a last time. "I do not want him to die for me! I'm ready to go back with you—"

"Not on your terms, girl. Be silent, there's men's work to be done now! Felipe, to the circle, and you, boy, look your last on the girl—you'll have little chance to think of her once Felipe's knife finds your heart or your tripes!"

Carmencita, bursting into tears, pressed herself against Catayuna, who put her arms around the sobbing girl and tried to console her.

They entered the circle, warily appraising each other. Gonzalez, short, squat, but powerful and experienced in the deadly art of knife-dueling, moved carefully to his right, his eyes unwaveringly fixed on the tall, slim young Comanche. The spectators were silent, and only Carmencita's muffled sobbing could be heard. Friar Bartoloméo crossed himself and prayed silently.

The villagers had thronged toward the entrance of the stronghold to watch the spectacle. For the young braves, it was a reminder of the times when they had been little boys and their fathers had boasted to them of the victorious raids against the hated *mejicanos*. And yet, despite their friendship for young Kitante and their respect for him as Sangrodo's son, they did not believe that he could defeat so formidable an opponent.

The two men circled slowly this way and that, till at last Gonzalez tauntingly exclaimed, "Are you afraid of the sharp *cuchillo, niño*? Are you already sorry that the *muy linda* Carmencita looked at you with soft eyes? They will not comfort you when you feel this *cuchillo* bite into your flesh, *indio!*"

Kitante's jaws compressed, but he was not goaded by the taunt, and Sangrodo silently nodded to Catayuna in approval of his young son's resistance of that trap. Now Gonzalez advanced a few steps and then lunged forward, only to draw back with an alacrity surprising for a man of his bulk and his years. Kitante made a stabbing motion toward him, but did not complete it; the Mexican had purposely attempted that feint to force the young Comanche to strike at him and thus lay himself open to a mortal wound.

"Oh, *Dios*, I cannot bear to watch—Mother of the Blessed Child, help Kitante!" Carmencita moaned.

The *bandidos* waited, astride their horses, calling exhortations to their *compañero*, while Caldera watched with a mocking sneer on his bearded face. Once again, Gonzalez taunted his rival: "Are you a coward, that you fear the first taste of my steel? Come, *niño*, end it before you puke out your guts with terror. Step outside the circle, and I promise I will give you a merciful thrust in the heart!"

Kitante ground his teeth together. His face was flushed with anger at this humiliating sally, but again he restrained himself. Crouching, the knife extended in his right hand, which was lowered to his knee and ready to stab upwards into the Mexican's belly should the chance present itself, he awaited the latter's attack. And at last it was Gonzalez who took the initiative, uttering a loud bellow to take his opponent by surprise as he came agilely forward and feinted toward Kitante's face with the point of the knife. This time, Kitante made the error of trying to parry it, and with a cry of triumph, the Mexican slashed the young Comanche's left shoulder, then leaped back as Kitante's sweeping lunge missed his throat. "I've scored first blood, *niño!*" the Mexican mocked him. "And now I will not promise you such mercy. I will kill you slowly; I will cut you to pieces till you bleed to death. Come now, taste my steel again, frightened boy!"

The wound was only superficial, but it bled profusely. Catayuna, looking toward the portly friar, herself began to pray silently and, with one hand, made the sign of the cross on her forehead, as she watched Sangrodo's courageous son fight for his life.

Felipe Gonzalez squatted for a moment, his left hand gathering up some of the loose earth near his feet, while he held his knife out straight beyond his chest, ready to parry any attack. Kitante saw this and understood what the Mexican intended to do. By way of coolly answering his rival, he imitated him, stooping and seizing a handful of earth, then rising and making two or three steps forward, as if about to attack.

"The boy learns quickly," the Mexican jeered. "But you are still a child when it comes to fighting one so expert with the *cuchillo* as Felipe Gonzalez. Come now, your lesson continues!"

Once again, he began to circle the young Comanche, who imitated him. Caldera swore under his breath, "Do not play with him, you imbecile! Finish him! We've a raid to be planned."

"Look there, *niño*, a *halcón* swoops down on you!" Gonzalez suddenly cried as he pointed his left forefinger above Kitante's head. Momentarily, the young Comanche glanced upwards, and at that moment Gonzalez swiftly ran forward and flung the handful of dirt into Kitante's face, then slashed viciously at his belly with the knife. Stumbling back, the Comanche luckily avoided all but a slight nick of the sharp blade. A thin ribbon of blood stood out on his coppery-skinned chest. Recovering and lunging to the right, away from his opponent, he flung his own handful of dirt into the Mexican's face, and then slashed at him from below—up toward the Mexican's heart. Instinctively, Gonzalez parried the blow, and the clash of knives rang out, as

244

both men stood struggling. Kitante seized Gonzalez's right wrist with his left hand and, exerting all his strength, forced the knife away from him, then slashed in a sideways lunge toward the Mexican's throat. But Gonzalez leaned back, uttering a vile oath, and his left hand gripped the young Comanche's right wrist as they stood swaying and twisting together, their eyes glaring with hate.

"I'll cut out your gizzard, I'll feed it to the coyotes, *niño*!" the Mexican hoarsely panted. And then, angered at not being able to free his wrist from the youth's grasp, he suddenly brought up his right knee into Kitante's groin.

There was a cry of alarm from the watching Comanches; and Sangrodo, betraying more emotion than was his wont, caught his breath and leaned forward, his face harsh with anguish.

Kitante uttered a cry of pain, stumbling back until he reached almost the fatal edge of the circle. Instantly Gonzalez was upon him. But in his conviction that his opponent could not meet his charge, Gonzalez thought only of delivering a single blow to the throat, which would finish the fight. As he reached Kitante, he thrust out his left hand, intending to twist his fingers round Kitante's braid, tilt back his opponent's neck, and deliver the death stroke.

His face contorted by the agonizing pain in his groin, Kitante still had presence of mind enough to twist away. Just as Gonzalez reached for him, he lunged upwards with his knife till it was buried to the hilt in the Mexican's belly.

Felipe Gonzalez screamed, staggering back, dropping his knife, clutching his belly with both hands. His eyes, glazed and widened, fixed on the handle of Kitante's knife. Then, with another agonized cry, he pulled it out of the wound and, clutching it, stumbled toward the young Comanche, mouthing, "You've done me in—but I'll kill you all the same—I'll kill you—I'll—"

Kitante got to his feet and, weaponless, watched the burly Mexican stumble toward him. His eyes ghastly, his mouth agape, Gonzalez made a weak lunge with the bloody knife and then, his eyes rolling in their sockets, sprawled face down. His outflung arms extended just beyond the circle.

The watching Comanches shouted their acclaim of Sangrodo's valiant son, and Catayuna ran to Kitante, tears running down her face. "You are truly the son of your great father, Kitante! Come, you have lost much blood, I will clean your wounds and bandage them."

Sangrodo flashed his son a look of intense pride, and then turned to Jorge Caldera. "You will keep your word, *jefe de bandidos*. The fight was a fair one, you saw it."

"I saw it," Caldera snarled. Then, fatalistically, he shrugged. "So let your son keep the girl. She does not want to be my daughter anyway. And besides, I've more important things to do than thrash or scold her. *Adios*, Carmencita. *Hombres*, back to the camp. We finish plans for the raid, and because we've lost Manuel and Felipe, there'll be more plunder for all of us, *no es verdad*?" He turned his horse's head back and galloped off, and his men followed him.

The governor of the province Caldera and his band had so successfully terrorized had at last, after many impassioned pleas to the commandant general in Mexico City, received reinforcement troops. He had ordered his young aide, who had a talent for mapmaking, to prepare a map of the several villages already raided by Caldera's band, and he had calculated that they would most likely strike again in the vicinity of Coalixa. In order to trap the elusive *bandidos*, he had sent spies disguised as runaway peons to spread the word that the *alcalde* of Coalixa was enormously rich and had buried a chest full of silver pesos in his garden. That lure would be sure to draw so greedy a *bandido*.

That was why, when Jorge Caldera's men rode swiftly toward the village, they were already riding into a trap. *Federalista* troops, stationed within a radius of a dozen miles in all directions, saw the approach of the bandits and closed the trap on all sides.

Suspecting nothing and seeing nothing because they were beginning their attack in the dead of night, Caldera himself led the first wave of men against the sleeping village. Before he could ride into the square, murderous rifle fire felled him and several of his men. The others, hearing the volleys, turned to flee, but troops on either side of them pursued them and cut them down. Only five men of his band escaped, two of them critically wounded. One was left behind by his fellows, too weak from his wounds to ride; the *federalista* officer who came upon him barked out a curt order, and without being given time to be shriven by a priest, the bandit was dragged to a tree and summarily hanged.

The other four were not much luckier. Pursued by the victorious *federalistas*, they were eventually caught, taken to the provincial governor's prison, and, after a brief trial, sent before a firing squad to pay for their crimes as outlaws and murderers.

CHAPTER TWENTY-TWO

Life was serene for Arabella Bouchard Hunter in this forty-ninth year of her life. All the tribulations, the heartaches, the flirtations, the yearnings of past years had been serenely channeled into the new life in Galveston which she and her soft-spoken but always firm and dependable husband, James, had begun eight years ago. They had come through much together since those terrible days in 1865 when Union troops had destroyed the red-brick chateau of Windhaven Plantation, and the Hunters, along with their children, Melinda and Andrew, had joined others of the Bouchard clan who were emigrating to Texas. During those grim days—and in every crisis since—Arabella had experienced repeatedly the security and peace that James provided as a bulwark against life's vicissitudes.

There had been frequent crises in their first years in Texas. Soon after they had come to Galveston, Arabella, who had begun to fear that she was no longer attractive as a woman, had indulged in a mild flirtation with Durwood McCambridge. And when James had befriended an attractive young widow whose Mexican husband had been killed during a revolution in Mexico, she had accused him of infidelity. He had taken his hairbrush to her, but then consoled her so ardently that, at the age of forty-five, she had given birth to a daughter, Joy, now three and a half years old.

Arabella's older daughter, Melinda, was a beauty, and for a time Arabella had almost jealously regarded her as a rival. But Melinda was now married to Lawrence Davis, and had a son, little Gary. A year away from her fiftieth birthday, Arabella was reveling in being a mother and grandmother, and this only added luster to the maturing woman's considerable charms.

Her husband, James, was prospering. He had resigned his post as sales factor for his cousin Jeremy's cotton mill, and was now enjoying a new career as a partner and sponsor of enterprising Charles Douglas, whose Galveston department store was flourishing even beyond Charles's most optimistic hopes. Andrew, who had been so trying as a little boy and so jealous of his older sister, Melinda, was, at nineteen, working for Cousin Jeremy. Just last week he came to Arabella, dressed in his very best and with as serious a mien as he could muster, to announce that he had just become engaged to Della Morley, the honey-haired, seventeen-year-old daughter of Cousin Jeremy's mill foreman.

Arabella sat before her mirror on this already hot May morning, combing her hair and scrutinizing herself. Much to her pleasure, there were only a few tell-tale streaks of gray in her luxuriant, glossy black hair. Her voluptuous figure had ripened into a matriarchal beauty, serenely gentle and yet secretly thrilling to contemplate, still very desirable to her husband. If the passions of youthful love were banked, then at least the comfortably warming fires of mutual respect and devotion still brightly glowed.

It was indeed very possible, Arabella smiled at herself in the mirror, that within another few years she would be a grandmother twice or even three times over. Yesterday evening, she had acceded to Andrew's request that he be allowed to invite Della Morley to supper. She had been touched by her handsome young son's old-fashioned solicitude for the traditional laws of etiquette. James was away in New Orleans purchasing artistic ornaments and paintings for Charles Douglas's department store, so Arabella had presided at the dinner table.

All during the meal, Andrew had appeared proud and a little stilted, and Della had been absolutely adorable—gentle, sweet, and shy, the ideal daughter-in-law for a concerned mother to welcome as a future member of the household.

As for her little Joy, Arabella was convinced that the little girl, now so pert and affectionate, would one day be as lovely as Melinda, or even Arabella herself, as she had been in those idyllic days before the guns had thundered at Fort Sumter.

Yes, life was very rich and very good. Arabella did not really fear the approaching landmark of her fiftieth birthday. Not with James still loving her, not with her young son looking forward to the ecstacies and the trials of a loving marriage, and not with Melinda so evidently happy with her Lawrence. James's new career had, it seemed to her, enlivened him, made him much less silent, and given him a highly engaging personality which she found divertingly new and rewarding. He was more demonstrative, more outspoken in his affection for her; in the past, she had always known he loved her, but there was no one alive who did not like, on occasion, to hear the words of avowal.

That was why she was smiling at herself in the mirror, thoroughly content. This afternoon, after lunch, she promised herself, she would sit down and write a long, chatty letter to dear Luke at Windhaven Plantation. He would want to know about Andrew and Della and how well James was doing at the department store. She remembered that she must say something about the prosperity they were all enjoying here in Galveston. Luke's last letter had contained a gloomy reference to his distress about the nation's economy after Grant's reelection. Well, he had only to come to this thriving port on the Gulf and his fears would be swept away at once. The theater, the symphony, even the opera, were well received in Galveston. More churches and houses were being built or remodeled. The ships that docked at the harbor in Galveston Bay continued to bring more trade goods for which there was a growing demand. The only fly in the ointment was that every summer one worried about the danger of a yellow fever epidemic from the marshlands. Last summer ten people had died, but the city physician had pompously declared that these were only isolated cases and that if one took proper precautions yellow fever would not be a problem, as it had been and, in some instances, still was in the port city of New Orleans.

Arabella rose from her dressing table. At that moment there was a loud, repeated knocking at the front door. Frowning—for she was expecting no one—she hurried to the door, calling to her maid, "It's all right, Annie dear, I'll answer it." When she opened the door, she saw her married daughter standing before her. She was about to greet Melinda with an expression of surprise and joy at her visit, when the young woman burst into tears and flung herself into her mother's arms.

"There now, Melinda honey, what's all this? Now stop crying—I declare, I don't understand this—"

251

"Oh, Mama, I'm so miserable, I'm so unhappy! Oh, I just have to tell you, I just have to!" Melinda hysterically entreated.

"Of course, darling. Come sit down here on the sofa. Now try to stop crying. What in the world is this all about?"

"It's—it's—it's L-Lawrence, Mama," Melinda sobbed as she fumbled in her reticule for a kerchief and tried to dry her tears, but without much success.

"Melinda! What are you trying to tell me?" Startled, Arabella put her arm around her daughter's shoulders and drew her close, her face taut with concern.

"Oh, Mama—Lawrence, he—he's been seeing someone—"

"No—you don't know what you're saying, Melinda!" Arabella gasped.

Melinda raised her lovely, tear-stained face and nodded. Her lips were trembling, and she struggled to control her unsteady voice. "Yes, Mama, it's—it's true. About—about three weeks ago, he met this woman—"

"Now, Melinda honey, you mustn't jump to conclusions. You know," Arabella magnanimously confessed, "I wouldn't have you think that everything went smoothly between your father and myself all the years of our marriage. I'll admit to you now, though you're not to tell a soul, that I used to flirt, even after I was married. Thank heavens your father knew how to bring me to my senses. You remember Durwood McCambridge, don't you?"

"Yes I do, Mama, but this is different—oh, I'm so unhappy. I—I just want to die!" Again Melinda burst into hysterical sobs, pressing her face against her mother's bosom and clinging to her while Arabella did her best to try to soothe the hysterical young woman.

"Now, now, just have a good cry and get it out of your system. You'll tell me when you want to. It's all right, honey, we're all alone and no one's going to overhear us. There, there, honey, it hurts me to see you like this. Now there's nothing to worry about; I'm here with you. You just tell me what you want, and I'll listen," Arabella murmured.

At last, Melinda drew back, took several deep breaths, dabbed her eyes, and then, staring straight ahead of her, began, "It's just awful, Mama. This woman—he's been to see her more than once, I know it. Oh, he—he won't come straight out and admit it, but I know he has."

252

"Do you know who she is?" Arabella asked.

"Oh yes! I could—I could just scratch her eyes out, Mama!" Melinda burst out and then, as another crisis of sobs assailed her, bowed her head and covered her face with her hands, as she gave vent to her despair.

"And—and the worst of it is, Mama, I—I think I'm going to have another baby. I knew it two weeks ago, just a few days after I found out about Marianne Valois."

"Oh honey, that's dreadful!" Arabella solicitously gasped as she hugged Melinda to her. "That's a French name. However did he meet anyone like that? Come on now, it'll do you a world of good to tell me all about it. When you get it out of your system, you'll see, you'll feel a lot better."

"I—I guess I have to—I just have to tell someone—and you're the only one—I'd die if I had to tell Papa—"

"You won't, I'll see to that. Besides, maybe it's not so bad as you think. Now out with it, you saucy little minx." Arabella pretended to take an airy tone to ease Melinda's anguish, but already her apprehension had completely driven away the happy, nostalgic mood she had known before her mirror.

"Yes, Mama, she *is* French. And she's a widow, which makes it so awfully worse. She's old, too, Mama, she's all of thirty."

Arabella did not know whether to laugh or cry at this naive declaration. She contented herself by noncommittally remarking, "Well, you see, honey, a mature widow is always a danger to a man, especially if he's young and susceptible. But I'm sure you haven't given him cause to wander, darling."

"Mama, how can you even think such a thing!" Melinda disengaged herself from her mother and indignantly sat up, staring at Arabella as tears streamed down her face. "I declare, I love Lawrence just as much as I love you and Papa—of course, in a different way, you know. But—but—oh, she runs a little hat shop, Mama, on Dressler Street. And he went there to buy a hat for me—"

"That was very thoughtful of him."

"Oh, Mama, now that I know what I know, it was as if he'd played Judas to me!" Melinda burst out, then began sobbing again.

Arabella sighed and shook her head. "But that's harmless enough, and it was certainly thoughtful of him to buy

253

you a hat. Now how do you know that he has actually had an affair with this woman?"

"B-because, Mama. You know that Lawrence works in the city hall with his papa, who's the city treasurer."

"Yes, I know that, but he's a smart young man, and there's really no nepotism in it. And he's honorable. Your father and I like him very much."

"Oh Mama, now you're taking sides with him!" Melinda reproachfully blurted out.

"I'm not taking sides with anyone, honey. And don't you think that I'm not hurt by hearing that you're hurt. I want my little girl to be happy for the rest of her life, the way I've been with your father. Now please, try to take hold of yourself and give me facts, not just frantic accusations. You must remember, I'm older than you are, and I think I know something about infatuation and flirtations. Maybe it's nothing stronger than that, you know, Melinda. And you certainly wouldn't want to break up your happy life with Lawrence, not with little Gary and another baby on the way, just over a supposition."

"But—but it's *not* a supposition, Mama. As I said, she's French, and so was her husband. He died last year from the yellow fever."

"You know, that yellow fever worries me. When we were in New Orleans eight years ago, getting ready to come out here, I was scared to death; we were in the city during that warm time of year when they always had epidemics. Fortunately, God protected us all, honey. But your father's told me that there have been quite a few cases of yellow fever over the last few years right here in Galveston. But do go on—I didn't mean to interrupt."

Melinda twisted her fingers together and stared unseeingly at the wall beyond her. "It was a lovely hat, Mama. I asked him where he got it and he told me. Then he started talking about what a sweet woman Marianne Valois was and all she had to go through after her husband died, trying to get clerks to help her in the shop and such."

"But that doesn't prove he was unfaithful to you, honey," Arabella murmured.

"No, Mama, it doesn't. But only about two weeks ago, he sent a messenger over from the city hall to tell me that he couldn't come to supper because he had some tax books to check. And when he did come home, it was nearly midnight, and he—and he smelled of another woman's perfume."

"You poor darling."

"But that's not all, Mama. Since then, twice more he's had someone come over to tell me that he wouldn't be home to supper. I smelled that perfume again, and I knew, Mama, that he'd been with that woman. Oh, whatever am I going to do?"

Arabella sighed and shook her head. She put an arm around Melinda's shoulders and drew the girl to her, and then said gently, "But you still love him, don't you?"

"You know I do, Mama!" Melinda reproached her through her tears.

"Well, then, we must both be very calm and think what's best for you, and for your marriage in the long run. Now let me think . . . yes, I think I see a way. . . . Oh, my darling, this is going to be very hard for you, I know, but Lawrence has to be brought to his senses. There are times when firm action is the best—sometimes it prevents things from getting worse." Arabella blushed now, remembering James's hairbrush. "I don't know why Lawrence went to see that woman in the first place, but obviously he has, and more than once, and we have to do what's best for you—"

"I don't want to give him up, Mama!" Melinda wailed.

"And you'll do no such thing," Arabella firmly interjected. "Both of you are Catholic, so it's not even possible to think of that. But, child, I know what you can do." Arabella took hold of Melinda's soft, rounded shoulders and gave her daughter a little shake. "Now you listen to me. You'll tell Lawrence that you think it best that the two of you separate for a time. You'll tell him that he knows why. And you'll tell him that when he's ready to make a clean breast of things, you'll decide whether you can go on together. Also, I'd make a point of telling him about the baby. If he has any moral decency at all—and I'm sure he does—he'll stop seeing this woman, rest assured."

"Do—do you really think so, Mama?" Melinda anxiously inquired.

"Of course, I do, you sweet child. Now then, I think we should both enjoy a little lunch together, and then we'll go for a carriage ride and see the bay. It's such a beautiful day, even if it is a little warm, it'll drive all these unhappy thoughts out of your mind, darling."

"Oh, Mama, I knew you'd help me! Yes, that's what I'll do. When Lawrence comes home tonight, I'll tell him that I think we ought to take a—kind of vacation from each other."

"That's the idea!" Arabella smilingly approved.

"And—and I'll tell him that I'm going to have a baby, and that I love him very much, and that I want time to think things over. He—he'll know what I mean, Mama, won't he?"

"I'm sure he will. I think that's all you have to do, honey. Now then, let's go to the kitchen and see what we can find for a nice lunch. We'll have a happy afternoon, just you and I, as in the old days."

Marianne Valois wore her dark-brown hair coiffed in a chic pompadour. She was of medium height and her hairdo made her seem taller and more elegant. She was alluring in a green silk dressing gown, which covered camisole, drawers, and beige silk stockings, and she had doffed her stylish high-button shoes, which she wore at her hat shop on Dressler Street, in favor of comfortable gilt-decorated bedroom slippers. She turned from the tabouret of her salon in the little house on MacComber Avenue to hand Lawrence Davis a glass of red Bordeaux, and took hers over to the armchair at the opposite end of the room. Melinda's handsome young husband stared ruefully at her, lifted his glass to his lips, hesitated, then grumbled, "I thought you liked me, Marianne. And there you go to the other side of the room, as if you wanted to shun me!"

"*Chéri*, you may be a married man, even a father, but you've a lot to learn about women. Please to remember, it was you who sought me out, so it's for me to decide just how long this little friendship should be continued," she rebuked him, softening the impact of her words with a piquant little smile.

"I—I know. I'm sorry, Marianne. But I can't help it—you're so beautiful, and I'm wild about you."

"So you have said—and shown me. But I must think things over very carefully. I know how easy it is for a man. You are married, you become bored, you see a woman and say to yourself, 'Here is a woman I desire, she is a widow, which means she knows what love can be between a man and a woman; she has no man now, so I will amuse myself with her for an indefinite period of time.' "

"No, no, that's not the way it is at all!" he protested, his face flushing. He stared doggedly at her, lifted his glass, and downed it almost at a gulp.

"And that, M'sieur Lawrence, is surely no way to treat a vintage Bordeaux," she reproved.

"Marianne, I—I can't help it, I—I'm just trying to tell you how I feel about you—have felt about you from the start—"

"Ah, do not speak to me of your passion, my friend. Let's at least be honest. For my part, I'll admit you're decent, handsome, young—and it's been a while since Gaston died and I have love. This is a pleasant adventure—but if you protest to a great passion for me, then I will say, *non*, it is *finis*—finished. And anyway, what about your wife and child?"

"Let's not talk about my wife and boy, please, Marianne—"

"Conscience so late?" she twitted him, and when she saw him wince and look away, she rose felinely and went to him. "That was cruel of me, I'll admit. You're obviously upset and confused. I do not like to think that I am coming between a man and his wife. And yet I don't want to be treated like a *putaine*—a slut—either."

"Marianne," he breathed, "I've never thought of you that way, and you know it. I don't know what will become of me or my marriage. All I know now is that I'm mad for you, I must have you—"

"Well then, *allons-y, mon cher*," she murmured huskily, as she pressed her mouth to his.

CHAPTER TWENTY-THREE

After spending March and April in Galveston, checking on the operation of his department store, Charles Douglas had gone back to Chicago in May to be reunited with his family: Laurette, his wife; the twins, Kenneth and Arthur, now seven and a half; Howard, four and a half; and the baby, Fleur, who had been born in November of last year and named after Dr. Ben Wilson's first wife, Fleurette.

Charles spent two days conferring with his partner, Lawrence Harding, who in March had at last married Sylvia Cross, an attractive, reddish-blond schoolteacher of thirty-five and the niece of William Young, alderman of the ward in which the Douglases maintained their Chicago home. Laurette had written to Charles about the upcoming marriage, and without undue modesty had taken credit for having been the matchmaker who had brought about the happy union.

In the course of their discussions, Lawrence Harding gave his enterprising partner a complete overview of the excellent financial condition the Douglas Department Store in Chicago had maintained since its reconstruction after the great fire of 1871. This report convinced Charles that he could continue to leave the store in Lawrence's hands while he occupied himself with the possibility of opening a third branch store; this one in Houston. Harding was as expert a merchandiser as Charles himself, and there was complete trust between the two partners. So, after spending two weeks with Laurette, romping with his three sons, and spoiling his infant daughter, Fleur, by bringing her many presents from the store, Charles prepared to leave again for Texas, promising that he would be back after he had looked into the matter of a Houston subsidiary.

Three days before he left on the train which was to take him to New Orleans and the packet bound for Galveston, Charles had a picture taken of little Fleur. Just as he had hoped, the newest addition to the Douglas family had Laurette's bright red hair. As he said to Laurette, "I couldn't be happier, my darling. You remember when you told me that you were carrying Fleur, I said I wanted it to be a daughter with your red hair and that combination of fiery temper and loving kindness that makes you the best wife a man could ever have? Well, I guess I was prophetic. It's still true, about you, for certain. And one of these days, darling, we're going to have to decide whether we're going to move to Texas so that I won't have to spend four or five months a year away from you while I supervise my stores in Galveston and Houston. I don't want to be away from you a single minute more than I have to. If I've been away a lot up to now, you know that it's only because I've wanted to make a future for our children while we're still young, and it's been necessary for me to travel."

"I understand that, darling," Laurette tenderly whispered, as she linked her arms around him and gave him a long, lingering kiss. "And you're not to worry about me. In fact, when I'm away from you, I think about you all the time. And then when you come back, it's like a second honeymoon."

"You're an angel, Laurette. Just the same, I hope it won't be long before we're settled permanently in one spot. Then there won't need to be any second honeymoons—just a prolonged, lifetime one. By the way, are you happy with the new governess?"

"Oh yes, she's a treasure! I still miss poor Polly, and there are times when I wish—well, no matter."

"I know, Laurette honey. But then, if she'd lived, you'd have lost her to Eddie Gentry. And from what Lucien Edmond Bouchard writes me, Eddie has found someone to take poor Polly's place. A very sweet Mexican girl named Maria Elena Romero, whom he rescued in Abilene from a dance-hall owner who was going to turn her into a fancy girl. Well, I might just surprise you and come home early—or, better yet—maybe I'll send for you in just a few weeks, so you can come and see if you'd like Texas as a permanent home."

"That would be wonderful, darling. And you know, Lawrence and Sylvia Harding have moved into their new house in the next block. If you send for me, Lawrence has already said that he and Sylvia will be happy to take the children so that I can join you. We could pretend we were getting married all over again. Wouldn't that be exciting?"

"Oh yes!" Charles said fervently as he held her to him in a tight embrace and kissed her eyes and mouth. "I'd love to have you with me. It's a long way off, and a man like me gets lonely."

"Not too lonely, Charles," she giggled, as she shook a reproving forefinger at him. "Just don't forget I still love you very much and that I can make you happier than anybody else you'd find in either Houston or Galveston."

"My, you're not the kind to leave a man much leeway, Laurette honey," he said softly and fused his mouth with hers in a passionate embrace.

The next day, Charles Douglas closeted himself with Viola Elbridge, the governess. She had come as a replacement for poor, deranged Agnes Strion, who last year had kidnapped little Howard. Charles had already had ample reason to be grateful to Viola, because a month before the birth of Fleur, when the twins, Kenneth and Arthur, had fallen ill after eating lunch, Viola had recognized the symptoms of food poisoning and taken the proper steps to help the children until the doctor could arrive. When the doctor did come, he said that thanks to Mrs. Elbridge's quick action, truly grave consequences had been averted.

"Mrs. Elbridge, you've been a godsend," Charles told her. "My partner, Lawrence Harding, and his wife have volunteered to take care of our children in case I send for my wife to follow me to Texas. On the other hand, since you've already done so well with them and our baby daughter, Fleur, seems to get along so well with you, I wonder if you could look after all of our children if Laurette and I decide to spend a few months in Texas."

"I'd be delighted to do that, Mr. Douglas, and thank you for your confidence in me. I love your children, and I think I could keep them happy and active all through the summer," she smilingly responded.

"That's fine. I'll send you a telegram in the event that things turn out the way I hope they can. Meanwhile, I'm increasing your salary, Mrs. Elbridge. I think you've earned it, what with all you've done for us."

"Oh, thank you, sir! I'm delighted to be able to help out in any way I can. I might tell you that when school is out, I can help Kenneth and Arthur brush up on their lessons. I used to be a teacher myself in a rural school in Indiana just before I got married, and I've already been helping the boys during this school year."

"Well, that's certainly very good to know, Mrs. El-bridge." Charles grinned and then looked thoughtful. "As a matter of fact, that gives me an idea. The more I think about it, the more I'd like to have Laurette go along with me now, and bring little Fleur, too. She's still nursing her, and after all, the boys have been to Texas already, so the prospect might not be too exciting for them. They'd have to wait until school was out in June anyway, and I'd much rather arrange my plans with Laurette and Fleur now than send for them in a few weeks and disrupt everything. What you just told me—and I'm certainly very glad you did—has just about decided me."

So unexpectedly, to Laurette's delight, Charles invited her to accompany him on the journey to Galveston. However, the twins, Kenneth and Arthur, and little Howard also, did not look upon their father's and mother's "vacation" with the indifference which Charles had believed they might, in view of their having already spent a good deal of time at Windhaven Range. Indeed, it was only by fervently promising each of them that he would have a pony of his very own to ride when Charles returned toward the end of the summer that he was able to console them.

That evening, Charles invited Lawrence and Sylvia Harding to the house for dinner, and the personable couple was told of the Douglases' plans, including the fact that Viola Elbridge would be able to look after the three boys in their parents' absence. Sylvia Harding smilingly proposed, "I have a still better idea for you, Laurette and Charles. Why don't the boys come to stay with us, as we originally planned? Viola could come and live with us too, so as to be close to the boys and continue their after-school lessons." Then she added, with a shy glance at her genial husband, "Having the boys with us would, you might say, be a kind of preview of having children of our own."

"Oh, Sylvia, that's a perfectly wonderful idea!" Laurette beamingly enthused. "Charlie, honey, you see what a clever matchmaker I turned out to be?"

"You're incomparable in every respect, my darling," he told her.

The news that they were going to live with "Uncle Lawrence and Aunt Sylvia," for whom they had already developed a considerable affection, together with the promise of the ponies, convinced the twins and Howard that the oncoming summer would be even more exciting than accompanying their parents to Texas again. Before the Hardings left, Mrs. Elbridge was apprised of the new situation, and she declared that she would be delighted to stay with the boys at the Hardings' home; at the same time, she would watch over the Douglas house in their absence.

"Look here, Bella," James Hunter irritably declared at the supper table the evening after Melinda's tearful visit to her mother, "this is a pretty kettle of fish. What I ought to do is have a talk with young Davis and remind him of his responsibilities, which he seems to have forgotten."

"That would be absolutely the wrong thing to do, James," Arabella protested. "If he went back on that basis, he'd start feeling sorry for himself, and a situation like the present one might occur all over again. No, dear, I think the separation would be the best for both of them. That way, once Lawrence sees that he might lose the fine girl he loved and who gave him little Gary and is about to bear his second child, he'll come back and want to be forgiven, you'll see."

James chuckled, as he helped himself to another portion of jambalaya, the recipe for which Arabella had picked up in New Orleans and supplemented with a few creative touches of her own. "This is absolutely delicious, Bella! I must confess that I never thought I'd live to see the day when you could sit back like the matriarch of the tribe and make calm, balanced, and accurate judgments about difficult matters—particularly, may I say, about marital indiscretions." At this, his eyes danced with wicked amusement.

"Well, I like that, Mr. Hunter!" Arabella bridled prettily, then met his eyes and could not help bursting out laughing. "Never you mind, I know what you're referring to, and I've certainly learned my lesson."

"If you're referring to the hairbrush, it's in a special place of honor in the drawer of my study," her husband teasingly remarked. "I'll admit that we men have it a bit one-sided. Now, if Melinda had been the errant one in this domestic spat, I'd have recommended to Lawrence that he borrow my hairbrush and use it where it would do her the most good. But I'm afraid that one could hardly expect so

well-bred a girl as our daughter to apply corporal chastise-
ment to a very misguided young husband. As it happens,
I've met this Valois woman."

"You have? James Hunter, you can be the most exasper-
ating man! Why didn't you tell me?" Arabella indignantly
demanded.

"First of all, because it was quite by chance. A few days
ago I visited the department store to take a look around
and see how things were going. There is, as you probably
know, a fairly decent millinery department at the back of
the store."

"Yes, yes, I know all that! Get to the point!" Arabella
impatiently interposed.

James Hunter reached for his glass of Madeira and sa-
vored a lingering sip, relishing the bouquet and holding the
glass up to the light, while Arabella fumed and frowned at
him. He was amused at her display of curiosity and pique,
and he took his time before answering. "We must really
put in another case or two of this superb Madeira, Bella.
Now then, where was I? Oh yes, the Valois woman. As I
say, I was walking in the direction of the millinery department when this very handsome young woman came by,
looking around as I was, and accidentally bumped into
me."

"That hussy!" Arabella's face clouded with jealousy. "I
suppose she was setting her cap for you."

"Her hat, don't you mean, my dear?" he twitted, and
when she uttered an exasperated gasp, he went on, "You
know, I've always thought it best to modify familiar quota-
tions where appropriate. And in this instance it would be
'hat,' wouldn't it?"

"Will you please get on with it, James Hunter!" Arabella
rolled her eyes ceilingward as if to imply that Providence
had saddled her with the most annoying man in all of
Texas.

"By all means." He took another sip of his Madeira.
"She apologized very prettily, and I did the same, and then
she introduced herself and I gave her my name as well."

"She didn't seem surprised, I'll wager!" Arabella said
half-aloud with a grim little smile.

"Now stop putting two and two together and making the
five you think it's adding up to, because it's not. For your
information, she went on to say that she was thinking of
selling her shop. It seems that a very good milliner has just

264

come here from Baton Rouge to live with her sister and has had plenty of capital left to her by a grandfather. So Mrs. Valois mentioned that she was thinking of investing the proceeds when she sold her shop, perhaps in city bonds, or, barring that, in shipping. It seems she plans eventually to go to San Francisco where her older sister is living with a husband and four children. She thinks there might be much more business in that thriving port than in our own—and besides, she isn't too fond of our atrociously hot summers."

"Well now," Arabella breathed, "you certainly managed to elicit a great deal of information from her on such an accidental meeting. I declare, James Hunter, you're still a force to be reckoned with when it comes to attractive women."

"Gently now, Bella dear," he chuckled, "don't forget the hairbrush is still very accessible. But this time, I rather doubt that it would have such a delightful after-result as Joy."

His wife turned a furious scarlet at this remark. When she had recovered her aplomb, it was to say, in a stiff, strained voice, "Well, at any rate, I hope she leaves for San Francisco quickly, so that Lawrence will go back to poor Melinda."

"I'm sure it will all work out very well in the end. As a matter of fact, there was a legitimate reason for her to have consulted with him, since after all he does work in the city treasurer's office and would have a pretty fair knowledge of commercial bonds and stocks and the like."

"Oh, you men, you're all alike, you stick together!" Arabella had, as usual, the last word.

James Hunter had insisted that Charles and Laurette Douglas be guests at his spacious house during their stay in Galveston, and on the Thursday in June which marked the day of their arrival, after having spent a delightful week in New Orleans shopping and dining and enjoying the Old World charm of the French Quarter, the two couples sat at the dinner table renewing acquaintanceship with one another. Little Joy had been put to sleep by her nurse after the excitement of welcoming the visitors to her parents' house, and by the time coffee and port were served, James invited Charles to enjoy these with him in his study while

265

Arabella and Laurette went on gossiping to their hearts' content.

"So you and Laurette decided to spend a few months here in Galveston, Charles?" James said as he poured out a generous gobletful of tawny port and handed it to the sturdy Chicago merchant. He had closed the door of the study, for he wanted a really serious chat with his partner.

"Things worked out very well. I'd originally planned to come here by myself and then perhaps send for Laurette. But then there was the problem of the children, especially little Fleur. So I decided to bring Laurette and Fleur with me, leaving the boys with Lawrence Harding and his wife. The boys' governess, Mrs. Elbridge, is also staying with them—she's been helping with their lessons, and will continue to prep them during the summer. I couldn't resist having what's usually referred to as a second honeymoon. It'll do Laurette a world of good, particularly after that tragic affair with Agnes Strion."

James Hunter soberly nodded, shook his head, then took a sip of his port. "I remember what you told me about that, Charles. It must have been pure hell for both of you, thinking your son was kidnapped by a deranged woman and not knowing exactly where to find her."

"Yes, God was very good to us, and we were very lucky. Agnes Strion's in a sanitarium now, being looked after— but I'm afraid she can never go back into society, the poor woman. She was victimized by an unscrupulous lover. There are many such people everywhere who sustain a crisis too great for them to bear alone, and if they don't have the fiber to rebound from it, they give way. This time, we had a chance to examine Mrs. Elbridge's references, and we happen to know one or two of the people for whom she'd worked before."

"Good, good! Now let me give you a report on your store here in Galveston, Charles. Have some more port."

"Good gracious, no, James! Laurette and I ate and drank far too much in New Orleans, and I must be careful not to overdo things now. This glass will do me fine."

"Well then, let me say I'm very happy that you persuaded me—with your enthusiasm as an absolute newcomer to Galveston—to take part in your venture, Charles. I'd say it's doing sensationally well. If anything, you've got a few disgruntled merchants in town just because it is doing so well."

"Oh? I don't want to put anybody out of business just because I opened a department store here, James. But as I recall, there were one or two small shops you could call variety stores, but nothing that handled the broad inventory of a department store. You see, even when I was living back in Tuscaloosa, I thought it was only logical that if you could have a lot of things that families needed, they'd come more and more to do all their shopping at your store. You might call it a one-stop shopping facility."

"I like that concept."

"Mark my words, James, you'll see a great deal of it in the big urban centers, as this country develops. Why," Charles grinned infectiously, "I hope to live long enough to see greengrocer shops expand to have produce and meats and canned goods and even nonfood items. Once they do, the housewife won't have to go to so many places so often during the week to provide for her family. It makes good sense."

"You are a very far-seeing young man, Charles," James sighed. "There are times when I wish I was your age. I'll admit that you've given me an inspiration to start a new career rather late in my life, and now that I look back, I'm happier being a partner with you in this department store in Galveston than I was as a factor selling cotton for my Cousin Jeremy. I daresay some of that is because the cotton business was getting monotonous, the same thing year in and year out. But in your department store there are new products all the time—like this newfangled typewriter Remington's bringing out. The changes make things exciting."

"That's my feeling too, James. Now you know, when I was here the last time, I had a bee in my bonnet about starting a store in Houston. I haven't given it up, either. Now that the Galveston store is doing so well, I'd still like to think about opening a second store in that thriving town. Tell me very frankly, have you changed your opinion at all about it?"

James Hunter leaned back in his chair, frowned thoughtfully, and took another sip of his port. "I know you had a bad run-in with those two crooks, Shottlander and Jemmers. At the time, I'll frankly admit that I was doubtful about the prospect. And, of course, the way our authorities have maintained restrictive tariffs made me feel that the venture might be a bit costly for you. However, there are a few new developments you ought to think about."

267

"I'd be very interested in hearing your views, James. I can rely on you for accurate and honest information about Galveston, certainly. You know the ins and outs of the town."

"Not entirely, but certainly since I shipped cotton for so long for Cousin Jeremy, I had my share of dealings with the port authorities, and I know the way they think. They don't like to see Houston prospering at the possible expense of Galveston. But, aside from that, there's another problem. We've been plagued by quite a few cases of yellow fever. They always occur during the summer months, because then it's the hottest, and the humidity and the mosquitoes, or whatever it is the doctors think cause yellow fever, seem to be most prevalent during that time of year. As a result, the authorities in Houston have put up a quarantine against Galveston traffic during the summer months. You'd be unable to ship any goods at that time."

"That certainly is a distinct disadvantage," Charles replied, "though I suppose some way could be found to build up an inventory of goods right in Houston prior to June, to prepare for the summer quarantine. There must be warehousing facilities in or near the city. But before I can even think about warehousing I have to think about getting the goods physically from Galveston to Houston. You'll remember that last year I talked to an old-time clerk of the Galveston, Houston and Henderson line, and he told me that he thought the smaller-gauge track of that line wouldn't be able to handle my freight goods. I suppose that picture still holds true. Do you have any information about that—more recent information, I mean?"

"Well, Charles, since you were here last, I took it upon myself to do some more checking with the freight agent of that line, Mr. H. B. Andrews. He gave me some insight into the real problem. You see, there are other railroads in Texas whose gauges differ; and so the main reason that the Galveston, Houston and Henderson line hasn't been used much for freight is that a great many shippers into Galveston want to go beyond Houston into other parts of Texas. They don't want to have to pay the cost of having freight transferred in Houston between lines of differing gauges. As a result, the Galveston, Houston and Henderson has never been able to attract the big shippers, and they have never adequately developed their capacity for hauling heavy freight. Their business has all been with small and local shippers—farmers, mostly. So you were smart last year when you decided not to rely on them to carry your goods."

James took a sip of his drink and went on, "The future should bring some changes reasonably quickly. Because of the quarantine, there is a lot of interest in building other lines to reach the interior of Texas, bypassing Houston. Just last week, a charter was granted to the Gulf, Colorado, and Santa Fe Railway Company, for the purpose of building such a line. Meanwhile, Mr. Andrews tells me that the Galveston, Houston and Henderson is planning to extend its service beyond Galveston—to construct extensions which, hopefully, before another year, will reach the northernmost boundary of Texas. Then, you see, they'll have connections with roads coming toward Texas from St. Louis, Cairo, Memphis, and Vicksburg."

"That sounds very promising, but you see, I'm not really concerned with going beyond Houston, at least for the moment."

"Nevertheless, you'll stand to benefit, because all this competition—plus the Galveston, Houston and Henderson's own plans to extend their lines—will inevitably result in better service on the line that already exists between here and Houston. Mr. Andrews assures me that his line has already added more and heavier freight cars, and more handlers. Now, if we can only solve that problem of yellow fever in the summertime, we'll be all set. I confess that I'm rather frightened of that disease. I knew one of the people who died from it last year, and I'm told that there have been a few more cases already this year."

"That's very bad," Charles Douglas agreed, pursing his lips and staring at the floor for a moment, as he collected his thoughts. "Nevertheless, I'm not easily discouraged, so what I might do is run up to Houston while I'm here and see about buying the land for the store. Dennis Claverton of the Houston Bank assured me last year that he'd help me out in the matter. Shottlander and Jemmers aren't doing business there any more, from what I understand."

"No, they're not. And I read that Jemmers died of a heart attack last year. Well, by all means, I would start things moving in Houston. If we can lick this yellow fever problem, then you'll be in business."

"Yes. I guess that's true. Well, James, I'm obliged to you for all the research you've done. You know, I just might spend a few weeks in Houston. Laurette hasn't seen it, and she might enjoy it. Now let me come back to your earlier remark—you remember, about some merchants who didn't like the fact that I was taking business away from them. Is that a serious problem?"

James Hunter frowned and studied his goblet of port, then took a reflective sip as he pondered. Presently he said, "There does seem to be one merchant who's been quite unhappy ever since your store opened, Charles. His name is Henry McNamara. For the last few years he's run a store on Edlinger Street, McNamara's Variety Store. It's a rambling, one-story affair, which takes up about a third of the block, and he's something of a sharp operator when it comes to prices. He has a habit of buying up goods from other storekeepers which they've refused or haven't been able to pay for, and in some cases, they've been waterlogged or even damaged by fire. Then he puts a little advertisement in the newspaper and boasts of the amazingly low prices for top merchandise—which, of course, it isn't."

"Those are shoddy selling tricks I'll never use, James," Charles emphatically declared.

"And you won't have to. I've been keeping a close eye on your books, which are being scrupulously maintained by Alice Steinfeldt. Even though she's happily married to our fine contractor, Max, she insists on keeping her hand in with the accounts. In spite of the tariff set by our port authorities, Charles, you're doing very well—as I said at the outset. You'll have a handsome profit to show for this first year of operation."

"I'm grateful to you, James. I intend to see that you get a fair share, because if it hadn't been for you, I might not have had a store here at all."

"You give me too much credit. But needless to say, I'm grateful. As partners, we'll always be able to communicate and there's a great deal of trust and friendship between us. That's the way it always should be in an enterprise like this. But to get back to this fellow McNamara. The only reason I know about him is that some time back, just before I went off to New Orleans on a buying trip for you, I saw him down at the dock waiting for some cargo to be unloaded. I heard him say to one of the port authority officials, 'I'll bet you wouldn't charge that fellow Douglas what you're charging me for this load. One of these days, things are going to be different.'"

270

"Hmm," Charles frowned. "Well, I really don't make anything too serious out of that remark. Seems to me that if I were in his shoes I'd be annoyed that somebody else was taking away business. But our operation is entirely legitimate, and I certainly didn't go out of my way to hurt him. His location is a good mile away from mine, to begin with. I'd say that, in all this time, if he'd dealt fairly with people, he would have retained a loyal patronage which even my store couldn't take away from him."

"But the point is, he doesn't. And that's why he's probably steadily losing business. I'd keep his name in the back of my head anyway, if I were you, Charles." James rose and stretched, finished his port, and set the goblet down with a clatter on the sideboard. "Well, I think I'd like a walk in the cool night air." He patted his stomach. "Bella's spoiling me these days. I enjoy it, I don't mind telling you. But at my age, it's not a good idea to put on too much weight. What do you say we go for a little jaunt around the block and then see how the ladies are doing?"

"I'm all for that, James." Charles Douglas rose, smiling.

Marianne Valois turned to Lawrence Davis and smiled to herself as she made out the silhouette of his handsome face in the shadowy darkness of her bedroom. She put out a slim hand and softly touched his cheek and jaw, and he mumbled in the drowsy torpor of well-being that had followed their *amour*.

"Are you awake, *mon cher*?" she murmured.

"Y—yes—sure—I—I guess so, Marianne."

Lawrence sat up, blinking his eyes. The tangy scent of her perfume filled his nostrils, and the warmth of her flesh lingered on his, and again he felt the sudden swift restoration of carnal desire as he reached for her.

But Marianne gently disengaged his hands from her high-set, firm breasts, and with a sinuous felinity slipped out of the rumpled bed. *"Non, mon amour, c'est assez pour ce soir,"* she gently remonstrated. "Lie still, I'll bring you a glass of wine."

"I'd rather have you, Marianne darling." His voice was unsteady, husky with the advent of his revived ardor.

"You're a very flattering *amant, mon ami,* and you've been good for me. But you and I both know very well this can't go on endlessly."

"Do we have to talk about it now?"

271

She reached for the kerosene lamp, turned up the knob, and the flame rose from the wick like a pure tongue of light, cutting through the darkness. She turned to stare at him, and smiled knowingly at the mingled anxiety and irritation on his face. Swiftly she reached for her discarded camisole and donned it before he could reach for her again. "Lawrence, we must be sensible. I told you before, there's nothing here for me in Galveston, and I'd like to go to San Francisco and stay with my sister Odalie."

"Not yet, please Marianne."

"Ah, I see," she nodded. "You'd rather wait till you're tired of me, is that it?"

"Now you're accusing me of saying things I never said or thought," he grumbled.

"But I want you to know, *mon cher*, that I, not you, shall be the one who says it is over between us. That is my right as a free woman. If you were free, then it would be your right. You can't have it both ways, Lawrence."

"But I *am* free—free to do whatever I want!"

She shook her head. "Don't try to spoil things by saying what isn't so. You know, by now you may have broken your poor Melinda's heart—she's very young, you know—and she is the mother of your child."

"Marianne—"

"No, listen to me. I didn't tell you, but I met your father-in-law, oh, about three weeks ago. He's a very fine man. I met him in the department store—I was looking over my competition, *tu vois*."

"You didn't tell me—"

"There wasn't any need before, but now I think there is. Oh, don't misunderstand me—I didn't say a word about you and he didn't, either. But just the same, you can be sure that he knows by now what there is between us, and he's hoping it won't hurt Melinda. And I'm going to make sure it doesn't, Lawrence. I've been making plans to leave Galveston."

"But—but—Marianne—"

"Now don't protest and don't pout. It's unmanly and not at all worthy of you. We cannot go on this way indefinitely, *mon cher*, playing the deceitful lovers as if we didn't care about what happens to others who are concerned with us."

"But—we've known each other such a short time—why

do you have to go now? I don't understand—haven't I meant anything to you?"

"Of course you have," she replied, and then seeing his anguished expression, she added, "Now don't look so tragic. Our little interlude has been charming and memorable, and you must let that praise console your ego. But, *mon ami*, there is a time when such things must end. After all, what future could we have together? Are you ready to give up your Melinda and your little son, Gary? No, and besides, I wouldn't allow you to."

"If you loved me—"

"You use the past tense correctly, *mon ami*. I *have* loved you—but not in the way you have sought. You have not been my entire world, only a pleasant and at times exciting diversion. Be content with that. Go back to your family. Melinda is young; she will one day be all the woman you ever need."

"I—I want to see you again, though—"

"Yes—but not to come to my bed, *mon cher*. Tonight was lovely—and it was for the last time—a memory to cherish. One we shan't spoil by hurting anyone else, least of all ourselves. Now dress and leave me, *mon amour*."

CHAPTER TWENTY-FOUR

Henry McNamara had already done a good deal more to show his hostility against the new department store in town than to express annoyance to a port authority employee while unloading his cargo at the Galveston dock. Only a month after Charles Douglas had formally opened his store, McNamara had engaged the services of Clarence Portman, a fifty-year-old attorney of questionable ethics and somewhat mysterious background, to dispute the Chicagoan's clear title to the land on which the store had been built. Charles Douglas was not aware of it, but the judge who heard Clarence Portman's appeal summarily dismissed the charge as lacking in substance. This land, on Demmering Avenue, had been recommended to the enterprising Chicagoan by the Galveston banker Mason Elberding; there was no question whatsoever about the legitimacy of the title, which had been thoroughly investigated when Charles bought the land and before his contractor, Max Steinfeldt, had broken ground on the site.

Henry McNamara was forty-eight. He had inherited his father's store in New Orleans, and when General Butler's troops had occupied the Queen City, he had been damned as a traitor for catering almost exclusively to Union officers, who had plenty of money to spend. His wife—a Louisiana sugar-cane plantation owner's daughter and ten years his junior—had left him, not only because of his turncoat activities during the war, but also because of his repeated infidelities with girls who worked in the fancy houses on Rampart Street.

McNamara did not miss his pleasant-featured, soft-spoken wife, for he had already obtained a handsome dowry from her father at the time of their marriage. As

275

soon as General Butler's troops left New Orleans, McNamara, having drawn out all his cash and put it into a valise, boarded a packet boat bound for Galveston and there opened his present variety store.

He prospered because there was little competition at the outset, and several of his smaller competitors either had bad luck with damaged shipments or found themselves short of cash to pay for the goods they had ordered from New Orleans. These goods McNamara appropriated, paying about ten cents on the dollar for them. And although it could never be proved, rumor had it that he also hired a stevedore who had been fired for drunkenness off the Galveston docks to set fire to the store of a rival who had refused to sell out to him. The stevedore vanished almost immediately after the fire and was never found. A few days later, Henry McNamara approached the impoverished storekeeper and made him an offer for the goods that could be salvaged. These he advertised and sold at a handsome profit.

In Galveston, just as he had done in New Orleans, he continued his liaisons with women of easy virtue. There were actresses in minor roles and singers in the chorus of the Galveston Opera Company. There were also some itinerant young women who had had misfortunes in Mobile or New Orleans and sought to recoup their losses by plying their ancient trade in the busy port of Galveston; ultimately most of these women would go on to San Francisco or—if they could not raise the fare for that long journey—to the gaudy saloons of Wichita and Dodge City.

Henry McNamara had also changed his name, as a precaution against any possible reprisal from the patriotic residents of the Queen City. Since his merchandise had come by steamship to the levee in New Orleans before the war, and there were still steamship lines that plied the route between New Orleans and Galveston, it was quite likely that he might have been traced had his actual name—Carter McNally—ever appeared on any cargo manifest of goods bound for Galveston.

Currently, he was indulging in a liaison with a pretty black-haired *soubrette* from the Galveston Opera Company, Pansy Lowell. She was twenty-six, opulent of build, and her sweet, pure soprano was pleasant enough to gain her a post in the chorus, though her musical ability did not warrant her rising to any leading operatic roles. At sixteen, enamored of the colorful life of the theatrical and operatic stages, as well as with a singing teacher in his mid-forties, Pansy Lowell had run away from her home in Natchez, been abandoned a year later by her teacher-lover, and, after various adventures in New Orleans, had drifted to Galveston when she had heard that the opera company was offering opportunities for singers in the chorus. Henry McNamara, who prided himself on his cultural outlook on life, had attended a performance, been smitten by her full-blown charms, and soon thereafter had installed her in a little house on Jasmine Road.

The career of McNamara's lawyer, Clarence Portman, paralleled that of his client and rivaled it for chicanery and lechery. Portman had been the black sheep of a middle-class Philadelphia family; he had been admitted to the bar at the early age of twenty-two, and promptly got himself involved in land schemes that resulted in the loss of his license and a suspended sentence from a circuit judge. From there he went to Haverhill, Massachusetts, where he married an attractive mill girl who had been discharged as the result of his urging her to try to get her companions to stand together against the bosses for better hours and wages. The marriage lasted exactly eighteen months, by which time Portman had deserted and divorced his young wife, leaving her to fend for herself as best she could with a six-month-old daughter.

From Haverhill, Portman's wanderings took him to Roanoke, Virginia, where for ten years he behaved decorously. He studied for the bar, was admitted to practice, and married a tall, stately blond girl of nineteen by whom he had two small sons. But his natural aptitudes for turning a quick, if illegal, profit involved him in acting as the lawyer for a tobacco-processing plant which was nearly bankrupt and which was trying to raise money by selling fraudulent stock. When the scandal broke, Portman's license was revoked by the state bar, and his wife, a highly moral Methodist, divorced him.

Footloose and fancy free, Portman saw no reason why he should again pursue the unadventurous course of matrimony, and took himself to New Orleans. There he set himself up as a lawyer, after studying for a year and meeting the Queen City's requirements for attorneys at the bar. During the Civil War, he added to his growing bank account by running contraband to the North and—since he had no patriotic scruples—smuggling for the South as well. Although he never met Mark Bouchard, some of his invested capital went to pay for the building of the ship on which Mark was killed by a cannonball. It was in New Orleans that Portman met Henry McNamara; appropriately enough, that first meeting took place in one of the elegant bordellos on Rampart Street, for it appeared that the two men shared a carnal interest in buxom young women.

Portman left New Orleans a year after Henry McNamara. He had made the social error of approaching an attractive young woman who was dining alone in one of New Orleans's most fashionable restaurants, only to learn that she was the mistress of the proprietor. The young woman complained to her lover, who promptly challenged Portman to a duel. Portman left New Orleans in the dead of night six hours before the duel was to have taken place, chartering a packet to take him to Galveston. Within six months he had set up his law office and, having by this time met Henry McNamara, entered into an amoral legal alliance. Several of McNamara's financially distressed rivals, whose merchandise the storekeeper managed to obtain by either legal or illegal means, were brought to terms by Portman's threat of suit for damages against them. On one occasion, Portman, who openly envied his associate's sponsorship of Pansy Lowell, had so importuned the storekeeper that the latter complacently ordered the young *soubrette* to service his good friend and counselor, on pain of his turning her out of the house in which he was keeping her.

On the Friday afternoon of the second week of June, Henry McNamara glumly looked around his shop and, seeing only two or three customers in it, sharply bade his twenty-four-year-old, underpaid clerk, Alexander Gorth, "Mind you, Gorth, I'm going out on business now. Look after things, and less of your dawdling, man. And if folks come in, don't let them just wander around; try to push something. You're here to move merchandise, to put money in that till for me—that's where your wages come from, and don't forget it."

"Why, yes, s-sir," Alexander Gorth stammered. He was thoroughly miserable in his situation, but there was little he could do about it. He had studied for the ministry in a St. Louis seminary but he had failed because, as his stern fa-

278

ther had thundered at him: "You're too fond of the devil's fleshpots, boy, and they'll be the doom of you."

Two years ago, his zealot, Bible-selling father and his ailing, palid mother had come to Galveston to visit a cousin. They had fallen victim to a yellow fever epidemic, and their only legacies to Alexander had been his father's well-worn Bible, seventy dollars in hard cash, and his mother's fearfully whispered last words, "Alex, boy, the ministry's not for you. It'll stifle and crush you, as your father did me. Best get out into the world and fend for yourself."

After his parents' deaths, Alexander had received no help from his father's cousin, who, a week after his parents had been buried, gave him to understand that he did not need another mouth to feed. Then there was an opening at Henry McNamara's store, for the previous clerk had resigned, and Alexander had started right away. He had worked here eighteen months now, and he was constantly· browbeaten and threatened with immediate discharge.

As a consequence of McNamara's threats, Alexander worked harder than any other clerk the storekeeper had ever had. But to add to his tribulations, he had developed a bad case of acne at about the time he had fallen hopelessly in love with Katie McGrew, a saucy, red-haired, nineteen-year-old Irish girl, an orphan like himself, who worked in Adolf Gottlieb's bakery on Sussex Street. Alexander went there two or three times a week to buy a loaf of bread and some milk for a frugal supper. The widow from whom he rented a shabby little room, three miles from work, served meals to her boarders, but Alexander's wages were too meager to allow him to sit at her table seven days a week. What little money he could spare went to a disreputable doctor on the edge of town who prescribed potions and even bloodletting to cure his pimples. Doubtless they were the effect of his overwrought nerves and unbalanced diet, and his father might have scornfully added another cause: "The flux of carnal lust, boy—it stamps a man's face for what he truly is." Whatever the cause, the ailment persisted, despite the purgatives and ointments and lotions for which poor Alexander spent his money.

Alexander's visits to the Gottlieb bakery were the high points of his week. He used these occasions to steal glances at the piquant young Irish girl. Katie, for her part, divined his infatuation. The two other girls who worked with her, Jennie Calloway and Esther Christopher, both older than

279

herself, began to tease her about the shy admirer and to make deprecating remarks about his acne, but Katie compassionately ignored these personal references. For herself, she was already discontented with Galveston and especially with her employer, a heavy-set widower in his sixties who was determined to remarry. Indeed, one evening last month, he had insisted on taking Katie to supper and had rather clumsily revealed that his marital choice had fallen upon her. Katie, who needed her job—for she, like Alexander, lived at a cheap boarding house—had taken pains not to offend her employer; at the same time she had indicated that she was too young to think of marriage. For the time being, that had sufficed Adolf Gottlieb, but she feared that he would soon press his suit more forcibly. In the meantime, she took what pleasure she could from Alexander's shy admiration.

After leaving his shop, Henry McNamara went directly to the office of Clarence Portman. His irritable mood had deepened, mainly because of how few customers were in his shop today; in fact, business had been steadily dropping off over the past six months, and McNamara was sure he knew the cause.

"Clarence, we've go to do something about that damned Douglas fellow," he began without preamble, bringing his pudgy fist down on the edge of the attorney's desk.

"Now then, Henry, don't get yourself all riled up," the lawyer soothingly responded. "Business tends to be a little slow this time of year anyway. We're in for a hot summer, and you know yourself folks are fretting about this business of the yellow fever. I do wish our city fathers would get some really good medical assistance and clean it up once and for all. I remember only too well the worries we all had up in New Orleans."

"So do I," McNamara growled. This reference to the Queen City evoked memories that had nothing to do with yellow fever, and he was not particularly grateful to the attorney for mentioning the city. "You didn't get anywhere when you tried to bring that claim before Judge Duggery. I've been wondering whether you've thought up something that'll work this time. I tell you, Clarence, this fellow Douglas is going to drive me out of business if he keeps on bringing in cargoes from St. Louis and New Orleans and expanding his store the way he's been doing lately. You know yourself he's managed to hire the best help in town.

280

All I've got is a pimply-faced clerk who isn't worth the ten dollars I pay him for a six-day week. If this keeps up, I'm going to have to think of moving out, maybe to San Francisco. And I'm reasonably comfortable in Galveston."

"I know, Henry. Now don't get excited. I'll think of something. Wait a minute—did you see this morning's paper?"

"I have it in my office, but I didn't have time to read it. I've been busy going over the ledger, and business has dropped off alarmingly in the last three weeks."

"Well, it seems that Charles Douglas and his wife Laurette are visiting friends right here in Galveston, Henry. It says so in the paper."

"I don't care if I ever see his face in this town. I'd like to see an end of his store, that's all I can tell you," McNamara grumbled.

"Now wait a bit," the lawyer craftily counseled. "Don't go knocking domestic bliss and marital virtue. It seems to me they could be turned to your advantage, Henry."

"How's that?"

"Well, short of committing arson or murder—and I wouldn't advise either action on your part, Henry—you can't do much about getting rid of Douglas's department store. But if you were to get him involved in a little scandal, shall we say, one that would make his devoted wife leave him, one that would get some mention in our worthy daily journal, he might just decide to pull up stakes, sell out, and try his luck elsewhere."

McNamara stroked his chin and leaned back in his chair, reflecting. Then he chuckled evilly. "That's not a bad idea. I should have thought of that myself. Well, how do you propose to go about it?"

"Why, it's very simple. Your charming companion Miss Pansy Lowell ought to be able to assist in the enterprise," Portman grinned and winked.

"The hell you say—now, come to think of it, she just might, yes, she just might at that. She's beholden to me, as you well know, Clarence. That's why you were able to get to bed with her that time."

"Ah, yes!" Portman sighed and looked up at the ceiling with a smile of an infatuated adolescent. "And I don't mind admitting that I'd be enchanted to enjoy her favors again, whenever the occasion presents itself."

"That'll be enough talk about that, Clarence Portman!"

McNamara angrily snapped. "I did you a favor because I owed a little settlement. But don't go expecting Pansy to leap into bed with you whenever you fancy. I've got her properly trained, and she serves me very nicely. Yes, I think if I have a little talk with her, she'll find a way to cozen this Douglas fellow and compromise him very nicely. I'll have to do some thinking about it and see how we can bring the two of them together."

"Couldn't she pretend to be looking for a job in his store, Henry?" the lawyer proposed.

"Yes, that's one way," McNamara grudgingly conceded. "But let me think about it a little bit. If she came looking for work, that would be a purely business proposition, and I don't think Douglas would want to follow her back to her house and give her a chance to tickle his fancy. There must be some other way she could meet him and attract his attention." He put a finger to his bulbous nose, squinted into space, and pondered a moment. "She'd have to catch him alone when he wasn't with his wife, of course, and do something that would get him to come to her house of his own will."

"Yes, that's logical enough."

"Sure it is. Now maybe, if she sprained her ankle, and he had to hire a horse and buggy and take her home, and she invited him in for a cup of tea or something like that—" McNamara mused aloud, still thinking.

"Excellent, Henry!" the lawyer purred, rubbing his hands with glee. "Once he's inside the house, she can always claim that he made an attack on her virtue. Then she'll come to me and I'll bring suit against him for carnal assault."

"Now you're beginning to think like the lawyer I hired you to be, Clarence." McNamara chuckled. "I think we're on the right track. I'll have supper with Pansy tonight, and I'll cue her in."

"You think she'll go along with it?"

"She'd better, if she knows what's good for her. I happen to know one of the directors of the opera company, and a word to him might just get her fired. Plus which I'd kick her out of the house so fast it would make her pretty head swim, and she wouldn't have a thin dime to her name after that. No, I think she'll go along with the idea. She doesn't have that much of a voice to earn her living as a singer, even if she tried it in San Francisco. I know because Mr.

282

Muir told me as much—he's heard her sing. Fact of the matter is, so have I. It's a nice bedroom voice, but it's no good on stage, not to make people buy tickets to hear her, anyhow. Oh yes, she'll do what I tell her to. Otherwise, she'll wind up a whore, and they don't last long, certainly not here in Galveston."

CHAPTER TWENTY-FIVE

"I—I had to see you one last time, Marianne," Lawrence Davis said as he entered Marianne Valois's bedroom.

The attractive widow looked up from the valise she was packing. "And so you do, *mon cher*. What I'm doing should tell you that I'm leaving Galveston, just as I told you I would."

"Oh, Marianne, I'm so confused—I can't bear the thought of your leaving like this. Can't you put it off—a week, a month?"

She straightened, put her hands on her hips, and forced a cynical smile to her full lips, looking like a genuine Parisian *bourgeoise*.

"I could, *vraiment*, but to what end? So that you could take your time, dally with me a little longer? No, *mon ami*, it is as I said last time: we have enjoyed each other, but it is finished. You should go back to your Melinda."

"I—I suppose I must. If you're really determined to leave me, where else do I have to go?"

"Ah, no, my friend, do not say you *must* go back. After all, you do have a choice. No, you must *want* to go back. And it is not so very hard to do, for I know that in your heart you love her. She will be good for you. You should teach her the arts of love, even as I have taught you. Sometimes, my friend, even when a marriage is young—perhaps *because* it is young and the lovers are inexperienced—things can be—routine. Try adding some spice. You know how—I know you do." She smiled at him saucily.

"Marianne, you know very well that Melinda would never permit—well, we could never do—some of the things you and I—you know."

"Come, come, *mon ami*, do not be so sure. She may be

285

shy, but she is a woman. If you are gentle and considerate, she will love you all the more for helping her to understand just what it is a man desires. Believe me, you should try to place your trust in her. That's just as important as love, in a marriage. Don't be afraid. Your love will make you strong."

"Oh, Marianne, sometimes I think you must be the wisest woman in the world. You seem so—so sure of everything. If only you didn't have to leave—but, if you've made up your mind, and I see you have—well, then, I guess I'll just have to accept it. But—but—darn it, do you really think Melinda would—would respond to me, the way you say? You think I ought to be less—less of a gentleman, you might say?"

"Of course I do, that's what I've been saying. Now you really must go, if I am to finish this packing. I'm leaving tomorrow morning. Remember that I'll be thinking of you, wanting things to turn out right."

"Will you give me your address, Marianne? I could write to you—"

She smiled and shook her head. "I think not. It is best if everything is over now. Come give me a kiss and then be off."

He did as he was bidden, then, picking up his hat, which he had let fall in a chair, he stood for a long moment, staring at her and twisting the hat in his hands. Then, with a little shrug, he turned and strode out of the house.

Marianne Valois sighed and shook her head. There was the glint of tears in her eyes as she turned back to her valise.

On the day after Lawrence's parting from Marianne, Charles Douglas paid a visit to his own department store, with James Hunter taking the role of guide, much to the Chicagoan's amusement. Arabella's husband had shown a zest and gregariousness in his new role, which was quite far removed from his former employment as a cotton factor. When Charles humorously remarked on this subject, James replied with some asperity, "I'll have you know, Charles, that I've never believed the old adage that you can't teach an old dog new tricks. And it's made a new dog of me too, if you must know. Now you see, while you were away, I suggested that more space be devoted to these displays of new furniture. I mean to say, there's no reason why we should stick with the old, primitive log-cabin type the settlers had, is there?"

"Of course not, not at all. That's why I asked my friend back in Indianapolis, whose factory provides this furniture, to send us his very latest line."

"And a good thing, too," Charles said with great emphasis. "That earlier line we had was just about useless."

It was all Charles could do to keep from smiling and perhaps offending his partner's sensibilities; it was quite obvious that Arabella's husband was both enjoying his new career and taking it seriously.

"Fortunately," James continued, "the new line has been doing very well, and that's why I thought more space ought to be devoted to it."

"I quite agree," Charles rejoined. "You should try to introduce new items, and when you do, devote a small space to them at first, using the space effectively. Then if the new products catch fire, you can always increase the floor space. That's a happy problem for any storekeeper to contemplate, believe me. More and more people are flocking to the West and the Southwest, and I'm convinced we'll be entering an era of strong merchandising and suggestive selling geared to reach a large population. It won't be enough just to open the doors of a store and have things standing there and expect the customers to walk away with them. No, sir. You'll have to create a desire to buy, and the more new things you'll be able to show them, to make their lives more comfortable—and flatter their egos in the process—the more profits you'll make." Thus Charles Douglas explained his business philosophy.

This same afternoon, Laurette paid a visit to the house of Max Steinfeldt and his lovely wife, Alice. Charles had told her how helpful Alice Fernmark had been to him when he visited Houston the year before with the intention of buying land and planning for a second store. Employed by the unscrupulous and perverted Arnold Shottlander, Alice had caught wind of the shady deal that Shottlander and the banker Calvin Jemmers, who had constantly tried to importune her into becoming his mistress, had concocted to defraud the industrious Chicago merchant. She had revealed it to Charles, and Arnold Shottlander had been in the process of beating her when Charles Douglas had come into his office, rescued Alice, thoroughly thrashed the crooked realtor, and then arranged to send Alice to Galveston to work in his store. There, she had met the genial contractor who had been responsible for hiring the crew and supervising the building of the Douglas Department Store, and a fortuitous accident had literally thrown her into Max Steinfeldt's arms.

Laurette found herself quite at home with the personable young woman and was overjoyed to learn that the Steinfeldts were expecting their first child around the beginning of next year. Miraculously—though she had believed herself to be hopelessly barren—Alice had discovered that she was blessed with a normal pregnancy.

"I almost envy you, Alice," Laurette told the blushing young woman. "It's wonderful to be in love and to be sure of your husband, but when the two of you know that you're going to have a baby, then it cements the relationship in the most wonderfully rewarding way. I know. And I was doubly blessed, you see, because I had my twins, Kenneth and Arthur. Maybe your first will be twins too."

"Oh my goodness!" Alice gasped, then blushed and turned away while Max Steinfeldt rose, went over to her chair, bent, and kissed her. "I'm so happy about it, I don't care whether it's a girl or a boy," he declared, which earned him still another kiss.

So thoroughly did Laurette enjoy herself that when Max suggested she have supper with them, she readily assented. She went home briefly to feed the baby, then returned in the early evening to share the Steinfeldts' delicious meal.

Meanwhile, Charles Douglas and James Hunter were winding up their tour of the department store. About half an hour before closing time, Arabella's husband took out his watch and frowned. "You know, I think I'd like to pay a visit to Melinda and see how she's getting on."

"Of course, James. I was sorry to hear about her trouble. I hope it doesn't mean a permanent rift."

"Oh no! I'm convinced it doesn't. I suppose every young man has to sow his wild oats, and the only trouble was that young Lawrence didn't sow them before he married my daughter. But I like the boy, I've always liked him, just as I do his father. He has good stuff in him; I think he's bound to come to his senses soon enough. He's been discreet so far, and there hasn't been any scandal. I think if there had been, it would be hard for Melinda to take him back. Well, I'll join you at the house for dinner, then."

"I've a feeling that Laurette might stay over with the

Steinfeldts, James. If you don't mind—and believe me it's out of no disrespect for Arabella's wonderful cuisine—I'd just as soon try my luck at a restaurant this evening," Charles proffered.

"Certainly. Matter of fact, if I stay any length of time with Melinda, I may finish up by taking her to dinner myself. I told her this morning I wasn't exactly certain what my plans were for this afternoon, and not to go to any fuss preparing supper. Besides, with warm weather like this, most of the week we eat very simply. I do have to watch my waistline, you know." James self-consciously patted his still-trim waist, then shook hands with Charles and left the store.

While the two men had been conversing, an attractive, black-haired young woman in a long hobbled skirt and high-button shoes, wearing a broad-brimmed hat with an artificial flower adornment, had been watching them. Earlier, when she had noticed the deference with which the clerks treated the two men, she had inquired of a girl at the handkerchief counter and been told that these were Charles Douglas, the owner of the store, and James Hunter, his Galveston partner.

As soon as she saw James take his leave of Charles, she slowly and hesitantly approached and, as Charles was inspecting the display of a small kitchen table with four matching chairs, politely inquired, "Is it true that you're the owner of this beautiful store?"

Charles turned and smilingly nodded. "That's right, miss. I'm Charles Douglas, and I'm very glad you approve of the store."

"Oh, I do, Mr. Douglas, I think it's just beautiful. Galveston has needed a store like this for ever so long. My name is Pansy Lowell, by the way."

"It's a pleasure to make your acquaintance, Miss Lowell. Were you looking for something special?"

"No, but I come here to shop quite often. Actually, I was thinking of some earrings."

"We've an excellent jewelry department, Miss Lowell. Permit me to escort you there."

"That's very kind of you, Mr. Douglas." She accompanied him farther down the floor, giving him a coquettish smile from time to time. Pansy Lowell had taken pains to look demure and decorous, and had refrained from using too much lip rouge or rice powder. Her dress was high at the neck, and its color was subdued. Nonetheless, her heart-shaped face, her expressive dark-brown eyes and full, sensuous mouth, together with her enthusiastic compliments about his store, made Charles Douglas aware of her decided feminine allure. As he chatted amiably with her, he learned that she was a singer in the chorus of the Galveston Opera Company, and since he himself was a music lover, this led to an enthusiastic discussion of the latest operas he had seen and heard in Chicago. Pansy expressed an admiration for the Italian composers Bellini and Donizetti, neither of whose leading roles, alas, she was able to sing. The effect was to leave Charles with the impression that here was a lovely, cultured young woman as sophisticated as could be found in all of Chicago, and it flattered him to think that the Douglas Department Store could count on her patronage.

At last, Pansy decided to buy a pair of amethyst earrings, prettily admitting to Charles that this was her birthstone. Smiling, he watched as she held up a pair to her ears, while the salesgirl stood by attentively. "Do you think they're becoming, Mr. Douglas? I really value your opinion," Pansy exclaimed effusively.

"Oh yes, they're quite becoming. And they're the latest fashion too, because a pair like those were selling in Peacock's in Chicago just before I left."

"Oh thank you so much for telling me! Then I do want them. But I confess I only hope it won't hurt too much when the doctor pierces my earlobes so that I can wear them," Pansy explained, giving him a soulful look and fluttering her lashes at him.

Despite his poised demeanor, Charles could not help flushing. Unquestionably, Pansy Lowell was seductive, yet so far she had played her hand so well that he was not in the least aware that their meeting had been artfully contrived. He hastened to reassure her that it was only a moment's discomfort; once that was over with, she would be delighted with the earrings, for they would make every woman in Galveston look upon her with envy. He expressed himself more effusively than was his wont, which undoubtedly could be attributed to Pansy's undeniable attractiveness. He did not associate her with a woman like Carrie Melton, who had approached him five years before in his Chicago department store and tried to lure him into her bed. Carrie had come from the Bridgeport slums and lived by her wits most of her life. Pansy Lowell was far better educated; she also had lofty ambitions, and if her talents did not quite qualify her to fulfill them, that was not to her discredit.

As she put the tissue-wrapped packet of earrings into her reticule and turned to go, Pansy seemed suddenly to lose her balance: she stumbled forward and uttered a sharp cry of pain. Charles swiftly steadied her before she could fall and anxiously inquired, "Are you all right, Miss Lowell?"

"Oh dear—I—I do believe—I—I've turned my ankle—it hurts—I don't think I can walk. Oh, I'm ever so sorry—it was clumsy of me—I don't know what I was thinking of."

"You weren't clumsy at all, and you mustn't blame yourself. Miss Evans, would you be kind enough to go out to the street and call a horse-and-buggy driver?" Then, to the black-haired young woman who had put an arm on one of his shoulders to steady herself, he said, "I'll drive you home, Miss Lowell. It's the very least I can do, hurting yourself here in my store, and right in front of me. I must have the floor examined. Perhaps it was irregular or there was a knot in the wood—"

"I—I don't know—but it does hurt—it's so very kind of you, Mr. Douglas. I'm sorry I'm giving you so much trouble."

"But it's no trouble at all, I assure you. Well now, Miss Evans has stopped a driver. He'll be waiting for you. Come now, lean on me, and I'll see you safely home."

Perhaps Pansy was not an accomplished soprano, but she was assuredly an accomplished actress. She grimaced, she courageously hobbled; she did not utter too many fluttering little cries to indicate her pain, but her occasional grimaces, which Charles clearly perceived, indicated that she was trying her very best to be brave about what was obviously a painful injury. He helped her into the buggy and, after inquiring her address, gave it to the driver and settled back in the seat beside her, his handsome face taut with concern. "I do hope you'll be all right, Miss Lowell. Do you think we should stop at a doctor's office before we go to your house?"

"Oh no! I—I think that if I were to heat some water and put my foot into it, it would be all right. Maybe some salts in the water—I'm sure I have some. It's so thoughtful of you to be concerned about me, Mr. Douglas. I feel just dreadful, spoiling your whole evening."

"But you didn't, and you needn't apologize. You were telling me that you sing in the chorus—will you have a chance to sing some of the important roles in the fall season this year, do you think?"

"I don't know. There are so many fine singers visiting this country, you know, Mr. Douglas, and I'm just a simple Southern girl who's had a little training. I'm doing well enough in the chorus, though, and it is regular work, thank goodness."

"But it's good to have ambitions. One should always try to achieve one's potential, Miss Lowell." He gave her his characteristically boyish grin. "I guess that's what made me think of coming all the way down here and building a store after mine was burned in the big Chicago fire."

"Oh yes, I read all about that! It must have been just awful, all those people killed and homeless, and the looting and the mobs—"

"Yes, it was terrifying at the time. But we're rebuilding, and now it's as if it never happened. You'd like Chicago, Miss Lowell. It's a bustling, friendly city with big ideas and plenty of people who share those ideas and are ready to back them with capital. One of these days, I shouldn't be surprised, we might be the biggest city in this whole country. Maybe even by the centennial."

"You're really a very nice man, Mr. Douglas. And so cheerful all the time. I guess that's what makes your store so successful. Well, here we are now. I really don't want to trouble you any more—"

"No, I insist in seeing you safely inside. Wait here, driver, if you please."

He helped her down as Pansy Lowell, leaning on his shoulder with one arm around his waist, hobbled slowly toward the door of her little house. She unlocked it and invited him to enter.

"Let me heat some water for you, so that you can soak your foot right away and ease the pain, Miss Lowell," he volunteered.

"Oh, I really couldn't ask you to do that, Mr. Douglas! What must you think of me?"

"No, I want to. After all, you hurt yourself in my store, and I feel responsible. Believe me, I'll feel much better if you'll let me help. And if the pain doesn't go away, I'll get a doctor for you. Now tell me where the kitchen is—oh yes, I can see it from here. You go sit down and rest and I'll heat the water."

"The salts are in the cupboard to the far right, Mr. Douglas. I really can't believe I could have been so clumsy and that the famous owner of the only department store in Galveston is looking after me just like a nurse," Pansy giggled, as she carefully lowered herself into an overstuffed armchair and leaned back with an audible sigh of relief.

When he returned with the pan of water, into which he had poured a sizable quantity of salts, she had already eased off her high-button shoe and had whisked up her skirt and petticoats to reveal delectably plump calves and thighs sheathed in black lisle hose with fancy pink garters. She was in the process of slowly doffing the right stocking when he entered. He turned crimson with embarrassment, then turned his back and stammered, "Ex-excuse me—I didn't mean to embarrass you."

"It's all right. I do feel a little better now, and I'm sure the hot water and salts will help tremendously, Mr. Douglas. If you'll set the pan down, I'll put my foot into it. Just a second till I get my stocking off—there. Oh my, it's very nice and warm. This is so much better! I think I'll be all right."

"Are you sure?" he solicitously inquired.

"Oh yes!" Then she giggled softly. "If I can stand this pain, I guess I shouldn't be a baby about having my ears pierced, now should I?"

"No, I suppose not, Miss Lowell." He chuckled, relieved to find her better. "Now are you quite sure you wouldn't want me to call a doctor?"

"Oh, no. I think if I just rest here for a while and soak my foot in the good warmth, I'll be fine."

"Try to move it around every now and then," he suggested. "Get the muscles back into tone. But don't try walking on it for a bit. And if you do feel any discomfort later tonight, I hope you've a neighbor who'd get a doctor for you."

"Oh, yes, I do, there's Mrs. Garrity; she's a nice, motherly old soul, and she'd get one in a minute, if I needed him. But I think I'll be all right. You've been ever so kind, Mr. Douglas."

"It was my pleasure, Miss Lowell."

"I wonder—" Her voice trailed off, and she looked at him with widened, misty eyes.

"Yes?"

"I was thinking—oh no, it's silly of me, I'm behaving very badly, Mr. Douglas."

"No, tell me."

"Well, even if I'm feeling better in the morning, I was thinking that Mrs. Garrity could call the doctor over tomorrow afternoon just to check my ankle, and he could put in my earrings for me. And then maybe you'd like to drop by and see how they are? After all, it was on your word that I bought them, you know."

"Well, I suppose I could," he hesitated. "I don't see any reason why not. You're my responsibility till I'm sure everything's all right. After all," he chuckled, "you know a customer can sue a store, if she hurts herself in it and it's the owner's fault."

"Oh, I'd never think of suing you, Mr. Douglas! Not after you've been so kind and helpful to me. I'd be the most ungrateful girl in the world if I did that. But maybe you could come by about, say, four o'clock tomorrow afternoon, if that's convenient?"

"I'll make a point of doing that. Well, I'll let myself out now, and bid you goodnight. I do hope you'll be better in the morning."

"Oh yes, I'm beginning to feel better already, thanks to you. You're ever so kind. Thank you so very much, Mr. Douglas."

"You did fine, Pansy girl, just fine." Henry McNamara took his black-haired mistress into his arms and kissed her resoundingly. Pansy Lowell had made a miraculous recovery. About an hour and a half after Charles Douglas had left her house, McNamara had come by and she had cooked him a beefsteak and roast potatoes; now, clad only in her camisole and stockings, they were sitting on the wide bed as she helped him remove his shirt and cravat.

"He's a very nice man, Henry. He told me all about his children. And he likes opera; he knows a lot about it."

"So?" he coldly retorted as he rose, tugged down his breeches, then pulled her down on her back and lay down beside her. "He's driving me into bankruptcy with his being a nice man and having kids and knowing about opera. Besides, Pansy, get it out of your head once and for all that you're ever going to amount to anything as a singer. You do fine enough in the chorus, where nobody can hear you by yourself, but don't ever expect to stand up there on the stage and have everybody cheer you and bring you flowers like they do for Jenny Lind."

Pansy Lowell pouted. "You're cruel, Henry. I can sing very well."

"Don't try now, honey; you've other talents I'm much more fond of. Now listen, and listen carefully. You say Douglas is coming over here about four tomorrow? That's fine. Clarence and I will be waiting outside the back door, you understand? You get him into your bedroom by hook or by crook, even if you have to take off all your clothes to do it."

"Henry McNamara, sometimes you can be the most vulgar man!"

"Yes, I can," he sneered, and reached out to pinch one of her nipples so cruelly that she squealed in pain and struck his hand away. "That's just a sample. You flub this, Pansy, and you'll be out in the street without a red cent to your name, just don't forget that. And you won't have a job in the chorus, either, I'll see to it. Now, to go on with what I was saying. You'll get him in here, and then you'll want to show him your ankle, see? Then you'll tear the top part of your dress and what's under it, so he can see your tits, you understand me? Then you'll scream, and Clarence and I will come in; we'll have him where we want him."

"All—all right, Henry," Pansy whimpered, wincing and cautiously touching her bruised nipple.

With a lecherous laugh, the shopkeeper ripped off her camisole and then, his mouth crushing hers to stifle her protests, savagely possessed her.

What neither Pansy nor Henry McNamara and Clarence Portman had reckoned with was Charles Douglas's innate honesty in keeping nothing from his wife. The episode with Carrie Melton back in Chicago had made him aware of how susceptible he could be to exploitation by attractive young women. Moreover, he could never forget how Laurette, learning what Carrie had done, had brought a horsewhip, gone to the bank where Carrie worked, and whipped her until Carrie tearfully confessed her plan to seduce Charles and then blacken his reputation.

So, after a leisurely dinner at one of Galveston's best

restaurants, Charles walked back to the Hunter house at just about the time that Laurette was descending from Max Steinfeldt's buggy and saying her goodnights to him and Alice. Charles called a cheerful greeting to Max and Alice and then gave Laurette his arm, escorting her toward the house.

"Well now, you seem very pleased with yourself, Laurette darling," he jocularly said as he stopped before the door to kiss her.

"Do you know something, Charlie? Alice is going to have a baby. Isn't that just too wonderful? Especially because, with her first husband who was killed, she'd had doctors tell her she never could. They're such a nice couple, so devoted to each other. I'm so glad for her, she's a wonderful girl and Max is the salt of the earth."

"That he is, and he built me a marvelous store. I'll use his services in Houston, if I can swing a deal there, Laurette. Now let's go in. James ought to be back by now, unless he's spending the evening with poor Melinda."

"I do hope Melinda and Lawrence get back together, darling," Laurette confided, as she reached for the door knocker and gave it a couple of taps. "After being with Max and Alice this evening, I just feel so romantic that I want everybody who's married to be happy—including us, of course, that goes without saying."

"I haven't given you any cause for complaint yet, have I, darling?" he laughed softly and bent to kiss her just as Arabella opened the door.

"My gracious! Look at you!" Arabella giggled. "An old married couple like you stealing a kiss out there in front of God and everybody. Come in. James got home a few minutes ago. And he brought wonderful news: it seems that everything is going to be fine between Melinda and Lawrence."

"I'm so glad, Bella dear," Laurette confided. "I was just telling Charles that I want everybody who's married to be happy. There's really going to be a reconciliation, then?"

"Oh yes. It seems that Lawrence came over this noon to visit Melinda, and he apologized and said he'd been a fool and it would never happen again. The Valois woman evidently left town today. And he said he'd make it up to Melinda, and of course, she was just so lonesome for him, she broke down and cried, and I'm sure it's going to be wonderful from now on. Shall we have some wine as a nightcap?"

"Not too much." Charles ruefully shook his head. "But I will have one glass to drink to Melinda and Lawrence, to you and James, to Max and Alice, and last, but far from least, to Laurette and myself."

"Hear, hear!" Laurette laughed softly as she linked her arm with his.

As they sat on the living room sofa with James in his favorite armchair and Arabella bustling about with a tray filled with glasses of wine and English tea biscuits, Charles turned to his wife and declared, "I had a rather amusing experience this afternoon in the store."

"Oh?" Laurette's eyes widened, and she turned to look at him with interest. "Tell me about it, darling."

"Of course, I intend to. As a matter of fact, James, it concerns you a little bit too, because the young lady in question was praising several of the departments you had a hand in."

"What young lady in question?" Laurette's eyes narrowed and the smile left her face.

"Why, after James left me, there was a very personable young lady who bought some amethyst earrings. She was very complimentary about the merchandise in the store, especially the furniture, and she liked the kerchief display also, I believe."

"And what happened?" Laurette demanded impatiently.

Charles grinned sheepishly. "I catch your drift, honey. Don't worry, it's nothing at all like what happened with poor Carrie Melton Haines. Yes, I was thinking about her just now, remembering all that. At any rate, the young lady's name is Miss Pansy Lowell, and she sings in the chorus of the local opera company. Unfortunately, she twisted her ankle, so I got a horse and buggy and drove her home."

"That was very gallant of you, dear," Laurette said with an edge to her voice. "And, of course, I suppose she was extremely attractive. What happened then?"

Charles fidgeted and had the good grace to blush. "She very sensibly suggested that she should soak her foot in hot water and salts, and I prepared them for her. Then she said she'd like to have me come by tomorrow afternoon to see if everything was all right, and since she'd bought the earrings at my suggestion and would have her ears pierced for

297

them when the doctor came to examine her ankle, she'd like me to see how they looked on her."

"And I suppose you said you'd drop by, dear." Laurette's sarcasm was hardly veiled.

"Well, er—yes, I did. But I didn't see any harm—after all, you know perfectly well that if a customer hurts herself in a store, she can bring suit to recover damages. I want to be sure that nothing is wrong with Miss Lowell, because she did turn her ankle while I was standing there talking to her at the jewelry department," Charles explained rather uncomfortably.

"Just a minute," James put in, his brows furrowed with concentration. "Did you just say that this young woman sings in the chorus of the opera company?"

"Why, yes, James, that's exactly what she told me."

"Hmm. I'm just wondering now—I have it! You remember I mentioned that disreputable storekeeper Henry McNamara, who has a habit of offering damaged merchandise at high prices and has a reputation for driving his smaller competitors out of business by rather shoddy practices?"

"Yes, I do. But I don't see the connection—" Charles began.

"This might be very interesting, Charles. You know, McNamara's name stuck in my mind after I had told you about him, and I made some further inquiries about him. It appears that he has, shall we say, an inamorata whom he's keeping in a house he owns, and it just so happens that she also sings in the opera."

"There, you see!" Laurette indignantly declared. "Charles, you're so naive at times about women, it's a good thing I came along with you on this trip. I'll just bet that if you go over there tomorrow afternoon, she'll try to trap you. This McNamara may be trying to hurt your reputation so that you'd have to sell your store and leave Galveston."

"You know, Charles," James thoughtfully mused, "your charming, intelligent wife might just be right about this. And I wouldn't put it past McNamara to try that ancient dodge. You see, Charles, I'm familiar with what is vulgarly known as the badger game. One of my friends in Tuscaloosa long before the war, even before I met my charming Bella, had just such a little dodge tried on him. He was squiring a girl of about sixteen who professed to be

298

considerably older, and, alas, he was somewhat in his cups when he had a tryst with her. It turned out that when he and the young lady found themselves in an intimate situation, a man burst into the room and threatened my friend first with murder, and then with a lawsuit and imprisonment because his daughter was being forced against her will. And my friend was so frightened that I'm ashamed to say he paid off the blackmailer. It later turned out that the blackmailer had worked this scheme in various cities and the girl was one of many protégées whom he had very skillfully coached."

"My gracious, James," Arabella giggled, "I've had to wait all these years to learn one of the most colorful episodes of your entire life. And here I thought you such a paragon of virtue."

"Careful, Bella," her husband observed with a twinkle in his eyes, "I didn't say that I was involved; the fellow just happened to be a very close friend of mine from college days, that's all. I'll have you know I was never thus entrapped. And you were, and still are, the only girl I've ever been interested in."

"That's very sweet, dearest." Arabella got up, went over to her husband, and gave him a hug and a kiss, which considerably eased the tension. However, Laurette was still up in arms at what she had just learned: "That's all very nice, but what are you going to do about this little assignation of yours tomorrow afternoon, Charles?"

"Well, I don't know now. Perhaps I'd better not show up there—and you know perfectly well, Laurette, I had no illicit intentions."

"I should hope not, for your sake, darling," she said sweetly. "But I think you're going to keep your appointment—except that I'm going with you. I'll wait outside the house after you've gone in so that if this little adventuress tries a scheme like the one James has just told us about, I'll be there to defend you."

"Now that isn't a bad idea at all, Laurette," James proffered. "The friend I talked to yesterday about McNamara thinks it would be good riddance if Galveston could see the last of him. And if you were to spike his guns, so to speak, a good many businessmen would be quite grateful to you."

"It's going to be fun tomorrow afternoon, Charles," Laurette smiled expectantly. Then she added, as she put her arm around her husband's waist and pressed her face against his shoulder. "After all, a loyal wife should always stand behind her husband in time of crisis. And you, Charles Douglas, happen to be the only husband I'll ever want to have, so I don't want you to get into any more trouble with unattached females."

At four o'clock, Charles Douglas put his hand to the knocker of the front door of Pansy Lowell's little house and rapped three times. Laurette had walked slowly about half a block behind him, and watched from across the street until he was admitted by the black-haired young woman. There was just time enough for Laurette to see that Pansy was wearing a very becoming red velvet dressing-robe, and her lips tightened with vexation, which boded no good for the buxom young chorine.

She waited a few minutes, and then walked slowly across the street toward the little house, stationing herself outside the door. She put her hand to the knob, tried it, and smiled to herself to find that the door had been left unlocked.

"It was awfully sweet of you to come see about me, Mr. Douglas." Pansy Lowell favored him with a dazzling smile as she led the way into her bedroom. "You see, I can walk ever so much better. The hot water and salts did the trick. Dr. Norman came over this noon and examined me and said that it was only a mild sprain and would be healed very quickly. He told me I should walk about on it and get the blood back into circulation. And he pierced my ears, too. See my earrings? Do you like them—may I call you Charles?"

"If you like, Miss Lowell. Yes, they're quite attractive. And I'm glad to hear that the injury you sustained in my store proved to be so inconsequential. I just wanted to hear from your own lips that you don't plan any suit for redress."

"Why, whatever gave you that idea, Charles? It was my own fault; I was clumsy, and just twisted my ankle, that's all. Of course, I wouldn't dream of asking for damages for such a silly thing as this." Again, Pansy gave him a dazzling smile, then, somewhat petulantly, she added, "Of course, I did have to pay Dr. Norman—"

"I'd be glad to take care of that for you, Miss Lowell. That much, at least, is my responsibility." Charles Douglas took out his wallet, extracted a ten-dollar bill, and handed it to the young woman. Pansy put the bill into the pocket of her robe and, in so doing, surreptitiously managed to loosen the belt so that the robe swung open. It disclosed a white silk negligee whose bodice was cut low enough to reveal the cantaloupe-like curves of an opulent bosom. This done, she suddenly moved close to him and, an arm around his waist, murmured seductively, "You've been so nice, Charles, I want to kiss you and say thank you."

Charles Douglas stood stiffly, though the temptation of Pansy Lowell's soft red lips approaching his, together with the generous display of bare flesh her décolletage revealed, was a considerable temptation.

"I want you to kiss me, Charles," she murmured huskily, clinging to him with her left arm. But when he made no move to accept her amorous invitation, she swiftly put her right hand to the bodice of her negligee and ripped it, then screamed and cried out, "Don't you dare! I didn't think you were that kind of man!"

Exactly on cue, the back door opened and Henry McNamara entered, followed by Clarence Portman. As the two men came through the kitchen into the front of the house, McNamara called out, "Pansy—Pansy, are you home? I hope you don't mind my barging in like this, but I've brought Mr. Portman to see you about that will you wanted to have drawn up." Upon reaching the door to the bedroom, which was just off the living room, McNamara cried out in mock horror, "But what's this? Why, I believe it's Mr. Charles Douglas. Pansy, what's the meaning of this? Has this gentleman been taking advantage of you? I thought I heard someone cry out—"

At this, Pansy, who had hastily belted her robe so as to appear respectable, now ran to McNamara as if for protection. "Oh, Mr. McNamara, you can't imagine—it's just the most awful thing—this man—" she gasped.

"Now, Pansy, it's all right. I'm here now. But I mean to get to the bottom of this." He turned to Charles, an expression of feigned outrage on his face. "See here, Douglas, what kind of lecherous rogue are you? A supposedly reputable married man, the owner of Galveston's finest store, attempting to overcome a virtuous young woman's will by brute force—you'll regret this, mark my words."

"I don't think he will," came Laurette Douglas's voice. Having heard Pansy Lowell's shrill soprano scream, she had opened the front door and marched straight into the bedroom, just in time to hear the lawyer's denunciation of her husband.

"My God!" McNamara ejaculated, his jaw dropping and his eyes widening with disbelief.

Clarence Portman whirled, his face pale. "Who—who are you, madam?" he asked in a faint, tremulous voice.

"I happen to be Charles Douglas's wife. And I see exactly what little game the two of you have tried to play on my husband. Oh yes, he told me all about Miss Lowell last night. And James Hunter, whom I daresay both of you know to be my husband's partner, warned me that Miss Lowell might try to enact this naughty little farce. Which one of you is Henry McNamara?"

The two men exchanged a frantic look, and McNamara, pulling a kerchief from his coat pocket, mopped his brow and stammered, "I—I am. But I assure you—"

Charles now stepped forward. "I don't think, Mr. McNamara," he angrily declared, "that you and I have anything of any importance to say to each other. You're not going to get me out of town, certainly not by such a laughable stunt as this. May I ask the name of the other gentleman?"

"I—if you must know, I—I'm Mr. McNamara's lawyer, C-Clarence Portman." The attorney's voice shook with consternation.

"I thought as much. Well, gentlemen, with my wife here as a witness, I don't think you have any case at all. In fact, if anything, I may have a case against both of you."

"Now don't be hasty, Mr. Douglas." Clarence Portman finally found his voice, but his face was contorted with apprehension. "I assure you that my client wants to forget about this misunderstanding, as I do."

"I'm glad to hear that. And if anyone's going to leave town, Mr. McNamara, I think it ought to be you, and you can take your lawyer friend with you. James Hunter knows a few of the judges in Galveston, and if he were to tell them how a lawyer acted in collusion with his client for the purpose of entrapping an innocent man, it's very likely they might take steps to disbar you from any further legal work in Galveston."

"Come on, Henry, we'd better get out of here," Portman hoarsely exclaimed.

McNamara turned to glare at Pansy Lowell, who had started to cry. Then, with a muttered oath, he pushed past

Laurette Douglas and made his way to the door, Portman following close behind him.

"I—I'm sorry, Mr. Douglas—I had to—Mr. McNamara—well, I'm beholden to him—" Pansy tearfully began.

"You don't have to tell me, Miss Lowell. I suppose he threatened you with loss of your job and stopping further financial support if you didn't go through with this. But I'll tell you what I'll do. If you want to work at an honest job and earn money in addition to what you bring in by singing in the chorus, I suggest that you might make a very personable clerk in my store."

Pansy stared at him, her eyes wide and wondering. "You—you really mean that? You're not—you're not mad at me?"

"No, dear, neither of us is angry with you," Laurette smilingly interposed. "All's well that ends well. But there's just one thing. If you do take that job in my husband's store, my advice to you is to look for a man of your own age who isn't married and who has honorable intentions toward you."

"Oh, Mrs. Douglas, I swear I wouldn't ever think of— you know what I mean—I'm ever so grateful—I'll work hard—you'll see—" Pansy babbled.

"I'm sure you will, Miss Lowell. When you feel up to it, why don't you go over to the store and talk to Mr. Philip Richter? He's my employment manager, and he'll give you every consideration." He turned back to his smiling wife and, linking his arm with hers, said, "And now, Mrs. Douglas, I'm going to buy you the finest dinner in Galveston."

"Yes, I rather think I deserve it, darling."

Once outside the house, Charles Douglas exhaled a gasp of relief and shook his head. "Well, Laurette darling, that just about convinces me that honesty really is the best policy after all. I'm certainly glad I told you about my little encounter with Miss Lowell yesterday afternoon. Otherwise, I might easily have found myself in a very embarrassing situation."

"That's true, my dear. But I know you well enough by now to be sure that even if I hadn't gone along, you'd have turned the tables on those two disgusting men. I trust you, and I'm not at all jealous. And I think I'll go back to Chicago in a few days. I've enjoyed being here with you, and

303

visiting Arabella and James, but I really do miss Howard and the twins, and I want to see how they're getting along with their lessons. You told me you wanted to go to Houston and arrange to buy some land for your store there."

"Yes, I was planning to do that this week."

"I'm very proud of you, my darling. One of these days you're going to have a big chain of stores all over the country. And we'll be telling our grandchildren about them and hoping they'll grow up to run them when the time comes, just as cleverly as you're doing now."

"I love you very much, Laurette." Then Charles laughed and kissed her. "I think I knew when I first met you that a girl with red hair like yours would never give me a dull moment."

"Just you remember that when I'm away and not around to defend you against scheming females, darling." Laurette smiled tenderly at him, linked her arm with his, and, walking close together as lovers do, they went down the street to the restaurant.

CHAPTER TWENTY-SIX

Laurette Douglas boarded the packet at the Galveston dock bound for New Orleans. From there she would take the riverboat to St. Louis, to connect by rail to Chicago. Her husband deferred his trip to Houston to see her off with a tender farewell and urged her, during her brief stay in the Queen City, to obtain presents for the three boys and little Fleur, as well as a gift for the children's devoted nurse.

On the previous night, Melinda and Lawrence Davis had come to dinner at the Hunter house. They were happily reconciled and outwardly as much in love with each other as they had been before Lawrence's brief infatuation with the attractive milliner. Hence it was in a spurt of blissful domesticity that Laurette took leave of Charles, who promised to return to Chicago within a month after he had successfully negotiated for a feasible site for his Houston store and conferred with Max Steinfeldt over hiring a reliable crew to build it.

On Thursday, since the Houston yellow-fever quarantine was in effect on the railroad connecting the two towns, he saddled a horse and rode to Houston. Since it was a fifty-mile journey, he spread it over two days, camping out at night near the bayou and reviving the pleasant memories of the journey he had taken last year from Windhaven Range to Houston, via Corpus Christi, in the company of Eddie Gentry, Simata, and Lucas. The four of them had had to beat off an attack by six outlaws who had robbed a bank in Austin and then ravished and killed the beautiful squaw of a Kiowa Apache chief. In that fracas, Charles had taken a bullet through his arm, but he had acquitted himself heroically.

As he camped out this Thursday evening, listening to the

croaking of the frogs and the twittering of the night birds, eating a simple meal and drinking water from his canteen, Charles reflected on the curious destiny that had linked him spiritually to Luke Bouchard, who in many ways represented the undeviatingly high moral credo of old Lucien, his grandfather and the founder of the Bouchard dynasty. He recalled that Luke, after the death of his first wife, Lucy, had taken the long ride from Windhaven Range to Corpus Christi, on his way back to New Orleans and—as fate would have it—a happy marriage to Laure Prindeville Brunton and a return to Windhaven Plantation. He thought, too, of Laurette's mother, Maybelle, once married to the dissolute Mark Bouchard and now serenely happy as the wife of Henry Belcher and foster mother to his children, Timmy and Connie, who by now had grown to marriageable age.

Alone with his thoughts in the stillness of the night, Charles reflected not only on the realization of all his ambitious dreams, but also on the future of the children Laurette had given him. Endowed with the good blood of the Bouchards, brought up by so dedicated a mother and so steadfast a companion, they would come to real maturity toward the turn of the century. What might they not achieve in their own right! Why, one of the twins or even Howard might one day be president of these thriving United States in the century ahead!

On the same day that Charles Douglas had begun his ride to Houston, Henry McNamara strode into his store and scowlingly confronted his young clerk, Alexander Gorth. He had already liquidated his savings at the local bank into a negotiable draft and packed one valise, and he was bound for San Francisco. Clarence Portman had decided to take down his shingle and look elsewhere for a place in which to practice law. He had chosen Lawrence, Kansas. There would be settlers throughout Kansas, he believed, and he thought also that one day Indian Territory might be open to statehood, once those murderous savages cooped up in reservations were driven away for good. There would be plenty of opportunity for speculation in land and the verification of titles to it, and with a fresh start, a man could turn a pretty penny in a location like that.

"G-good morning, Mr. McNamara," Alexander Gorth nervously stammered.

"It's far from that, Gorth," his employer snapped. "Now listen here. I'm leaving town for good. This store is a liability, and I've no further interest in it, where I'm going."

"You—you mean I'm f-fired, Mr. McNamara?" Alexander quavered.

"You might say that." Henry McNamara uttered a sardonic laugh. "But I'm going to make you a proposition. Personally, I don't think you've got the brains or the guts to handle it, but because I'm in a hurry and want to clear out and not worry about this place, I'll tell you what I've got in mind. How'd you like to buy this store and own it yourself?"

"Why—why—Mr. McNamara, yes—but I don't have any money—I couldn't possibly pay you what it's worth—" Alexander could not believe his ears and stared wide-eyed at his scowling employer.

"I'll sell it to you for two thousand dollars. And I'll tell you what. I owe you two weeks' wages, and we'll consider that a down payment to bind the contract. I'm going to draw up a promissory note, and you'll pay the difference off when you can and as you can, understand me? You can send a draft to me every now and again care of General Delivery in San Francisco." He laughed again and shrugged. "I expect you'll have to close your doors a week or two after I've left, because you're such a lily-livered pup; you're certain to drive away customers by yourself, if your pimples don't."

Alexander turned crimson with humiliation at the scurrilous allusion to the problem that plagued him, but the sudden prospect of being his own master unexpectedly stiffened him. Drawing himself up, he indignantly retorted, "At least I'm more polite to customers than you are, Mr. McNamara, and I've wanted to say that for a long time. I'll take you up on your offer. And I'll pay you regularly, as I can. Maybe I'll just surprise you. One thing's for sure: I won't overcharge, and I won't handle the shoddy goods you've forced me to sell to decent people."

"Well now, the worm turns, doesn't it?" McNamara guffawed. "All right, then, Gorth, I'll just call your bluff. And I'll make you another proposition, a sporting one. If you're in business six months from now, you can stop sending me

307

any more money—how's that, now? Because personally, as I just said, my guess is you're going to have to close down in a couple of weeks, once you're on your own."

"Draw up that paper, Mr. McNamara, and I'll sign it. And I'll take your bet."

"Done!" McNamara burst into hilarious laughter as he drew a sheet of paper from his frock coat pocket, took out a pencil, and began to scribble on it. "I haven't time to make it nice and fancy and legal, Gorth," he explained as he wrote. "My attorney has decided to seek his fortune elsewhere. But this is just between the two of us, and I'm trusting you the way you're trusting me. Here, sign it. You'll notice that I've written down the purchase price as two thousand dollars less your down payment of twenty dollars, which represents the two weeks' wages I'll owe you as of tomorrow. Agreed?"

Alexander nodded, seized the pencil, and wrote down his name with a flourish, then straightened. "And now, Mr. McNamara," he said coldly, "I'd be obliged if you'd leave my store."

Henry McNamara stared at him blankly for a moment, then burst into laughter again and slapped his thigh. "It's almost worth giving this store away to hear you talk to me like that, seeing as how you've been afraid of your own shadow ever since you came here puling and whining, looking for a job. Well, you won't see me again. And I still don't guess I'll be hearing from you much."

Before he reached the front door, Alexander called after him, "As long as the mail runs from here to San Francisco, Mr. McNamara, you'll be hearing from me all right. Good day to you."

The store was empty. Alexander gripped the counter with both hands till his knuckles were white, and took a deep breath. His eyes were shining. He suddenly thought of Katie McGrew. But then the immediacy of his new situation diverted him. He turned to look at the shelves and the counters. He grimaced with distaste; it was high time the store was cleaned from top to bottom. There wasn't any other clerk to help, so he'd just have to do it himself.

He took off his coat, rolled up his sleeves, took a broom, and began to sweep vigorously. After he had done that, he filled a pail with water from the little sluice well in the back of the store, and got down on his hands and knees to scrub the dingy floor. He was interrupted several times by customers, to whom he explained that he was the new owner and who were thunderstruck to hear that he was planning a sale in which all prices would be cut in half to clear out the merchandise. As a preview of the sale, he immediately deducted ten percent from the cost of all items, and the customers went away marveling at the bargains they had been able to find. By the end of the day, Alexander counted sixty-nine dollars and forty cents in the till.

He cleaned himself as best he could from a fresh pail of water, put his coat back on, and combed his straggly dark-brown hair, reflecting that it was high time he had it cut. He had completely forgotten about his acne. If he hurried, he told himself, he could just catch Katie McGrew leaving the Gottlieb Bakery.

Henry McNamara had given him the keys to the store once he had signed that promissory note. He took a deep breath again as he locked the door and stepped back to survey the establishment in which he had slaved and felt thoroughly miserable. Now it seemed magically to have changed. It would never be anything like the Douglas Department Store, he knew, but it could very well be an honest, decent shop where people could buy what they needed at not too high a price—just enough to give him a decent livelihood.

He turned and began to run down the street, and he was just in time. Katie McGrew, in her drab little bonnet and dull blue cotton dress, was coming out of the bakery with the other women who worked with her. They caught sight of him and whispered and giggled to the pretty Irish girl. Alexander swallowed hard and could feel his Adam's apple grow to intolerable size. He was perspiring, too, and suddenly he was conscious of his acne.

"I'm afraid we're closed," Katie turned to say to him in a sweet voice.

"I know. I—I didn't come here to buy any bread."

"No?" She waited, her face expectant, while her companions, having gone a little way down the street, turned back to watch, giggling and whispering to one another.

He took his courage in both hands. He had nothing to lose now, and besides, he wasn't just a humble, browbeaten clerk; he was the owner of a store. "No, I came to see you, Miss."

"My name is Katie—Katie McGrew," she volunteered.

"And mine's Alexander Gorth. I was wondering—I mean—I used to work at McNamara's store—"

"I know where it is. Yes?"

"Well, I—I'm running it now."

"Oh, I see. You mean your boss went away and left you in charge?"

"Not exactly, no. I mean, the fact is, I—I bought it from him today. I own it now." It came out in a rush, and yet it had been easier to say than he had thought it would.

Her eyes seemed to widen, then to consider him with more than impersonal interest. "Oh?" Her voice was soft and friendly now.

"Yes. Miss McGrew, I—I hope you won't think I'm too presumptuous, but I would like—I want to—if you're free for supper, I'd like very much to take you to a restaurant."

Katie McGrew blushed. She looked at Alexander Gorth, and she did not see his pimples. She saw instead a resolute but very shy young man who was just as lonely as she was. Then she smiled, and it was the most radiant smile Alexander had ever seen in all his life. "Wait just a minute, Mr. Gorth," she said gently. Then she walked quickly down to where her companions were waiting and said something to them. Alexander heard their collective gasp, then saw them nod, turn, and walk away. His eyes widened and his heart began to pound as Katie came toward him.

"I'd like that very much, Mr. Gorth. Thank you for asking me," she said.

CHAPTER TWENTY-SEVEN

Charles Douglas rode into Houston about two-thirty the next afternoon, stabled his horse, took a room at a nearby hotel, and after freshening up and having a quick meal, went to the city hall to ask for Mayor Scanlan, whom he had met the year before, after Calvin Jemmers and Arnold Shottlander had tried to swindle him. He was told that the mayor would be back late in the afternoon, so he made an appointment and then went across the street to the Houston National Bank.

Wiry old Dennis Claverton, president of that thriving institution, remembered him and came out of his office to welcome him to Houston.

"Thanks, Mr. Claverton. You remember that last year, after I very nearly got fleeced by Jemmers and Shottlander, I asked you to act as my agent in finding a decent piece of property on which I hoped to build a department store that would be as successful here as mine is in Galveston?"

"I remember that very well. And don't think that I've been idle all this while, Mr. Douglas." Dennis Claverton opened a drawer in his desk, drew out a sheaf of neatly arranged papers, and placed them before Charles. "There are several possible sites, Mr. Douglas, you might choose from. Of course, as I recall, you weren't certain last year exactly when you planned to begin construction here. Wasn't it a matter of the railroad?"

"It still is, in a way, Mr. Claverton. I've found out about the quarantine you put on the Galveston line in the summer."

"Yes, I'm sorry to say there's a great danger, and I share the majority view of the citizens here that even if we lose

311

trade as a result, it's far better than to let that deadly yellow fever into our midst."

"I've been doing some thinking about that on my way here. It wouldn't be so difficult as it first looks. Most of my goods come into Galveston from New Orleans and St. Louis in the early spring and early fall, with a third, smaller shipment toward winter. Provided I could find a suitable warehouse or some other storage facility here in Houston, I could arrange to get my goods here before or after the quarantine season—though I'm afraid the cost of warehousing will cut into my profits a good deal. But first of all, I have to deal with the other major problem—the condition of the railroad between here and Houston. From what my partner, James Hunter, tells me, that line is being improved. It should already be a good deal better than it was last year. Do you know anything about that?"

"Yes, indeed," Mr. Claverton replied. "The line is getting better. Competition is the answer: more lines are being built, so the ones that already exist have to improve their service. Why, for years there has been only one railroad bridge across the bay, between Galveston and the mainland. Now the Gulf, Colorado, and Santa Fe is probably going to build its own bridge, and that will in turn open the way for more lines to come into Galveston. I think you can count on reasonably good service in the future."

"I'm glad to hear that, Mr. Claverton. It looks as if I'll be able to set my plans in motion, so what I'd like to do is transfer some of the capital in my Galveston bank to your bank here. And you'll want to draw up a legal agreement whereby I formally appoint you as my agent—or whatever title you think would be in order—to act for me in acquiring suitable land. I'd like to think about opening the new store by 1874. I've got a fine contractor who built my store in Galveston; I could bring him here, and I'm sure he'd be able to find a crew of good, dependable workers."

"I'm sure he could," Dennis Claverton smilingly agreed. "And politically, it would be a very good thing for you to use Houston labor rather than men from Galveston. It would set well with the town and help your business later on."

"Yes, I've thought of that. Then you'll act for me?"

"I'd be honored. You see, Mr. Douglas, we've already had word of how successful your store in Galveston has been, and we people of Houston are a mite envious. Don't forget, we took the name of our town from good old Sam Houston, who led the fight for Texas independence, and we don't feel like taking second place to Galveston or any other Texas town. For that matter, not even to your own fine city of Chicago."

"Mr. Claverton, I'm going to like doing business with you. Here's my card with my permanent new address in Chicago. I'll rely on you, knowing the area as well as you do, to pick a logical site where I can get traffic and yet not obstruct any residential plans the town has for the future. Meanwhile, when I go back to Galveston, I'll have my bank send you a draft for one thousand dollars as a starter."

"I think I could get you a very nice piece of property for that."

"Thanks, Mr. Claverton. I'll keep in touch with you. I'm going to see Mayor Scanlan later this afternoon and tell him about my plans. May I tell him that you're going to represent me?"

"By all means, Mr. Douglas." Dennis Claverton shook hands with the energetic Chicagoan.

Soon after the death of Captain George Munson and most of his troops in the Cañon de Uvalde, the War Department in Washington sent a grizzled old colonel, George Pastor, and a contingent of troops to restore Fort Inge, in Uvalde County, to its previous strength. Colonel Pastor was two years away from retirement, a mild-mannered man without imagination, who unquestioningly carried out orders and whose only irritating foible, so far as his soldiers were concerned, was his insistence on excessive military maneuvers. When he retired in November of 1872, he was replaced by Major Dana Creston.

Dana Creston was forty-eight, tall, athletic of build, with trim gray beard and sideburns. As a lieutenant in an Illinois regiment, he had been decorated for exceptional valor during the first battles of the Civil War, promoted to a captaincy on the battlefield six months before Appomattox, and appeared to have a bright military future ahead of him.

However, his failing, so far as the War Department was concerned, was humanitarianism, which was not confined to the men serving under him. For several years prior to his posting to Fort Inge, he had inveighed against the ruthless treatment of Indian tribes by military forces, and argued that a policy of peaceful treaty and decent treatment would accomplish far more than bloody forays by way of punitive reprisals. He had told one brigadier general, "Sir, it's only natural that the Indians should fight to defend the land they have lived on when white settlers and soldiers suddenly pour onto it and start acting as if the Indians were intruders. You can't blame them for fighting back when a lot of peaceful Indians who just want to trade or to get acquainted with their new neighbors are shot down."

The brigadier general had delivered a scathing lecture to this brash officer, and conferred with some of his associates who were responsible for the disposition of officers and troops throughout the country. The result was that Dana Creston found himself given the command at Fort Inge with the commission of major, and, through the oblique wording of a communiqué from an obscure colonel whose name he did not recognize, was given to understand that this would be his last assignment in the service. There would be no further chance of promotion. And there was a particular irony in Creston's assignment: the frontier of Texas at this particular moment was entirely without defense, and Indians seemed to be everywhere; Creston would be under orders to wage war on them—against the dictates of his conscience. Formerly it had been the army's policy to let the Indians roam at will and simply protect the settlements against them, but now the army commanders in Washington were convinced that aggressive military campaigns should be conducted to drive the Plains tribes entirely out of Texas into Indian Territory. With more and more settlers flocking into Texas every month, perhaps such a course was inevitable, but it wrought terrible consequences on a man of Dana Creston's convictions. He would be sorely tried by the orders to take the field against those whom he regarded innocent of wrongdoing.

Fort Inge had been rebuilt since the days of the vaingloriously ambitious Captain Munson. About half the troops under Major Creston's command had served in the Civil War, returned to their homes, married, and had families. They brought their wives with them to the fort. The rest of the men were single; they were recruits and volunteers who had seen at most a year of service, and seasoned veterans, bachelors in their early thirties, who had decided that the

314

security of a military career was preferable to civilian life and domestic responsibilities.

There were barracks for the soldiers, separate quarters for the married men and their wives, and houses for the married officers—the largest of which was reserved for Major Creston and his thirty-year-old wife, Stella.

Stella Anderson had been a slim, honey-haired girl given to daydreaming and writing poetry. She had grown up in Galena, Illinois. She fell in love with Dana and married him when she was eighteen. Her parents, farmers, had been secretly glad to see her married, for in their opinion she shirked her chores and had fancy ideas of rising above her station in life. In Dana Creston she thought she had found a man of innate decency and honor, sensitive enough to comprehend her vague yearnings for a life that would not be encumbered with the prosaic duties of a farm or a store.

Three months after they had been married, Dana—who had been a schoolteacher in Galena—enlisted in the Union army. Stella was incredulous when he announced his decision to her. He was already thirty-six, she had argued; surely there were plenty of young men who could fight the South. But he told her that it was his duty, and that what had most impelled him toward this drastic step was his hatred of human slavery; his was a kind of holy war against the tyrannical plantation owners who valued human life so little that they bought and sold human beings like cattle.

Because of his education and his swift adaptation to army life, Creston was quickly commissioned as a lieutenant. He managed to go through the war without a scratch, and his medals for bravery made him something of a hero in Galena whenever he returned on furlough. To be sure, he had become somewhat hardened and cynical by the end of the war, like so many sensitive men on both sides who felt compelled to fight. General Grant's unwavering belief in the military necessity of slaughtering the enemy's main armies, with the resulting loss of life on both sides, agonized him. And when the war was over and he returned to Stella, it was to find that already an invisible rift had grown between them.

First of all, Stella had discovered that she could not bear him a child. She felt herself flawed as a woman, and subconsciously resented her husband as if he were somehow

315

responsible for her barrenness. Furthermore, she found she was unable to reconcile his gentleness and his discussion of literature and poetry with the stern, incisive officer who returned to her, already feted as a hero in his home town.

Stella Creston had hoped that at the end of the war he would resign from the army and resume his teaching, so she was particularly disappointed to discover that he had decided to continue his career as an officer. His argument was that in the peace to follow—a peace he knew would be far more aggressive and punitive than could have been foreseen at the outset of the war—it would be essential that there be officers in command who would practice the restraint and tolerance necessary to heal the wounds of the terrible Civil War.

There followed six years of service at forts in Kansas, Wyoming, and Missouri, each seemingly more desolate and hopeless than the last, until Creston's assignment to Fort Inge last year. During these years, Stella grew increasingly more bitter, and by the time of her husband's assignment to Fort Inge she openly resented him.

For Stella, Fort Inge was bleaker than any of the earlier posts, and when her husband candidly revealed to her the import of the communiqué informing him that he would enjoy no further advancements in his career, her mood became one of complete despondency. Yet the social requirements of the post obliged her to play the role of hostess to the junior officers and to those competent noncommissioned men whom her husband had singled out as worthy of promotion. The effort required to carry out her duties as commanding officer's wife left her drained of all emotion, and she was utterly unable to respond to Creston as a man. When, a few weeks after their arrival at the fort, he hesitantly tried to make love to her, she turned from him wordlessly in a fit of bitter weeping, which he understood to be a rejection of his love. With a murmured, "Forgive me, Stella," he turned away from her and pondered through a sleepless night. He could foresee that the ensuing years would deepen the bitterness between them, just as he could see with pitiless clarity that no matter how well he performed his duties, no matter what devotion he displayed in carrying out distasteful military orders, he was, for all purposes, abandoned by the War Department.

Yet outwardly, with enormous self-discipline, Creston did not show his pain. For her part, Stella tried to ignore

316

her sufferings and to be gracious to the officers who were invited to dine with the fort commander and his wife. She was consoled at least in part when one of the sergeants, Maxwell Kenton, a bluff, personable man who had been a soldier for seven years and had joined the army when his wife and only child had died in childbirth, was thoughtful enough to plant a little garden in the yard outside Major Creston's house. Stella was deeply grateful to him for this thoughtful gesture.

There were periods when she felt an enormous guilt in denying herself to her husband, the more so because he had been a model of fidelity and devotion ever since he had courted her back in Galena. She knew herself to be less than adequate as a woman and a wife; and yet, ironically, she was in some ways even more attractive now than she had been as the emotional young girl whom Creston had married. Through all of her husband's assignments, there had been soldiers as well as officers who had eyed her appraisingly, and she had comprehended their desire even while remaining totally aloof from it.

Three weeks after she had come to live at Fort Inge, her husband invited Captain Anthony Brent to dinner. He had arrived two days before, having been transferred from a desk job in Washington. Brent was thirty-three. He had been seriously wounded at Gettysburg and decorated for his bravery in that battle. At the end of the war, his knowledge of tactics had brought him an assignment to an important post in Washington, where he made himself indispensable to his superior officers. But he had been determined to transfer into active service away from Washington because he had become embroiled in an affair with a congressman's wife and the affair had threatened to explode into a major scandal. So anxious had he been to leave Washington that he had accepted the first available assignment—to Fort Inge—even though that post was not one he considered worthy of his attainments as an officer.

He was tall, towheaded, inordinately good-looking and well aware of it. He wore a Vandyke beard and neatly trimmed moustache, and his large, innocent-looking light-blue eyes invariably entranced any attractive woman to whom he paid gallant attention.

At that first dinner for Captain Brent, Stella was instantly aware of his animal magnetism and his conceit; yet his flattering remarks about her—which he addressed to

Major Creston—could in no way be taken as offensive, and indeed, they caused Stella's husband to glance at her with a sheepish pride. But in the days and weeks that followed, Brent was able to discern that his commanding officer and the latter's wife were at odds with each other. Since she was intensely desirable to him—actually, she vaguely resembled the congressman's wife whose lover he had been over a year—it was inevitable that he should come to regard her as the woman who could assuage his carnal needs, and he felt he could satisfy her needs, which he felt certain her husband denied her.

CHAPTER TWENTY-EIGHT

By the end of July, Lucien Edmond Bouchard and his partners, Joe Duvray and Ramón Hernandez, had sent off three shipments of cattle to Fort Duncan and Fort Inge. The last two shipments had been of a hundred head each. When Simata and Eddie Gentry returned from the last drive to inform Lucien Edmond that the new commander at Fort Inge was anxious to meet the head of Windhaven Range and work out a regular arrangement for the purchase of cattle, Lucien Edmond readily agreed.

Already there were rumors from the East that Congress was trying to cope with speculative investments and rising prices for food products and clothing. On the first Thursday in August, Lucien Edmond conferred with Ramón, Joe Duvray, Simata, Eddie Gentry, and Lucas and Nacio Lorcas, who were being brought into the managerial discussions for the first time. Together the seven men planned a program of balanced sales and crossbreeding for the remainder of the year.

"I'm pleased with what we've already accomplished in selling to the army forts," Lucien Edmond declared energetically. "I think we were very wise in not trying to drive to the Kansas market. Prices there have already dropped from ten dollars a head to as low as six dollars. And we've avoided a three-months' expenditure of time, to say nothing of the potential losses to rustlers and bushwhackers. It's true that our dollar profit will probably look small compared with last year's, but to offset this we've cut our costs to the very bone. And after the news I've heard from the East, I'd just as soon continue this way for the rest of the year, until we can see which way the economy's going to go."

"I have no arguments, Lucien Edmond," Ramón concurred. He looked around at the others and all of them nodded. "I guess it's unanimous. We work together, we build for the future, we take what profits we can make close at hand, and we wait to see what will happen by the end of the year."

"Fine," Lucien Edmond said. "And this time I'll ride with you to Fort Inge. We'll take a hundred and fifty head there, and another hundred on to Fort Duncan." Lucien Edmond chuckled. "We'll let Simata go to Fort Duncan, for reasons you already know. We'll only need about five vaqueros for the trip to Fort Inge. The others can do useful work here—remodeling, painting, checking our boundary markers. The way I see it, 1873 is a year of survival for Windhaven Range, a time to avoid needless risk. I've never been greedy, and what we may bypass in dollar profits this year we'll realize in the years ahead, when things have straightened out."

"There can't be any objections to that sort of reasoning, Lucien Edmond," his Mexican brother-in-law reassured him.

"I agree," Joe Duvray concurred. "I think we're sitting pretty. We have plenty of cattle for crossbreeding; we don't have any neighbors who want to grab our land, as we had in the past; and we're stronger because of your policy of uniting all our properties to build one huge ranch. And the day isn't far off when we'll have railroads down here to transport our cattle to a market we can control, a market that will seek us out and pay decent prices. Until then, I for one am quite willing to mark time and build for the future."

"Then it's settled. We'll leave next Monday, and we'll all look forward to a pleasant social get-together at Fort Inge. Simata will have a somewhat more important stake in his ride to Fort Duncan. He's still a bachelor, and I believe he has some more serious purpose in mind."

Amid general laughter, Lucien Edmond rose and called a halt to the conference.

By the middle of the following week, Lucien Edmond, Joe Duvray, Eddie Gentry, Nacio Lorcas, Simata, and eight vaqueros were driving two hundred and fifty head of cattle toward Fort Inge. Part way along the trail, Simata and three of the vaqueros, including the genial young Mexican Gregorio Salamancár, veered from the group, heading toward Fort Duncan with a hundred head of cattle. Lucien Edmond raised his hand to Simata as the Kiowa scout led his men and cattle toward Fort Duncan and his beloved Najalda. In return, Simata brandished his fist and shook it with exultance. A cloud of dust hovered over the departing herd as the ranch owner rode on toward Fort Inge.

As Lucien Edmond directed the movement of the cattle through the gates of Fort Inge and into the corral, Major Dana Creston came out of his house in full-dress uniform to pay his respects to the blond trail boss of Windhaven Range.

"I'm happy to meet you, Mr. Bouchard. My cook, Corporal Denburg, who used to be a butcher back in Cairo before he joined the army, tells me this is the finest beef he's seen in years."

"Thanks, Major Creston. I've looked forward to meeting you. We're quite happy with the arrangement we've worked out, and we'd like to continue this for as long as you need meat," Lucien Edmond declared, smiling.

"Nobody else has approached me, Mr. Bouchard, so you've got a head start on all your competition. And I've been completely satisfied with my dealings with your outfit so far. By the way, can you and your men stay to dinner this evening? We're having a dance, as it happens. Even out here in this vast, lonely country, I like to think that we can enjoy a pleasant social life, and keep up a close relationship with all the men and their families."

"That's very generous of you, Major Creston. I'm in no hurry at all, and we hadn't really planned on going back for a couple days, in any case. And at some point I'd like to sit down with you and talk privately about a contract for regular deliveries of beef in the future."

"That's just the idea I had in mind. I think I know enough about cattle myself—even though I was a schoolteacher back in Galena—to say that you're going to get all the business Fort Inge can provide so long as I'm commander here. My quartermaster feels the same way."

"That's good to hear, Major Creston. I've brought along one of my partners in Windhaven Range, Joe Duvray, and his assistant foreman, Nacio Lorcas, as well as Eddie Gentry, here—one of the best cowhands I ever had the pleasure of hiring."

"I'm pleased to meet you gentlemen, and I look forward

321

to getting to know you better at supper tonight. One of the settlers yesterday brought in a pair of lambs, and my chief cook was in seventh heaven. I hope you've no objection to good roast lamb, even though you're cattlemen?"

"None whatsoever. It'll be a welcome change from beef." Lucien Edmond grinned as they shook hands.

Stella Creston watched from her curtained window as the plump, glossy yearlings were being herded into the wide corral. She took particular notice of the tall, blond, handsome leader of the cowboys, and then she let the curtains fall together and turned away from the window with a sigh. Her husband had told her of the arrangement he had made with a prosperous Texas rancher to provide beef for the fort, but the news had meant nothing to her. Yet now, seeing Lucien Edmond Bouchard riding in, she experienced a curious yearning to meet him and to converse with him. She sensed that he might provide a link to the outside world, of which she had heard so little over the past years, during her husband's shifting army assignments. The man she saw riding the cattle in seemed pleasant and kind, although she knew nothing about him except that he represented a way of life beyond the narrow confines of the desolate army post.

Major Creston had gone to the barracks to chat with Sergeant Maxwell Kenton and to give orders for a dinner in the officers' mess, which would test the camp cook's capabilities to the very utmost. "I'd also like the fiddlers to be in especially fine form for the dancing tonight," he had added. "I think our visitors will enjoy that, and certainly it will help morale."

"I agree with you, Major," the sergeant energetically nodded. "There's been some grumbling lately, especially from the new recruits, about how far away we are from anything that matters. The man you replaced, if I may be so bold as to tell you this in confidence, Major Creston, had us sweating like blazes on drills and full-dress marches, till we downright hated his guts. Your pardon, sir."

"No offense taken, Sergeant Kenton. As you know, I don't see any need for West Point-type maneuvers in a place like this. We're saddled with one another here, and we've got to get along, because it's just possible that one of these days I will get orders from the War Department to go

322

out and attack the hostiles. And I'm praying you and I won't have to do that."

"I know exactly what you're getting at, Major. If you won't hold it against me, I'd like to say right now, sir, that I don't hold with mowing down Injuns who haven't done us any harm just because we're told they could wipe us out in our beds."

"You're a good man, Sergeant Kenton. I won't officially remember what you just told me, just as you won't remember how I feel about the whole Indian business. Anyway, I'm counting on you to make tonight something special."

"I'll do my best, Major Creston, you can rely on me."

"I know I can. Thank you, Sergeant Kenton."

About an hour before the dinner, at which the men from Windhaven Range were to be honored guests, Lucien Edmond freshened up in the enlisted men's barracks, putting on the brand-new fancy shirt Maxine had ordered for him from Charles Douglas's department store in Galveston. Then he walked out toward the stable to inspect the horses. He paused just outside the stable door, watching as the blazing August sun dwindled in the west, and he noticed that there was an almost deathly silence about the fort, as if this place were utterly without relationship to the rest of the country.

At this moment Stella Creston peered out her window again. She saw Lucien Edmond standing alone by the stable, and as she watched him, she was beset once again by a feeling of desolation. The sight of so distinguished-looking a man from the outside world only made her feel all the more choked and frustrated by her own tiny sphere. She felt more useless than ever. She did not know how long she could go on being loyal to Dana. She admired—she had always admired—his unrelenting idealism. Only now it was so futile, and out here where there were only barren stretches of plain to contemplate, it seemed the more out of place. He was being punished, and she was doomed to share his punishment against her will.

She could not explain what impulse made her turn to the mirror on the commode, critically examine herself, dip a cloth into a pan of water no longer cool, and dab at her face to make her seem more youthful. All she knew was the oppressive heat and the dreariness of the long day, and

323

even the prospect of a gala supper and music and dancing left her emptied and alien. She felt she could no longer enter her husband's world: he had defined it narrowly, and in so doing, he had put her outside the boundaries. She had never told him that Captain Brent had several times eyed her with such a cynical, appraising look that he had made her feel contaminated and cheapened; there was no longer any intimate communication between them, and she had already begun to conclude that it no longer mattered to him. Oh yes, he would be faithful, he would be unswervingly scrupulous in observing all the niceties of marriage— but without the need for affection, without beseeching her help to get him through this purgatory to which she knew he had been sentenced precisely because of his ethics and high-mindedness.

Her husband, she knew, was conferring with the fort cook, Corporal Carl Denburg. How curious it was, she thought to herself, that so many of the enlisted men and noncommissioned officers at Fort Inge came from so far off and from such diverse backgrounds. Each man had his own story. She remembered Dana's telling her that Denburg had once been a waiter at Delmonico's in New York, and had acquired enough money to buy a little restaurant on the East Side. He had devoted all his energy to making it a success, but because Denburg was a French Jew, one night some East Side toughs had thrown bricks through the glass windows of the restaurant and then stormed in and terrorized the patrons. The next day Denburg had sold his restaurant and joined the army. He was a superb cook: the miracles he could achieve with a few wild vegetables and fruits, eggs, flour, and even buffalo meat or *jabalí* showed creative talents which, Stella was convinced, were wasted out here in this barren land.

While still engaged in her fretful musings, Stella had left her room and come out onto the parade ground. Then, without knowing quite why, she wandered in the direction of the stable. Lucien Edmond, meanwhile, was inside the stable, moving along the stalls. He smiled as some of the horses softly nickered to him, and as he approached one of the middle stalls, a chestnut mare thrust her muzzle at his shoulder and playfully tried to nip him. With a friendly chuckle as he quickly moved to one side, he stroked the mare's nose and soothingly praised her spirit.

At the very end of the row of stalls, Captain Anthony

Brent, in fatigue trousers and shirt, was squatting down examining the fetlock of his black gelding. He was about to rise and greet Lucien Edmond when suddenly he heard footsteps entering the stable. To his quick ears they were not those of a soldier but rather the softer tread of a woman. A curious smile curved his lips. He continued to hunch down, stroking his gelding's leg and whispering, "Shh, Robey, we've got company."

"I see you've introduced yourself to my mare, Mr. Bouchard," Stella Creston said with a soft laugh.

Lucien Edmond turned, his eyes widening with surprise for a moment, and then smilingly rejoined, "She has a good deal of spirit, ma'am. But—I'm afraid, ma'am, you have the advantage of me: are you by any chance Mrs. Creston, the major's wife?"

"Yes, I am. We haven't been formally introduced, though I'm looking forward to our conversation over dinner this evening, Mr. Bouchard. But—well, I saw you riding in at the head of those cattle you brought to the fort, and I—I admired your horse," she lamely finished. A warm flush suffused her cheeks and she lowered her eyes. "We don't get too many visitors, you see."

"I understand," he murmured sympathetically. "Do you go riding a good deal?"

"Several times a week, yes. But lately the weather's been so terribly hot and dry, and my husband doesn't want me to go alone. Not that he's afraid of Indians, you understand—"

"I can reassure you a little on that score, Mrs. Creston," Lucien Edmond broke in. "To the best of my knowledge, there aren't any hostiles for a radius of fifty miles. There used to be buffalo, which the Indians hunted not far from here, but they've long since been slaughtered or driven off."

"Yes, Dana—I mean, my husband—told me. He—he has a great deal of sympathy for the Indians, you know." She uttered a bitter little laugh. "Sometimes I think he's too noble for his own good."

"On the contrary, Mrs. Creston, I admire him a good deal for a stand like that. It takes a lot of courage these days. The military powers-that-be in Washington don't appear to share your husband's opinion, unfortunately. As for myself, I've had only the friendliest of dealings with Indians, even the much-feared Comanches."

325

She looked at him directly, and the flush deepened on her soft, suntanned cheeks. "Thank you for saying that, Mr. Bouchard. You're a very understanding and sympathetic man. The fact is, I'm afraid that Dana—my husband—well, this is just about the last post he can count on because he stands up for the Indians the way he does. And it isn't pleasant to be stranded out here in what's practically a desert, with only a few settlers miles away."

"Yes, I can see how hard it must be for you, Mrs. Creston." Lucien Edmond's voice was tinged with warm sympathy.

A momentary silence fell upon them both, and then Stella Creston reached out her hand to the mare, which nuzzled her palm. "Good girl, Delia," she murmured. "Maybe, if the sun's not so hot tomorrow, we'll go riding, I promise."

"Where did you come from, Mrs. Creston, you and your husband?"

"We both grew up in Galena, Mr. Bouchard. I—well, I didn't think Dana would go off to the army when the war broke out. And I certainly didn't expect him to want to stay in it after it was over—but, as you can see, he did." She gave a hopeless little shrug and turned away, her face suddenly shadowed with dejection.

Seeing the change in her expression and hoping to lighten her mood, Lucien Edmond cheerfully remarked, "It was good farming country where you both came from, Mrs. Creston. Just the same, I've a feeling that before too much longer, there'll be more and more settlers flocking into Texas. A great many of them will be homesteaders, wanting to farm, not caring at all for grazing cattle. I don't think it'll be too long before you'll have neighbors, and that will mean more of a social life for you, I'm sure."

"You—you're very kind. I—I must apologize. I didn't mean to burden you—"

"But you didn't. May I walk you back to your house? And I'll look forward to dining with you tonight."

"There's to be music too, you know." She suddenly brightened, a little smile playing on her lips as she met his gaze. "My—my husband doesn't enjoy dancing—he did when we were first married, but he's so serious now about his duties that I'm afraid he doesn't look upon dancing as very important." And then, quickly contrite and as if to defend her husband, she added, "But it's thoughtful of him to have music and dancing so that the other men and their wives can enjoy it. It'll almost be like a social, you see."

"I'd be honored if you'd save a dance for me, Mrs. Creston. That's one of the social graces I've tried to keep up even on my ranch. We've a spinet too, and my wife, Maxine, plays wonderfully. Music is a joy."

"Yes, I know." Again her voice was wistful. "My mother played the church organ, some Bach and Handel, but I don't think I've heard good music since Dana entered the service." She uttered a nostalgic sigh, raised her eyes to fix him with an intent look, then added, a tremulous smile on her lips, "Mr. Bouchard—your life sounds just wonderful. Even though in some ways you're as isolated as I am here on this army post, you're blessed by having a feeling for music and making it part of your life. That must compensate a lot for the long hours you have to spend on your range, I should think."

Lucien Edmond nodded. "It does indeed, Mrs. Creston. And it helped too, when I was a boy, to have a father who cared for books and music just as much as for supervising his plantation."

"Oh, yes, that was very important," she eagerly concurred. Then, almost hesitantly, "You and your wife have children, I suppose?"

"Yes indeed, Mrs. Creston." His smile broadened. "I've a twelve-year-old boy, Hugo, and four daughters—there's Carla, thirteen; Edwina, four; Diane, two; and our latest, Gloria, just eight months old."

Stella sighed again and shook her head. "How I envy you and your wife, Mr. Bouchard! A family like that shows what love can be between two people who care very much for each other." Then she uttered a nervous little laugh, and—by way of breaking the tension that had taken hold of her after this spontaneous and treacherous self-avowal—put a hand up to press back a wayward curl and said in a tone that strove to be airily casual, "You know, Mr. Bouchard, ever since I was a little girl, I've had what you might call a fixation for tall blond men on horseback. But they had to like the finer things, not just be strong, outdoor physical specimens. Now you see, I saw you riding in, just like the pictures I used to have in my mind when I was little. And now I learn you like music and books, and have a family to whom you're obviously devoted."

Lucien Edmond shifted nervously. Underlying Stella

Creston's pleasantly conversational tone, he could hear loneliness and frustration, and what was more, he could
sense that all was not entirely well between her husband
and herself. He felt himself to be an intruder on the private
world of her unhappiness, and it made him ill at ease.

"My gracious"—again she gave a nervous little laugh—
"you mustn't mind me, Mr. Bouchard. I do go on sometimes, but that's because I have so few visitors to meet out
here. Please forgive me—" She put out a hand and touched
his shoulder. As she did so, a vivid blush suffused her face,
and Lucien Edmond trembled despite himself; in that
touch, in the swift, almost pleading glance she had just
given him, there was a declaration of unmistakable yearning, almost an invitation—the attitude of a woman starved
for affection and lonely in the midst of many whose lives
were totally alien to her own.

"There's nothing to forgive, Mrs. Creston. It's been a
pleasure meeting you and chatting with you, and, as I said,
I'll look forward to dining with you tonight—as will all of
my men. Maybe I'd better go back to quarters and see that
they're ready—are you sure I can't walk you back to your
house?"

She bit her lips, shook her head, flashed him a quick,
mechanical smile. "No thank you, Mr. Bouchard. I want to
look after my mare a bit before I go back. But—well, I
hope this won't be your only visit to Fort Inge. I—I'd like
very much to talk about books and music with you when
there's more time."

"I'd like that too, Mrs. Creston." He chuckled softly.
"Assuming your husband likes the quality of beef I'm
bringing in and keeps on ordering, chances are I'll be visiting Fort Inge again in the not-too-distant future. Till tonight then." He gave her a gallant little half-bow and left
the stable.

Stella stood staring after him, a hand pressed to her
heaving bosom. Again she bit her lips and then quickly
blinked her eyes to clear the tears that stung and blurred
them. Aloud, to herself, she said, "Oh God, what a fortunate woman his wife is—and how happy he must be with
her! What I wouldn't give to have a family like that—a
man like that who could share more than just the routine
of living with me—"

She bowed her head, then put her hand to her mouth to

suppress the forlorn sob that surged to it. After a moment, taking a deep breath, she walked out of the stable.

As she disappeared, Captain Anthony Brent rose, and thoughtfully stroked his crisp, trim beard. His sensual mouth curved in a knowing smile. Then he turned back to his gelding and chuckled. "That was quite a conversation, wasn't it, boy? A most interesting one. I think the lovely wife of our commanding officer might also have been indiscreet then and there if that Bouchard fellow hadn't been such a confounded gentleman. But as for myself, I don't have his involvements—no wife and brats to cramp my style. And learning that our delicious Stella feels the way she does leads me to think that if I play my cards right, she can be led to come to my bed of her own delightful accord."

Then whistling tunelessly and softly, his smile mockingly sardonic, he went back to his quarters to dress for the gala dinner.

Unlike many fort commanders, Major Dana Creston believed in establishing close personal relations with his noncommissioned officers. So Sergeant Maxwell Kenton sat at his commanding officer's left, at one end of the mess table, while two corporals and three other sergeants sat to the commander's right. These five noncommissioned officers had, in Major Creston's opinion, shown exceptional merit in their assignments.

As befitted his status as second-in-command, Captain Brent, resplendent in full-dress uniform, sat at the opposite end of the long table, with Lucien Edmond Bouchard at his left and Joe Duvray and Eddie Gentry at his right. Nacio Lorcas sat next to Lucien Edmond. The captain conversed with Lucien Edmond and his three companions, but with no more than token interest; from time to time, as he cut the roast lamb or paused to sip an excellent claret which Major Creston had himself purchased out of his own pocket, he eyed Stella Creston, who sat at her husband's left beside Sergeant Kenton. She was particularly attractive in a high-necked, long-skirted blue cotton dress, her hair austerely put up in a heart-shaped chignon at the back of her head. Several times during the dinner she saw Brent eyeing her, and at once she turned to one of her neighbors to engage in conversation that would ease the nervous strain she suffered from Brent's insulting glances.

After dinner, the guests moved to the large hall adjacent to the refectory, where the musicians were already tuning up their instruments and a lanky private from Wisconsin was preparing to be the caller for the dancing which would follow.

Major Creston took Stella out to the center of the hall to begin the dancing, and held her stiffly, his face expressionless. Lucien Edmond Bouchard watched, standing against the wall with Joe Duvray, Eddie Gentry, and Nacio Lorcas. He watched Anthony Brent dance with the young second lieutenant's pretty, auburn-haired wife. He observed also that Captain Brent seemed far more interested in the major and his wife than in his own winsome and merrily talkative partner.

With the second dance, Captain Brent genially approached his commanding officer and requested permission to take his wife as partner, which was readily given. Stella flushed nervously, and passively let herself be led out onto the floor as the musicians began a familiar waltz. Captain Brent whispered something, and Stella's flush deepened as she lowered her eyes and seemed to ignore her partner's remark.

"That captain's a right handsome fellow, isn't he, and doesn't he know it!" Eddie whispered to Lucien Edmond.

"That's quite evident, Eddie. Unless I miss my guess, he's the kind who has a wandering eye. I shouldn't be surprised if he had quite a reputation for womanizing before he came to Fort Inge," Lucien Edmond replied.

Stella had two other partners—both junior officers—for the next two waltzes, but for the fourth dance, Brent returned. When that dance ended he stayed with her, as the private who was leading the musicians called out boisterously, "Now then, folks, choose your partners for the square dancing, and follow my calls as best you can." Nodding to the fiddlers, he gave the signal to begin a jaunty tune, as the couples formed their squares.

Captain Brent followed the calls with flawless precision, moving from female to female with polished grace. When he returned to Stella Creston, however, he seemed to hold her closer and to continue his whispering. Several times she glanced nervously at her husband, who was standing at the other end of the hall conversing with Sergeant Kenton.

During a pause between dances, she watched Captain Brent bow to her with mock gallantry to thank her for being his partner. Then she turned on her heel and walked to the other end of the hall. "Dana, I've a headache. Would you please excuse me and make apologies to our guests?"

"Of course, my dear. I'm sorry you're not feeling well."

"Maybe it's because it's been so hot today, and all these preparations—do forgive me."

"Of course, my dear."

"I—it seems cooler outside now, and I'll go for a little walk and then I'll go straight to bed. Good night."

"Good night, Stella."

"Good night, ma'am," Sergeant Kenton inclined his head toward her. She smiled wanly at him, nodded back, and then left the hall.

A few minutes later, after the next dance, Captain Brent excused himself from his partner, approached his commander, and casually remarked, "By your leave, sir, I'd like to go out to the stable and look over my mount. He's been having some trouble with a fetlock, and since we're going on maneuvers tomorrow afternoon, I thought I'd just make sure he's all right."

"Of course, Captain. Maybe you'd like to have Corporal Sadley go with you—you know, he's got a way with horses."

"I know that very well, sir. But this is nothing really serious. I think a little linament will do the trick."

"Just as you say, Captain. Good night, then."

"And to you, Major Creston." Captain Brent gave him a smart salute. Very casually, without haste, he left the hall after exchanging a few pleasantries with two of the lieutenants.

Stella Creston had walked out into the starry night, exhaling a deep breath and wearily closing her eyes for a moment. Happily, the night air seemed cooler, and it was a relief to emerge from the noise and the music and especially the irksome attentions of Captain Brent. She detested him, and yet there was a magnetism about him which almost fascinated her. Perhaps it was because she knew exactly what he was thinking, and the prospect was so at variance with the life of denial she had been leading with Dana that it had a singular kind of hold upon her. She shook her head, impatient with herself, and walked slowly toward the stable. At least with Delia, her mare, there was no misunderstanding, nothing except pleasurable communication with an animal who sensed her every mood. What a pity that relationships between people couldn't be sorted out as easily!

She entered the stable and went to the mare's stall. Delia nickered with delight and rubbed her muzzle against Stella's hand. "You're a beauty, darling. It's so easy to be with you and we get along so well," she said softly.

"A very touching picture!" She heard the suave, baritone voice of Captain Brent behind her and whirled, a hand at her mouth.

"I'm glad you came here, Stella. I've wanted to have a little chat with you."

"I—I don't think we have anything to say to each other, Captain Brent."

"On the contrary, my dear, I think we have a great deal to say. At least, I do. And it would do you no harm to listen, Stella."

"I resent your using my first name so familiarly, Captain Brent. You're forgetting that I am the wife of your commanding officer." She drew herself up and stared indignantly at him.

"That's precisely why I'm talking to you as I am, my dear," he chuckled. "I know that you and Dana haven't been hitting it off too well. It's no secret around the fort."

"How dare you discuss my personal relationship with my husband, Captain Brent! You forget yourself!"

"And you'd like to forget yourself, too, wouldn't you now, Stella girl?" He approached, a smug smile on his sensual lips. "Admit it, you're a beautiful woman who's being neglected by a husband who acts more like a teacher than a soldier. You're not happy at Fort Inge; anyone who isn't blind can see that at once, just by watching you."

"Oh yes, and I'm sure you've done that ever since you came here. I'd much prefer it, Captain Brent, if you'd remember that my husband outranks you and I haven't the least interest in your personal feelings about me."

"I think you'd better reconsider that rather brash remark, Stella. You see, I was looking after my horse earlier this evening when you and Mr. Bouchard were here."

"You—you contemptible—" she began in a choked voice, her face flaming.

"Gently, Stella. You as much as flung yourself at Mr. Bouchard. Oh, don't try to protest. I could overhear your conversation, you see. You wouldn't have minded at all if he'd taken you in his arms and kissed you. He's a tall, blond man just like me, my dear. Only he's already married and has a ranch to look after and he'll be leaving in a few days. But I'm here, and I'm not married, and I'm as lonely as you are, Stella.".

"How dare you talk to me like that! Get out of here!"

Stella uttered a strangled cry of shame and rage, turned, and began to walk out of the stable. Captain Brent grasped her by the shoulder and spun her around to face him. "That won't do, Stella dear." His eyes were mean and narrowed, his voice insinuating. "We haven't settled this matter yet."

"I'll tell my husband how you're behaving toward me, Captain Brent!"

"I don't think you will. I've done nothing, actually. I've just told you that I overheard a conversation. And if I were to tell your husband what I heard, I'm sure he wouldn't particularly like the implications of it."

"You've no right to assume—"

"I've every right. I want you, Stella. I'm convinced that there's nothing between you and Dana, probably hasn't been for a long time. You see, my dear, I've had considerable experience with women—"

"That I'm sure of," she said with icy sarcasm, jerking herself away from his restraining hand on her shoulder. "I'll slap you if you touch me again, I mean it, Captain Brent!"

"Just hear me out a bit more, my dear. Now look, as I started to tell you, I can tell when a woman's satisfied in bed, in or out of marriage. And you're definitely not—but you're the sort of woman who needs loving, Stella. I'm exceptionally good at providing it, and we're here together in a lonely, abandoned fort the army doesn't really give a damn about. There's ample opportunity for us to enjoy each other, and for you to feel yourself a beautiful, desired woman again."

"You—you despicable, shameless scoundrel!" she panted, her eyes sparkling with fury. "I'm going now, and you'd better not try to stop me."

"In that case, I'll have to have a little chat with Dana, I'm afraid. And when I tell him what I heard you saying to Mr. Bouchard, he's going to be very put out with you, Stella. Now wouldn't it be simpler for us to become lovers, discreetly, and enjoy the fact that we're here together because you've no man to satisfy your needs?"

With a choking gasp, she drew back her hand and slapped him across the face. "That's enough! Don't you ever come near me again with your filthiness!"

"Ah, Stella, but you're saying that just out of form's sake; you know you really don't mean it. That lovely body of yours is eager for passion, and I know how to fulfill your needs. You don't love Dana. No you don't!—" This was spoken as she tried to strike him again. He caught her wrist and twisted it till she uttered a cry of pain. "Just think over what I said, Stella darling. You'll see things more sensibly in the morning. But if, by sundown tomorrow, you don't come to me and tell me you've changed your mind about us, I'll definitely have that talk with Dana. Good night!"

It was nearly midnight when Major Creston, having concluded the festivities and bidden his guests good night, made his final rounds of barracks and officers' quarters, chatted pleasantly with the sentry guards, and then slowly walked toward his house. The evening had been a great success, and the men had thoroughly enjoyed themselves. Yet he had felt a nagging sense of discontent, as if there were something indefinable that was wrong; it had troubled him on and off all evening.

He quietly let himself in and went directly to his small study, for it was his inflexible practice to keep a daily journal of what had happened both in a military sense and in a social and domestic one. He lit a kerosene lamp, sighed wearily, and then drew out the notebook, opened it to the correct page, dipped his pen in ink, and began to write.

There was a soft tap at the door and he looked up, startled. "Come in!"

Stella entered, wearing a long, yellow robe over her nightgown. He glanced at her and saw that her eyes were red and swollen. He rose quickly. "What's the matter, Stella dear?" he solicitously asked.

"Dana, I—I wonder if I could talk to you for a few minutes. I—I just have to."

There was such a desperate anguish in her voice that he felt a sudden contrition, an awareness that, somehow, he had failed her. Stammering, he responded, "Why, why—of course, dear. There's something troubling you. I—I can see it. Have I done anything to offend you?"

She seated herself on a leather-upholstered couch, her

face turned away from him, leaning forward with her hands clenched and pressed against her knees. "No. No, it's not that, exactly. Dana, it's—it's hard for me to say this, so please bear with me."

He took a step toward her, and then he thought better of it. There had been a constraint and a distance between them for so long now, that he hesitated to make any overt gesture which might seem either possessive or condescending. He stood beside his desk, and in the gentlest tone he could find, urged, "Take your time, Stella dear. I guess I might know a little of what's behind the way you feel tonight. It's being out here at Fort Inge, isn't it? So far away from where we grew up."

"That's only partly it, Dana." She did not turn, but stared at the curtained windows, her body still tensed, her fingers tautly clenched together. "And—and some of it's my fault, too."

"You mustn't blame yourself. I know we've been transferred a good deal the last few years, but I was hoping that—" he helplessly shrugged, "—well, that the contingent of officers and enlisted men here would be a bit more congenial for both of us. And there really are a few fine men here, Stella."

"Yes, I know." She hesitated a long moment, then suddenly turned to stare at him, her eyes wet with tears, wide and imploring. "Dana, you're so wrapped up in your career that you've forgotten to let me into your life. That's a good deal of it, but there's even more. It's—it's about us, personally."

"I didn't know—" he faltered and then was silent.

"Before dinner tonight, Mr. Bouchard went to the stable to look at the horses. I went out there, too. I wanted to look after Delia, and—well, perhaps I wanted to see Mr. Bouchard, too; he seemed so good, so decent."

"He's certainly that, Stella dear. And we're all going to be very grateful to him for the beef he'll provide us with. But tell me—"

"Let me finish in my own way, please, Dana." Her voice was strained. She took several deep breaths, fighting for self-control, swallowed hard, and then went on: "Mr. Bouchard and I—we got to talking. I—I made the mistake—because he was so sympathetic—of letting him guess just how lonely I'd been."

"I'm terribly sorry."

"And then—and then—" She seemed not to hear him, but went blindly on: "then at the dance I said I had a headache. It wasn't that, it was just that I felt so wretched, with everyone having fun except me. So I went out to see Delia again and get some cool air before I went to sleep. And—and Captain Brent followed me to the stable."

"Oh?" His eyebrows quizzically arched.

"You see, Dana, he'd been in the stable attending to his horse when Mr. Bouchard and I were talking, only we didn't see or hear him. So—well, he heard what I said to Mr. Bouchard. And then, late tonight, he told me that he'd heard and that he was going to tell you that I practically threw myself at Mr. Bouchard. He said—" Again she stopped, closed her eyes, trembling.

"What did he tell you?" Major Creston softly demanded, but his voice was compassionate and not accusing.

"It's an ugly thing, Dana, but I have to tell you. And I'm partly to blame, I know I am. Well, Captain Brent said that he would tell you unless—unless I gave myself to him. He said that he knew you and I couldn't have much to do with each other—that way—and that he could pleasure me—he knew how to make a woman happy."

Major Creston stiffened, dug his nails into his palms, and was silent, seeking the words to ease his wife's agony of soul. Her eyes, glistening with tears, fixed on him beseechingly, and then he came slowly toward her, put an arm around her shoulders, and said hoarsely, "I wish to God I'd known this. I wish I'd had the brains to understand why you were unhappy with me, Stella. I know now. I've shunned you, stupidly, because I was clinging to a dream. The dream's gone, and I know it now, but I was too afraid to admit it to myself."

She stared at him uncomprehendingly, without a word, and he felt himself wrenched by the sudden, long-pent-up need to confide in her, to justify himself. "I felt myself so much more idealistic than all the others in the service, Stella. I made the fatal mistake of ignoring what was really happening to us both, justifying it all this time by thinking my own humble efforts could change things. I know now how wrong I was."

She put out a hand, and tears ran down her cheeks as she stammered faintly, "I wanted so much to be a part of you, Dana, but you'd never let me. You shut me out."

"I know, my darling." He bent to her and kissed her forehead. "I was so wrapped up in trying to make things right, and I was only one man against many. And in doing that, I kept you away from me all this time. I can see now what's happened to us, Stella. Please don't blame yourself. It's my fault, mine entirely."

"Oh no, Dana—" she sobbed.

"Hush, dearest Stella." Again he kissed her, one arm around her shoulders as he took her hands and held them to his chest. "I was so sure I was right, I wanted to change all the minds of my superior officers in the War Department, make them realize how biased they were. I know now it can't be done. They've sent me out here, and it's almost as if they'd cashiered me to tell me that I'm powerless to fight them. Well now, at last I see that. I've been such a fool! And—and—do you know what else I'm beginning to realize, Stella?"

Wordlessly, she shook her head, still looking at him with a yearning hope.

"I—I'm beginning to see that I've wasted years of our lives, Stella, all because of a notion that couldn't be realized. I've hurt you and I've neglected you, but—but I want to change that—and I think I can. From now on, I'm not going to care at all what happens to me in the army, Stella. I'm going to try to make it up to you for what we've lost, the two of us. That is, if you'll still have me—"

"Oh, Dana, Dana my darling, of course I'll have you—I've been so alone, so hurt, so unable to come to you and tell you what was happening to us—" She sobbed and reached for him.

"Hush, Stella dearest. I very nearly lost you, and I'd have deserved it, if it had happened. But from now on, you've my promise things will be very different between us. First off, I'm going to transfer Captain Brent. And after that, maybe in six months, I'll consider sending in my resignation to Washington, and then we'll both go back to Galena and start all over again."

"Perhaps it's not too late?" she wistfully murmured.

"No, it's not. Maybe we can have a family, too—we can adopt children. Things will be just as they were back when I first met you, Stella. And if God is good, maybe we'll have some years left so I can make up to you for what I've cost you in love and trust and respect. Forgive me, Stella."

She burst into tears and rose to put her arms around him, tendering her lips, and it was a sacrament of love, pledged anew.

"You sent for me, Major Creston?" Captain Anthony Brent saluted smartly and then stood at ease, a triumphant smirk on his lips.

"Yes, Captain Brent." Major Creston, his face expressionless, reached for a paper on his desk, folded it, and extended it. "I'm transferring you to Fort Belknap in Young County. As it happens, Colonel Struthers needs a qualified officer. You'll still be second-in-command there, and I think you'll be happier."

"May I ask what's displeased you about my work here, Major?"

"We don't have to discuss that, Captain Brent. Let's just say that I think you'll be happier."

"I think I understand, Major Creston. You know, if we could both forget our rank, I think I could say something—"

"I don't want to hear it, Captain Brent. It's not necessary to go into detail. Let's just say you've made several errors of judgment. That's all I have to say on the matter. You'll receive your orders when the transfer is approved."

"I see." The blond officer smirked and stroked his crisp beard. "Well, there are other fish in the sea."

"There are, Captain Brent." Major Creston stared coldly at the younger man. "And you'd best forget everything you thought you were going to tell me about my wife, because I know it in advance. You see, my wife and I trust each other. And I've nothing but contempt for a man who would resort to blackmail to gain his ends."

"You don't—"

"I said that's all we have to say to each other. You may consider yourself confined to the post until transfer orders are approved, and then I wish you well in your future career."

For a long moment, the handsome junior officer stared at Major Creston, and then, with a casual shrug, saluted, turned on his heel, and left the major's study.

When Lucien Edmond Bouchard, Joe Duvray, Eddie Gentry, and Nacio Lorcas mounted their horses and prepared to return to Windhaven Range, Stella Creston came to the stable to wish them a speedy journey home. She went

338

to Lucien Edmond, her face serene, her eyes joyous, and said simply to him, "I'm very grateful to you, Mr. Bouchard. I think your wife's a very lucky woman, and I wish you both long, happy years."

It was indeed a time for fresh beginnings—for others as well as Dana and Stella Creston. Far, far to the south, across the border, near the little village of Miero, Friar Bartoloméo Alicante had begun his own new life, learning the ways of the once-marauding, hunting tribe of the Wanderers, now at peace under the leadership of their revered chief, Sangrodo, and celebrating the union of brave Kitante and his young squaw, Carmencita Caldera.

And in Wichita, Dr. Ben Wilson and his wife Elone brought their two-month-old son to the Quaker meeting house on the first Sunday in August for baptism by Pastor Jacob Hartmann. True to his vow, Elone's husband, when asked what baptismal name he had chosen for the baby, replied, "Let it be Jacob Wilson."

CHAPTER TWENTY-NINE

For a young nation struggling toward its centennial, seeking a renewed sense of unity after the divisiveness of a civil war, the Ides of September were to be as fateful as the Ides of March had been to Julius Caesar. The first ominous sign that foretold the economic crisis, which in its own way would be even more devastating than the Civil War, took place on September 8, 1873, with the failure of the New York Warehouse and Security Company. That disaster cast a pall of gloom over the business world.

Ten days later, the banking house of Jay Cooke and Company was forced into bankruptcy. Jay Cooke, regarded as the leading American financier, had marketed the Civil War loans of the federal government. But he had become overinvolved in financing the Northern Pacific Railway, which he had managed since construction had begun on the line three years earlier. Regarded as the most powerful banker in America and presumed to be a model of business probity, he had gone bankrupt because he speculated recklessly in railroad securities. His failure was to precipitate the business panic of 1873, which would lead to four years of severe depression. And two days after Jay Cooke's failure, the New York Stock Exchange closed its doors. Before this ominous year was over, there would be five thousand business failures.

Already there were the signs of collapse: unemployment, falling farm prices, and business stagnation—exactly those calamities Luke Bouchard had foreseen.

It was a sign of the moral deterioration of the chaotic times that the Reverend Henry Ward Beecher of Plymouth Church in Brooklyn, America's best-known preacher, became involved in a private scandal which ended in a trial

341

for adultery. There were further scandals in Grant's administration, too, and as a result the tide had begun to turn against the Republicans. The *Nation* editorialized that the punitive Republican policies of Reconstruction against the South must come to an end; the South must be given home rule so that the country would "once more resume the path of careful and orderly progress from which the slavery agitation and its consequences have, during the last generation, driven us."

Once again, America was beset by crisis, all the more disturbing because the leaders of the country were seen to have feet of clay. Ulysses S. Grant, once the great military hero and the embodiment of many national virtues, though he himself was personally honest, was now associated with corruption and the debasement of the Civil Service. All over the nation, the common people, frightened and confused by the events of this September, flocked to the churches to pray for the nation's and their own salvation.

Although Charles Douglas had arranged with the president of the Houston Bank to transfer some of his working capital there for the purpose of purchasing land and building his second Texas department store, the reports he had from his Chicago partner, Lawrence Harding, on the economic times ahead made him decide to wait at least a year before undertaking the new enterprise. It was more important, for the immediate future, to consolidate the growth of the Chicago store, rebuilt after the great fire two years earlier, and to maintain a steady flow of merchandise to the Galveston store. For most of the month of August, Charles spent a great deal of time with Lawrence Harding at the Chicago store and with his Chicago banker, though he managed to find weekends for recreation with Laurette and the children. To the boys' delight, he kept his promise about getting ponies for them, since the stable attached to their spacious new house could easily accommodate them, and the yard was large enough so that the children could ride in perfect safety under the supervision of their parents or their governess.

Laurette's time was taken up not only with little Fleur, who was cutting her first teeth, but also with new neighbors who had moved into the red brick house directly south of the Douglasses. These were the Jurgensons, Andrew and Penelope; they were both thirty-five and childless. Andrew was a stocky, bluff, genial man with reddish-brown hair and not an ounce of deception to his good nature. He had volunteered to serve in an Illinois regiment during the Civil War, risen to the rank of sergeant and had been decorated for valor at Manassas; after Appomattox he had become a schoolteacher. His wife Penelope—tall, soft-spoken, light-brown-haired—had been a teacher in the same school, and they had fallen in love and married eight years ago. What touched Laurette Douglas most about the Jurgensons was their obvious love for children and, as she quickly learned, their sorrow that they had none of their own. Penelope Jurgenson had consulted with several physicians and had learned that her only hope of a child was through adoption. Consequently, she and her husband became attached to the twins, Kenneth and Arthur, little Howard, and the baby Fleur. Several times, indeed, the Jurgensons had invited Laurette and Charles to have supper with them and had always urged, "Please do bring the children; we love them so!"

The first week in August had been exceptionally humid and oppressive, with only the unfulfilled promise of dark clouds to herald a welcome rain and the freshening of the sticky atmosphere. On this Friday evening, Laurette and Charles Douglas were preparing to visit their next-door neighbors for supper, and Laurette was dressing baby Fleur for the occasion.

"It's such a shame, Charles dearest," Laurette confided, "that Andrew and Penelope can't have children of their own. It just about breaks my heart when I see them look at ours and when Penelope begs me to let her hold Fleur for just a minute."

"Yes, it's a shame indeed, they're such nice people. And they're in the right profession too, teaching children. Maybe in a way that's a consolation for them," Charles vouchsafed as he adjusted his cravat, then sighed, "Tarnation, I never can tie a proper knot. I wish I didn't have to wear a coat this evening. I'm starting to sweat already."

"Correction, darling," Laurette playfully jibed at him as, putting Fleur down in her bassinette, she came over to adjust the cravat. "Famous, wealthy businessmen like you perspire, poor people sweat. And you'll have to admit, Charles, that you're not poor common folk any more. Do you know, the *Tribune* had a story today mentioning the leading businessmen of the city who have pulled themselves

343

up by their bootstraps after the great fire, and your name was sixth on the list. I'm very proud of you, darling."

"Thanks, but I'm still sweating," he chuckled. And then, when she made a mock face of annoyance at him, he resoundingly kissed her and gave her a playful slap on the behind. "That's just to show you I'm common folk, honey. And you're as beautiful as you were when I first married you, so you know I don't go around doing that to other girls."

"Well, you'd just better not let me catch you, that's all I have to say to you, Charles Douglas!" Laurette threatened, smiling and shaking a reproving finger. Then, serious again, she wistfully added, "I still wish Penelope and Andrew could have a family of their own. But Penelope says it's no use, and she's just about resigned herself to the doctors' verdict. When I asked her, in a very tactful way, of course, what she thought of the idea of adopting, she said she and Andrew weren't sure, because you couldn't know what background the child came from. All the same, I think if they keep on being as lonely as they are and seeing our children around all the time, they might just decide to do it anyway. I certainly hope so. With parents like them, both teachers, I'm sure any child, no matter what its background, would benefit from the love and concern and education they'd be able to provide."

"I thoroughly agree with you, honey. Oh say, that reminds me, don't forget there'll be someone new to meet over at the Jurgenson's tonight—Andrew's younger brother, Danny."

"Oh yes, I knew he had a brother, but I didn't know that he'd be there tonight," Laurette responded.

"There now, that cravat's the way it ought to look, thanks to you." Charles glanced into the framed chiffonier mirror. "Danny's been working in the stockyards, but he gave up his job two weeks ago, and from what Andrew tells me, he's going to live with them for a while."

"I wonder why he gave up a job there; I should think he would have made a good deal of money."

"Yes, that's true. He's only nineteen but he'd been doing quite well before he quit. Maybe we'll find out more tonight. Well, honey, I see you've picked out the blue dress that's a favorite of mine. You look absolutely scrumptious." With a conspiratorial wink, he leaned toward her and, cupping a hand to his mouth, whispered, "Mrs. Douglas, do you think you could be induced to forego the party and stay home and console your yearning husband?"

Color flamed in Laurette's cheeks and she could not suppress a giggle as she primly retorted, "There'll be time enough for that when we get home, my impatient husband." Then, relenting at the sight of his long face, she giggled again and whispered back, "All the same, it's wonderfully reassuring to a staid old married woman of thirty-six to learn that her husband still wants to go to bed with her. Now stop your foolishness and let's be on time. Penelope's a wonderful cook."

In many ways, Laurette decided, Danny Jurgenson resembled Lucien Edmond Bouchard. Like the latter, he was tall and blond with frank blue eyes and a ready smile. To be sure, since he was only nineteen, he had a callow forthrightness which was at once disarming and ingenuous. Yet at the same time his manners were impeccable, almost those of a romantic gallant, as Laurette discovered when he hastened to draw out her chair from the dining-room table and seat her after they had been introduced.

Unlike Laurette, Penelope Jurgenson had no servants, and her husband proudly announced, "Penny is such a good cook, she couldn't abide having someone in her kitchen." His pride in his wife's cuisine was more than justified. There was an admirably cooked saddle of lamb with mint jelly, accompanied by side dishes of cauliflower, snap beans, tiny roasted potatoes, and a salad of vegetables picked from Penelope's own garden. For dessert, she had made a delectable blancmange, accompanied by bowls of fresh fruit and exceptionally strong black coffee served in Wedgwood cups.

Danny Jurgenson ate with typical youthful appetite till he came to the coffee. He took a sip and frowned, then looked at his sister-in-law. "That's Cuban coffee, isn't it, Penny?"

"Why yes, Danny dear. Why do you ask?"

His face hardened and he set down the cup. "It makes me think of what's going on there right now," he declared bitterly. "Haven't you read about the way the Spanish government is oppressing the Cubans? Why, they live like slaves, and the Spanish authorities and the soldiers punish them cruelly if they speak out against what's being done to them."

345

"I'm sorry, Danny." Penelope was abashed and looked helplessly around at her guests as if for succor. "I didn't know you felt so strongly about it."

"Yes, Danny," his older brother interposed. "I'm curious, too. You haven't said much since you came to me two weeks ago and said you'd quit your job with Armour and Company and asked if I'd mind if you stayed here with us for a spell. And, naturally, we're delighted to have you."

"I—I don't want to offend Mr. and Mrs. Douglas." The blond youth lowered his eyes, his face flushing. "And their kids—though maybe young as they are, it wouldn't hurt them to know what's going on in the world."

Laurette had seated baby Fleur in a highchair beside her, carefully watching her throughout the dinner and feeding her from a spoon dipped into crumbled bread and milk. The three boys were on Charles's side of the table, and they peered quizzically and wonderingly at Danny because of the vehemence of his tone.

"I'm sure, Danny," Charles said soothingly, "that no one here will take exception to what you're saying; in fact, I'm sure you have a good reason for saying it."

"I do, sir!" Danny turned to him, his eyes bright, his face eager. "I—I want to help the Cubans. You know, they've been at war with Spain for five years now. They want to be free, and I don't blame them—and neither would you, if you knew everything that's happening."

"Suppose you tell us, then, Danny," his brother suggested.

"I mean to. The Spaniards tax the Cubans to death, and they enforce all sorts of cruel trade restrictions. Not only that, there's hardly a single Cuban in the government."

"I'd no idea," Laurette murmured.

"Oh, Mrs. Douglas, the Cubans have already set up a rebel republic and they've had to go to war—of course, they're outnumbered and they don't have arms, but they do it guerrilla-style."

"You say you want to help them, Danny," his brother slowly said. "In what way? How can you help, other than by showing your sympathy?"

"By volunteering to fight on their side, that's how, Andy!" the youth fervently averred.

"You must really be out of your mind! What chance do you think you'd have against crack Spanish troops? Guerrilla warfare is always waged against enormous odds and the reprisals are terrible. I think you should take a long look at this matter before you go off and do anything foolish, Danny."

"Look, Andy, I know you're my older brother, and I'm grateful to you and Penny for taking me in. But—well, you might as well know it now, because it means so much to me—I—I've met a girl, Concepción Perez. She and her brother escaped from Havana and got to Florida, and they came here to Chicago to live with their Uncle Esteban."

"And I suppose she's told you about what's going on in her country," his brother remarked.

"Yes, she has, Andy. And she's not telling any lies, believe me. I—I love her, Andy."

"But how did you come to meet this girl, dear?" Penelope Jurgenson asked.

"Her brother, Rolando, got a job in the stockyards, and he worked for a time on the same shift I did, and we got to talking. One Saturday evening he brought me over to his uncle's house, and I met Concepción there. Since then, we've been seeing a lot of each other." He drew a deep breath and looked down at his plate. "If you could only hear her, Andy—hear her tell about the things that have happened to people she knows, friends she's had, why, you'd know just how I feel. I've made up my mind, I'm going with a volunteer group to Cuba and see if we can't help win freedom for those poor people!"

"Danny, this is very serious. We're going to have to talk about this later in private," his brother remonstrated, giving Penelope an anxious look.

"You might as well know it now, Andy, it won't do any good. I'm going." Then, abashed, he looked around and stammered, "Excuse me, Mr. and Mrs. Douglas, I didn't mean to sound off this way. But I wouldn't feel right unless I could do something to help Concepción's people."

"Don't apologize for taking the side of the oppressed, Danny, that's a wonderful trait. I can only pray that you won't suffer for your convictions. Don't forget, you were too young for the Civil War and a great many young men died there, or were wounded and disabled for life." Charles shook his head. "Wouldn't it be enough if you contributed money?"

"No, I have to go myself, Mr. Douglas." He saw that the twins and Howard were staring open-mouthed at him, and, flushing again, leaned toward them and said, "Don't be scared, everything's fine. Now you eat up the rest of your dessert, because Penny's the best cook in all Chicago."

A ripple of laughter eased the tension, and as Charles and Laurette exchanged a wondering glance, Kenneth and Arthur and Howard dug into their food again.

On a rainy Friday evening in early September, Danny Jurgenson climbed the rickety stairs of a shabby little flat on West Lake Street and knocked at the door. His face brightened when he heard a girl's voice call out, *"¿Quién es?"*

"It's Danny, *querida*!" he eagerly called.

The door opened and a black-haired, olive-skinned girl of eighteen appeared, her heart-shaped face dimpling with an exquisite smile and her black eyes flashing warm and wide with recognition. *"Mi corazón,* I prayed you would come to me tonight! Rolando and Tío Esteban have gone to the meeting for Cuban independence—they will not be back till very late. Oh, but I am so sorry this place is so ugly and so dirty. It's all that Tío Esteban can afford. Still, they like him at the shoe factory, and the foreman says he will soon have more *dinero.* Then perhaps we can find a better place." Her face grew grave all of a sudden, "But no, that is being selfish. I do not care where we live, so long as our people can be free, Danny."

"I know that, sweetheart." The blond youth took her in his arms and kissed her. Concepción Perez drew back for a moment, and then with a little sob, flung her arms around him and returned his kiss with tempestuous fervor.

"Now you will think I am bold, you will think me a *puta,*" she murmured, adorably blushing as she at last freed herself from his embrace.

"You know better than that, sweetheart," he indignantly reproached her, as he took her hand and brought it to his lips. "I want to marry you, Concepción. I want to be not only your *novio,* but your *esposo,* just as soon as possible—you must know that by now. I've saved some money from the job I had in the stockyards, and I've put it away; my brother is letting me live with him and, of course, he's not charging me anything. I've had a few odd jobs, but I've been waiting to know when I can join the others and go down to Florida and then sail on to Havana with the volunteers."

348

"Rolando says there is already talk of a ship being cutfitted. It will carry men and weapons for the glorious fight of our independence against the Spanish tyrants, *querido*," Concepción rejoined. "It is called the *Virginius*. Rolando says it will fly the American flag, and that will get it through the Spanish blockade in the harbor. He says it will be next month."

"Good! I want to see your brother, sweetheart. I want to find out when I should go to Florida and start training. You know, I've never fired a gun in my life, but I want to learn how. I want to do everything I can to help free your people, and then I'll come back and we'll be married."

"Oh, my love, my sweet Danny, that, too, is what I pray for!" She put her head against his chest and sighed, "If only many, many *americanos* like you would fight to save my country, the cruel Spaniards would be driven away forever. I think it is a little miracle that you, who knew nothing of us until you met my brother at the stockyards, should feel and think like one of us. And most of all, it is a miracle that you should love me, for I am only a simple peasant girl from Havana."

"You're more than that to me, darling. I love you, I want to marry you, I want you to bear my children, Concepción."

Her eyes shone with joy as she looked at him, and she murmured softly, "That, too, I wish, so very much, *querido*! You are my one, my true love, my *esposo*."

"Oh, my love, I want you so—"

"It is what I desire also, dearest." She cupped his face with her soft little hands and, standing on tiptoe, kissed him ardently on the lips. "Let us make a pledge of our love, and seal our promise to one another. Do not think I am bold, it is because I love you—"

As a reply, Danny took hold of her shoulders and kissed her mouth. Instantly, Concepción's arms curved round him and drew him to her and to the fulfillment of their love.

CHAPTER THIRTY

The panic of September began in New York and swept through Chicago, as it did through all large urban centers. But Charles Douglas, who had paid all his bills and retained ample working capital for the future, did not suffer unduly from the business slump. He could weather the next few months, during which time there would be few customers in his store with money to spend. There was widespread unemployment in the city, and every day at least ten jobless men or women visited the personnel director of Charles's store to ask for work of any kind, no matter how low the wages. Out of compassion, Charles authorized the hiring of two part-time clerks for the furniture department, which—contrary to trends elsewhere—was holding its own and even showing a slight increase in business over the previous years. Charles himself hired three married women whose husbands were out of work and who had families to support.

Andrew Jurgenson had at last, but most reluctantly, lent his young brother sufficient funds to finance his trip to Florida and his sojourn there until his ship could sail for Havana. First, however, he engaged Danny in a long, serious conversation in which he brought all his eloquence and logic to bear on the folly of a young American plunging headlong into a rebellion which did not yet concern his own country and which could easily cost Danny his life. He even played on the youth's avowed and faithful love for Concepción, saying, "You haven't even married her yet, Danny. Think of it, if you should die over there needlessly, perhaps even before reaching the shores of Cuba, what would you deprive her and yourself of—a long, happy life together, children, a home, and your own choice of a pro-

351

fession. Damnit, Danny, forget your romantic crusade. I'm a schoolteacher, as you well know, and I could quote you the pitiful story of the Children's Crusade and how the Pope blessed them—and not a one returned. They were all sold into slavery, or else perished miserably."

But Danny was not to be shaken from his resolve, and on the seventeenth of September he departed for Florida, where he would train with other American volunteers and Cuban expatriates until the *Virginius* was ready to sail.

Five weeks later Andrew received a letter from his brother, short but enthusiastic, telling how he was quickly adapting himself to the brief, but intensive military training, how he had learned to use a rifle and even a bayonet, and that he expected to leave the Florida harbor within the week. He did not mention Concepción Perez, but Andrew concluded that his brother had doubtless sent her a personal letter of far greater length and more detail.

And then there was nothing. Nothing until the twentieth of November, when the postman came with a letter from Danny dated November 1. But by that time Andrew already knew his brother's fate.

The *Virginius* had taken a circuitous route to avoid Spanish patrol boats, and, as planned, it had flown the American flag so as to reach Havana in safety. But it had been intercepted by a Spanish gunboat off the Cuban coast on October 31. A week later, the *Chicago Tribune* had reported that fifty-three passengers and crew, including many Americans, had been taken in irons to Havana, there to be tried and summarily executed by firing squad. One of the names of the victims had been that of Danny Jurgenson.

Secretary of State Hamilton Fish had at once communicated with the Spanish authorities, doing his best to prevent a war between the United States and Spain. By the twenty-ninth of November, the Spanish government agreed to pay indemnities of eighty thousand dollars to the families of those Americans who had fallen before the firing squad. Thus war was averted, but the incident foreshadowed the Cuban War of Independence of 1895, and the eventual Spanish-American War of 1898.

Andrew Jurgenson, his eyes wet with tears, handed his brother's letter to Penelope. Then he turned and walked to the window of the living room and stared unseeingly out into the street.

Dear Andy:

I guess you might say the jig is up. I'm smuggling this letter out by one of the guards. I gave him ten pesos and he promised he'd get it off. I hope he does, otherwise you might not be hearing from me for a while.

We thought we were safe with the American flag, but a gunboat got us on the high seas about fifty miles before we reached Havana yesterday, and took us directly to this dirty, crowded jail. The food is just awful, and there are cockroaches and rats. But the worst of it is, I heard one of the guards saying to an officer—you see, Concepción taught me enough Spanish so I could make myself understood—that we'd probably be tried and sentenced to death as spies.

If it happens—though I think our government will certainly try to stop it, because we're not at war with Spain—I want you to know I'm not sorry. Well, maybe I'll be terribly sorry that I might not ever see Concepción again—but at least if I have to die it'll be to help her people. You kept reminding me you were a schoolteacher, and you're a darned good one, Andy. Then you ought to remember how a lot of farmers who'd never gone to war before fought British troops at Concord and Lexington, and how we beat the British again when old Andy Jackson smashed them in the Battle of New Orleans. And then there was the Mexican War. Anyway, I'm not sorry—and I don't want you and Penny to worry about me. I had to do it. God bless all of you.

Your brother,
Danny

"Oh, Andy, that poor boy—God rest his brave soul!" Penelope's voice was choked and barely audible as she rose, went to her husband, and put an arm around his shoulders. He turned to her, tears streaming down his cheeks. They clung to each other wordlessly, seeking comfort, helpless before this loss whose cause still seemed so alien and irrational to them.

They sat alone by themselves at supper that evening, trying not to speak of what oppressed them. Halfway through the meal there was a knock at the door and Andrew gestured to his wife that he would answer it. When he opened the door, it was to find a lovely young girl dressed in black, her eyes swollen with tears, clutching a crumpled letter in her hand.

"Are you Señor Jurgenson, the *hermano* of—of Danny?" she quavered.

"My God—yes—you—you must be Concepción Perez!" Andrew Jurgenson blurted.

"*Pero sí*. He—he wrote me this—this *carta*, and he told me to come to you if—if—oh, Señor Jurgenson, you know—"

"Yes, Miss Perez. We know. Please come in," he gently urged her.

Penelope had risen from the table and come out into the living room. She looked swiftly at the girl and then at her husband, and then she burst into tears and held out her arms to Concepción, who, completely breaking down, hurried to her and began to weep bitterly.

"There, there, honey, cry it out, that's right," she urged Concepción. "We tried our best to stop him—but he wanted to do it. You have to think that it was for a good cause, honey."

"I know, señora. But they had no chance, none of them—how we prayed and hoped, Rolando and I and my Tío Esteban, that they would reach Havana and stir the poor people to rise up against the tyrants! And now—now it was all for nothing. And the Spaniards will be crueller than ever. Oh, *Dios*, and he—he said he wanted to marry me—" Concepción raised her tear-swollen face to Penelope and then falteringly stammered, "And it was our pledge together; we loved as *esposo* and *esposa* and now—now I carry his child—and my uncle will turn me out, I know, and my brother will think I am a *puta*—"

"You—you're pregnant by Danny, then?" Penelope gasped, and when the black-haired girl tearfully nodded, she turned to look at her husband and she said softly, "Andrew, perhaps this is the will of God. You know how both of us have wanted children so badly—and I've failed you, I can't have them, not ever. But Concepción is bearing your brother's child, Andrew. Couldn't we—why shouldn't we bring it up here as our very own—if—if you're willing?"

"Yes, by God!" Andrew huskily responded, furtively rubbing the back of his hand against his tear-filled eyes. "Why couldn't Concepción live here, and raise her child with us; we could be sort of godparents to it, and help to raise it, too. If, that is, Concepción is willing—"

"Oh yes, yes, the Holy Mother of our dear *Señor Dios* will bless you and keep you in Her Holy mercy for saying that to me now, Señor, Señora Jurgenson!" Concepción sobbed. "I have nowhere I can go; I know my Tío Esteban will not want me living with him—and I have no money. But if I could stay with you and have my *niño*, and raise him to revere the memory of his beloved father, with you as his guardians, too—oh, that is too much, I have more than I deserve!"

"Now don't cry," Penelope took the weeping girl into her arms. "Andrew and I would love to have you and the baby with us, and I promise we'll be very good to you both. We will be so happy to see the youngster growing up. Perhaps, some day, if you are willing, we can adopt him legally—so that he'll be really and truly a part of Danny's family, a Jurgenson. As you are, too, my dear, in every way, for all the kindness and love that you have given our poor Danny—" Here Penelope turned away, stifling a fresh access of tears as she did so.

"I will pray for you, Señora Jurgenson, and you, too, señor. You are too kind. Oh *mi novio, mi esposo querido,* if you could only know this! And if the *niño* is a boy, I will name him Danny—"

"That would be a fine thing to do, honey. Now then, you just sit down and rest a bit," Penelope said. "I'll bet you haven't eaten anything all day long, and you need food if you're going to have a good, strong baby, you should know that. I'll get something right away. Andy, get her some hot tea, the pot's still on the stove," Penelope ordered briskly. Drying her eyes, she smiled radiantly. "Everything's going to be all right, you'll see, honey. Danny will live for all of us through your baby. Bless him for writing you to come to us. We wouldn't have known where to find you otherwise."

"Yes, that is what I think, too. I did not want to come at first, Señora Jurgenson. I did not want to be a burden to you and your *esposo*—"

"Now you stop such silly talk, honey. You're here, and this is going to be your home from now on. Everything is going to be wonderful. Ah, here's the tea. Now you try to drink as much as you can and then lie back and rest. I'll get some supper in a jiffy."

CHAPTER THIRTY-ONE

As the new year of 1874 dawned, it became increasingly evident that the nation was facing a political crisis in addition to the economic recession which had already swept through every major city. The New York *Tribune* and the *Nation* were ardently demanding an end to Radical Reconstruction, because it was paralyzing Southern business and discouraging those who had capital to invest in that part of the country. William E. Dodge, a New York capitalist and a Republican supporter of Grant, declared, "What the South now needs is capital to develop her resources, but this she cannot obtain until confidence in her state governments can be restored, and this will never be done by federal bayonets. . . . As merchants, we want to see the South gain her normal conditions in the commerce of the country; nor can we hope for a general revival of business while things remain as they are." And he went on to say that, as for the Southern Negroes, it had been a mistake to make them feel that the United States government "was their special friend, rather than those with whom their lot is cast, among whom they must live and with whom they must work. We have tried this long enough. Now let the South alone!"

At Windhaven Plantation, Luke Bouchard, with Marius Thornton continuing as foreman, concentrated more and more on produce, cattle, pigs, almost to the total exclusion of cotton. Burt Coleman was still managing the four hundred acres which had once been the property of old Edward Williamson. He and Marius often conferred, and Burt had shown himself to be as expert in planning profitable crops at a minimum of cost as Marius himself. What pleased both Luke and Andy this year was that Burt had gone to Mobile for a week with the Ardmore brothers, to buy supplies, and there he had met a pretty dark-brown-haired girl of twenty, Marietta Wolman, the only daughter of an elderly storekeeper. Burt had fallen in love at first sight with the girl, and the two of them were now corresponding weekly. As the fall harvest neared, Burt sheepishly asked Andy if he might take off a week to go get married. Needless to say, Andy gave the hardworking, genial Southerner not only his blessing, but also a cash bonus to spend on his honeymoon.

Letters from Lucien Edmond to his father indicated that, just as last year, Lucien Edmond and his partners would sell the Windhaven Range cattle in specified lots at various times during the year to the two army forts. Lucien Edmond had added a few Brahmas and Durhams to his already prime-quality herd, and, as he wrote Luke, "When the market steadies and prices go up, we'll have the finest beef in all of Texas. Besides, it won't be too much longer before there'll be feeder lines established by the railroads right down into Texas, so that drives will take perhaps a week at most instead of three and four months, as in the old days when the frontier was new."

There was a postscript to Lucien Edmond's letter: Major Dana Creston had resigned his command in June and he and his wife, Stella, had gone back to Galena to resume their lives there. The retired officer would go back to schoolteaching, and had bought a little farm for which he had appointed a capable manager.

There was a letter from Arabella Hunter, too, in the fall of 1874, happily informing Luke that Melinda and Lawrence Davis, who had been blessed the previous December with a second son, named James in honor of Arabella's devoted husband, would be having their third child in the spring. As for James Hunter himself, he continued to show great enthusiasm in his work as a co-partner in the Galveston department store and was looking after Charles Douglas's enterprise with as much enthusiasm and concern as if it had been his own. He had sent off several telegrams and long, detailed letters to Charles, reporting on the economic situation in Galveston, and these had helped the aggressive Chicago merchant to amend his buying and shipping plans, so that he would not overload his Galveston store with expensive and slow-moving merchandise. Finally, there was news from Lucien Edmond that in November, Joe and

Margaret Duvray had become the parents of a baby girl whom they named Marguerite, after Margaret's French mother, who died three months after giving birth to her.

Although Andy Haskins—because of his exemplary record and reputation for honesty—was reelected to a second term in the Alabama House in November, he was one of the few Republicans to survive the tidal wave of popular reaction against the dissolute Republican administration in Washington. In the Congressional elections across the country, Democrats made great gains, and for the first time since the Civil War the federal House of Representatives had a Democratic majority. This meant that there would be no further protection given by the federal government to Negroes; the Reconstruction policies of previous Republican Congresses were now deemed a total failure, and the fate of the black man was largely left to white Southerners.

During the same month, the War Department inaugurated a more vigorous and aggressive frontier policy, restoring autonomy to Texas and permitting the use of state troops. The Texas Rangers were reformed to patrol the desolate outposts where settlers were beginning to homestead, and the extermination of the buffalo herds was encouraged. With this, the days of the Plains Indians were numbered.

On November 24, 1874, a patent for barbed wire was granted to Joseph F. Glidden, a farmer in DeKalb, Illinois. Using an old coffee grinder, Glidden manufactured the first coiled barb. His invention was to transform the entire cattle trade; barbed wire would mean the end of free grass and water forever.

Many Texas ranchers resisted this newfangled means of making boundaries effective along their range, fearing that the barbed wire would cut up their cattle and that the injured animals would die of screw worms. When the Texas legislature threatened to make the wire illegal, two extraordinary salesmen, Henry B. Sanborn and John "Bet-a-Million" Gates, were sent to the ranching country as missionaries for the new product. A barbed-wire corral was built in the main plaza of San Antonio, and a hundred head of longhorns were placed inside it. The demonstration convinced a number of Texas cowmen that the wire would hold cattle satisfactorily and without injury. To prove further the advantages of barbed wire, Glidden and Sanborn established the first barbed-wire enclosed ranch in the Panhandle, on Tecoras Creek in Potter County. From the activities of this test ranch, the town of Amarillo developed, one day to become the largest city in the region.

Beyond what had once been Robert Caldemare's acreage and which was now Joe Duvray's through his marriage to Margaret, Caldemare's only heir, there was a wide stretch of excellent grazing land. Lucien Edmond and Joe Duvray had discussed buying this land several times over the past two years, but their well-grounded apprehension of a national recession and the swift drop in cattle prices had diminished their interest in any immediate acquisition. On a windy, sunny day in early March of the year 1875, Lucien Edmond, Ramón Hernandez, Joe Duvray, and Eddie Gentry were breakfasting in the ranch house and discussing the news of President Grant's opening of territory in Oregon to settlement, land that had been occupied by Nez Percé Indians since the treaty of 1855. "Maybe," Joe humorously proffered, "nesters will decide to settle over in that untouched land, instead of flocking down here to Texas. For my part, I don't really think we need any more neighbors—at least not until this cattle market straightens out, and I'm not looking for that to happen until the centennial, if you want my opinion."

"I'm inclined to agree with you, Joe," Lucien Edmond smilingly concurred. "But, you know, there's something else going on in this country besides homesteading. It seems like there's a big religious revival under way. There's a story here about a huge evangelistic revival in the East led by a fellow called Dwight Lyman Moody. Seems that thousands of people are crowding to hear him and pray for salvation. The story says he's a former shoe salesman from Chicago whose principal aim in life is to reduce the population of hell by one million souls."

"Amen to that!" Eddie Gentry chuckled. "I only hope some of those crooks in Washington get the message. Especially the fellows in on that Whiskey Ring. You remember, Mr. Lucien Edmond, how last year when the President appointed Benjamin Bristow as secretary of the treasury, he started digging into the records of the Internal Revenue, checking out tax collections against liquor shipments. And he found that distillers had paid taxes on only a third of the whiskey they'd shipped out of St. Louis. There have been rumors that General Orville Babcock, the President's

360

confidential secretary, was in on the whole deal. A scandal like that's bound to hurt the Republicans in next year's national election."

"You're right, Eddie. We're a long way from Washington down here in Texas, and what we have to do first of all is to worry about protecting our investment and minimizing our loss of profits from the old days of the drives, because I believe, just as you do, that next year is going to see a turnaround in our political and economic situation."

There was a knock at the front door. Lucien Edmond frowned, then rose, excusing himself to his friends, and went to open the door. It was Nacio Lorcas. His face was begrimed by dust and contorted with anxiety. *"Señor patrón,"* he excitedly began, "something is very strange just beyond the land of Señor Duvray. There are men there putting up wire. It has points and it is sharp. I do not like the way it looks, and I do not like the look of those men."

Lucien Edmond turned to his three friends. "Did you hear that, *amigos?* Joe, you were saying you hoped there wouldn't be any more neighbors and that settlers would go to Oregon instead. It appears that at least one of them hasn't. We'd best find out who this new neighbor is. And I don't like the feeling I suddenly have—I'm thinking of Andrew Moultrie and also—"

He did not finish; Joe finished it for him: "And of Margaret's father, yes. I'm thinking the same thing, and God knows, I hope I'm wrong."

CHAPTER THIRTY-TWO

In the summer of 1874, some twenty miles from Sacramento, Emory Carruthers had owned a ranch of four thousand acres, a small part of which he had devoted to raising cattle. The rest of it, sectioned off by wooden fencing, was devoted to fruits and vegetables, and he had already become rich through truck farming. Much of his beef had been sold to Sacramento butcher shops and some of it had even been shipped on to San Francisco. He was forty-one, the only son of a man who had struck it rich during the 1849 Gold Rush.

Oddly enough, despite his father's wealth, young Emory had been much more interested in working the land than living the life of a rich gentleman of leisure. This was in marked contrast to his father, Leo Carruthers, who had started out as a none-too-well educated storekeeper's clerk. Leo had been obsessed with a desire to see his only son ascend into the upper stratum of society. Emory's mother had died a year after his birth, and his father had bought a mansion on Nob Hill and an elegant carriage, and had sent his son east to school. Nevertheless, Emory had wanted to work on the land, and he had finally persuaded his father to lend him money enough to buy the ranch near Sacramento. To his father's surprise, he had turned it into an extremely profitable venture, and he had quickly reached a point of complete financial independence.

When Leo Carruthers died at the age of fifty-two, he left young Emory a hundred thousand dollars in gold and the Nob Hill mansion. Emory Carruthers promptly sold the mansion and put the money toward improvements on the ranch and the purchase of some prize bulls. Also, at the age of thirty-six, he married Lois Haverford, the beautiful,

363

capricious, twenty-five-year-old daughter of a Sacramento politician.

Carruthers soon discovered that Lois had no interest in giving him a child and that she chafed at his insistence that they live in the magnificent but isolated ranch house he had had built. Because of a curiously puritanical streak in his nature—perhaps a reaction to his father's fondness for shallow, sensual mistresses—he knew little about the ways of women. Being totally infatuated with Lois, he tried at first to win her love by indulging her every whim. Indeed, for the first two years of their marriage he proved indulgent to a fault, taking time off from the duties of the ranch to take her on trips to San Francisco and Los Angeles, and once even to New Orleans and New York.

At about this time Carruthers hired two foremen. One of them, Ernest Johnson, came from Montana and had considerable experience in handling cattle. The other was a suave, personable half-breed named Antonio Mercado, whose mother had been Mexican and whose father Irish; he had taken his mother's maiden name upon his father's death. Mercado was twenty-eight and had been a foreman for an Encino truck farmer. When his employer had died, young Mercado had come to work at Carruthers's huge ranch, at a salary double what his former employer had paid him.

With Antonio's coming to the Carruthers ranch, Lois Carruthers at last seemed ready to accede to Emory's repeated demands that she be content to live quietly at the ranch. She even intimated that she might at last give him the child for whom he had longed. She seemed, too, to take a particular interest in the planting and growing of crops, and Emory Carruthers began to believe that at last she would be the kind of wife he had envisioned for himself.

But one late June afternoon in 1874, when Carruthers returned from a brief visit to San Francisco, he found Lois absent from the ranch house. When he inquired as to her whereabouts of her maid—another concession he had made to his importunate young wife—the girl became evasive and then frightened.

Carruthers was tall and heavyset, with a strong Roman nose and a firm jaw, and his black hair already showed streaks of gray. He cut the maid short, his large gray eyes growing cold and narrowing, went to his study, opened the drawer of his desk, and took out a revolver. Then he walked slowly out to the groves of oranges and lemons, peaches and apricots, till he came to the little brick cottage where Antonio Mercado lived. He tried the knob of the door, found it locked, and hammered on it with his fist. He heard a frightened cry and recognized his wife's voice and then the hurried voice of his foreman. With an oath, he lunged at the door and broke it down, to find Lois and Mercado cowering naked on the bed. He stared at them for a moment, while Lois began to babble explanations. Calmly he leveled the revolver at her lover and killed him, then put a bullet through his wife's heart.

He was in complete control of himself, and he considered swiftly what must be done. Although he had acted by the unwritten code of justice and was certain that no California jury would convict him—particularly if he forced his wife's maid to testify truthfully as to her mistress's clandestine visits to the cottage—he was also sure that the scandal and Lois's father's political power could very well turn public opinion against him. He might even face hanging, for he remembered his father's lurid tales of the vigilantes who had tried to put an end to murder and thievery in the days of the gaudy Barbary Coast.

There were only two persons he knew he could trust. One was Frank Caswell, a young Sacramento attorney whom he had met a decade earlier, and whom he had financially backed until Caswell could pass the California bar and set up his own practice. The other was Ernest Johnson, his second cattle foreman, a dour, zealously honest man in his late thirties who, he knew, had privately held a low opinion of his employer's faithless wife, though he had always shown her the most careful respect whenever he was in her presence.

Leaving the cottage, Carruthers went to a nearby stable, saddled his horse, and rode over to the other section of the ranch. Ernest Johnson returned with him. During their ride back, Carruthers told his foreman about what had happened and enlisted his aid. The two men buried the bodies, wrapped in tarpaulins, in the bed of a dried-up creek some ten miles away. Emory Carruthers then dumbfounded his foreman by saying, "I'll sell you my ranch, Ernest, for two thousand dollars. Obviously, it's worth a lot more, but I don't need the money, and I'd like to give you this opportunity. As for myself, I'll buy me a prize bull and a few heifers, and I'll start all over again in Texas. How does that strike you?"

When Johnson had recovered his wits, he blurted out, "I can't believe it, Mr. Carruthers, but if that's what you want to do, you've got a deal."

A week later, Emory Carruthers visited Frank Caswell's office in Sacramento and appointed him factor. He told the young attorney exactly what had happened; and Caswell agreed that while his client had been morally justified and would very likely be acquitted in a court of law, it would nevertheless be a wise move for him to lose himself in Texas.

Frank Caswell had a close friend, David Simmons, whom he had met in San Francisco, and who now lived in Texas. Simmons worked in the land office at Austin, so Caswell sent him a telegram, informing him that he represented a wealthy Californian who was anxious to acquire a Texas cattle ranch. The telegram also stated that a detailed letter and a bank draft would shortly follow.

Upon receipt of the letter, David Simmons selected for Caswell and his client, Emory Carruthers, six thousand acres of prime grazing land whose eastern boundary lay about a quarter of a mile from Joe Duvray's spread. Then, after conferring with an experienced cattle buyer, Simmons purchased a pedigree bull and a dozen heifers. The buyer then recommended a foreman currently out of work, who in turn engaged a dozen vaqueros and six laborers to build a ranch house and start the nucleus of Emory Carruthers's new Texas enterprise.

After having disposed of the Sacramento ranch to his trustworthy cattle foreman, Carruthers left California and traveled for a few months through the Midwest, paying particular attention to the Armour stockyards. He learned the ins and outs of the Kansas rail centers and their distribution of herds. Then he journeyed on to Texas, in time to see the Glidden demonstration of barbed wire, and the idea appealed to him on several counts: first, to protect cattle against rustlers and Indian attacks, but most of all to ensure the privacy he sought because of an inner fear that one day he might be held to account for his vengeance against his faithless wife and her lover. When he finally arrived at the Texas ranch in January of 1875, it was with

366

a herd of some five hundred cattle and a dozen new vaqueros, many of whom had been hired because they were
pistoleros.

By then, the ranch house he had ordered had been built,
and he moved into it. He had decided to remain a bachelor,
for his experience with Lois had soured him to the point of
being almost a misogynist. If occasionally one of his vaqueros brought a pretty *muchacha* to the ranch for his
pleasure, that would suffice: he would never remarry.

Though Carruthers steadfastly believed that he had cast
off the traumatic influence of a marriage in which he had
never realized his hopes for a son, he was already committed to the life of an outlaw, and he was morbidly fearful of
intrusion and even neighborly interest in his activities.

On that afternoon in March 1875, when Nacio Lorcas
had first seen Emory Carruthers's men putting up barbed
wire around their property, Lucien Edmond and his companions rode over to the edge of the boundary that marked
the westernmost edge of Joe Duvray's acreage and the eastern edge of the Carruthers land. As they reined in their
horses, Lucien Edmond shook his head. "It's true, then,"
he said wonderingly, "there's wire all around. But you'll
notice that it's a very different kind of wire from the kind
Margaret's father once put up on the land, Joe."

"Yes, Lucien Edmond, I can see that. His was a kind of
mesh; this has barbs on it. My God, if one of our bulls or
prize heifers got near it, there could be real damage!"

"Now that I think of it, I read in the San Antonio paper
that some experiments were being made with barbed wire
to keep away the rustlers and the sheep raisers and to pen
in the cattle. If memory serves me right, the Texas legislature was taking it under advisement. But here we've a real-
life example of what it is."

"Do you think, Lucien Edmond," Ramon spoke up, "we
should protest it?"

"Not right now. After all, our cattle haven't been hurt by
it. And we'll try to let them graze a little closer in. But if
there is trouble, I'd simply ask in a friendly way to have
that section taken down. After all, we have no intention of
going in on this man's land. We just want to make sure that
this boundary here between Joe's land and his doesn't inter-
fere with our own breeding and grazing. Let's go back
now."

With a last look at the formidable-appearing, taut strands of barbed wire between solidly implanted wooden stakes, Lucien Edmond Bouchard turned his horse's head back toward Windhaven Range.

CHAPTER THIRTY-THREE

The big, black Brahma bull was skittish, and Domingo Huerta, a twenty-year-old vaquero from Chihuahua whom Nacio Lorcas had hired in January, should have known better than to let it waste its strength galloping this way and that, pawing the ground and snorting as the heifers scattered. But he did not think there could be any harm. He rode along on his mustang toward the western edge of Joe Duvray's acreage. There were not many cattle at this end of the ranch.

Domingo was thinking of his *novia*, flirtatious seventeen-year-old Rita Sanchez, who had finally promised to marry him as soon as he had secured his position and put aside six months' wages to satisfy her irascible father. Rita's father did not really like Domingo, but the young vaquero knew that this was because Rita kept making eyes at nearly every personable suitor. Now that he had been here since January and sent several letters off to Rita in Chihuahua, to inform her proudly that he was putting away his wages, he was sure that they would be married well before the end of the year.

So he was riding in a pleasant, contemplative mood, not watching the Brahma bull as carefully as he should. Before he knew it, the bull had rushed at a heifer, which avoided it, and came up against the strange new fence, the likes of which Domingo had never seen before on the range.

The bull went down because of a gopher hole and with a wild bellow of pain it fell on its side against the sharp strands. The newly erected fence did not give way. Besides, one of Emory Carruthers's vaqueros had set it up the wrong way for some seventy-five feet along the western side of Joe's boundary, so that the barbs pointed upward rather than downward. The Brahma bull was bleeding badly. It lifted its head and emitted another agonized bellow of pain.

Horrified and believing that his daydreaming had caused the damage to a bull, which he knew to be a costly addition to the *patrón*'s herd, the young Mexican leaped down from his mustang and ran toward the bull. It thrashed and kicked, and he could see with a gasp of horror that its left foreleg was broken.

As he straightened, he saw the drops of blood along the strands of the barbed wire fence, and with an angry cry, distraught because of his own error of judgment, he looked about for some weapon with which to destroy this destructive fence. Not far away was a sharpened wooden stake, which had been left on Joe Duvray's side of the ground. Disregarding the bull's agonies, Domingo Huerta seized the stake and, swearing volubly, tears in his eyes, began to smash at the fence.

There was an angry shout beyond him, but he disregarded it. He went on striking and striking until at last the taut stretch of wire between two stakes began to sag. Then suddenly there was a shot, and just as he was in the act of raising the stake to strike again, he stiffened, his eyes widening and then glazing over. The stake dropped from his lifeless hands and he crumpled slowly to the ground, rolled over, and lay with one arm outstretched toward the thrashing, bellowing Brahma bull.

A stocky, heavily mustachioed Mexican in his early forties, Julio Marquez, walked slowly up to the wire fence, blowing the smoke away from the muzzle of his revolver, and then contemptuously shrugged. He watched the Brahma thrash and writhe, cocked the revolver, and put a bullet through its head to end its suffering. Then, with another shrug, he holstered the revolver, walked back to his gelding, mounted it, and rode back toward the bunkhouse to tell his *compañeros* what had taken place.

It was nearly sunset before Nacio Lorcas—riding out with some concern to look for Domingo Huerta because the young vaquero should have returned at least an hour earlier—discovered what had happened. Crossing himself and staring aghast at Domingo's inert body and that of the bull, he galloped back to the ranch house to find Lucien Edmond Bouchard in the midst of a conversation with Joe Duvray.

"*Patrón, patrón,* something terrible has happened! It is poor Domingo, he has been shot, and the new black bull is dead also. It is by the wire fence. It is terrible, *patrón!*"

"My God," Lucien Edmond gasped, as he rose from his chair, "it's happening all over again, Joe. You remember how Caldemare's foreman shot poor Ignacio Valdez? It's my fault. I should have called on this new neighbor of yours and found out exactly what he's up to. Come on, Nacio, arm yourself and join us. Joe, get two of the Spencer carbines. If they'd shoot down both poor Domingo and that fine young bull, they might be the sort of vaqueros who'd fire on anyone who rode up peacefully. No sense taking chances!"

A few minutes later, the three men rode toward the boundary of Joe Duvray's ranch, dismounted, and stared down at Domingo's sprawled body. Lucien Edmond crossed himself, uttered a muffled groan, and walked over to squat down and examine the dead bull. "It broke its foreleg," he reported. "Look, I see what did it—there's a gopher hole right by the fence. The bull got too close to it, caught its foreleg in the hole, and then toppled sideways down onto these strands of wire. Let's have a closer look at them—well, look here, the barbs are up at an angle. That can't be right. There's something very wrong here, Joe, Nacio."

"I think so myself, *patrón,*" Nacio solemnly replied. "And see, poor Domingo must have tried to break down the fence, when he saw what had happened to the bull. Do you see the stake that lies near him? And the wire is dented and loose between the two posts which hold it up."

"Yes, that's very plain. One of the vaqueros on that ranch must have seen him doing it—my God, and then he shot him down, just like that!" Lucien Edmond ejaculated, his face angry and drawn as he rose to his feet.

"We're going to go calling on this fellow, whoever he is, aren't we, Lucien Edmond?" Joe angrily demanded. "We'll have to ride due south for a spell till there's a break in the wire—a gate or something. See, there's the bunkhouse over yonder, quite a distance away. And beyond it is the house of whoever owns this property. No, it was just as much my fault as yours, not thinking of paying a social call on this fellow and finding out just what he had in mind. I didn't

371

like wire when Margaret's father had it put up, and I like this still less. I don't care what the newspaper says about its being safe, you can see it wasn't here. It not only cost us a bull, it got this fine young vaquero murdered in cold blood!"

The three men mounted their horses and rode south till they reached a gate, then turned in toward the clearing and made for the bunkhouse in the distance. As they neared it, they saw two vaqueros adjusting the saddles on their horses. One of them, seeing Lucien Edmond and his two companions approach, cupped his hands to his mouth and shouted something toward the ranch house.

"There's no help for it now, they know we've come calling," Joe Duvray said grimly, pulling the Spencer carbine from its saddle sheath and quickly inspecting it to make certain that it was fully loaded and in working order. "I'm going to hold this carbine up, just so they'll see we're not in a mood to get what poor Domingo got."

"Good idea, Joe," Lucien Edmond tersely concurred as, gripping the reins of his gelding in his left hand, he pulled his carbine from its sheath and brandished it aloft in his right hand.

Emory Carruthers and Julio Marquez came out of the house together. The new owner of the ranch wore a pair of holstered revolvers, while the glowering, moustachioed *capataz* had his right hand hovering near his holstered weapon.

"You're on private property, mister," Carruthers insolently called to Lucien Edmond, who rode slightly ahead of his two companions.

"I know that, but I've something to say to you. One of our men was shot down near your wire fence, and one of our prize new Brahmas with him. I'd like to have an explanation."

"And who might you be?" Carruthers stopped and stood, his hands on his hips but dangerously near the holsters, his eyes narrowed and cold. Julio Marquez turned to mutter something to him, but Carruthers shook his head.

"My name is Lucien Edmond Bouchard, this is Joe Duvray, my partner, and Nacio Lorcas, our *capataz*. I don't believe I know your name yet," Lucien Edmond replied as coldly.

"I'm Emory Carruthers. About your vaquero, Julio here tells me that he caught him in the act of trying to break

372

down my fence. The fencing is legal, in case you didn't know it."

"It's also barbed wire, and the Brahma was cut by it."

"I find that hard to believe, Mr. Bouchard. Perhaps you don't know it, but Joseph Glidden, who invented the fencing, brought it to Amarillo and proved to a very skeptical group of cattlemen that it was safe. I've been a cattleman for some years, and I saw this for myself: they penned a hundred head in a corral at Amarillo, and not a one of them was cut."

"Then it was put up wrong here. The barbs were up at an angle, and that doesn't seem logical."

"Logical or not, Mr. Bouchard, your vaquero was trying to break down my fence, and my *capataz* wasn't going to let him get away with it," Carruthers replied. "Once again, I'll remind you that it's legal, that the Texas legislature is approving the use of barbed wire, and that I intend to use it, just so that your cattle won't wander onto my land and vice versa. I think that's all I have to say to you."

"It's not all I have to say to you, by a damn sight, Mr. Carruthers." Lucien Edmond was very close to losing his temper. "Domingo Huerta wasn't carrying a gun. There wasn't any reason for your *capataz* to shoot him down. At least he could have warned him, or fired a warning shot over his head and told him to get away. Domingo Huerta was an honest, hard-working young man who wanted nothing more than to live his life in peace. He was aiming to get married, and he was saving his wages for it. He wasn't the sort to pick a fight, or to ignore a warning—if, that is, he'd been given one."

"I did warn him, señor," Marquez drawled with a covert wink at his employer which Lucien Edmond perceived with rising anger. "I called to him, but he kept on smashing the stake against the wire fence. I could not stand by and let my *patrón's* property be damaged."

"You still didn't have to shoot him, when you saw he had no gun," was Lucien Edmond's angry reply.

"I had no way of seeing that, señor. And it is not my fault if he was a fool and did not carry a gun when he rode with the *ganado*."

"You're a liar and a *cobarde*!" Nacio Lorcas flashed.

"No man calls me that! *Señor patrón*, must we stand here listening to these men who come to insult you?" Julio Marquez demanded of his employer.

373

"Get off my land, Mr. Bouchard! And I'm warning you, if any of your men try to break down my fencing, I won't be responsible for the consequences," Emory Carruthers snarled.

"So that's your answer," Lucien Edmond Bouchard said, his voice shaking with rage. "I think I'd like to know a good deal more about you and your background, Mr. Carruthers. You've let me know only that you're new to Texas. That's not the way neighbors behave out here in Texas, let me assure you. I think I'll ride over to the land office and do a little investigating of you and your property."

At these words, Carruthers turned pale, took a step backwards, and then both hands plunged down toward his holstered revolvers.

"Look out, Lucien Edmond!" Joe Duvray cried as he raised his carbine. But before he could fire it, the arrogant Californian had drawn both revolvers and fired them simultaneously. One of the bullets took Lucien Edmond in the left shoulder. Joe Duvray's carbine shot caught Carruthers in the chest and flung him backwards, staggering. He dropped his revolvers, turned to one side, and then fell to the ground. Julio Marquez, with a vile oath, flung himself down on the ground, his revolver drawn, and fanned it with his left hand to empty its contents. Nacio Lorcas uttered a cry and clutched at his right thigh, dropping his own revolver from the unexpected pain of the bullet, which shattered a bone. But Lucien Edmond whirled and leveled a shot with his carbine, and the moustachioed *capataz* bowed his bloody forehead to the ground and lay still.

"My God, why did he go for his guns?" Joe groaned as he hurried over to his wounded partner. "Is it bad, Lucien Edmond?"

"No, it throbs a lot, but I think it's just in the fleshy part of the shoulder." Lucien Edmond gritted his teeth against the pain. "Nacio's hurt worse, though. It's his leg. We'll have to help him onto his horse."

"Look out, some of the vaqueros are coming out of the bunkhouse," Joe warned. "I'll handle them!" Swiftly mounting his gelding, he brandished his carbine and shouted in Spanish, "We came in peace, *hombres*! One of our vaqueros, who carried no weapon, was shot down by your *capataz*. And one of our bulls with him. We came only to ask your *patrón* why this was done, and he and your *capataz* drew their guns and fired at us. We had to defend ourselves. We want no fight with you, *comprenden?*"

The vaquero who had run to the ranch house to inform Emory Carruthers and Julio Marquez of their arrival moved closer to his horse, turned his back, then suddenly whirled and fired his revolver directly at Joe Duvray. Joe reeled in his saddle as the bullet pierced the fleshy part of his right arm. But he was able to lift the carbine and trigger a shot that dropped the vaquero in his tracks. Instantly, the other men who had come out of the bunkhouse raised their hands and cried out that they wanted no part of this fight.

"Let's ride back as fast as we can, Lucien Edmond," Joe hoarsely panted. "Nacio's leg is bad, it needs attention. The bone might be broken. Can you hold out till we get back to the ranch, Nacio?"

"*Sí*," the *capataz* gasped, wincing at the pain.

Joe transferred his carbine to his left hand, holding the reins laxly in his right, as his wound began to throb. He rode up to the frightened vaqueros lined up against the side of the bunkhouse and, gesturing with the carbine, demanded, "Which one of you knows anything about your *patrón*? Where did he come from, does he have kin, what can you tell us about him? He is dead, and so there is no owner of this hacienda, of these *ganado*. There will be no jobs for you. There will be no one to pay you. Come now, which of you can tell me anything about him?"

"I—I can, señor." A stout little man in his early forties timidly moved forward, his hands still raised in surrender. "It was our *capataz*, Julio Marquez, who told us about the Señor Carruthers. He had an *abogado* in Sacramento who handled his affairs."

"*Gracias.* Do you know his name?"

"No, señor." The stout little vaquero shook his head, frowning with intense concentration. Then he brightened and volunteered, "But there is certain to be something in the hacienda, among the papers of the Señor Carruthers. Perhaps a letter from this *abogado*."

"Do you read and write, *hombre?*" Joe Duvray demanded, fighting off the waves of pain that assailed him.

"*¡Pero sí!* I will go into the house and try to find it for you, señor. We are peaceful men. There are others here who were hired as *pistoleros*, in case of trouble. But my *amigos* in the bunkhouse have already told them what has

375

happened, and they do not have any stomach for a fight, not when there is no one to pay them. Wait here. I will go to the house and find you what I can about the *abogado*."

Three weeks later, Frank Caswell arrived at Windhaven Range to confer with Lucien Edmond Bouchard. Joe Duvray, Eddie Gentry, Ramón Hernandez, and Nacio Lorcas were present. One of Lucien Edmond's vaqueros had ridden to San Antonio to bring back a doctor to set the shattered bone in Nacio's thigh. He was able to walk now on improvised crutches, and the doctor had assured him that by the end of the year he would be fit again for the saddle.

After Frank Caswell had heard Lucien Edmond and Joe relate their part in the needless murder of young Domingo Huerta and the Brahma bull, which had resulted in the unforeseen gun duel that had killed his client, he somberly shook his head and was silent for a long moment.

"Perhaps it's as well," he said at last. "Emory Carruthers was a man haunted by a tragedy that was, in its way, just as senseless as this one. He wanted a ranch, a home, a wife and children. He married the daughter of a Sacramento politician who was exactly the wrong woman for him. And when he found her and his foreman in bed together, he killed them and had their bodies buried where they wouldn't be found."

"My God!" Lucien Edmond said softly.

"He put me through law school, he gave me a career, he was kind and generous to me. To my mind, he acted from one of the oldest motives known to man, the unwritten law, as we call it. But his wife's father was a powerful politician, and Emory was afraid that his story might not be believed and he might even be hanged for double murder. That's why he sold his ranch and came to Texas."

"If only he hadn't gone for his guns that day," Lucien Edmond gloomily mused.

"I think your remark about investigating his background on going to the land office in Austin was what set him off. I think he was driven by the fear that, some day, lawmen might find him and bring him back to answer for what he had done to his wife and her lover. You can't be blamed for that, Mr. Bouchard, you couldn't possibly have known it."

"But what's to be done about his land and the cattle?" Joe Duvray spoke up.

"I've thought of something." Frank Caswell was silent for a moment, pondering. Then he nodded decisively. "Yes, it makes as much sense as anything else. You see, he had no kin at all. And certainly the property can't be left to his dead wife or to her father. I've a proposal. Since I was his attorney and was empowered to act for him—which holds over until he's officially pronounced dead in a California court—I could sell you this property. I would donate the proceeds to worthy charities, taking only a token fee to cover my expenses for the time I've spent in this matter."

"That's damned decent of you, Mr. Caswell," Joe exclaimed.

"I owe him a debt I can't ever repay. Maybe some of the money could be used for scholarships at California schools in his name, or be given to hospitals. That way, it would be a memorial to him, and all the money he had, which unfortunately never did him very much good, could be well spent. So, if you're agreeable to such a proposal, let me work out the details and draw up a deed."

"We'll have to do that at the land office in Austin, Mr. Caswell. We'll ride over there tomorrow, if it's convenient for you. And we'll pay you a fair price," Lucien Edmond said. Then he turned to Joe Duvray. "It's adjacent to your holdings, Joe. You're the one to supervise it. And I've an idea, Mr. Caswell, which may pay a kind of late tribute to an unfortunate, misguided man who probably was more sinned against than sinning. The cattle on that range will be branded C & C, after you and Emory Carruthers."

CHAPTER THIRTY-FOUR

It was the Year of the Century. It was the year of the stolen election. It was the year in which a great national hero, ending his second term as President of the United States, came to see himself vilified and denigrated, not for what he had done, but because of what his trusted associates had done under cover of his shortsighted management. It was the year of the Centennial Exposition in Philadelphia. It was the year of Custer and of Sitting Bull, in which a supposedly great military hero and his gallant men were massacred by a supposed arch-villain. It was the end of one era, the chaotic beginning of another. It was also the year that marked the sixtieth birthday of Luke Bouchard.

For Luke Bouchard's native state of Alabama, it was also a new era. Slightly more than a year before, George Smith Houston had been inaugurated as governor of Alabama, restoring Democratic, white government to the state. With that inauguration, Radical Reconstruction ended; now began the period of reactionary "Bourbon democracy," which took its name—and its inspiration—from the Bourbon king of France, Charles X, who declared that the French Revolution and all its ideals meant nothing to him. Just as Charles X had expected life in France in 1824 to be the same as it had been under the old regime, so the Democratic leaders of Alabama now expected a return to politics as they had been before the Civil War.

In one respect, the Alabama political climate was not wholly reactionary: last year the Alabama legislature had adopted a new constitution which was moderate, in that it neither abolished universal manhood suffrage, nor repudiated popular election of the executive and judicial officers; in short, it did not attempt to disfranchise the Negro.

379

It also put forward some measures of reform: it sought to restore credit, cut expenses, correct government abuses while preserving state's rights, develop mining and advancement of manufacturing, invite immigration and capital into the state, and encourage education for children. It encouraged railroads and industry, while disavowing the scandalous corruption of the Alabama and Chattanooga Railroad.

For all this Democratic surge in Alabama, the leaders of the new era were more often former Whigs than lifelong Democrats. The fact that Andy Haskins was a Republican in no way militated against his popularity. His forthright stand on the theme that government should be the servant, not the master, of the people, his voting on bills whose purpose was to benefit the small towns as well as the urban centers and encourage individual enterprise, had won him acclaim among all political leaders of Alabama, Democrats as well as Republicans. There was even thought, during this spring of 1876, of encouraging the one-armed Tennesseean to run for the state senate.

On Luke Bouchard's sixtieth birthday, his devoted wife, Laure, held a festive party in the large dining room of the red-brick chateau. Dalbert and Mitzi Sattersfield attended with their four children, Mitzi having given birth in February to a girl whom she and her one-armed storekeeper husband had named Julia. Andy Haskins and Jessica were there, with their two children, for in January Jessica had given birth to a son she had insisted on naming Andrew after his father. Andrew's birth had given Jessica particular pleasure, for she had suffered two miscarriages since the birth of Horatio in 1872.

Marius Thornton, his Clemmie, and their six children had places of honor at the birthday table, as did Burt Coleman and his wife and their infant son. Buford Phelps and his wife and infant daughter also attended; the once-belligerent representative of the Freedmen's Bureau had just been promoted by Dalbert Sattersfield to manager of the latter's store in Lowndesboro, for last fall Sattersfield had opened a second store in a small town ten miles down-river, and he was concentrating most of his attention on the new branch. And Lopasuta Bouchard, now one of the most prominent attorneys in Montgomery, sat at Luke Bouchard's right hand, with Laure and the children at Luke's left.

At the conclusion of the festive dinner, Luke rose, wine goblet in hand, and at the urging of his guests proposed a toast. Tall and erect as ever, his hair and beard now completely gray, his eyes youthful and serene, he contemplated the smiling, attentive faces around him, and then said, "To the centennial, to the progress of our beloved country and our state. To Grandfather and his Dimarte, who made Windhaven Plantation possible and whose love and compassion have helped it to endure." After that toast had been drunk, he turned to Laure and, lifting his goblet toward her with a courtly bow, added, "To my wife, whose love and loyalty have made me forget my having reached this venerable age of three score. May God grant me many more happy years to enjoy her company and to see the wonderful children she has given me begin to take their places in the society of the future."

Laure then rose, her eyes wet with tears, and kissed her husband amid affectionate laughter and applause.

On the very day of Luke Bouchard's sixtieth birthday, Charles Douglas was cutting the red, white, and blue ribbon across the door of his Houston department store. Max Steinfeldt, who had been the contractor and supervisor of the highly successful Galveston store, had agreed to take the post of manager in the new branch, and he and his wife, Alice, had moved to Houston to take up residence in their new house about ten blocks from the Chicago businessman's latest venture. Their little boy, John, born in January of 1874, was now a strapping youngster whose lively antics were the delight—and sometimes the bane—of his doting parents.

Thanks to the enthusiastic cooperation of Mayor Scanlan, Charles Douglas had managed to overcome the difficulties of building the modest but attractive two-story edifice and arranging for the transportation of merchandise from the port of Galveston to Houston. The mayor had suggested that Charles build a warehouse just twenty miles from Houston, near Buffalo Bayou, for the storage of goods during the summer months when Houston still maintained its apprehensive quarantine against shipments from Galveston. This arrangement proved to be ideal; instead of having to ship his goods by rail all the way from Galveston, Charles could have them brought by boat up the bayou and unloaded at the warehouse before the start of the quaran-

381

tine season. Then, even in summer, the merchandise could be loaded on freight cars and carried into Houston via a brand-new extension of the Galveston, Houston and Henderson Railroad.

James Hunter was on hand also to participate in the official opening of the Houston store. He and Charles had spent a week in Galveston prior to the opening in Houston. James had the air of a man who was well content with his achievements in life. Melinda and Lawrence Davis now had two sons, Gary and James, and a tiny daughter, Denise, born in the spring of 1875. And Andrew had married Della Morley, the daughter of Cousin Jeremy's mill foreman, and the couple had gone to settle on a small ranch near Austin. Arabella had become a patroness of the Galveston opera and symphony, and was also spending a good deal of her time raising money for the construction of a new hospital.

The hospital staff saw frequent cases of yellow fever, which was a source of great concern to James. As he said to Charles, "I think all of us are more and more concerned with this fever, Charles. So far, our health officers say only that a previous warm winter and a hot, moist summer are favorable to the disease, but they don't know exactly why. And they still haven't found out what causes it. Some of them still think that it's the porous soil which—as they phrase it—exhales insalubrious vapors and miasmic germs. But if that hospital succeeds in cutting down the number of deaths we have every year in Galveston, it'll be God's own blessing."

Wichita was booming, for it had successfully weathered the transition from a cattle town to a farming and trading community. Settlers were pouring in, closing the range to the great cattle drives of earlier years. Now many of the Texas ranchers were sending herds up through Colorado, some to feed the booming gold camps of the Black Hills. The reservation Sioux, who still claimed the Hills, threatened them at times, but a few head of cattle were usually all that was required to pacify them, for they were beginning to starve for want of buffalo meat.

Dr. Ben Wilson, now in his early forties, had become one of the most beloved citizens of Wichita. He and his wife, Elone, and their children were admired and respected. Only once did any newcomer make the mistake of

382

calling the earnest Quaker doctor a squaw man. If he did it in the hearing of oldtimers, he was swiftly warned to forget that disparaging term.

Elone had always understood that her gentle white-eyes husband was unlike any other white man she or her people had ever known. This was the reason for the empathy that had sprung up between them from their very first meeting at the Creek reservation; this was why she had known deep within her heart that this man was good and kind, and that marriage to him would be the fulfillment of dreams she had scarcely dared have. Always, from her childhood, she had known that she might be wed to any brave who could provide food and shelter for her parents. Such unions were mainly economic, and rarely did love grow out of them. Furthermore, her abduction by the Kiowas and enforced union with the chief had brought her to a fatalistic acceptance of her lowly destiny as a female. Yet now, she found her dreams fulfilled. She found herself loved, respected, cherished. To walk with Ben Wilson on the streets of Wichita was an incredible daily proof that he set as much store by her as if she had been white.

Along with her mastery of the English language, she had begun also to think as a white woman would, caring for her man and loving him as an equal. She had harbored misgivings that there would be hardships for him, here in Wichita, where he might be mocked as a squaw man. But what had reassured her and shown her that there was little to fear on that score was the friendship that had developed between Ben and two of his former patients, Dave Haggerson and Dallas Masterson, men whose personal lives seemed to have nothing in common with that of the kindly Quaker doctor.

Dallas Masterson was by now the best gambler in Wichita, having quit his job as trail boss for a Texas outfit four years ago, to become a faro dealer in a local gambling hall. He had never forgotten how Dr. Ben Wilson had saved his life, three years ago, after he had been shot near the lung by a man who accused him of cheating at the card table. Nor had Ben forgotten how Dallas subsequently had thrashed a loud-mouthed drunkard who had called the Quaker doctor a squaw man. In the years since then, Dallas had continued to be Ben's most admiring champion in Wichita.

Last year, Dallas had befriended a young waitress who

383

had run away from a squalid home in St. Louis, where her stepfather had turned her into a virtual slave. Pretty twenty-year-old Flora Colcroft fell in love with the mature cowhand-gambler; having learned from one of his intimates that he stayed aloof from women because of a disappointing love affair years before in New Orleans, she had taken her courage in her hands the previous September and boldly declared her love for him. "I want to be your wife, Mr. Masterson, and I'll make you a good and faithful one, I promise," she told him. He tried to dissuade her, but Flora only persisted the more till at last, secretly aware of his own loneliness, he agreed. Now once again Dallas Masterson was thinking of changing his profession, because gambling wasn't really a proper calling for a family man.

On a pleasant fall evening in 1875, soon after Flora had made her astonishing avowal, Dallas called on Dr. Ben Wilson at the latter's house, and when Elone opened the door, doffed his Stetson and stammered, "Evenin', Mrs. Wilson, ma'am. Do you suppose, if it wouldn't bother him too much, I could have a word with your husband?"

Elone served tea to the two men, along with biscuits and honey, then excused herself temporarily to look after the children. She was pregnant again, and Dallas Masterson looked after her, sighed, then turned back to Ben. "You know, I've been thinking a heap of gettin' hitched myself."

"It would be a fine idea, Mr. Masterson. Every man needs companionship, especially as he grows older. You can see how I'm blessed."

"Damn right you are—excuse my language—and I don't mind saying I'm downright envious. You know"—he stared almost defiantly at the Quaker doctor—"I can see right off what you and your missus have here is a lot happier than the setups I can see between lots of nice, big-talking, high-muckity-muck folks here in Wichita. I see them go to church on Sunday, then I catch word of how they squabble all the time. But this house has got plenty of love in it. Yes sir, Dr. Wilson, I think I'm going to marry this li'l girl Flora. Er—would you mind if I brought her over some evening? I'd powerful like to have you and your missus—well, you know—look her over—she doesn't have many friends here—"

"Of course, Elone and I would be very happy to make her welcome, Mr. Masterson."

After a few more minutes of serious conversation, in

384

which Elone participated, and in the course of which Dallas Masterson confided some of his cherished hopes for the future, the gambler rose to take his leave. "Thanks for everything, Doc, and thanks to you too, Mrs. Wilson. You're real good friends. Just let me catch anybody in Wichita looking even sideways at you folks, they won't find it healthy to stay in town much longer. Well, good night. And thanks, Mrs. Wilson, for the feed. It was great." He chuckled. "I don't mind telling you, knowing that Flora's a good cook and enjoying your biscuits the way I did tonight, I'm certain I'm going to take her up on this marriage business."

"You do that, Dallas—do you mind if I call you that?"

"Hell, Doc, who's got a better right? You saved my life." Dallas put out his hand and Ben Wilson shook it.

"I'd like it if you'd invite Elone and me to the wedding. And I'd be proud if you'd accept my offer to be godfather to your first baby—after I deliver it, of course," Ben smilingly proffered.

Bluff Dallas Masterson went red in the face and fumbled with his Stetson. "Hey now, Doc," he protested, "better wait till we get hitched up before you talk about babies. Well, I'm much obliged for the talk and the refreshments. Thanks again!"

Dave Haggerson, tall, graybearded, and in his late forties, had been a schoolteacher in Iowa before the Civil War. He had married one of his pupils, a gentle girl far more mature than her eighteen years might suggest. During the war he had served for two years in an Iowa regiment, been wounded and mustered out three months before Appomattox. After the war, a cousin of his who had moved to Wichita died and left him a small farm on the outskirts of the town, and he and his wife, Elaine, eagerly moved to it. A year before Dr. Ben Wilson first visited Wichita to buy supplies for Emataba and the Creeks, Elaine died in childbirth, and the sickly boy followed her to the grave eight short days later. Dave Haggerson went back to teaching. At times on a Saturday night, when he felt the pangs of loneliness most keenly, he would visit the gambling hall where Dallas Masterson ran the faro table, and the two men became fast friends and confidants.

Indeed, a week after the gambler had first intimated to Dr. Ben Wilson that he was thinking of marrying, both he and Dave Haggerson visited the Quaker doctor to announce the marriage would take place in two weeks and that Haggerson had volunteered to be best man. Ben and Elone came to the church to witness the ceremony, after which Elone cooked a bridal feast for the happy couple. With these two loyal male friends, Elone happily felt certain, there could no longer be any question of her beloved husband's acceptance in Wichita. And at the meeting of the Society of Friends the following Sunday, presided over by Pastor Jacob Hartmann, she gave thanks to God for the happiness He had granted her and her husband and for the true friends who had enriched their lives.

In March of 1876, Elone presented Ben with a little girl, whom they named Amy. Then, on Luke Bouchard's sixtieth birthday, Elone and her husband and Amy began a journey to the Creek reservation in Indian Territory, while Pastor Jacob Hartmann and his wife, Tabitha, looked after the other Wilson children. Word had come the previous week from an army rider that Emataba, *mico* of the Creeks, was ailing. The rider told Ben that the fort doctor, whom the Indian agent Douglas Larrimer had appointed to make regular visits to the reservation, was greatly concerned about Emataba's rapidly failing health.

"I must go to him, my darling," Ben had said. "It was through him that I met you, and him I must thank, as well as our dear Lord, for the joy and the new life you and the children have given me. If I had not come to the reservation when I did, I should not have found you," Ben had told Elone. And she had nodded, with a quiet little smile, and said, "And I must go also, for I owe him great thanks for the shelter he gave Tisinqua and me when I fled to him and his people."

He had attempted to dissuade her from making the long journey with him by horse and buggy, but she had shaken her head and smilingly responded, "But I shall nurse Amy, as I would do if I stayed in Wichita. We will be together, my husband, and Emataba will see that we bring forth new life and take joy in each other. Have you not often said that he and his people are penned away like animals, and that the young men grow old and resentful with no hope of a good life before them? He will see, when I bring little Amy, that you and I remember the vow we both took when we were in his village, that we would tell all who come after Emataba and his people of their honor and dignity, of their love for peace and for truth and for friendship." And she had added sadly, with a sorrowful look on her lovely face, "What I read in the newspaper of the way in which the white man looks upon the Indian as a hateful, murderous savage often makes me weep. Will it always be so, my husband?"

"I don't know, Elone, my darling. But so long as there are people like you and me to tell others what we know, what we have learned by living with them, perhaps one day there will be understanding and tolerance. I pray for it constantly."

They rode into the village of the Creeks on the first day of May, but Emataba did not emerge from his tepee to greet them. With a feeling of foreboding, Ben helped Elone down with the baby in her arms, and as they walked toward the rickety gate, Sipanata, who was standing nearby talking with two of the younger braves, hurried forward to meet them.

"It is good to see you, Sipanata," the Quaker doctor exclaimed as he gripped the hand of the brave who had helped teach him the Creek tongue and who had told him that Elone longed to be his squaw, in those desolate days when he had believed that his grief for Fleurette would overwhelm him. "I have heard that Emataba is ill, Sipanata. And when he did not come out to greet us, my fears redoubled."

"Yes, he is dying, shaman. The shaman from the army saw him three days ago, and told us that he could do nothing. He wastes away. I do not know whether it is from the grief he had borne so long since all of us came to this lonely village, or whether it is a sickness which perhaps he acquired from the white-eyes." Sipanata made a bitter gesture. "The white-eyes who are not like you, shaman, have given us much in return for our land. They have enslaved our people; they have brought sicknesses to us which we never knew before; and now it is said that the Great White Father himself in Washington would be happier if none of us were upon this land. You know now why, when you first came here, I hated you. But you, blood brother to Emataba and good shaman and friend to the Creeks, are not like those men, so do not think my angry words touch you."

"I have never thought that, Sipanata. May I see him?"

"Yes. He has spoken of you these last few days, hoping that he would see you before his time comes. I will take

387

you to him. One of the old squaws does what she can for him."

"Elone and our new child will come with me also, Sipanata."

"It is Elone!" Sipanata turned and smiled at the gentle young Aiyuta woman. "You and the child are more than welcome here. You bring life, in the midst of death. It is a good thing. Come now."

His heart heavy, Ben followed Sipanata to the tepee of the *mico* of the Creeks, and Elone, carrying Amy, came with him. The Quaker doctor saw at once that the tall Creek leader was wasted, his eyes hollow, his breathing forced and heavy, and the white-haired squaw who rose quickly when they entered shook her head, her eyes filled with tears.

"I welcome the shaman of the white-eyes," she murmured, as she stopped a moment to give him a long, meaningful look. "The Great Spirit will soon call him. He has been our life, and now he is to be taken from us."

"I will pray to the Great Spirit to look well upon this great chief, Jusunte," Ben reverently murmured.

He knelt down and reached for Emataba's hand. The Creek chieftain slowly opened his eyes and stared, at first blankly, then with a faint smile of recognition. "My—my brother. You have come. I prayed that you would, for I do not think that I shall see you again upon this earth."

"I have brought Elone and our new child, a little girl whom we have named Amy, Emataba."

"Let me see the child."

"Do not try to move, rest yourself, Emataba," the Quaker doctor compassionately urged, as quickly and deftly he felt for the *mico*'s pulse and then the heartbeat. They were weak. Just then Emataba coughed, and Ben bit his lips. The signs were all too plain: an advanced case of consumption for which his own science had no remedy.

Elone knelt down and held up the baby, staring with tear-filled eyes at the *mico*'s gaunt face. "Here is our child, my *mico*," she murmured. "I asked my husband to bring me to you, that I might thank you for the refuge you gave me and Tisinqua when we fled from the evil men who killed the Kiowas. If you had not taken us in, I should not have met this man who has fulfilled me as a woman and mother, and thus I shall owe you to the end of my days a

388

debt that cannot be paid, except in my heart and my prayers."

The faint smile returned to Emataba's lips. He closed his eyes and seemed to rest a moment. Then he murmured, "Now I am at peace and I await the summons of Him who is the Giver of Breath, Ibofanaga, who knows all things and the thoughts of the lowliest as the highest."

Ben could not see Emataba's face for his own tears which he fought to control. He reached for the *mico*'s hand and pressed it to his own heart and murmured, "You are my blood brother. Your Great Spirit is mine also, Emataba, as He is Elone's and our children's. And for all your people and those who will come after them, it will always be the same. Elone and I will teach our children to respect all that you've stood for, all that you and your people once were and still are, even if mine look down upon you. This I swear to you by the bond that has made us brothers."

"It is good. I do not fear the call of Ibofanaga now. I do not—" A rattling cough shook the wasted body. Emataba opened his eyes, feverish, unseeing, and then he slumped back on his pallet. The faint smile on his face lingered.

Jusunte peered into the tepee. She saw the *mico* lying still upon his pallet and uttered a wailing cry. She turned and hobbled toward the center of the village, her undulating voice ascending in the stillness as the sky turned purple and red with the oncoming twilight. The villagers came out of their tepees to chorus her lament; the women went to the campfires and rubbed ashes upon their foreheads and their braids.

At dawn the next morning, Dr. Wilson and Sipanata dug a grave for the *mico* at the eastern end of the little village. They chose a site beyond the rotting fence as a symbol that, at last, the leader of the Creeks had found liberation from his oppressors. As the villagers stood, Ben delivered a simple speech in the Creek tongue: "Henceforth his name shall not be spoken, but his deeds and most of all his love for the Creeks will dwell within our hearts and our souls. It will be told of him that he brought his people from the land of the Creeks to a far-away place where the white-eyes herded them in, as was done with the black slaves of the land they had left so long ago. I stand before you as his blood brother, and therefore, brother to all of you this day, and with me stands Elone, my wife who was Aiyuta, then

389

Kiowa, and is now of my white-eyes faith. She, too, and our children with us both, will remember the name we do not speak henceforth. And our children will go forth among the white-eyes to say that the Creeks were noble and strong, and that they bowed to no man, and that even in their betrayal by the white-eyes they did not lose their courage and their honor. And it will come to pass, long after our names and yours are said no longer, that the wise ones will look upon the Creeks and say, 'Here was a race blessed by Ibofanaga and cherished eternally by Him who knows that which is good and that which is evil.' Now your *mico* has joined Him in the skies and watches down upon you. May you be blessed always by that knowledge, though you do not say it even among yourselves."

He and Sipanata had dug the grave and placed the body of the *mico* in a sitting position, that he might answer the summons on that day when all men are judged. And then the earth covered him forever.

Many miles to the south, near the little village of Miero, which had become the stronghold of the Wanderers, Sangrodo walked with Catayuna near the pleasant little creek from which the villagers drew their water. The lovely, stately Mexican woman carried in her arms a month-old boy, whom she had named Nahubiyaa, He Who Sings a Song for Someone. For almost at once after birth, the baby had gurgled and cooed, smiled joyously and waved his tiny hands. Catayuna had said to her Comanche husband, "He wishes to talk, to sing, to bring happiness to his people. So let us give him this name, that it may become his destiny."

"I give thanks to the Great Spirit for our little son, beloved woman." Sangrodo turned to Catayuna, his eyes glowing with warmth as they fixed on the baby she carried at her breast. "And the name you have given him is a prophetic one. It is my wish, remembering how the young brave Lopasuta brought honor to all our tribe, that when our little son grows to manhood, he will study the books of the white-eyes and perhaps speak out for our people, as Lopasuta does. Truly have you named him to accomplish this, my beloved woman."

"It is my joy to find favor in the eyes of my husband," she murmured, eyes downcast.

His face grew thoughtful. "And yet, riders come to us from the north and tell us that the People, like the Penateka, are driven by the soldiers of the white-eyes and by those who hunt buffalo. It is as if the white-eyes wish to be rid of us for all time. And if this is truly so, then it is well that we remain here in our stronghold across the Rio Grande and accustom ourselves to this strange new way of tilling the soil and being content with its bounty."

"I echo your words, my husband, for they are my thoughts also," Catayuna softly replied.

"Kitante will one day prove himself to be a worthy chief of the Wanderers. It is good that he is no longer restless with the life we lead here. He has his mate, and she has given him a strong son, Kwaku-h, He Who Wins Out. This, too, is a name that pleases me, Catayuna."

"Yes, for it shows that your oldest son accepts his fate and yet is determined to do great things with his life and to teach his son, in turn, how to live with honor and with a straight tongue."

"Catayuna," he turned to her and took her by the shoulders and smiled at her, "if someone had told me long ago that you, a *mejicana* and the *esposa* of a man who was our enemy, would one day be the beloved woman of our tribe and to me beloved in more than this, I would have laughed and said that he had eaten too much loco weed. I have learned much from you in all this time. You have shown me that one may conquer with love and gentleness and peace, instead of by force and in battle. I am content, and I am teaching my people to be content also. All of us work for the good of our people, so that no man or woman or child may go hungry or without shelter, or without those who are friends when friends are most needed. This is what you have taught me, Catayuna." He uttered a soft laugh and then added, "I do not think ever in the history of the People there has been a squaw who wore a chief's bonnet. But I say this to you, beloved woman, that if I were gone and if I had had no sons by you, if you were to wear the bonnet, our people would be strongly led."

"My husband pays me too much honor, I am not worthy." Catayuna bowed her head, but the way she hugged her tiny son to her and the ineffable look of love in her dark eyes spoke better than words between them.

CHAPTER THIRTY-FIVE

Charles Douglas and James Hunter stayed on for a week in Houston to see how the new store would catch on with Houston shoppers, and both expressed themselves delighted with the initial crowds. News of the store reached Galveston via a highly laudatory—and even somewhat envious—article about it in the local newspaper. Alexander Gorth—who had by now married his pretty Katie and become the father of a little girl, Jennifer—read the article with interest and resolved that if he could, he would not only make the acquaintance of Mr. Douglas, but would also make a trip to see his new Houston outlet.

The Gorth store was drawing its own share of patrons, because its young, enthusiastic owner was more than willing to work on a small profit margin, devoting long hours to his work, and he had eliminated shoddy merchandise from his counters and shelves. One evening, over the supper table, he told Katie, "Some day, honey, we're going to have a store just like the Douglas stores, you'll see." To this, his practical young wife saucily retorted, "Never you mind, Alex, I didn't marry you to be the wife of a rich tycoon. And you might just consider the possibility that if you can't get any bigger, Mr. Douglas might sit down with you and buy you out. He'd probably give you a darned good job in his store and then you could spend more time home evenings with your wife and family."

Charles Douglas left for New Orleans, to buy Laurette and the children some presents and to enjoy a week's vacation. He would be glad to return to Chicago, and he was grateful now that he and Laurette had decided not to move to Texas, after all; Charles had become a thoroughgoing Chicagoan, and hated the thought of moving.

Before leaving Galveston, Charles noticed that his partner was looking somewhat peaked, and he advised James that a few weeks' vacation wouldn't do him any harm. They shook hands at the dock, and Arabella's gray-haired husband said almost wistfully, "Well, time enough for a vacation once I'm sure that both our stores are on an even keel, Charles. Who knows, I might even bring Bella along and pay a visit to Chicago. I've never seen it, you know."

"You just let me know when you want to come, and I'll take both of you on a guided tour as my very special guests," the Chicago businessman promised as they parted.

One of Max Steinfeldt's own ideas, with which Charles had heartily concurred, was the use of gracious, well-informed, but never obsequious floorwalkers who would suggest special sale items to customers. The floorwalker, in Max's opinion, should greet the customer, approach her if she seemed uncertain as to what she wanted, and then casually mention that there was such and such merchandise on sale and where to find it. The idea had already been put to work in Galveston, and Max's energetic wife, Alice, during her stint as a bookkeeper, had observed a noticeable rise in the volume of special-sale merchandise which could be directly attributed to the efforts of the floorwalkers. Max had promised Charles Douglas that he would try to select an especially good one for the Houston enterprise. And, just a week after the Chicagoan had gone back home, he believed he had found one.

The man was Keith McNallis, thirty-four, black-haired, suave, dapper, and very neatly groomed. He had come into the store, looked around for a bit, and then asked one of the clerks somewhat diffidently whom he might see concerning a position. The clerk had referred him to Max Steinfeldt who had interviewed him.

As it chanced, Alice had visited her husband that afternoon to give him a report on the previous week's business, having left her son, John, in the care of his nurse. She had become an expert bookkeeper and sometimes she teased Max, saying that he really ought to pay her a salary for making her work on the books at home; but she really enjoyed being able to contribute. Max had proved to be a devoted husband—a considerate and gentle lover who fulfilled her as a woman and an admirable father to their son, who was now a little more than two years old.

Alice was just leaving Max's office when Keith McNallis was waiting to be summoned for an interview. Alice looked him up and down and took an instinctive dislike to him. When Max returned home that evening, he mentioned that he had hired the man as a floorwalker.

"You mean the man who was waiting outside to see you, Max dear?" Alice incredulously asked.

"Yes, the very one. From your tone, I gather you didn't take a fancy to him."

"Max, you're a wonderful husband, you're all a girl could ever hope for. But you can't possibly have a woman's intuition about people. To me, that man is someone I'd be distrustful of from the very start. He's too smooth-looking, and he knows just how handsome he is. Oh, I'll grant you he could turn a girl's head in a jiffy—except he wouldn't turn mine, not with someone like you around."

"Now that's what I like to hear from my girl," Max chuckled, as he pulled Alice to him and gave her a hugely satisfying kiss. Then he added, "But, honey, you can't really expect to judge a man properly just from a casual glance, and that's all you had. You didn't hear his story. He's really been down on his luck. He's been used to better things, obviously, but he came in here humbly and eagerly and looking for a job, so I'm going to give him a chance."

"What did he tell you, darling?"

"Well, that he used to own his own store in New Orleans. He played cards occasionally, and he ran afoul of a cardsharp who not only cheated him out of the store, but also romanced his wife behind his back and made her run off with him. Now that's really hard luck."

Alice frowned and shook her head. "And if I'd been sitting there, I don't think I would have taken that story without a full saltshaker. Max, if the man was steady and reliable, why in the world would he gamble away his store?"

"I thought of that too," Max sheepishly admitted. "McNallis said that this fellow let him win a few pots every now and then, just enough to lure him on. Before he knew it, he was playing for big stakes and going well beyond his capital. Then, like a great many amateurs, he got desperate and tried to win everything on the luck of one hand—now that could happen to anybody."

"Not to either of us, and you know it, Max Steinfeldt," Alice insisted. "You mark my words, he may bring in business for you, but he'll be up to no good around the pretty clerks you've got working for you. I only wish you had let me interview him."

"Well, we'll see. Anyway, I just wanted to thank you for doing that sales report for me, sweetheart. I can see a few areas of effort to be worked on in the store next week. We aren't doing what I'd hoped for in the jewelry department. Maybe a small advertisement in the paper and cutting a few prices on simple things that younger women would like and can afford, like bracelets."

"Now there I can really be of help to you. We'll talk about that. You just finish your supper while it's still hot, Max Steinfeldt!" Alice laughingly ordered.

President Grant had already declared that he would not seek a third term, and he had a preference for the flamboyant senator from New York, Roscoe Conkling. If women could have voted then, the romantically handsome and sartorially elegant Conkling would undoubtedly have been the popular choice of the fair sex. For Conkling's running mate, the Republican ticket-makers favored Rutherford B. Hayes, Governor of Ohio.

As the Republican National Convention opened in Cincinnati in June, Conkling was joined in the running by a strong challenger, Congressman James G. Blaine of Maine, Speaker of the House. In January, Blaine had made a name for himself by proposing a motion to deny amnesty to Jefferson Davis, former President of the Confederacy. But Blaine's candidacy was hampered by the threat of scandal, for a month before the Republican Convention, the House Judiciary Committee began an investigation of his acceptance of favors from the railroads during his term as Speaker. Blaine countered the challenge: a week before the convention, he made a dramatic speech on the floor of the House, depicting himself as an honest man maligned by thieves. That speech turned the tide and put him back in the lead for the presidential nomination.

Hayes, believing that Blaine would win the presidential nomination on the first ballot, urged his campaign manager to withdraw his name; he had an aversion to being a candidate on a ticket with a man whose record had been questioned. But after five ballots, Blaine's total began to drop, and Hayes himself was now being favored for the presidential nomination. He was not well known to the general public, but he was thoroughly acceptable to the reform wing of the party. On the seventh ballot, Hayes won the nomination.

Since the New York delegates had made the Hayes victory possible, they received the honor of naming the candidate for Vice-President. Roscoe Conkling spurned the nomination, so they chose a second-rate politician, William A. Wheeler, who was no better known to the American voters than Hayes.

President Grant was delighted with the ticket, for Hayes had a good reputation as an upright man who could save the Republican Party from the disgrace now darkening Grant's final days in office. The overtones of the Whiskey Ring scandal of the previous year had suddenly turned into a discordant symphony whose sounds were deafening Grant's ears. His secretary, Orville Babcock, had been definitely implicated in the Whiskey Ring. Babcock was found not guilty largely because of a deposition from Grant asserting his secretary's innocence. He returned to his duties at the White House after the trial, but shortly thereafter Grant summarily dismissed him.

In March, William W. Belknap, Grant's secretary of war, was cited by a committee of the House of Representatives, which recommended that the secretary be impeached for malfeasance in office. Between 1870 and 1876 Belknap had received more than twenty-four thousand dollars for having awarded the post-tradership at Fort Sills to one John S. Evans. Belknap resigned his post, but the resulting scandal was still another blow to Grant's administration.

On June 25, General George Armstrong Custer and his entire force were massacred at Little Big Horn River in Montana by Sioux Indians led by Sitting Bull. The chief had been angered by the advance of the whites, the reckless slaughter of buffalo, and the gold rush in the Black Hills which had drawn hordes of white miners to Sioux lands. The massacre stunned the nation. Custer had been a national celebrity, adored by women and admired by men. He was also a gifted publicist, which had helped his career a good deal.

Earlier, Custer had been summoned to Washington to testify in the Belknap impeachment proceedings, and under the adroit questioning of Heister Clymer, the Democrat who had exposed Belknap in the Fort Sills affair, Custer related an incident that implicated the president's brother, Orville Grant, in the sale of corn stolen from the Indian

397

Bureau. Custer went on to criticize Grant's order extending the Great Sioux Reservation, intimating that it only gave the post traders ample opportunity for illegal profits.

Two days after Little Big Horn, the Democratic National Convention met at St. Louis and swiftly nominated Samuel J. Tilden of New York for President.

As governor of New York, Tilden had won national acclaim for ousting the corrupt boss of Tammany Hall, "Boss" Tweed. He would run on a platform of reform, and already it was believed that he was sure to be the next president. He was rich, cultured, incorruptible, and a bachelor. For thirty years he had been a corporation lawyer, investment broker, and financial advisor for ailing railroads.

To discredit him, the Republicans thought of bringing Tweed back to New York to give damaging evidence against the man who had ousted and jailed him. For William M. Tweed had escaped from a New York jail to Cuba last year, and the government had traced his flight to Spain. But President Grant firmly refused to allow this contrivance. Thus the lines were drawn for the battle for the presidency: a battle destined to be won by a single electoral vote only two days before the inauguration on March 4, 1877.

It was, indeed, a year of deceptions and disasters, of homilies and hopes, of glowing images which, when studied close at hand, proved to be as nebulous as smoke rising from a dying campfire. And the image that personable Keith McNallis had created to deceive trusting, good-natured Max Steinfeldt was nebulous indeed. He had never owned a store in New Orleans. The truth of the matter was that he had been discharged from a New Orleans store for theft at about the same time he had been caught having an affair with the owner's wife; the latter fact very nearly cost him his life and it compelled him to flee in the dead of night from the Queen City.

Nevertheless, he was a consummate actor and realized that as he was unknown in Houston he had a golden opportunity to create a new life for himself. And so for the first few weeks he worked at his job so zealously that the impressed Max Steinfeldt increased his wages and complimented him.

With his curly black hair and neatly trimmed beard, his

flashing dark-brown eyes, and his soft and often florid speech—marked by a Southern accent which enchanted the female shoppers of Houston—Keith McNallis had already received many sidelong glances from flirtatious wives and several of the attractive young clerks in the Douglas store. With what seemed Spartan self-discipline, however, he did not allow himself to be enticed by these unspoken invitations; indeed, he appeared to maintain decorum and probity in his business and his personal life. Quite without Max Steinfeldt's knowledge, however, he had already entered into a brief liaison with an attractive young widow who worked as a seamstress for middle-class Houston families. When he discovered that she hoped for marriage as the logical end to their relationship, he abruptly ended it.

By the middle of July, therefore, McNallis found himself deprived of carnal love, and by this time also, his role of gracious but personally aloof floorwalker was becoming onerous to him. He began to consider replacing the widowed seamstress with one of the store clerks. He had just about decided on one of them when Max Steinfeldt unknowingly took a hand in revealing McNallis's true nature.

On Tuesday of the third week of this exceptionally warm July, Max was ascending the stairway to the second floor when a pretty, coppery-haired girl of about seventeen scurried down, rudely jostling him. At the same time he heard a cry from upstairs from one of his male clerks, "Stop her; she's stolen some jewelry!"

"Just a minute, miss!" Max exclaimed, as he turned to pursue the frightened teenaged girl. Though she had managed to stumble down to the first-floor landing, she lost her balance and sprawled ignominiously on her stomach. Shoppers stopped to gape at her and to whisper among themselves, while Max hurried down and bent over her, concerned that she might have hurt herself. "Now then, miss, are you hurt?"

"N-no, just let me be—please, let me go!" the girl stammered in a voice strident with near hysteria.

"I'll help you up. Now, let's see what this is all about, shall we?" he said, not unkindly. At the same moment, the clerk who was an assistant in the jewelry section at the far end of the second floor ran down and, out of breath, gasped, "That's the one, Mr. Steinfeldt! I saw her steal a bracelet and two little garnet rings, and she tucked them into her shirtwaist."

"I didn't—let me go—you haven't got any right to hold me—I swear I didn't do it!" the girl protested. Max Steinfeldt had helped her up, but kept a firm grip on her arm. Her tousled curls, her disheveled clothes, and her grimy face piqued his curiosity.

"That's all right, Dell, I'll take care of this," he said to the jewelry clerk. The latter nodded, looked dubiously at the frightened girl, and then went back upstairs.

"Suppose we come into my office at the back of the store, miss," Max softly suggested. "You don't want to cause a scene with all these people watching, do you? That's a good girl. Nobody's going to hurt you, I promise. You can tell me what it's all about."

"You—you won't land me in jail, mister?" the girl stammered, fearfully eyeing him and ready to bolt as soon as he released his tightened grasp of her arm.

"I give you my word of honor. Come along now. What's your name?"

"M-Mabel—H-Harston. I didn't mean to—I mean—oh Lordy, I guess that does it. But I had to—I haven't—I don't have any money, and I haven't eaten in two days—"

"Shh, Miss Harston, you can tell me all that once you get into my office where nobody else will hear. Be a good girl and come along," he compassionately urged.

Once inside the office, Mabel Harston revealed that she had run away from a small farm about thirty miles northwest of Houston because her widowed mother had married her hired man, who had lost no time in trying to compel Mabel to yield herself to him in the barn, threatening to whip her if she did not do so.

"That's a terrible thing, Miss Harston. How old are you, really?"

"I—I'll be seventeen the tenth of August, mister. Are you sure—you—you won't send me to jail? Here—I—I'll give you back what I took—I was going to—I hoped maybe I could sell them and get something to eat—that's the truth, so help me," Mabel blurted out and then, modestly turning to one side, delved into her shirtwaist and produced the bracelet and rings.

"I'll tell you what I'm going to do, Mabel—it's all right if I call you that, isn't it? After all, I'm old enough to be your father, but I assure you that I won't behave like your

400

stepfather. I'm married and I have a very nice wife and she's a wonderful cook. You come along to dinner with us tonight. You'll get a good meal and a bath, and you can stay at the house. And maybe we'll talk about giving you a job in the store—that is, if you'd like it. By the way, my name is Max Steinfeldt, and I manage this store."

"Oh my gosh, Mr. S-Steinfeldt—you mean it? And I wouldn't have to go back to my stepfather?"

Max Steinfeldt frowned. "Technically, you're a minor and under your mother and stepfather's supervision. But after what you've told me—and I believe you, Mabel—I wouldn't send you back there. Do they know you ran away and where you were going?"

The girl vigorously shook her head. "I left a couple of nights ago, and I just ran. There was a fellow coming to Houston to buy some supplies, and I told him my sister was sick and I just had to get here, so he gave me a lift in his buggy."

"I see. Well now, we'll be closing soon; you just stay here and lean back and try to rest a little, till I lock up the store. Then I'll take you home to my wife, Alice."

The next day, Mabel Harston went to work in the Douglas Department Store. At first, Max gave her simple errands to run and let her help out behind the counter when the clerk in charge had several customers to deal with at one time. By the end of the week, he discovered that she was quick to learn and knew a good deal about women's clothes. By the end of the second week, she was standing behind a counter and selling, bright and cheerful to customers, several of whom went out of their way to praise her to Max Steinfeldt himself.

Keith McNallis had noticed the lovely newcomer at once. She was slim and willowy, with an oval-shaped face, large, expressive, gray-green eyes, and a small but full mouth—physical attributes he especially relished. By the end of the second week he had asked her to supper with him, but Mabel had firmly declined.

Not to be denied, and certain that an impressionable young girl would fall easy prey to his suave lovemaking, McNallis casually did some investigation on his own. He had seen the incident of Mabel trying to run out of the store and heard Dell Baxter calling after her.

And so, on the Tuesday of the third week of her employment, toward the close of the day, he made it his business to go up to her, and seeing no one around, murmured, "Mabel, if you haven't got a fellow, there's no reason why you couldn't have supper with me tonight. I haven't got a girl, and I'm lonesome in this town."

"I'm sorry, Mr. McNallis, I—I don't go out with anybody. So, if you will excuse me—"

"I see. Well." Again he glanced around, and then leaned forward and, in an insinuating whisper, remarked, "I know you're a little shoplifter, Mabel girl. I heard Dell Baxter yell that you'd taken a bracelet and some rings. Now maybe Mr. Steinfeldt gave you a job, but you're on trial here. And I'm the floorwalker and I have a lot to say about who works here and who doesn't. You'd better be nice to me, or you might not have a job here any more."

"That's mean! You haven't any right to talk to me like that! I'm a good girl, and I know your kind."

"Oh, you do?" He chuckled knowingly. "Well then, in spite of your being so young, I'd guess you had a few experiences to be able to say a thing like that to me, when you don't even know me. All right, there are other fish in the sea."

Her obstinacy only heightened his lust for her. She had a creamy skin with rosy flecks, and the swell of her breasts made him remember that it had been many weeks since he had enjoyed the delights of Venus. Besides, Mabel Harston was a great deal prettier than his widow.

At the close of business on Friday, he managed to get up to the second floor and, when Dell Baxter was talking to another clerk, he deftly dropped several garnet and onyx rings and three bracelets into his pocket. This done, he waited until the store had nearly closed and, seeing that Mabel had momentarily left her counter, swiftly went behind it, stooped and opened the little drawer into which cash was placed, deposited the jewelry, then closed it and went down the floor toward the main entrance, nodding pleasantly to customers whom he recognized.

When all the customers were out of the store, he walked over to Mabel's counter and saw that she was very red in the face and nervous. "Dell's just told me that some jewelry was missing from upstairs, Mabel honey," he began at once in a low voice. "I'll bet I know where it is—in your cash drawer. Now, if Mr. Steinfeldt finds out about this little stunt of yours, I'm sure he'll send you to jail. But I promise I'll keep my mouth shut—and I'll even pay for the stuff you've taken myself—if you're nice to me. Understand? You can start by having supper with me."

"Oh my God, Mr. McNallis, I didn't take that jewelry, and you know I didn't! I—yes, I found it in my cash drawer just now, but I swear I don't know how it got there!"

"Come on now, Mabel, do you take me for a fool? You've done it once, you'll do it again—it's part of your nature. But I'll cover up for you, if you're nice to me. Or do you prefer that I go to Mr. Steinfeldt and tell him straight out? You'd better make up your mind before we open for business tomorrow, unless you want to find yourself in jail."

With this parting sally, he walked off with a smug smile of triumph.

As it happened, Max Steinfeldt was not in the store on this particular afternoon, and Mabel was in a quandary. With a heavy heart she went home to the inexpensive little room in a nearby boarding house, which Max had found for her.

She came to work the next morning after having spent a virtually sleepless night, and her eyes were red and swollen from crying. Keith McNallis observed this and gleefully rubbed his hands. He would wait a few minutes, and then tell her what she had to do. He would take the jewelry back upstairs, explain that he had found it near the entrance—some shoplifter must have had a siege of conscience and thrown it away before walking out of the store with it. It would be very easy.

But Max Steinfeldt was down to work early this morning, and he also observed Mabel Harston's distraught appearance. As she slowly took her place behind her counter, took out a handkerchief and blew her nose, he approached her, a sympathetic smile on his genial face.

"Good morning, Mabel. My goodness, what a long face! I hope it's nothing to do with your situation here. You're getting along well with your fellow employees, aren't you? I've heard some very nice things about you. In fact, if you keep this up, you might find a small increase in your wages very soon."

"Oh, Mr. Steinfeldt—I just have to talk to you—I don't know what to do—" She wrung her hands and burst into tears.

Max glanced around and saw that the doors were about

403

to open and customers were already waiting outside. "Let's go into my office and discuss this in the right place, Mabel," he suggested.

Once inside his office, Mabel told him that she had found some rings and bracelets in her cash drawer the night before, and that Keith McNallis had told her that he intended to tell their employer that she had stolen them, unless she agreed to be nice to him. As she blurted out the telltale words, Max Steinfeldt's face grew grim and his eyes narrowed with anger. When she had finished, he abruptly rose and said, "You just go back to work. Everything's going to be all right. And by the way, send Mr. McNallis into my office at once, please. I'm glad you told me this, Mabel. I know you didn't take that jewelry."

A few moments later, Keith McNallis, cocky and self-assured, sauntered into the manager's office.

"Close the door, McNallis. Now, Mabel Harston has just told me of your filthy little scheme. I'll tell you just one thing about her. Yes, she did take that jewelry the day I hired her, but she did it because she'd run away from a stepfather who tried to force her to go to bed with him and because she was hungry and hadn't eaten in about two days. In my book, she had a valid excuse. But you, McNallis, you're a disgusting specimen of what I wouldn't even call a man, trying to blackmail a decent young girl like that into a situation that certainly isn't much better morally than what she tried to run away from."

Keith McNallis's mouth fell open with astonishment. He had not expected to be so quickly challenged, before he had had a chance to tell his story. With Max on the offensive at once, McNallis was completely at a loss for words. His face reddened, and finally he began to sputter incoherently. "I—but—"

"Of course, you're fired, McNallis," Max cut him off. He opened a drawer and took out some greenbacks, counted out a few, then thrust them at the stunned floorwalker. "Put these in your pocket; that's your pay. Wait—before you go, there's just one thing more."

"I don't—you've misjudged me—I didn't—" McNallis finally managed a feeble defense on his own behalf.

He did not finish. Max Steinfeldt came swiftly from behind his desk, drew back his fist, and felled the dapper floorwalker with a right uppercut that would have done credit to a professional boxer in the ring.

404

"Now get out, and don't ever let me catch you in this store again, or you'll be the one who goes to jail!" Max growled.

Before the day had ended, he had sent for Mabel Harston again. This time, it was to tell her that not only would she receive a raise in wages, but that he was arranging to have her transferred to the Galveston store. There she could start a new life, farther away from her lecherous stepfather. He wrote a letter to the manager of the Galveston store, asking him to find Mabel a decent boarding house and to have one of the married female clerks look after her, until such time as she could begin to lead her own life and choose the sort of man she would like to keep company with.

That evening, when Max came home to supper, he casually mentioned, halfway through the excellent meal of chicken fricassee and dumplings, "By the way, I fired Keith McNallis this afternoon. He planted some jewelry in Mabel Harston's cash drawer and then told her that he'd report it to me, if she didn't accommodate him."

Alice smiled gently. And with a wonderfully commendable wifely restraint, she forebore from voicing her thought: *Didn't I tell you that I didn't like that man from the very start?* Instead, she nodded and said, "Mabel's a fine girl. You're a good judge of character, Max darling. Now have some more chicken fricassee. Otherwise, I'll begin to think you don't care for my cooking any more."

He looked suspiciously at his lovely wife for a moment, and then smiled and finally burst into laughter in which she merrily joined. "I'll certainly help myself to more of this fricassee, sweetheart," he told her when the laughter had subsided. "But first, I'm going to help myself to an extra-special kiss, if you've no objection."

Three weeks after Keith McNallis lost his job in the Houston department store, during the last week in August, James Hunter came down with nausea, intense pain in the back, head, and limbs, and an accompanying high fever. Arabella, hysterical with fright, rushed out to find a doctor, after first helping her husband to bed. The equally terrified maid had to be first bribed and then threatened with dismissal before she would agree to look in after Arabella's ailing husband, for she was certain that it was the dread "yellowjack," a term now in vogue throughout most Southern seaports because the orange-hued skin of the victim warned of impending death.

When the harassed little elderly doctor arrived, he took one look at James and pronounced it yellow fever. Quinine, with a calomel and castor oil to purge the bowels, was at once prescribed. And then he told Arabella something that terrified her even more.

"Ordinarily, when a man's this sick, I'd have him in the hospital, Mrs. Hunter. But our hospital's already crowded— we've an epidemic on our hands. All you can do is carry out my instructions, keep away from him as much as possible, and burn sulphur in the room. Oh yes, and if you change his sheets or any of his bedding, burn them a ways away from the house. I'll try to get back tomorrow, if I can."

After the doctor had gone, Arabella gestured to the frightened maid to leave the room, whispering, "I'll look after him myself for a bit, Annie. The way you're carrying on, you won't do him any good."

"But, Miz' Hunter, the doctor said it's awfully contagious!" the maid whispered as she backed toward the door, obviously only too eager to take Arabella at her word.

"I'll take my chances. Now go to your room and compose yourself, for goodness' sake," Arabella hissed, exasperated.

Once the young woman had left, Arabella dipped a towel into a bucket of cold water and, folding it, knelt down and gently patted her husband's forehead. Wanly James blinked his eyes and stared dully at her. Then with the ghost of a struggling smile, he whispered hoarsely, "Bella girl, I never figured you'd have to look after me this way."

"Now you just hush up and save your strength, James Hunter. The idea! Didn't it say for better or for worse, till death do us part, in the ceremony, darling? You're going to be fine. Just you rest, and Annie and I'll try to make you as comfortable as we can."

He sighed softly, turned his face to one side, and closed his eyes as a spasm of fever made him grimace with pain. Then, haltingly, his voice rough and unsteady, he averred, "No matter what happens to me, Bella . . . I—I want you to know—you've been the best wife a man could pray for. God—bless you—for loving me . . . and giving us . . . children we can be proud of—"

Arabella sought to hide her tears as she tried to joke,

406

"James Hunter, I do declare, just because you're lying in bed a little under the weather there's no reason to be solemn and try to preach a sermon. But, darling, I shan't ever forget what you just said. Now please try to get some sleep. I love you very much. I need you."

"As . . . I've always—always—n-needed you—Bella," his voice came faintly. Then his head fell back. Arabella slowly rose, her eyes widening with apprehension. He lay very still, and as she bent toward him, she could not detect the slightest flicker of movement of his eyelids, nostrils, or lips.

"Oh James—oh my dear God—oh my darling, my love," she groaned softly. Then, turning, she went to the maid's room. "Annie, please go bring Dr. Emory back at once."

"Yes, Miz' Hunter, right away—why, is the master worse?"

"Never you mind silly questions, girl!" Arabella fiercely declared. "Just go get him as fast as ever you can, do you hear me?"

After the girl had hurried out of the house, Arabella sank down on her knees in the living room, buried her face in her hands, and sobbed wildly. Somehow, the last decade of their union had redoubled her love for this compassionate, quietly assertive man. Her sense of irreparable loss was far greater than if he had been taken from her early in their marriage.

When at last she managed to compose herself, she clung to the consoling thought that because he had, late in life, involved himself with the new business interest of Charles Douglas's department store, he had enjoyed these last few years with the zestful vitality of a much younger man. And thanks to that, she told herself, unlike many women her age, she had been blessed with the felicity of his renewed desire for her. No, she would be strong now, remembering that, remembering that he had been spared a lingering illness. There could be no regrets for either of them—and yet Arabella knew the years ahead would be heart-rendingly lonely.

A week later, at the insistence of Melinda and Lawrence Davis, the bereaved widow took Joy and went to live with her daughter and son-in-law. Melinda would surely be glad to have her help, she knew, for there was now a third child in the Davis household—a little girl named Denise. And

Joy would benefit from growing up among other little children—who were in fact her nieces and nephews!

As the long centennial summer drew to a close and the presidential election drew nearer, Joe and Margaret Duvray were blessed with a second daughter, whom they named Ella. In Alabama, the three politicians who in 1870 had urged Luke Bouchard to run for the post in the House of Representatives which Andy Haskins currently held, informed the one-armed Tennesseean that his election as state senator was "practically in the bag." "By God, Andy boy," William Blount declared, "you're about the only real Republican we know of who doesn't have dirty linen to be aired. It wouldn't matter what party you're from, if you want the truth. People around here, like everywhere else, are sick to death of graft and bribery and scandals with loose women and such. So you'd better tell your sweet wife and your kids that you're going to be spending a lot more time in Montgomery from now on than ever you did when you were in the House."

Colorado had entered the Union on the first of August in this centennial year. Already it was being touted as a cattle market. By now the glories of the old Chisholm Trail to Kansas were beginning to fade, as some of the Kansas cattle towns were being filled up by farming families. And throughout the plains, the piles of bleached buffalo bones —the work of hunters—grew larger and more numerous; the days of freedom for the Indian tribes that had once hunted where they chose were almost at an end.

It was a cool evening during the second week of September. Sangrodo and Catayuna walked together, as was their wont of late. The beautiful Mexican woman had for some weeks now felt a strange premonition about these confidences between husband and wife, so uncharacteristic of the taciturn chief of the Wanderers.

She held her little son, Nahubiyaa, in her arms, and from time to time, she glanced up at Sangrodo. His hair was almost white now, in the fifty-sixth year of his life. He still rode his horse with the erect, vigilant attitude of a warrior. Yet Prissy, the squaw of Jicinte, who had seven children in their tepee, had told her something yesterday which she had not known—something that made these strange new walks between them seem even more ominous. Prissy had said that she had seen Sangrodo take his horse to the corral yesterday afternoon and then, when he had thought that no one watched, he had leaned his head against the topmost rail, and his body had been shaken by a fit of trembling. Prissy did not know what it meant, but she thought that Catayuna should watch him closely.

"Beloved woman," Sangrodo's voice was strangely hoarse as he stopped for a moment and turned to look at her, "I am sad tonight. I hear more with each new moon of how all our tribes and those of the other Indian nations are being driven from the land that was once theirs. They have no food, they are sent into what the white-eyes call reservations, but which are no more than prisons, for if they do not imprison the body, they imprison the spirit by showing them how the white-eyes hate and wish them dead. We can never go back to the land we knew, Catayuna."

"Do not be sad, my husband. See how happy your people are, that we are here and that we live, that the braves have squaws and the squaws have children. It is a good land, and we have food and we do not flee from the soldiers. And the white-eyes do not ride into our stronghold and kill the women and the old men. You can look back with pride that you have been the chief of these proud people."

"Yes, beloved woman." He drew a long breath and, for an instant, she thought she saw a grimace of pain on his face. "But do not think that my sadness comes from life with you, do not ever think that. You who were once my slave have become the great joy of my life, and here in the solitude of this new land where once we raided as warriors and where we now live in peace, you have brought me life and hope. I shall—*aiii!*"

He stopped suddenly, and staggered to one side. Catayuna uttered a cry of terror. They had come to the bank of the little stream. Out of the grass a huge scorpion, unseen and nearly stepped on by Sangrodo, had stung the tall Comanche's right ankle.

With an imprecation, he raised his other foot and crushed it with his moccasion, then staggered, groaning. "The poison is swift and strong, Catayuna! I did not think—Catayuna—beloved woman—I am weak, I cannot see—"

With a sobbing cry, she tearfully laid down her little son and took Sangrodo in her arms, bearing all his strong weight, to ease his shuddering body down to the ground.

She knelt over him, tears streaming down her cheeks. "Wait, I will hurry back to the village, I will bring our shaman—"

With an effort he shook his head. He opened his eyes and in a hoarse, rasping voice that fought for breath he panted, "Too late—Catayuna, beloved woman—let Kitante be chief. Let him follow in my moccasins—let him—I go to my forefathers, I—beloved one—I—" and then a spasm seized him and he was still.

It was Jicinte who rode to Windhaven Range to tell Lucien Edmond Bouchard of Sangrodo's death. He brought back to the stronghold, which mourned their chief whose name would not again be spoken, an invitation for Catayuna and her children to live at Windhaven Range. And because of the blood brotherhood between Luke Bouchard's oldest son and her beloved husband, Catayuna sent back word that she would accept.

On the day she made her journey, escorted by the four strongest warriors of Sangrodo's stronghold, she said to Kitante, "I will not be away from you for always, Kitante. The son of the *Taiboo Nimaihkana*, who also was blood brother of your father, will always welcome you and your people. But now you shall be chief, and you no longer have need of my counsel. Have strong sons by your Carmencita. Lead our people in peace—for truly I am one of you. That which was Mexican in me died forever when he took me and made me his woman. And now I am all Comanche— for did he not tell me this once when at last I had the child I yearned to bear for him, so that I might help our people?"

Kitante bowed his head and murmured, "I will walk in the moccasins of my father, but do you, Catayuna, pray to the Great Spirit to make me worthy of them."

CHAPTER THIRTY-SIX

The news of James Hunter's death, which he received by telegram from Arabella, grievously distressed Luke Bouchard. He rode to Montgomery to send off a telegram of condolence, and that evening shut himself up in his study to write a long letter. Though he knew the futility of words at such a time, he sought to cheer Arabella by reminding her of the unusual opportunity her devoted husband had enjoyed in being able to alter his career late in life and derive such undeniable pleasure and fulfillment from it. And he reminded her, too, as tenderly as he knew how, that she had contributed so much to James's success and contentment in life; and that Melinda and Andrew, under their parents' guidance, had found their own mature destiny.

But as he wrote, Luke could not help pausing to reflect darkly on the mortality of man; he could not banish from his mind that grim and always lurking shadow which darkens the brightest hopes and most dazzling ambitions of purposeful men and women. Yet how much better it was, he thought to himself, to have dreams and goals in life. These were what made life worthwhile. And if such dreams brought with them a certain restless impatience, that was a price well worth paying for the richness and joy and fulfillment the dreams also brought.

During the next few days he was drawn even closer to Laure, who was aware of his autumnal mood and was gentle with him. Theirs was a warm comradeship, though he still was her considerate lover. Now was the time, Luke reflected, to watch their children growing up, to see them developing the traits that would carry them through a lifetime, to strengthen their spirits by showing them how much they were loved and respected.

Luke had always taken pains never to be condescending or dictatorial. "Yes, Laure dearest," he told her, a few nights after he had received the news of James Hunter's death, "parents are certainly responsible for their children and have in that sense a proprietary right to steer them away from what they know to be injurious. But, at the same time, I've always believed that parents should be friends with their children, wholeheartedly and enthusiastically, till the children come to understand—through this kind of frank communication—just how much they, in their turn, contribute to their father's and mother's enjoyment of life itself."

Thus Luke Bouchard, in his sixty-first year, found himself more frequently looking back at the ledger of his life, remembering his faults as vividly as his virtues and achievements. It was not an egotistical summing up, but rather an impersonal appraisal, as if he were standing to one side, looking at himself from a distance, judging the man who was—who had been—Luke Bouchard.

At least his stewardship of Windhaven Plantation would surely satisfy that memorable man who had imparted such compassionate wisdom to him as a boy. There were times—in this mellow month of September when the fields of Windhaven Plantation were bountiful with crops nearly ready for harvest—when Luke walked out into the fields with Marius Thornton or Hughie Mendicott and the aging but still industrious Hannah. At such times he would look quickly up at the towering bluff near the river and feel that the spirits of Lucien Bouchard and his Dimarte were watching these fertile fields and approving of the harmonious commune established here.

On a mid-September afternoon, Luke Bouchard was finishing a letter to Lucien Edmond, a gossipy letter which mentioned his expectation of an abundant harvest this fall and the likelihood of Andy Haskins's becoming a state senator. He wrote also of the pleasure he took in seeing his ten-year-old son Lucien and seven-year-old Paul playing together and becoming good friends, without any hint—happily as yet and perhaps never, he devoutly wished—of sibling rivalry. Celestine, who was five, tagged along with her brothers, insisting on being included in their games. And Clarissa, at three, was a constant joy with her saucy

412

remarks and her enchanting habit of toddling up to him or Laure and groping for their hands to hold one of hers, with a happy little laugh. He congratulated his oldest son on the latter's good judgment in working out long-term contracts with the two army forts for the sale of prime beef, because the weather vane of the economy was still swinging this way and that, and the Montgomery *Advertiser* was constantly printing the doleful news of yet another business failure.

He concluded with a note on politics, telling Lucien Edmond that he had decided to vote for Tilden in the forthcoming national election on November 7. Though he had always been a Republican by preference, he believed that Tilden more nearly answered the national need for honest reform and an end to the scandalous corruption that had characterized the Grant administration. Of course, he humorously added, he would be sure to cast his vote for Andy Haskins here in Montgomery, regardless of party affiliation.

He went over the letter quickly, was satisfied with it, and sealed it. Then glancing out the window of his study, he saw that the first shadows of twilight were falling and decided on a walk before supper. Leaving the study and passing out through the front door, he descended the steps of the red-brick chateau and walked slowly toward the river bank. The soothing sound of the river never failed to bring him a feeling of peace and contentment, even after the most hectic events. Always it reminded him of his grandfather's journey up from Mobile three generations ago, to find this fertile land. How often his grandfather must have walked this very way, after his own many crises of grief and uncertainty, as he sought to realize that idealistic dream which had led him across the ocean toward his destiny.

How peaceful it was now, with the first shadows touching the twin towers of the chateau, with the sky changing from blue to the richer oranges and purples of the oncoming sunset. Then, without warning, Luke felt a sudden pain in his chest, as if an invisible hand had stealthily squeezed his heart and then released it. He swayed, blinking his eyes, and forced himself to turn, to stare up at the bluff where Lucien and Dimarte were buried. And in his mind came a frantic yet humble prayer: *Not yet, dear God; grant me a few years yet to watch my sons come to young manhood and the beginning of their own hopes, hopes which will surely surpass mine—and may they be realized with fewer errors than mine have been.*

The spasm passed as swiftly as it had come, and he drew in grateful breath after breath, waiting as if for a sign.

Some five days later, when he had the telegram from Lucien Edmond telling him of Sangrodo's death, Luke Bouchard's hand clutched the paper and he murmured to himself with a kind of awe, "It must have been at that very moment that my blood brother and friend was taken by the Great Spirit whom he revered. It was a sign; because we were bound in blood, I felt his passing as agonizingly as if it had been my own."

In an earlier letter this summer to Lucien Edmond, Luke Bouchard had already delightedly revealed the news that his adopted son, Lopasuta, who had now become famous throughout the country for his able defense of impoverished litigants in the courtroom, had become engaged. What most pleased Luke was that the young woman in question was white, from a leading Montgomery family. This paralleled, he declared to Lucien Edmond, his grandfather's marriage to the Creek girl Dimarte; in this alliance of a Comanche whose mother had been Mexican with an Alabama girl of good breeding and family, the unfailing credo of the Bouchards was demonstrated. Just as old Lucien had always believed that love, honor, trust, and moral decency were not limited to any one race upon this earth, so a courageous young white woman dared risk the opprobrium that was certain to follow her engagement to a man who was, in essence, a half-breed—a term that would never have occurred to his beloved grandfather or to him.

It had happened in June. Lopasuta Bouchard had represented an illiterate black freedman who had been engaged to work as a stonemason. The mason's client was a political scalawag who a decade ago had moved from Tuscaloosa to Montgomery, bought an old house and, upon marrying his third wife, decided to remodel the house for his new bride. He and the black man, Ezekiel Manson, had verbally agreed on a price. After the completion of the work, the politico disdainfully declared that he did not believe the work was worth the fee agreed upon, and offered Ezekiel Manson less than half the sum in question.

The black, who was partly crippled by arthritis and in

his early fifties, had hired two nephews to assist him in the work and had already paid them out of earnings derived from prior jobs. He had, understandably, included their estimated wages in his original proposal to the politico, and would thus—if he accepted the lesser sum now offered—find himself virtually unpaid for his own labors. Having been told of Lopasuta's willingness to defend those who had very little to spend on lawyer's fees, he applied to the handsome young Comanche lawyer, who agreed to take his case.

Ezekiel Manson proved to be an exceptionally convincing witness on his own behalf when cross-examined on the stand, and he steadfastly refused to be intimidated by the politico's crafty attorney. After the verdict had been rendered in his favor, he hobbled up to Lopasuta, shook his hand, and in a choked voice stammered, "Gawd bless you, Mistah Bouchard. Gawd bless you and keep you—ain't many men like you round these parts, dat's for certain!" There was a mild flurry of applause, which the solemn old judge promptly silenced with a bang of his gavel, but as he left the bench he was seen to smile approvingly.

As Lopasuta picked up his papers from the table in front of him, he was accosted by a young woman:

"Excuse me, Mr. Bouchard, but I heard your defense of that poor man, and I want to congratulate you. I was moved by what you said for him, and I've read about you in the past and have always admired you. In fact, when I read that this case was being argued by you, I decided to come for the express purpose of meeting you and telling you how much I admire what you're doing here in the South."

Lopasuta smilingly confronted the flattering spectator and his eyes widened with admiration. She was dark-haired, with an oval face whose high-set cheekbones and delicately aquiline nose bespoke breeding. Her eyes were animated, candid, brown with green flecks at the iris. She was five feet, six inches, with a slim, poised figure, and she was modishly clad in a brown cotton dress with high neck and puffed sleeves. Her voice had a sweetness and freshness which made her words sound all the more sincere.

"That's most kind of you, Miss—Miss?" he paused.

"Oh, I'm sorry, Mr. Bouchard. My name is Geraldine Murcur." Then she gave a deprecatory little laugh and

415

added, "You know, I'm sure you'll think it's silly and my parents think I'm out of my mind, but I've always had a secret desire to be a lawyer myself."

"But I don't think it's silly at all. I should think that a woman could plead even more eloquently because she has sensitive feelings, often beyond those of a man, and she has the gift of intuition. As you may know, Miss Murcur, I grew up with Comanches; my Mexican mother married a brave. And in the stronghold where I grew up, ruled over by the wisest of all chiefs of the Wanderers, Sangrodo, there is a woman named Catayuna. She is called the beloved woman, and she sits in the council with the men because they respect her wisdom. So you see, Miss Murcur, in one sense, we Comanches are already more progressive than the people we call the white-eyes."

She tilted back her head and uttered a delicious little laugh, then impulsively put out her hand. "I know I'm breaking all the rules of acceptable social conduct, especially in this town, Mr. Bouchard, but if you don't think me too outrageously shocking, I'd like very much to talk with you when you've some leisure time. What you've just said makes me feel all the more that I'd like to pursue this idea of mine. And you're about the only one so far who's given me any hope."

"I'd be delighted to talk with you about it, Miss Murcur. Perhaps sometime at your convenience we might have supper together?"

Geraldine Murcur frowned a moment, then brightened. "I think, for the time being, Mr. Bouchard, if you've no objection, we'd best make it luncheon. My father and mother are dreadfully protective, you see. If I went out at night by myself, even though I'm twenty-two, they'd be certain that I was seeing a young man on the sly. And, of course, I would be, wouldn't I?" Again she uttered that exquisite laugh, which drew an appreciative grin from the young lawyer.

Throughout July and most of August, Lopasuta Bouchard and Geraldine Murcur met at least once every two weeks and, on some happy occasions, once a week, at a little restaurant on the outskirts of the city, owned by an elderly black and his wife. Despite its really exceptional fare, it was almost never patronized by the white citizens of Montgomery. Lopasuta had discovered the restaurant when one of his black clients had insisted on buying his dinner there. He preferred it to the two or three supposedly elite restaurants which Montgomery afforded its more influential citizens.

Geraldine Murcur was an only child, and her parents were well-to-do, second-generation Alabamans. Her great-grandfather had come from London as an apprentice with the East India Company, but had become disenchanted with long voyages and decided to try his fortunes in America. He had settled in New York and become a prosperous greengrocer. His older son had married a Tuscaloosa girl who had come visiting in New York with her parents; he had returned with her to Tuscaloosa and there had opened his own greengrocery shop. His son, Geraldine's father, had married a Montgomery belle and now owned a small hotel.

Both he and Geraldine's mother had often been distressed over their daughter's nonconformity. She had plainly told them that she did not want to go to a nearby finishing school, but preferred instead to go east to school. Though scandalized, the Murcurs had at last given their consent and sent along as chaperone her father's older sister. When Geraldine returned, her parents tried unsuccessfully to marry her off to half a dozen eligible suitors from Montgomery, but Geraldine would have none of them. "I know you love me very dearly, Mama and Papa," she said, "but if I do marry at all, it's going to be for love and because I find him by myself. I don't believe in matchmaking, and so far there isn't anyone I've met through your good graces who is the sort of man I'd want to spend the rest of my life with."

During their meetings through the summer, Lopasuta became more and more enchanted by Geraldine's quicksilver mind and candid conversation. He realized at the very outset that he was already beginning to fall in love with her. But he remembered what he had told Luke about the difficulties of such an alliance; he thought too much of this alert, lovely, spirited young woman to condemn her to the snobbery and malicious gossip that would certainly be directed at her, if anything more serious than this casual companionship developed between them.

One early afternoon in mid-September, however, as they rose to leave the pleasant little restaurant, Geraldine exclaimed, "Lopasuta, you know we've talked so much about my wanting to study law. I really wouldn't know how to go

417

about it, but you know it's more than just a daydream with me. Maybe nothing will ever come of it, but I'd really like to do some studying. Do you—could you lend me any of the books you have, which would at least give me a foundation in how the law works?"

"Of course, I'd be happy to. You know, Geraldine, I've been meaning to ask you—do your parents know yet about our meeting?"

"Oh heavens, no," she laughingly shook her head. "I tell them I'm going out shopping—and I always do bring something back, you know, so I'm not a complete liar—or I go to the library or I read some of the old papers. Mama likes to think that she's a pioneer citizen of Montgomery, which of course she isn't, so when I tell her that I go over to the *Advertiser* office and read some of the fading, yellowing pages of the days before the Civil War, she's very pleased about it. In fact, she thinks it may be at last I'm settling down to the point where she and Papa can marry me off and not have to worry about my being an old maid any more."

"I'm sure you won't be that, Geraldine. All the same, it's probably wiser for both of us to meet secretly, the way we have been, because there are too many loose tongues in this town. There's a woman living across the street from me, a Mrs. Elizabeth Steers, who I believe was born to tell tales. Often when I go out on my porch of a pleasant evening, I've seen her across the way drawing aside the curtains and peering out at me to see what mischief I'm up to."

"Oh my goodness! The poor old soul, she probably hasn't anything better to do," Geraldine laughed, amused.

"I'm sure she's lonely," Lopasuta mused. "She's rather wealthy, from all I've heard, but her son and daughter live on the other side of town, and apparently they visit her only when they think it's fitting. Her grandchildren—a boy and a girl about eight and ten, I'd say—do come over more frequently to visit." He sighed and shook his head. "Last week, they were out there on her lawn playing some children's game, and she came out and scolded them in a very loud voice saying that they shouldn't make so much noise when they played, or she wouldn't leave them her money when she died."

"How pathetic, how terrible," Geraldine sympathetically murmured. "I was hoping we could pick up those books this afternoon, but maybe it would be better if you brought

418

them here. I think next Friday would be fine. I know that Mama and Papa are going to visit some friends in Tuskegee over the weekend, but I've begged off." Her eyes suddenly sparkled mischievously. "Do you know, I'd quite forgotten all about that until just this minute—there's no reason why we couldn't see each other while they're gone—that is, if I'm not being too forward again? I like our talks very, very much, Lopasuta."

"I'm glad. We'll think about it. But you know, I could give you those books this afternoon—I'm sure there won't be any harm if you stay in the buggy while I go in and get them and bring them to you. Then I could drive you back to where you want to walk on to your house."

"Of course not, there's absolutely nothing wrong with it at all! And I *would* like to study them over this weekend."

Lopasuta had left his horse and buggy down a side street, the reins tethered to a hitching post about half a block from the restaurant. He helped Geraldine into the buggy, then took the reins and drove to his house. Securing the reins, he said to Geraldine, "I'll be back in a minute, Geraldine. I think I know exactly which books will give you a good start in understanding the law—though I warn you, you'll think a great many of the statutes are antiquated by now."

"I think they always have been down through the ages, Lopasuta. That's why it takes people like you to stand up for the rights of others who can't make head or tail out of what's in the law books," was her enthusiastic answer.

Lopasuta disappeared into his house, and Geraldine sat back with a wistful smile on her lovely face as she looked after him. She, too, had begun to look forward with almost impatient eagerness to their next meeting. No man before had ever interested her as much as Lopasuta Bouchard assuredly did, and not only as a legal mentor.

Mrs. Elizabeth Steers was home this afternoon, feeling particularly sorry for herself. Her grandchildren, Beth and Everett, wouldn't be coming to visit her this weekend, she knew. Things were so awfully boring during the summer here in Montgomery. If it weren't for some of her old friends on Loftus and Evander Streets, she really wouldn't know what to do with herself. But the worst thing about this town was that they were letting all sorts of people move into the best residential neighborhoods. Take that man across the street in the little white frame house, for

419

instance. She'd heard he was a lawyer of sorts, but she had her own private opinion about him. He looked like a nigger; at least he wasn't all white, that was for certain. She had been watching ever since he had moved into that house, to see if some trashy nigger girl didn't come traipsing down and go into his place, because everybody knew that niggers were just animals when it came to—well, she didn't think about such disgraceful things.

Elizabeth Steers was sixty-eight. Her husband had died twenty years ago, henpecked and invariably fearfully apologetic in her presence. She had sniffed at him and called him a mealymouthed old fool more times than she cared to remember. At least, she often told herself, she had been smart enough to have him put his money in gold, especially when she knew that there was a war coming when gold would be all that could keep people going. A good deal of that gold was still hoarded in a small hope chest she had hidden carefully in the cellar of her old house.

She went to the window and, stooping down, stealthily plucked the chintz curtains apart with her bony fingers. Then she gasped with surprise. Why, that girl sitting there in the buggy was Geraldine Murcur, plain as day. And there—wait a minute—there was that nigger fellow, that lawyer, coming out of the house with some books under his arms, getting into the buggy and handing them to her, and then they were driving off together. What was the world coming to? A white girl and that nigger—why, it was unthinkable. And she knew George Murcur, because he owned the Murcur Hotel and his wife had been Angela Oldrick, who came from one of the very best Montgomery families. They would just faint away from shame, if they knew what their daughter was doing right this very minute—the shameless hussy, as bold as you please, sitting there in a buggy on the street where everybody could see while that nigger got in beside her!

She had to do her duty. It was very plain. Of course, the Murcurs didn't know what Geraldine, that poor misguided girl, was up to. Why, if she'd so much as dared think of going out in a public place with a nigger when she'd been a girl, her father would have taken his razor strap to her and lathered her till she couldn't sit down for a month, that's what. No, she had to save Geraldine from her folly.

Rising with a grimace and groan of annoyance at the pain in her back, she resolutely went to her dresser and

420

carefully chose her very best dress, which she had laid by itself in a single drawer atop two towels, so that it might remain fresh and smooth. A few minutes later, wearing a bonnet decorated with artificial flowers, she left her house and, with surprising agility for a woman of her age, began to walk in the direction of the Murcur Hotel.

"Come in here this very minute, Geraldine, I want to talk to you!" George Murcur, his lips tight and whitened, angrily exclaimed. His wife uttered a sobbing cry and wrung her hands. "Oh my poor darling, how could you disgrace us so? What in the world made you do it?"

"Papa, Mama, what are you talking about? I've done nothing!"

"Come into my study, Geraldine!" Murcur commanded, drawing himself up to his full height and glaring at his bewildered daughter.

Once inside the study, he turned to her and, in a voice shaking with anger, declared, "Is it true that you've been keeping company with a nigger, Geraldine? I want the truth now, girl. You're not a child any more, you're twenty-two; an age when most decent young women are respectably married and already having families. You've always gone your own way, but this time you've gone too far. Now I want an answer, and I want the truth!"

"I see," Geraldine quietly replied, straightening her shoulders and facing her father with a calm dignity. "It must have been that nasty old woman who lives across the street from Lopasuta Bouchard."

"I'm not the one to answer questions, Geraldine; you are!" he indignantly countered. "Now I want an explanation. How far has this—this disgusting affair gone?"

"Papa, you're insulting yourself as well as me when you talk like that. It isn't an affair, and it isn't disgraceful. And Lopasuta Bouchard is definitely not a nigger. He had a Mexican mother and a Comanche father. And he was adopted by Luke Bouchard, who, as I think you should know, has a family that goes back practically to when this country first began."

"A Mexican and a Comanche," George Murcur slowly, incredulously repeated. "Perhaps he's not a nigger, but he's not a man for you, not if you've any pride and decency."

"Now wait a minute, Papa!" Geraldine's face was crimson with indignation. "If you really want to know the truth,

Lopasuta Bouchard's blood is purer than yours or mine, and it's a good deal older. The Indians, yes, and the Mexicans too, were in this country a lot longer than any of us here, probably than anybody else in the whole country. And I love him, and he's the man I'm going to marry. You might as well get used to the idea, because I've made up my mind."

"How dare you speak to your poor father that way, you irresponsible hussy!" Angela Murcur burst into hysterical tears. "Oh, what have I done, George, to raise such a disrespectful, shameless daughter?"

"Mama, don't say a thing like that, you don't mean it—"

"But I do, Geraldine, may God forgive me!"

"Amen to that, Mama." She turned to face her by now speechless father, "Yes, Papa, I meant what I just said. Oh, don't worry, nothing has happened. As you say, I'm a decent girl. But I want to marry him, and if he doesn't propose to me, I'll ask him."

"Geraldine Murcur! If you dare do such a thing, I'll disown you. I promise you!"

"Very well, Papa, if that's the way you feel. Maybe you don't know what he's done in this town for people who wouldn't have a chance in the law court without his help."

"Oh yes, I daresay I've read about some of his cases, but that doesn't make him any the more acceptable as a husband for you. Do you realize what it would mean to you to live in this town and have people stare at you and say filthy, disgusting things about you?"

"Just like that Mrs. Steers did, I'm sure. Yes, I've thought about it. And if it gets too bad, Lopasuta and I can go live somewhere else. Only, he's a strong, good man, Papa, and he's not afraid to fight for what he believes in, either. Maybe you didn't know that the Ku Klux Klan burned his house and tried to kill him, but he had the courage to fight back at them. That's the sort of man I can respect and be proud of; that's the sort of man whose children I'd be privileged to bear."

"How dare you! Geraldine, leave this house. And you needn't return till you've come to your senses and are ready to apologize to your mother and me," George Murcur stormed.

Geraldine looked sadly at both of them, and then turned on her heel and left the house.

* * *

It was exactly a week later when Lopasuta Bouchard left his house and walked quickly across the street, took hold of the knocker on the house across the way from him, and banged it loudly three times.

Mrs. Elizabeth Steers opened the door and then, seeing who her visitor was, uttered a shrill, "I don't want to talk to you, do you understand me? Why don't you move away from decent folk? It won't do you any good—"

"I don't want to use force, Mrs. Steers. I respect your gray hairs, but you're going to talk to me whether you like it or not. And if you don't, I might just consider bringing a lawsuit against you for malicious slander. Not only on behalf of myself, but my fiancée, Geraldine Murcur."

Hearing this last, the crotchety old woman released her grip on the knob of the door and stepped back, dumbfounded. "Your—your fiancée?" she incredulously echoed.

"That's right. Thank you for being courteous enough to let me have my say, Mrs. Steers." Lopasuta inclined his head and walked inside the room, politely gesturing her to a seat. Dazed, her eyes fixedly gazing at him, she groped her way toward the overstuffed sofa and heavily sat down with a gasp.

"Let me tell you a little something about myself, Mrs. Steers, which you may not know. My mother was a Mexican, my father a Comanche Indian. Perhaps because of the color of my skin you mistook me for black—though what difference that makes, I can't tell. But my mother was well educated and wanted me to have advantages, and so I studied and I learned to speak Spanish and English, as well as the Comanche tongue of my father. And then the chief of our tribe, who had taken refuge in Mexico because he did not wish to war against the whites, sent me to Luke Bouchard, who was kind enough to adopt me. He had me instructed by that wonderful old man, the lawyer Jedidiah Danforth, and I was admitted to the bar of the state of Alabama."

"I—I thought you were a n-nigger," she feebly stammered.

"Now you know I'm not. But in a way, Mrs. Steers, I'm grateful to you."

She squinted suspiciously at him. "G-grateful?" she faintly echoed.

"Indeed. You see, I knew very well in advance what problems Geraldine and I might face if I declared my love

423

for her. I didn't want to expose her to gossip, to the knowing smiles and nasty comments behind her back, which she would certainly have had to endure if I had come out and asked her to marry me and she had accepted. And that was why there was nothing between us and there might not have been, except for you."

"I—I don't understand you—"

"I'll try to explain, Mrs. Steers. When you went to Geraldine's parents, they raged at her for daring to see me. To my astonishment, she defied them. She said that she loved me and that she would marry me. And she said that if I didn't propose to her, she would to me. And that's exactly what she's done, and we're going to be married in New Orleans next month, since there obviously would be a good deal of antagonism toward us if we legalized our marriage here in Montgomery. All the same, we shall return here to live and I shall continue my practice."

"Lands sakes—I can't believe—you mean you actually are—" Her voice broke off as she continued to stare at Lopasuta.

"Let me say one last thing to you, Mrs. Steers," he said gently. "I'm proud of my ancestry. Most of the Mexicans, though perhaps not my own mother, were little better than slaves, their lives ruled by rich masters. The Comanches, who once ruled the land of the Southwest before the white men came, looked toward marriage and family with perhaps even greater respect than many whites. But most of all, Mrs. Steers, Geraldine and I sincerely love each other. Out of this, we can make a life that will be happy. Even if we both must face hatred and bigotry—yes, even persecution—that love will be strong enough to make our marriage endure, to give our children courage and wisdom. Think what it is to have no one, to grow old and not to be loved. Geraldine would not have that, nor would I. And that's why I thank you for having told her parents what you did."

He turned to go, and Elizabeth Steers began to sob and put out a hand. "Please, Mr.—Mr. Bouchard—f-forgive me—I'm old, I lost my husband so long ago—I didn't know about you—please forgive me—"

"Do you go to church, Mrs. Steers?" he turned to ask her.

"Oh yes, every Sunday, Mr. Bouchard—"

"Then perhaps you will remember," he said, his voice soft with compassion, "how Christ upon the cross said, 'Father, forgive them, for they know not what they do.' When I have sinned, Mrs. Steers, I pray to Him whom my people call the Great Spirit to forgive, and I bid you do the same."

He let himself out of the house, and as he did so, he could hear the old woman sobbing and saying, "Oh, Mortimer, forgive me—God help me, I lost a man so long ago and I never let him think or know that I loved him—forgive me!"

CHAPTER THIRTY-SEVEN

Lopasuta Bouchard and Geraldine Murcur were married in New Orleans on the eighth of October, in the very church in which Luke and Laure Bouchard had exchanged their vows. A week before they left for New Orleans, Luke Bouchard received a telegram from Jason Barntry, the elderly manager of the Brunton and Barntry Bank which, thanks to his conservative and sound investment policies, had survived the panic of 1873 and the ensuing recession. Jason Barntry's wife had died in August after a long and painful illness, and her death had led him in his grief to tender his resignation to Luke and Laure. Luke had urged Lopasuta to visit the bereaved manager and persuade him to change his mind.

"You know, Lopasuta," Luke said philosophically, "now that his wife is gone, all he'll have left is his work, and it has been his life. He has run that bank as a kind of dedicated trust, and it has been an inspiration for him. But if he leaves now, saddened as he is by his loss, I fear he will follow his wife before long. Her memory is best preserved, in my mind, by his continuing at his post. Her devotion was an inspiration to him, and I wish that you would tell him from us both that if he reconsiders, he will deepen the bond between himself and the Bouchard family. We have relied so completely on him for all these years, and that goes back to the days of my grandfather."

So, by the time Lopasuta and Geraldine left New Orleans and returned to take up residence at Lopasuta's little house across the way from the repentant Mrs. Elizabeth Steers, Jason Barntry had indeed found consolation in meeting with the handsome young Comanche lawyer. And he had sent back a message to Luke and Laure: "Tell them

427

that I pray God to bless them, for the message they have sent me consoles me, and each day that I am in this bank, I shall remember how my wife stood by me and how the Bouchards gave me my chance."

Not long after midnight of November 7, 1876, almost every morning paper in the United States was preparing headlines announcing a close victory for the Democratic candidate, Samuel J. Tilden. At Republican headquarters in New York's Fifth Avenue Hotel, all but the diehards had given up and gone to bed. When it became evident that even New Jersey had gone Democratic, the Republican chairman, Zachariah Chandler, was convinced of defeat and retired to his room.

The popular vote showed a majority of a quarter of a million for Tilden over Hayes. But the election would be decided by electoral votes, and it would take 185 to elect a president. When New York Democratic headquarters telegraphed the *New York Times* to ask for the newspaper's estimate of electoral votes for Tilden, John C. Reid, the *Times'* managing editor, realized that the Democrats were not certain of victory. He had endured the horrors of Richmond's Libby Prison during the war and hated both Southern and Northern Democrats, whom he still considered traitors to the Union. He and his chief reporter checked over the latest totals and saw that if the three Southern states of Louisiana, Florida, and South Carolina went Republican, Hayes could win by a single electoral vote. Armed with this information, he went to Zachariah Chandler's hotel room and asked permission to wire Governor Chamberlain in South Carolina to ascertain whether the latter could hold his state for the Republicans. He also sent telegrams to leading Republicans in Louisiana and Florida. And that morning, when Zachariah Chandler awoke, he found that the *Times* was claiming a victory for Hayes, 185 electoral votes to Tilden's 184.

On December 6, as directed by the Constitution, electors met in each of the thirty-eight states, cast their ballots, and forwarded them to Washington. All through the remainder of the centennial year the issue was in doubt, for there were two conflicting sets of electoral votes from Louisiana, Florida, South Carolina—and also Oregon—and no clear winner of the electoral vote could be determined. Finally, on January 26, 1877, the House and Senate arranged to sign into law the establishment of an Electoral Commission, consisting of fifteen members, of whom five would be justices from the Supreme Court. Less than a week before the inauguration, the Electoral Commission voted eight to seven to give the disputed electoral votes to Hayes.

Rutherford B. Hayes of Ohio was duly elected President of the United States. His term was due to begin on the fourth day of March, 1877, but since that day fell on a Sunday, the inaugural ceremonies were postponed until Monday, March 5. And for the duration of his term in office, President Hayes's enemies would derisively call him "Old Eight to Seven."

When Lopasuta Bouchard and his devoted young wife Geraldine returned from their honeymoon in New Orleans, the couple took up residence in the new house Jedidiah Danforth had provided for him after the original house had been razed by the Ku Klux Klan. Though they did not discuss the family rift which Geraldine had incurred by her defiant resolution to marry Lopasuta, the latter had secretly hoped that once they had been married and had returned to Montgomery to begin their new life together, Geraldine's parents would overcome their hostility to him and be reconciled with their daughter. But it did not happen. In the two weeks that followed, there was no message from the Murcurs. Surprisingly enough, however, the day after Lopasuta and Geraldine moved into the house, Mrs. Elizabeth Steers paid them an unexpected visit. When Lopasuta opened the door to her knock late that afternoon, she stammered apologetically, "Please—I—I want to apologize for having been so nasty to you both. And—and—well, I baked some cornbread—I—I thought you and your sweet wife might enjoy it—"

"That's very kind of you, Mrs. Steers," Lopasuta said gently, taking the pan from her. "I know Geraldine would be delighted to thank you in person for your thoughtful gift. Won't you come in—she's in the kitchen."

"Oh—oh, yes—I—I'd like that very much—I do hope— you know, Mr. Lopasuta, I hope you've forgiven me for what I—I did—"

"I've forgotten it entirely, Mrs. Steers. What matters to me is your graciousness now. Geraldine will be very pleased to be welcomed home by a neighbor. Come this way."

And after the elderly widow had left, Lopasuta took Geraldine into his arms and murmured, "My dear one, that's a very encouraging sign. She was the most bigoted gossip in the neighborhood, and now she wants to be our friend. It was her loneliness which embittered her. If only all of us could reach out and communicate our true feelings to people, there'd be so much less hatred and prejudice in this world of ours."

"I know, my darling." Geraldine uttered a little sigh. "But it's much harder for you than for me, so that's why I'm going to be a real helpmate to you."

"You already are, and you're my love, which means most of all," he murmured tenderly.

Geraldine showed herself eager to participate in her husband's work and volunteered to spend several hours during the week at the library, looking up historical and legal references which would be of assistance to Lopasuta in his current cases.

But on Thursday of the second week after their return from New Orleans, Lopasuta concluded a claims case and returned home to see a sheet of foolscap thumbtacked to the front door of the house. His lips tightened in anger as he read it.

Montgomery's no place for niggers and redskins, specially one who's a lawyer for thieving niggers and soils the fair name of the South by forcing a decent white girl to marry him. You and her better leave town if you know what's good for you.

The tall young Comanche crumpled the paper in his hands, his eyes dark with anger. He was glad that he had arrived ahead of Geraldine; knowing how much she secretly mourned the rejection by her father and mother, he realized how reading this scurrilous anonymous denunciation could have upset her. When she did arrive, ten minutes later, he made a great to-do of telling her about the case he had won, and poking fun at his own courtroom eloquence so as to make her laugh delightedly.

Luke and Laure sent Dan Munroe into Montgomery with an invitation for Lopasuta and Geraldine to join the annual commemoration of old Lucien's birthday and to spend the weekend as their guests, and they enthusiastically accepted. Since no communication of any kind had come from Geraldine's parents, even with the joyous Christmas season at hand, Lopasuta welcomed this chance to be reunited with his adoptive family. The aura of the love and loyalty of the Bouchards and their workers at Windhaven Plantation would assuredly be compensation for Geraldine's separation from her parents.

The day before they were to visit Windhaven Plantation, Geraldine went to the library again. Lopasuta had the afternoon free, and since the weather was unseasonably pleasant and sunny, he decided to ride his horse beyond the city, both for the exercise and for a chance to ponder what he might do to reunite Geraldine with her parents.

Before he saddled the spirited roan gelding, he opened the last drawer of his bedroom dresser and took out his Comanche costume of moccasins, buckskin jacket, and breeches, which he had not worn since his arrival to begin the study of law under Jedidiah Danforth. Then he rode out to the west, and crossed the Alabama River on a narrow little bridge. He rode on till he came to a strip of land that had once been a prairie, but was now framed by tall gnarled oak, cypress, and cedar trees, and was profuse with tall grass and clumps of elderberry and sumac bushes.

Lopasuta had no way of knowing that this was the ancient gaming field of the Creeks—a place avoided by the supersitious townspeople of Montgomery, particularly at night, when it was believed the ghosts of the deposed Creeks returned to watch over this historic ground. Nor did he know that the disgruntled attorney, Vernor Markwell, had summoned Klan members to this place when he incited them to burn his house four years ago. But he did recall the stories Luke had told him of old Lucien's life with the Creeks of Econchate, and he thought of them now as he let his gelding take its own lesiurely pace.

But then his mind turned to the irksome problem of Geraldine's parents. He and Geraldine had determined to live in Montgomery and let his work and their fruitful union be the sturdy bastion that would withstand prejudice. Surely her father and mother could not blot her out of their lives so callously—especially when Geraldine bore her first child. Only last night she had whispered to him with a radiant smile, "We might just have another lawyer in the family, my darling."

431

Perhaps, Lopasuta thought, he could confront the Murcurs directly, asserting his love for Geraldine and his determination to provide every material security for her and their children. Then he changed his mind, realizing that the Murcurs might regard this as a kind of forceful intrusion. No, it might be better to send a little gift and a note, asking for the privilege of meeting with them. Yet he didn't want to take any step without consulting Gerladine; if his action served only to augment the rift, he would never forgive himself.

The sky had begun to darken, and a faint wind rustled the grass and the leaves. Perhaps, indeed, the ghosts of the Creeks were near, impatient for twilight to fall when they might begin their ancient revelry upon the land which had been their inheritance long before any white man had set foot upon Alabama soil. Lopasuta, preoccupied with his own troubled thoughts, was brought back to the realization that he had sat astride his gelding for an unconscionable time and the animal was restive; now it ambled off the path and toward a clump of poison oak. Lopasuta gasped out a cry of alarm, then jerked at the reins and leaned back—just as the sound of a shot rang out. He could hear the bullet whistle past his head. Galvanized, he leaped down from the gelding and crouched beside it, staring back to the east. He could see the shadowy figure of a man carrying a rifle; as he watched, the man ran toward a horse at least five hundred feet away, mounted it, wheeled its head toward the south, and galloped out of sight.

Who could it have been? Perhaps the same skulking, cowardly enemy who had written that vicious note and tacked it onto the door of his house? There was no point in his racing after the unknown assailant, nor in upsetting Geraldine by mentioning the incident. But he would have to be on his guard from now on, to protect her as well as their unborn child from the warped mind of anyone who could write such a note and stalk him with a rifle. Could it have been one of the defendants against whom his clients had won judgments? Very possibly. And then he remembered Vernor Markwell. It could even have been a rival lawyer like that intemperate man. In any case, he would have to be very careful—yet to be forewarned was indeed to be forearmed.

* * *

On December 18, 1876, Laure and Luke Bouchard, with Paul and Lucien, and Lopasuta and Geraldine, climbed to the bluff-top graves of Luke's grandfather and Dimarte, to commemorate the birthday of old Lucien.

"Grandfather," Luke began in a solemn voice, "we come once again to you and Dimarte and the child. We come to tell you of a cycle of the renewal of life. A cycle that—"

A sudden spasm seized him, and he swayed. Laure uttered a frightened cry: "Darling, what's the matter?"

Lopasuta came forward and steadied Luke, a strong arm around his shoulders. And then the spasm passed. Luke smiled wanly and nodded his thanks to Lopasuta, then murmured reassuringly to Laure, "It was nothing—the dizziness of the climb. After all, my darling, I'm almost sixty-one now." Looking up at the serene blue sky, in which there was scarcely a cloud, he murmured to himself, "I give humble thanks, my dear God, for hearing my prayer. Let me be spared yet a little longer, not out of selfish fear of death, which all men owe to You for the gift of life, but to remain as a guide and loyal ally to these people who are so dear to me, as they are to my grandfather."

"Luke, darling, are you sure you're all right now?" Laure took a step toward him.

"Yes, thank you, my dear. I'm fine now. God is very good to all of us and to me especially." Then, raising his voice, he declared, "Forgive me, Grandfather, for interrupting my birthday greeting to you. Here before you stand my adopted son, Lopasuta Bouchard, and his wife, Geraldine. You, Dimarte, and you, my grandfather, see them and how they love each other and how devoted they will be to each other just as both of you were so long ago. It is a cycle of life, the very one you taught me to understand, Grandfather. And Windhaven will renew its cycle, with the spirit of you and Dimarte watching over us and with the beloved compassion of God who has made all men and all races and wills them to live together in peace.

"This year has seen a crisis of our young nation, Grandfather. It has torn us asunder in many ways, almost like the war that ended more than a decade ago. We have come to the crossroads, we of the Bouchards, we of America. But we pledge to you here this day, Grandfather, that the Bouchards and our beloved country will go forward valiantly as you yourself did; love and truth and our belief in our Maker will strengthen us, as they strengthened you with your Dimarte."

He sank down on his knees and bowed his head before old Lucien's grave.